Scorpion East

Also by Jerrold Morgulas

THE TORQUEMADA PRINCIPLE

THE SIEGE

THE ACCUSED

Scorpion East

Jerrold Morgulas

SEAVIEW BOOKS NEW YORK

FIRST EDITION

Library of Congress Cataloging in Publication Data

Morgulas, Jerrold.
Scorpion east.
1. World War, 1939-1945—Fiction. I. Title

PS3563.087158S3 813'.54 80-52417
ISBN 0-87223-653-6

Designed by M. Franklin-Plympton

For *Rosalinde*

The war against Russia cannot be conducted in a chivalrous fashion. This struggle is a struggle of ideologies and racial antagonisms and must be waged with unprecedented, ruthless, merciless harshness. All officers must free themselves from outmoded traditional theories. I know that they cannot make these views their own, but I demand unconditional execution of the orders issued by me.

Adolf Hitler

May 17, 1941

Part I

1942

Prologue

The general sat for a long time by himself beneath the tallest of the few remaining trees in the grove. It was impossible to tell what kind of trees they had been. The limbs had been sheared off by shrapnel and the trunks were black with smoke. But the general did not care. He was concerned mostly with the dull pain in his left leg and the growing certainty that he had come at last to the end of his strength. So far, the cold had kept the wound from hurting too badly. The bullet had smashed into his leg just above the knee, barely missing the bone, and had torn a jagged hole the size of a kopeck piece in the muscle. Now, he was desperately afraid that if the temperature rose, even a few degrees, he would begin to feel the wound again and that he would become sickened by the pain and be unable to walk at all.

For two days he had managed to stay on his feet. Supporting himself on a crutch fashioned from a splintered German rifle, he had crossed field after field cluttered with the charred and smoking debris of fierce tank battles, the blood sloshing in his boot with every lurching step. The corpses of soldiers lay in piles everywhere, slowly freezing into the mud, identified still as human bodies only by the occasional arm or leg jutting up like a tree branch from the frozen muck. Along the roads and scattered all over the fields were hundreds of smashed tank bodies, panzers, T-34s, and the light BT-7s that burst into flame so quickly when hit that they were called "matchboxes" by their crews. The charred, still-smoking bodies of the tankers hung stiffly over their treads and turrets and lay scattered about where they had fallen trying to escape the blazing tanks. Hundreds of fires smouldered on the fields and in the forests of poplar and larch, leaving soft brown patches where the light snow had melted away and the mud had thawed. Crows wheeled in dense clouds over the corpses.

Everywhere the general had gone he had found only the dead. The booming of artillery and the clank of treads had seemed always to come from the forest just beyond the horizon.

Now he sat, waiting, his old, long-barreled Nagant pistol in his lap, his finger idly stroking the trigger. He had used a pistol just like it five years before when he had been in China, and his father no doubt had one just like it at Mukden, twenty-eight years before that. He stared at the oddly graceful ancient weapon, smiling sadly. He had had no intention of using it on himself. He was no Samsonov, to blow out his brains because others had betrayed him into defeat. The loss had not been his fault and he felt no obligation to sacrifice himself.

He wanted to live to accomplish something.

He could see his orderly, Dushkin, keeping a wary distance, crouched down behind a log and rubbing his hands together for warmth. Dushkin was older by ten years, and had been in the czar's army as a boy, and later, at Khalkin-Gol; he had seen much but understood very little. The general had no desire to speak to Dushkin now and was thankful that the man had enough sense, or perhaps enough love for him, to keep his distance and respect his anguish.

That anguish was deep and it hurt him far more than did the wound in his leg. There had been no reinforcements as he had been promised. There had been no medicine for the wounded and they had died. There had been no ammunition for the living and they, too, had died.

Not a single *Mule* had come down out of the flak-splattered sky to take out the dying. The offensive had failed. The Second Shock Army had not broken through to relieve Leningrad. For a few days they had held the ground they had gained on the far side of the Volkhov River, but then the Germans had regrouped and General Seydlitz-Kurzbach's panzers had gone through the exhausted Soviet regiments like a hot poker. There had been no possible way for him to hold. Finally the order had come over the closed phone line to Moscow—*"Otstupayetye."* Retreat. But retreat to where? And how?

In the end there had been nothing more for him to do, nothing that was possible. More than fifty thousand men had died. For no reason. The regimental commanders were all dead. Yakovlev had been crushed by a tank. Mamedov had been blown to bits by the Stukas while trying to hold the salient at Izvyak. The stout, laconic Grebvonka had gone berserk and led twenty men in a bayonet charge against a full battalion of Württemberg Jägers. The general had watched him literally be disintegrated by machine-gun fire. All of the fine young men had been killed: his former students at the academy, Lieutenants Luchenok and Timofeyev, and his favorite, Kurenko. Honor students. Corpses now. And for what? The Germans were everywhere. Brinapol had been overrun and the only remaining signs of Soviet presence were the thousands of corpses half buried in the black, freezing mud and the wreckage of downed planes, like the skeletons of pterodactyls, in the blasted tree limbs. In a few weeks the real freeze would set in. The weather would turn and the mud would go solid, and until the snowfall grew heavy enough, the panzers would race eastward, unthinkable, unstoppable.

The general's uniform had long since shredded on his huge, shambling frame. Dushkin was in rags, looking like a filthy mummy slowly coming unwound in the bitter, slashing wind. The general could hear the ragged streamers that had been Dushkin's coat snapping in the wind like regimental pennants.

He had to avoid Dushkin's eyes.

He would never again be able to look into the eyes of any man who had served with him in that hellhole. What he would see there would be unbearable. He knew that.

To the east he could hear the drone of the Heinkels again. Constant. As though all the aircraft factories of Germany were emptying them into the Russian skies in a never-ending stream. Now and then he heard, too, the whine of a distant Stuka. The Germans had installed sirens between the undercarriage legs so that they screamed as they dove.

He had been deliberately left to rot. It was not because the rescue attempt would have been futile that no attempt had been made. Such things had never deterred Stalin before. No, the choice had been a deliberate choosing. The Defender of Moscow was being left to die.

For himself, he did not much care. He expected little out of life now. He had lived through the bitter, confusing years in Chungking and Canton, through the purges, through the break with his wife. Ever since he had left her, he had been single-minded, dedicated to his duty. Obsessed, some called it. He had not realized at the time just how important his leaving her had been. Now he knew. More important, even, than the fifty thousand dead, terrible as it was to think such a thing. But not more important than the betrayal.

Nothing was more important than that.

He saw Dushkin rise slowly to a half crouch and the general instinctively touched his raw cheeks to see if any tears had fallen. If they had, the cold, scarifying wind had dried them at once.

Overhead, a gray-white crane passed, oddly graceful in its lop-winged passage across the iron-colored sky and the low banks of black clouds. A few insects buzzed near his hand. A bottle-fly, bright green, lit on his wrist. He made no move to brush it away.

Now Dushkin was pointing but still kept his respectful distance. Then the orderly rose up, a lumbering, uncertain figure in a shredded coat and a woolen balaclava taken from a dead German.

General Golitsyn turned his head slowly, reluctantly. From the west came a low grumbling sound. Motors. Probably tanks pushing through the half-frozen mud. A constant snapping sound too; not rifle fire but the cracking of tree limbs as the panzers rolled over the charred ruins of felled trees.

The wind shifted. For a moment he could even hear voices.

Dushkin came over at last. The man's eyes were red and ringed. But they seemed moist too. Why was it, General Golitsyn wondered, that Dushkin's tears had remained damp while his had dried?

"Over there, comrade General."

"Comrade, I hope," said Golitsyn, touching Dushkin on the shoulder, "but general? No more." He smiled faintly, amused at the way Dushkin still stuck to the correct form of address. Even there, in the mud, in the ruined forest.

Dushkin ignored the general's words and pointed again, his flat, Mongolian face still expressionless.

"They're coming. I can smell them. The oil, sir, the German oil has its own smell."

"You can hear them too, Osip Vissarionovitch."

It was true. Over the wind, the clank of treads and the snap of men's voices were quite clear now. Harsh, loud, contemptuous. As though they knew that there were only two Russians left alive in a hundred square *versts* of corpses.

"You must get away," said Dushkin. "We must hide, comrade General."

"From what?"

"Sir?" Dushkin looked westward again, toward the voices.

"From them? From *those* men?" The general rose. Shards of dried mud fell from his clothing. He pushed his steel-rimmed eyeglasses up along the bridge of his great, flat, lumpy nose. Rising there against the shattered tree trunk in the windings of his shredded greatcoat, he looked like some ancient Mongol chieftain determined to die standing, as Attila had demanded to die, upon his horse at the peak of a mountain so that his shadow should be cast every evening, reaching toward the west.

"There are woods to the south. Untouched, I think. There's been no firing from there for weeks, and the planes don't go there either and . . ."

"Osip Vissarionovitch, you don't understand."

"Sir?"

"I'm going to surrender," said the general.

Dushkin stared at him in disbelief. His eyes filled with the real, full tears that the general could no longer shed.

"But we can hide there, sir, I'm sure of it," Dushkin protested.

General Golitsyn shook his head. The clanking of tank treads and the snapping of tree branches was much louder now, much nearer. To the west, through a screen of blackened, limbless trees, darker shapes could be seen moving forward.

"There's a marsh to the south, to the *south,* comrade General. The scrub is too thick. They will not go there," said Dushkin as though he had not heard.

"And neither will I, my good friend."

"Well then . . ." Dushkin began.

"Is it settled? Are you coming with me or not? It's up to you."

Dushkin looked away; his old face wrinkled into a reddened mask.

"Are you coming with me? No? Then good-bye, Osip Vissarionovitch. Have no regrets. We must each of us choose for himself." The general sighed and pointed to the northeast. "Over there, do you see the woods beyond that ridge? The one that was hit by the barrage this morning? You'll be safe there for a while. The panzers won't try to go over all those heavy tree trunks."

Then the general holstered his pistol, and turned his back on his orderly. With the makeshift crutch tucked under his arm, he began to limp toward the treeline from which, just then, the first of the big Panzer IIIs was emerging. His free hand was held high over his head and from it fluttered a piece of filthy white cloth that had once been a leg wrapping.

Dushkin stood there, watching him go. His shoulders twitched. Something indefinable stirred under the shapeless ruin of his coat.

Then, with a shrug and a shake of his head, he trotted after the general, leaving a straight line of black footprints on the snow-dusted mud.

1

> Russians, Ukrainians, Georgians . . . members of all the races and tribes in the east have streamed in continually increasing numbers to the German armies for enrollment in a Volunteer Army, which is fighting shoulder to shoulder with the Germans against the Soviets. This army has at its disposal infantry, cavalry, artillery and engineers, that is to say troops and weapons of all kinds. They have shown surprisingly quickly that the true soldierly spirit can soon be kindled in them when a great idea is at stake.
>
> *Signal*, 1942

The dozen high-ranking military intelligence and NKVD officers who had gathered to watch the showing sat stone-faced and grim in the darkness. On their laps were small leather folders containing the *svodki,* the intelligence briefings they had been handed upon entering the overheated little room. A flicker of light shot from the projector lens to the opposite wall. The all-too-familiar runic symbols that identified an official Wehrmacht Signal Corps film flashed across the screen.

A picture came into focus.

The film was coarse and grainy, the camera hand-held. But the images were vividly clear.

It was midsummer and the sun blazed overhead. Grass grew high in the yards. Giant sunflowers were everywhere. The painted signs hanging from the shops and the market stalls identified the place as being somewhere in the Ukraine, a town of size and importance, not merely some outlying village. Large stone warehouses could be seen in the background and behind them the stacks of a brickyard and the squatter, wider chimneys of a foundry. A church cupola caught the glancing sunlight on its gilt surface.

A large crowd had spread out along three sides of the square, which opened toward the road that stretched off, out of the town, and into the flat, featureless steppe beyond. In the distance rose a vast, whirling cloud of dust.

In the center of the square a delegation of village elders waited. The oldest of them, a tall, gnarled man with a long white beard, stood like a tree, rooted to the spot, smiling nervously with anticipation. He held before him a large wooden platter on which lay a loaf of bread and a large cake of salt. On his left stood the other elders, on his right half a dozen children with their arms full of flowers. Many of the women in the crowd around the edge of the marketplace also carried flowers. They were all smiling.

The dust cloud to the west grew more turbulent. Shapes began to emerge, dark against a lighter background. Out of the dust crawled scores of motorcycles with sidecars. In the center of the phalanx of motorcycles rode a wide, open-backed command car with a stiff pennant jutting from the right fender. Bringing up the rear were masses of infantrymen and lines of enormous tanks and huge gun tractors stretching as far back as the camera could keep the focus.

The cameraman panned the crowd, catching more smiling, happy faces. Old men waved, women kissed each other in excitement.

The picture suddenly cut to the actual entry of the troops. Women embraced the German soldiers, threw flowers. A Panzer colonel in full-dress uniform smilingly took the bread and salt and thanked the elders with a courteous and elegant gesture. The crowd was obviously cheering.

There was an audible intake of breath in the room. One of the older officers began to curse.

The projector ground on, repeating the same scene with only minor variations in half a dozen other towns and cities. From the Ukraine in the south to Latvia and Estonia in the north. The last scene was clearly Poltava.

"These are nothing but propaganda lies. How do we know these scenes were not staged, perhaps even in Germany?"

"Use your eyes, comrade Colonel," came the reply. "You can *see* that it's all true."

"Yes, it *was* true, at the beginning. We have to admit that. But such things no longer happen. The fascists have made sure of it themselves."

"If that were so, comrade Lieutenant General, you would not have been brought here today. As you will see, there is much more of which you are unaware. So far, only STAVKA and the security services have been given the information. For obvious reasons, it would be most unwise if it were to become generally known."

There was a long silence. The projector continued to whir though the screen went dark for a moment. Some of the officers started to get up.

"Remain seated, please," came the curt command.

"Must we see more of this?"

"You need to see what's coming next, comrade General."

The screen lit up again, as though on cue.

The film now showed a vast, open steppe. In the distance one could see quite clearly a line of German PzKw IIIs and trucks. German soldiers moved in wide, massed formations across the wind-blown fields. Then a large group of horsemen appeared, a column perhaps half a mile long. In the front rode officers of the Waffen SS in camouflage jump suits, rifles slung over their shoulders. Behind, the horsemen were clearly Russians, of all nationalities. Cossacks with their characteristic cartridge cases sewn to their jackets, men still wearing remnants of Soviet army uniforms, Asiatics, blond Ukrainians. They were smiling and waved to the lines of German foot soldiers. The Germans waved back. Along the flanks of the main body rode officers also identifiably Russian, carrying drum-fed Degtyarev submachine guns and carbines and long-barreled Mosin-Nagant rifles of the kind that had seen service since czarist days.

Then the scene vanished. A beam of light from the projector illuminated the faces of the audience and caught the long curls of cigarette smoke that wound up toward the low ceiling of the bunker.

"This is intolerable," cried a gruff voice from the audience.

"It is true, however," replied the voice that had earlier silenced the officer who had said that the scenes had been staged; it came from a small, elderly officer who stood near the screen, holding a pointer. "And we must take it all very seriously."

"An isolated example. There have always been traitors . . . bandits."

The screen went black again. The calm voice continued out of the darkness.

"We have many, many more reels like that one, comrade. Some were captured, some were shot by our own brave cameramen from hiding. There are thousands of still photos and reports. We receive more every day. We cannot deny the evidence of our own eyes. We must recognize the truth and deal with it or it will destroy us."

A sober voice asked from the front row, "What is the best estimate we have as to their numbers? How bad . . . has it become?"

"We cannot be sure. So much is yet not known. But we do know there are thousands already marching in the Ukraine with Bandera and Melnik. There are between fifty thousand and a hundred thousand wearing German uniforms as auxiliaries. As for the Estonians and the Latvians, we have no idea as yet, but you can use your imagination there. They have come, all these men, from the prison camps, from the occupied towns and cities. They are being used by the Germans both as auxiliaries and in the front lines. Naturally, we have taken the most stringent measures to contain any knowledge of this situation. Those of our troops who have come in contact with these units have been . . . isolated wherever possible."

"Are all of these units under German officers? There are no Russian officers in command?"

"Only in the cossack units and even there only at the lower levels."

"Then they have no units of their own?"

"Thus far that is how it has been. There has been no leader, no single man the fascists could put forth. So far. . . ."

The projector clicked off. The lamp went out and the room was plunged into total darkness.

Senior Lieutenant Vassily Gregorovitch Kurenko was sure that he was freezing to death.

There was no sensation in his legs and he was beginning to feel warm all over. He tried to lift his right hand from the M38 semi-automatic he had been cradling in his lap and found that his fingers would not come away; the skin was frozen to the metal.

It was insane. Like everything else. The mud should still have been soft, the flies should still have been buzzing. The temperature should still have been well above freezing. He had been hiding in the woods for almost two weeks. It was still November but the weather was already like midwinter.

He swore viciously and looked around.

Beyond the wooded slope, in the slight valley that lay just before the land began its final convulsive descent to the Zbalga River, smoke still rose, a high, broiling tower of black, spreading out at the top like a fan and finally vanishing into low gray skies still troubled by snow. Now and then, over the tops of the ice-freighted trees, Kurenko could see a tongue of flame leap up, lick once or twice at the sky, and then fall back again into the oily black cloud that had enveloped the village of Kolabyansk.

Or at least he thought it was the village of Kolabyansk. There was no real way of telling. According to his map it should have been Kolabyansk but in the snow, with every house on fire and without a compass, he could not be sure.

He had picked up another survivor in the woods, a sergeant from the Forty-third Guards Division. The man had torn off his insignia of rank. The Germans, he said, were shooting all officers and *politruks* out of hand. It just wasn't safe for anyone above the rank of common soldier. They wouldn't even let you surrender.

The sergeant was hunkered deep down in the snow, barely visible. Only his eyes showed over the edge of the filthy leg cloth he'd wrapped around his face. He sat there, stolid and impassive, as though the rattle of machine-gun fire, which was now drawing closer through the woods, was no more significant than the sound of branches being snapped by a fleeing rabbit.

Kurenko wiped the snow from his eyes and tugged at the earflaps of his fur-lined *ushanka*. The frosty air burned his nostrils. Through a break in the tall, leafless trees, a long tunnel probably smashed out by a tank weeks before, he could see some of the houses in Kolabyansk burning. He knew that he should have moved deeper into the forest, where it would be harder for the Germans to find him, but he was fascinated by the sight of the burning village. There was an oddly tranquil beauty in the combination of flame, rolling smoke, and falling snow, as if nature was gently but firmly canceling all evidence of man's destructiveness.

In an hour there would be no trace.

"They're getting closer," Kurenko whispered. The sergeant

nodded, stroking the potato mashers that hung from a rope tied around his body; he preferred the German grenades, he said. They threw more easily. He had taken this particular string from a dead lance corporal only the day before.

It had all changed so suddenly, Kurenko thought. It was enough to drive anyone mad. The Germans had broken through the Third Regiment lines near Brinapol and crushed all resistance within a day. Waves of German tanks had moved rapidly forward over the suddenly stiff mud. New models, with treads that could cope easily with the snow. The shock battalions that had smashed through to the Volkhov River only a few weeks before had melted away like ice in a spring thaw. The mud that had been their staunchest ally had unaccountably stiffened, then frozen, betraying them utterly.

The sergeant loosened a grenade and shifted it anxiously under the blanket he wore as a winter cape.

"No, there's no point in that," said Kurenko wearily, sliding further down into the snow-filled ditch in which they had been sheltering.

"They know we're here, comrade Lieutenant," said the sergeant.

"They don't know anything at all," Kurenko said. He was bone-tired and his stomach was knotted with hunger. They'd been eating nothing but bark and roots for the last few days. But now, with the snow, even those were denied them. "Why should they care about us?"

"We fired on them. How can they not know we're here?"

"Knowing and finding us are two different things, just you remember that. You don't want to die for nothing, do you?"

The sergeant shrugged. A little snow fell from his shoulders. Kurenko raised his head just above the edge of the ditch. A flock of crows lifted suddenly from the forest's edge. Small dark shapes appeared among the trees. Above the crackling of fires and the groaning of the wind the sound of men and horses could be heard.

The first line of cavalry spread out fanlike across the field just as the second rank emerged from the treeline.

"Hurrah," cried the sergeant. "We're saved, we're saved." He grinned, displaying a mixture of steel and rotted teeth.

"Stay down, you fool," Kurenko snapped, pulling sharply at the startled man's arm. It was the first time he'd touched him and the sergeant, taken by surprise, drew back sharply. "Look again . . . can't you see . . . ?"

"See what? I see cavalry. They have to be ours. Look at the horses. They're Kabardians. The Germans don't have Kabardians, damn it. They don't have horses like those. . . ."

"And our lads don't wear uniforms like those either," Kurenko snapped. He thrust the binoculars into the sergeant's hands. "Look for yourself, and stay down while you do it if you don't want a bullet in the head."

"Bozhe moy," breathed the sergeant. "My God, you're right."

He handed the binoculars back to Kurenko with a shudder. Kurenko raised them quickly to confirm in detail what the shape of the helmets and the camouflage blankets on the lead riders had told him at once.

The line of horsemen moved straight out into the open field. The officers in front were unquestionably Germans. He could see clearly the coal-scuttle helmets, the long-barreled Mauser pistols, and the characteristic gourd-shaped water bottles hanging from their belts. But as he brought the faces of the second rank of riders into focus, he felt a shock of confusion run through his body like an electric current.

The faces of the riders were not German. They were Russians, without the slightest doubt. Some of them were Kalmuk or Kirghiz. And the uniforms were like none he had ever seen before, a jumble of Soviet army greatcoats, padded jackets, German helmets, shoulder boards oddly reminiscent of the old czarist uniforms, and boots of every variety known to man. On their coats were cossack *gaziri,* bullet pouches with nine pockets each. He couldn't quite make out the unit patches on their shoulders.

The officers in the lead shouted something; the words cut harshly through the bitter cold, the meaning lost but the shape and sound of the language clear and sharp. German. No doubt of it. Kurenko spoke fluent German himself, straight from the Frunze Academy; he'd been a first-ranking language student.

Then another cry went up, this time in Russian.

The horsemen hunched forward high in the stirrups and picked up the pace, urging their lines rapidly over the snowy field.

"Maybe they're Bulgars or Turks. . . . They say they look like us, some of them."

Kurenko didn't answer. What was he to say? He let the glasses fall onto his lap and ducked down. The sergeant pulled his white camouflage canvas down over his head.

When they looked up again the horsemen had disappeared into the smoke of the burning village.

"They were Russians, comrade Lieutenant, just like us."

"Not like us," Kurenko breathed. "And you'll forget you ever saw them if you know what's good for you."

The sergeant stared at him blankly.

"Not a word, do you understand?"

Kurenko didn't care whether the man understood or not. His teeth had started chattering and it wasn't from the cold. Kurenko was normally a brave man, at least so he had always considered himself, but he hadn't been prepared for anything like the apparition that had just flashed across the field in front of him. He'd heard rumors of such things but he'd never really believed they were true. After all, he'd never actually seen any of the turncoat units. As deep a hatred as he knew many people within the Soviet Union held for the government in Moscow, didn't they know how much worse the Germans were? He knew that there'd been trouble in the Ukraine and that some Georgian separatist units had gone into the woods and were fighting German and Soviet troops with equal ferocity. But what the devil were they doing here, on the Volkhov? Turkmen, Volga Tartars, cossack cavalry units? It made his head swim.

He looked despairingly toward the birch forest to the south. There were no Germans there, he knew. The panzers had all rolled on past, heading due east. There was nothing of importance to the south, only trackless, frozen marsh for a hundred *versts*.

To the south then, and a little east too, for good measure. Maybe they could make it after all, if they kept on pushing and kept out of sight. And didn't die of hunger or get picked off by German rear-guard patrols.

Time enough later to decide what to say or do about . . . the others. The cavalry, or whatever they were.

But, damn it, Russians riding with the Germans. That was going to make things difficult. He'd have to watch his step. If an NKVD squad got hold of him, he'd have to let them know who he was as fast as possible. They wouldn't dare arrest a member of General Golitsyn's headquarters staff, even if he had been behind German lines for two weeks or more. He hadn't surrendered. That ought to count for something. He'd fought his way out.

But he'd have to be very, very careful, and get rid of the sergeant as soon as he could. It wasn't safe to have the man around anymore. Not after what they'd both just seen.

But for the moment he had no choice. . . . It was move on to the southeast or freeze in his tracks right there. The temperature was dropping steadily.

When he was sure that the horsemen had gone into the village he nudged the sergeant.

"Come on. We have to find someplace to spend the night. Unless you want to freeze to death right here."

The sergeant rose uncertainly to his feet, a grenade in his hand, his flat peasant face without expression. He nodded glumly, turned, and started off to the south.

Above the forest, the crows were beginning to settle down again into the ice-glazed trees.

On the ridge, silhouetted against an angry, ash-gray sky grown feverish from the light of two burning villages not far distant to the west, a long line of gray Panzer IIIs could be seen lumbering slowly along with an appearance of stately majesty possible only at such a distance. Overhead the sky was dark but clear, the low snow clouds gone for the while and the sun a pale flat disc, grotesquely enlarged, like an object glimpsed at the bottom of a lake.

Signal Captain Martin Beifelder stood outside the shed and swore. He had been swearing since dawn, first at the hour, then at the suddenly terrifying cold, then at the Russians and, finally, at SS Oberstürmführer Hans Gruzenberg.

Beifelder rubbed his bare hands together briskly. How the devil was one to keep warm and function at the same time? The thicker the gloves, the better for warmth, of course, and that was essential. But the thicker the gloves, the more difficult it was to do anything meaningful with one's hands. If the command post were suddenly to be overrun by Russians, Beifelder doubted he would even be able to find the trigger of his Walther, much less pull it.

The shed in which Gruzenberg's regiment had set up its temporary command post had been used for animals and the place stank of pig urine, though it was really hard to tell just what the smell was in such cold. Frost reduced all odors to a wretched common denominator. The place smelled awful, and that was enough for Beifelder. Even the freezing air outside was preferable. Besides, there was no stove in the shed, so what was the sense in nauseating oneself from the stench?

No one else seemed to mind. Wires ran everywhere, and ran off—to nowhere. Beifelder was sad, pensive. His own division was in the attack again, and driving the exhausted Russians before it like so much chaff. But he knew perfectly well that every kilometer deeper they drove simply put them that much farther from their source of supply. As he had said to Gruzenberg repeatedly, it was like digging oneself into a long horizontal grave. SS Oberstürmführer Gruzenberg hadn't appreciated the analogy, and though he had said nothing it was easy to see that he was thinking. If he was thinking at all. Beifelder often wondered whether the Waffen SS really did think or whether they had simply been punched out for the proper, politically acceptable responses, like the little metal discs in a Swiss music box. He and Gruzenberg had been engaged in their own private war for weeks now, and it was a source of astonishment to both that they even talked to each other anymore. Nor could the two men have been more dissimilar physically. Gruzenberg was fairly tall, lean, with sharp, hawklike features, while Beifelder was heavyset, tending to fat, with a face that his friends cheerfully insisted looked as though it had been sat on. It was probably the fact that Gruzenberg looked almost Slavic while Beifelder, for all his Bavarian dumpiness, was acceptably blond, that had first nettled the SS lieutenant. Beifelder had more serious reasons to dislike Gruzenberg.

Overhead—from the southeast, Beifelder thought—a rackety clatter followed by a long whine and then the crash of an explosion was heard. The Stukas were at it again. Somewhere over the hill. There hadn't been a Russian plane in the sky all day.

As he watched, Beifelder saw a plume of smoke unwind lazily in the distance, far beyond the arrowhead wedge of panzers that had now climbed almost completely over the farthest ridge.

A voice . . . not speaking in German but in some other language, softer, at first not at all distinct, sounded behind him. Beifelder looked around, puzzled.

It was Gruzenberg again. Beifelder hadn't realized that the man had come up so close to him. The soft-sounding language was Italian. Gruzenberg was fond of declaiming the lines written by Mussolini's son extolling the beauty of bursting bombs. Every time a Stuka so much as dipped its nose, it was the damned poem again. It was enough to make a man vomit.

Just as Beifelder was about to say something unpleasant, Gruzenberg turned, his attention attracted by the appearance on the road of a line of open-topped armored Hanomag half-tracks escorted by motorcycles equipped with special tires—a new consignment, made of real rubber, not the ersatz *Buna* that froze stiff as wood the minute the mercury dropped below zero.

The head car in the column carried SS markings. Beifelder swore. Why did Gruzenberg's men always have to arrive first? Where were his own men? What was the point of being a liaison officer if one-half of the unit-pairing was always kilometers ahead of the other?

"Time to be off, Captain," said Gruzenberg in his irritatingly tranquil voice. "Unless you'd prefer to remain here, of course."

The stocky Beifelder climbed up into the lead half-track, taking up a position just behind the driver. He was barely tall enough to see over the armor plate shield. The column moved off again, leaving only a skeleton command staff in the stinking shed.

Gruzenberg put on a pair of slit snow goggles and squinted directly into the sun. The undulating flatland ahead of them was mostly dun-colored but already splotched here and there with islands of snow. The really rotten weather hadn't set in yet, though, God only knew, it was already cold enough.

To the left, at a considerable distance, a long line of men could be seen crawling up a shallow snow-dusted slope behind a fan of tanks.

Gruzenberg turned and smiled wickedly.

"There, Captain, *that* should satisfy you people at OKH, shouldn't it?" He pointed to the battalion advancing like ants over the snow-flecked steppes to the north.

"And why should that be, Gruzenberg?"

"Why indeed? Why? Because they're UVV—Ukrainians—Captain. Living proof that even the SS does not regard all Slavs as subhuman."

Beifelder remained doggedly silent. He recalled the memorandum he had recently dispatched to his nominal superior in Berlin, Captain Schreiber-Hartstein. Nothing but protest. Protest against the way the SS were treating Russian prisoners, leaving them to die of their wounds without any medical attention, to die of exposure in huge outdoor pens or shooting them outright. Even more vigorous protest against the brutal way the SS were dealing with the civilian population. He had dwelt lengthily and painfully on the disgrace that the massacres and hangings were bringing on the regular army, not to mention the insane problems they were creating by turning the whole countryside against them. A population that had earlier greeted the Wehrmacht with flowers, kisses, and cheers was now up in arms against them—man, woman, and child.

If Gruzenberg or any of his Waffen SS superiors ever saw the memorandum, Beifelder knew he could count on a bullet in the back of the neck within twenty-four hours. Thank God he'd soon be headed back to the capital.

But he spoke of none of this. Instead, he nodded and smiled at Gruzenberg in a vaguely patronizing way.

"Excellent fighting men, I suppose, Oberstürmführer?"

"I must admit, Captain, they're among the best."

The armored car continued to rumble along. A flight of Henschels, with their long antitank guns sticking out ahead of them like the proboscises of so many giant mosquitoes, whined overhead in the cold, clear sky.

"And they will, of course, be first in the attack also? Because they are such excellent fighting men?"

Gruzenberg gave Beifelder a sharp, irritated look. "Because of that and because, if you want to hear it, because I would rather lose a thousand Ukrainians than one Berliner. Does that satisfy you?"

"It does, it does. I would not have thought otherwise for a moment."

By the time the column of half-tracks, motorcycles, and tanks had reached the outskirts of the village of Teribyakino, they had already passed not only four formations of mixed Wehrmacht and Waffen SS moving forward but two long, gray columns of Russian prisoners moving in the opposite direction along the road. Beifelder noticed that not one of the prisoners was wearing winter clothing, though the temperature was already well below freezing.

Most of the men had on only their tunics. Some wore nothing heavier than a shredded uniform shirt. All but a few were without boots of any kind. The wounded were either being dragged along or left on the roadside. Twice, in the few minutes he watched, Beifelder saw a wounded prisoner shot for faltering.

The western periphery of Teribyakino had been occupied before the Heinkel 111s had come over by a molybdenum plant and a large brickworks that had covered the west flank of the town in a protective arc. Now, thanks to the bombers, there was nothing left but a seemingly endless swath of still-smoking rubble. German troops were already swarming through the town and only desultory rifle fire could be heard from the far eastern end of the place. Corpses, both Russian and German, lay everywhere. What resistance remained was not even serious enough to warrant automatic weapons fire.

Beifelder was pleased and displeased at the same time. Easy victories inevitably bred overconfidence and an increase in arrogance. The more easily the Russ were driven out of their towns, the more firmly entrenched became the belief of the Gruzenbergs of the world that the Russ were garbage, subhuman, beneath contempt or consideration of any kind—Ukrainians to the contrary notwithstanding. And sooner or later—sooner, if Beifelder knew his elementary psychology as well as he thought he did—that belief was going to bring on a disaster. It had already cost them a significant advantage.

The armored column came to a halt at the edge of what had been the marketplace. Here only the skeletal remains of a few buildings still stood to define the general outlines of the square. As they stood there in the cab surveying the scene, squinting into the acrid smoke haze, a few chickens ran squawking through the debris. Otherwise the marketplace was a silent jumble of wreckage and mounds of earth, shell holes, corpses—buried and unburied, some barely identifiable as human figures, others startlingly lifelike in frozen death—and scattered pieces of military equipment. A burning truck stood on end, its headlights on, sending a finger of light up through the smoke.

Then he saw it.

"What in God's name is that?" Beifelder cried suddenly, catching sight of something in the center of the ruined marketplace.

Even Gruzenberg seemed startled. He ordered the driver to turn off the motor and he clambered down, followed by Beifelder and a dozen wary Waffen SS men carrying submachine guns.

In the center of the square stood a rough, trestle-shaped gallows. From the crosspiece hung more than a dozen corpses, frozen stiff and swinging slightly in the wind like the clappers of so many bells.

The dead were not wearing uniforms. They were all Russian civilians, two women and an old man among them.

Beifelder was beside himself. How was it possible? They had only just reached the town. He had given specific orders, backed up by OKH. Such things were not to happen. Not without a full trial. Only regular Wehrmacht officers were to have jurisdiction in the area. Not the SS.

"You will find at once who did this, Oberstürmführer," Beifelder demanded angrily, forgetting for the moment that Gruzenberg was not under his direct command.

Gruzenberg, somewhat bewildered, shook his head and licked his lips. He paced up and down the line of bodies, hands clasped behind his back.

Then he stopped, a faint smile on his face, and faced Beifelder.

"I can assure you, Captain, neither I nor my men are responsible for this. I can also assure you, however, that it would have been my pleasure, if not for your directive. . . ."

"I'm sure it would have. Which is precisely why it is necessary to issue such orders in the first place. Now, you will do as I say and find out just who . . ."

Gruzenberg shook his head.

"I *know* who, Captain."

Beifelder stared at him. "How is that possible?"

"We were here before, Captain. Last week." He gestured toward the line of dangling corpses. "These very people welcomed us. The old man on the end was the mayor. The woman there ran the school. That blonde one turned over the keys to a granary to us. Then the Ivans drove us out again. Police troops, Captain. NKVD."

"Who then?"

"Who the devil do you think, you damned fool? What would *you* do to traitors?"

"The Russians don't hang people, they shoot them. . . ."

"Not when they want it to look as though we did it," Gruzenberg laughed. "Though the devil knows why they bother. We'll give them plenty soon enough."

Beifelder felt sick. He turned away in a hot sweat.

At that moment, a column of big black PzKw IIIs clanked up behind the half-tracks. In the turret of the lead tank Beifelder saw Lieutenant Pohl from his own battalion. He breathed a sigh of relief and went over to join him, trying not to look at the gallows.

He wanted to feel relieved but could not. In the last few moments he had inherited yet one more perplexing problem.

He knew he was in for a bad time of it, at least until he could manage to get out of that godforsaken ice hole and back to Berlin, where he could try to sort things out with Schreiber-Hartstein over a glass or two of good whiskey.

Kurenko had no idea where he was. The forests had closed in, blanketed now with thick snow, dark and trackless. Here and there were the charred remains of a fallen plane, an abandoned vehicle of some now-unidentifiable kind. Once they had come across the barely recognizable skeleton of an strange biplane. It was only after Kurenko had stood staring at the thing for a full ten minutes that he realized that it had been there since the first German war, twenty years before.

The sergeant had been no help. Kurenko had looked to him for a peasant's cunning. Instead he had found only a peasant's stupidity. The only thing the man knew how to do well was to forage for food. He knew the edible roots, the plants that could be chewed without causing violent cramps. Once or twice he managed to trap a small animal and ate pieces of it raw. There was no question of building a fire. Kurenko watched, nauseated. Hungry as he was, he could not bring himself to eat that way.

They trudged on through the dense forests, heading south. In the near distance they could often hear the sounds of battle. Flights of planes, heavy-engined bombers, blackened the skies to the north, and when the gray, lowering clouds cleared they could see the planes, distant, precise black shapes, little punctuation marks against the suddenly silvery sky.

When they heard rifle or automatic weapons fire, they hid, burrowing in the ground like animals, pulling their white canvas over them for further camouflage. Kurenko knew the sounds of German rifles and machine guns and could easily distinguish them from the sound of a Tokarev or a Pepesha. Twice he had to stop the sergeant from rushing blindly in the direction of the firing.

Toward evening of the second day after they had left Kolabyansk, they entered a deep birch wood that had been partially destroyed by heavy cannon fire. Vast areas had been blown away, then covered over by the fresh snow so that it appeared as though someone had tried to build roads through the forest. Jagged tree trunks, shattered by explosives, jutted up from the snow. As they pushed on farther into the forest, they came upon heaps of discarded equipment. Corpses sat frozen and oddly lifelike under trees where the men had dragged themselves to tend their wounds. Boots, canteens, shovels, even small arms. Soviet and German equipment mingled on the forest floor in a silent truce of mutual defeat. Here and there lay small piles of helmets and smashed ration tins. The smell of cordite and decay hung in the air.

On the ground before them, not entirely covered over by the fresh snow that had fallen that morning, were the tracks of many horses and brown patches of droppings. A cavalry unit had passed this way not too long before.

Then Kurenko smelled it, clear and strong, even in the cold. Dead horses. The stink of disemboweled animals.

They stayed close to what tree cover was left, moving cautiously and as silently as they could. The forest was still. The sergeant hung back, reluctant to go forward. Kurenko kept on, moving steadily south. If the man wanted to die there in the snow, let him. It was his own affair.

Then they came to a clearing. A dozen or more dead horses lay in the snow. Flocks of crows hopped and danced over them, pecking away at the openwork of ribs and at the eyes. Kurenko felt nauseous and looked away.

"It's them," whispered the sergeant.

"Them?"

"The ones we saw."

The sergeant was right. There were a number of corpses lying half buried in the snow in the clearing, fewer than the dead horses but almost as many. It was clear that the cavalry column had run into an ambush.

"Wait . . . listen for a minute. Do you hear anything? My head is ringing."

"Maybe you have a fever, comrade Senior Lieutenant."

"The hell with a fever. Are there any Germans around?"

"Only dead ones," said the sergeant, cheerful for the first time in two days.

Kurenko moved cautiously out among the bodies. The crows cawed and lifted from the horses' corpses, flapping and angry. On the other side of the clearing there were a few more bodies. He'd get to them later.

He leaned down over the first dead man he came to. The man's fingers were frozen stiff, grasping snow, the face blotted out by blood. A bullet had smashed the jaw on the left side. What was left was not a German face. The cheekbones were high, the eyes slightly slant—definitely Tartar—the hair black and glossy. Nearby was a dead German officer, his Mauser still in his hand, his pale boyish face a mask of surprise.

Kurenko knelt, touched the odd shoulder boards on the Russian's uniform, the cross straps, the flat brass buttons.

There was an odd elliptical cockade on the shoulder of the dead man's coat. Kurenko pulled at it and it came off.

"Do the others have this on their uniforms?"

The sergeant lumbered off, making a circle among the corpses. When he returned he had four more of the odd patches.

"What are they, comrade Senior Lieutenant? I've never seen anything like them before."

Kurenko shook his head. Huge whorls of black cloud pushed through the slate-gray sky above the clearing, obscuring the setting sun. But there was still light enough to see by if the little scrap of cloth was held up close.

A curious thing: a blue and red ellipse, the blue outermost. The dead man's shoulder straps were dark olive, with a red line through them and a little diamond-shaped gold pip set near the outer edge.

"I found these too," the sergeant said, handing Kurenko some papers and a little book that he recognized at once as a New Testament.

"Which one of them had that on him?" Kurenko asked, pointing at the Bible.

"Him, right over there, the one by the bay."

"And these?" Kurenko took the papers. They were regulation Red army document folders, but the unit designation was blanked out.

The sergeant looked puzzled. He pointed across the field, to the other side of the clearing where he had gone last.

"From the ones over there," he said. "I don't understand it, comrade Senior Lieutenant. It's enough to drive a man crazy."

"Damn . . ." said Kurenko. "What don't you understand?"

"They're Russians over there too, comrade Senior Lieutenant."

"What's so odd about that? A Soviet unit opening fire on . . . whatever these men are?"

"Yes, I understand about that, comrade Senior Lieutenant, but the men over there . . . the ones I took these papers from . . . ?"

"Yes, yes?" Kurenko looked up and saw that there was a genuine look of terror on the man's flat, normally expressionless face.

"They're wearing German uniforms," said the sergeant.

2

The sunset sinks in blood
From the heart, blood streams forth.
Weep, heart, weep . . .
There is no peace.
The mare of the steppes
Rushes on.

Alexander Blok

The cracked phonograph record sent Serge Lemeshev's silvery-sweet tenor spilling into the bleak, cold little room, the same words repeated over and over.

"The rosy dawn . . . the rosy dawn . . . the rosy dawn . . rosy dawn . . ."

"*Kak zhal,* what a misfortune. Such a lovely song and look what's happened to it now," lamented Basha Petrovna, a small, bundled woman from the floor below, who frequently came up in the evening to ease her widow's loneliness, thinking—of course—that she was doing a good turn for her neighbor.

"It's not really broken, only stuck," said Nina Andreyeva Golitsyna. "Like everything else. Broken. Sit still. I'll fix it."

She rose wearily from the sofa and went over to the table where the gramophone sat and resentfully lifted the arm from the record. A heavy winter silence flowed back into the small room, chilly and penetrating. She pushed the dark hair back over her high forehead, away from the lines that now showed there so clearly and caused her to start whenever her fingers strayed across them. Standing silently by the gramophone, she looked about the room as though expecting to see or hear someone besides her turnip-faced downstairs neighbor.

But there was no one else there and had not been for many months, not since she'd sent her ten-year-old son, Petya, to her cousins beyond the Urals. There was only Basha Petrovna, and the old photographs of her husband and herself when they'd been in China, a single photo of her father, long since faded and barely identifiable, a picture of her son in his Young Pioneer's neckerchief. A few medical books and a few books of poetry, a stamp album full of Chinese stamps, some phonograph records, mostly scratched. There was not even a carpet for the wall.

Just before the old woman had come up Nina Andreyeva had been rereading her most recent letter from Petya. He was doing well but missed her terribly. His cousin Tikhon always smelled of sour buttermilk, which he couldn't stand. When would the war be over, he wanted to know, so he could come home again? And could he have a cat then, please?

She lived alone in her dingy room. There had been those who had at first offered her a few luxuries, feeling it their duty to Alexander Semyonovitch, and not really understanding what had happened or why. The staff at the hospital suddenly all had become very solicitous. Some of Alexander Semyonovitch's old acquaintances—it could not be said that he had had any real friends, which was something that had always made the two of them even that much closer—had come around, openly at first, then furtively, looking more embarrassed than fearful or concerned. Extra food, a larger apartment, warmer clothing, a padded coat, even cosmetics. Some stockings. The former wife of a general, a hero of the Soviet Union, should not be without such things. She should not live in such a mean way, they said. She knew better, shook her head and gently refused. After a while they stopped offering things and left her alone. None of her husband's old acquaintances—those few who were still in Moscow—came around anymore. No one bothered her and she preferred it that way. There was not even a single sugar cube in the cupboard. She drank her tea bitter and scalding.

She was, in fact, even growing to like the solitude and the spartan existence. During the days she worked at the hospital, where no one any longer seemed to care who she was. At night she sat and listened to Lemeshev sing old love songs. They were her only solace. The government had requisitioned all the radios in Moscow the winter before when the German army had been only twenty-five kilometers from Red Square and the Twentieth Army, led by Alexander Semyonovitch, had pushed them all the way back to Rzhev. She had helped dig trenches and firing pits and had pushed the heavy steel "hedgehogs" into antitank barriers until her shoulders were raw and she thought she could not stand up another minute. That was all in the past. The snows had come and gone and come again. She could not bear to listen to the new patriotic songs that came booming out of the street loudspeakers all day long. What had they to do with her? Her world was her room, the hospital, and her son far away behind the Urals.

She placed the needle back at the beginning of the record, hoping that this time it might play through. It was a beautiful song, "The Rosy Dawn," and had always been one of her favorites. They had even had a gramophone record of it when they'd been in Canton. Now, even as the song began again, she thought that she was beginning to hate it.

"Such a lovely tune," said Basha Petrovna.

Nina Andreyeva did not respond. She wished that the old woman would leave. She wanted to read Petya's letter again, particularly the part about the Pioneers and his new mineral collection. She was bone-tired and wanted to go to bed before the cold in the apartment became so intense that she would have trouble getting to sleep. The year before, the government had ordered that there be no heat at all in the apartment houses. The pipes had cracked. Now just enough heat was allowed to keep that from happening. It was almost worse that way. If only Basha Petrovna would go while she still had some warmth left in her body. But the sad, wistful look on her neighbor's face was so deep that she could not bring herself to ask the old woman to leave.

Absently, she walked to the frosted window and looked out onto the narrow, dark street that ran before her building. A light snow was drifting down, the wind coming from the direction of the Moskva River. Long fingers of blue-white light from the antiaircraft searchlights continued to swing lazily back and forth across the sky, illuminating the snow in an aurora borealis of fragile beauty. There had been no German planes over Moscow now for at least a week and the weather had closed in so suddenly that it was unlikely that there would be any more bombing raids for some time.

She gazed out into the street for a moment without really thinking or really seeing what was there. Then, as though almost by accident, she noticed a big black American car and a green van with wire grating on the rear window standing a little ways down the street from the entrance to her building.

All at once she remembered with a dull ache the news she had read two or three weeks before. Of the disaster at Brinapol. There had been no word of Alexander Semyonovitch since then. And suddenly she knew.

"Go home, Basha Petrovna, go back to your room."

The old woman blinked at her, her wrinkled-apple of a face blank and expressionless.

"Please, you must go right away," Nina Golitsyna said. "I think I am having . . . guests. . . ."

She kept looking out the window as she spoke.

Two men had just gotten out of the front seat of the black car and were leaning against the rear door, talking to someone sitting in the back. She could just barely make out the man's profile. He was wearing a military *ushanka* with fur earflaps, and a heavy sheepskin coat with the collar pulled up to his ears. His dark silhouette cut across the slightly lighter interior of the automobile.

"Basha Petrovna, for God's sake, go. Please. Go to bed."

"What's the matter, Nina Andreyeva? You've gone white as milk."

The other two men, both in bulky overcoats and wide-brimmed felt hats, stamped across the street, rubbing their hands together, coming straight for the entrance to her building. She had no doubt who they were coming for. Who else in that dilapidated building could it possibly be but Nina Andreyeva Golitsyna, the former wife of a general who had just lost a terrible battle?

Basha Petrovna finally got up to go.

"God bless you." She understood at last and rushed out.

"Yes, yes. Bless you too. But go at once. Go, go."

The door slammed.

Nina Andreyeva went to the window again. The two men had already entered her building. The man in military uniform had gotten out of the backseat of the car and was pacing back and forth nervously in the light snow, examining some papers in the lamplight.

The motor of the big car, a Packard, was still running, the hood trembling slightly and catching the light on its shining curved surface. A trickle of exhaust melted a blue-black fan in the snow behind the van.

She took her robe off the peg, suddenly aware that she was wearing only her quilted housecoat, little more than a nightdress. Now she wondered why, exactly, they had come. There could be a hundred reasons or there could be none at all. Who she was was reason enough.

She waited, trying to remain perfectly calm. Her cousin would take care of Petya. They wouldn't dare take the child too. What had he done? Everything would be all right with Petya, she was sure of that.

But as she heard the knock, her heart began to beat more rapidly and she realized that she was no longer sure of anything.

Lemeshev's voice rose.

> Oh beautiful stars, your unforgettable shining
> brings me such poignant memories . . .

She opened the door. The younger of the two men looked down at a photograph in his hand, then at her.

"Nina Andreyeva Golitsyna?"

"At one time, yes."

"Come with us, please."

"For what reason?"

The man holding the photograph said nothing but glanced sideways at his companion. He flushed and seemed to her to be slightly embarrassed. At that moment there was a stamping of boots on the rickety wooden stairs and the man in the military coat and *ushanka* appeared, puffing and red-faced.

"Here, here, you forgot this," he exclaimed, highly agitated. He thrust a folded paper at the man who held the photograph. He took the paper, glanced at it, and then handed it to Nina Golitsyna.

"You must read this," he said.

She looked briefly at the paper; there was nothing there that explained anything.

"But *why* are you doing this? I'm entitled to know *why*. It doesn't say *why* here. . . ."

The man in the military uniform, a captain, backed off and spoke without looking at her.

"The order is for protective custody, as you can see, *gospozha*

Golitsyna. Your husband," he said, "has gone over to the Germans. We are taking you with us for your own safety. . . ."

Captain Schreiber-Hartstein was fuming.

It was bad enough that there were so many idiots in the world but it was a catastrophe when they were placed in positions of such power. It was both a catastrophe and, worse yet, a disgrace.

He was so angry that he almost lost his balance coming down the stairs of the General Headquarters building, failed to salute a startled artillery major with whom he almost collided on the first landing, and, finally, began shouting at his driver for no reason at all other than that he simply had to shout at someone.

He should have been used to fools in generals' uniforms by now, he told himself. God only knew, there had been fools enough of that same kind in the czarist army in which he had served as a young man. But, as a German Balt, he had always felt that things would be different in that marvel of modern science and technology, the Wehrmacht. How wrong he had found himself to be. The feeling of intense longing and pride that men so often feel for the homeland of their fathers—which they have never seen—did not long survive close-hand acquaintance. General Keitel, with his lilac pencil, was no better than the Russian Generals Samsonov or Deniken had been in the old days. A blind, conceited, rigid fool with a ramrod up his asshole and no understanding whatever of human nature.

Schreiber-Hartstein slumped angrily into the backseat next to Captain Beifelder, who had been waiting for him. Beifelder was pale, haggard, and showed clearly the marks of extreme fatigue and deprivation. When he was worn out, his small frame seemed even smaller, his normally gray complexion even sicklier. On top of it all, he had lost weight and was ill with a bad cold, blowing his nose constantly. He had just flown in from the front the day before with yet another satchel full of infuriating and sometimes puzzling documents. They had not been in time for inclusion in the memorandum Schreiber-Hartstein had set before Keitel but, as things had turned out, it would have made no difference at all.

Beifelder looked up, focusing his watery, inflamed eyes only with the greatest difficulty on his friend's long, schoolmasterish face. Schreiber-Hartstein had also lost considerable weight, though he could ill afford it, being normally lean almost to a fault. The bones of his pale intellectual's face were accentuated, the circles under his eyes behind the square-rimmed glasses deeper now, giving him the appearance of one of Klimt's elongated skull drawings. His hair, formerly almost colorless, was now turning distinctly gray. His lips had grown so thin that his mouth seemed not more than a brief hyphen in his face. At the moment, though, his brow was furrowed with worry, his eyes were bright and angry. A nervous tic had announced itself below his left eye.

"Well, Reinhardt, what did he say?"

Schreiber-Hartstein let out a heavy, exasperated breath.

"He told me to mind my own business—which, in his opinion, was making war, not political decisions."

"We might have expected that. . . ." Beifelder said dismally.

"Expected what? Martin, one must expect *nothing* of fools. And the man is a fool, plain and simple, that's all there is to it." He took the memorandum out of his briefcase and laid it on his knees. "Look at this," he complained; the pages to which he pointed were framed in sharp, lilac-colored scribblings. Schreiber-Hartstein had diligently collected his evidence and had prepared his memorandum as carefully as a legal brief. It was, in fact, a masterpiece of precision and documentation. But it had all been in vain. Keitel knew all about the now-infamous "commissar" order that provided that all Russian political officers, as well as all Jews and "Asiatics" taken prisoner, be shot out of hand. He knew all about the *Einsatzkommandos* and the mass killings. He knew all about the murderous treatment the Russian POWs were receiving. He knew all about the brutal treatment being meted out to civilians in the occupied areas. Such things were common knowledge, and a lengthy, boring report telling him what he already knew was hardly of any interest to the general. The general simply wasn't interested in such facts.

"He was concerned *only* with my 'presumption,' as he called it, in daring to set forth these 'facts' without having been first *asked* to do so *by him*," Schreiber-Hartstein snapped. "And how elegantly he puts it. . . . Here, read this."

In fact, what had upset Schreiber-Hartstein most was not the severity of Keitel's rejection, which he had more than half expected, but the language in which it had been expressed. The lilac comments were mostly gutter words of the worst sort.

Beifelder groaned and blew his nose. All he could think of was a hot bath, bed, and a glass of whiskey, preferably good English Scotch.

Schreiber-Hartstein leaned forward.

"Can't you go any faster, Rudi?" he shouted at his driver, though why he should want to get back any faster than he was going he would have been unable to say. The news he carried could certainly wait. And he was in no mood to repeat it all to Kreppel and Gottinger and Major Reiman, his fellow Slavophiles at OKH.

The driver, who knew his superior well enough, understood the question as rhetorical and did not presume to answer.

"You ought to go to bed, Martin," said Schreiber-Hartstein. "God only knows, we must look after ourselves. If we don't, what will happen to the rest of the country, eh?"

Beifelder blew his nose again and looked very uncomfortable. His eyes were partly closed. Even though he was now being driven along the Königstrasse in the heart of Berlin, it seemed to him that he was still on the freezing, snow-laden steppe somewhere east of Orel. Not even the Knight's Cross he had recently received was any real comfort to him. A little piece of iron. It might as well have been a bullet in his heart.

The trip back to the OKH offices on the Landeswehr canal took almost an hour because of the heavy truck traffic in the streets. By the time the two men had gotten themselves up the stairs to Schreiber-Hartstein's office, both Gottinger and Kreppel were waiting. Reiman had gone out to Tempelhof airport and sent his regrets.

Kreppel was a dark, heavyset young man who looked as though he had been a greengrocer or a butcher in another life but, in fact, was an engineer and quite a good one at that. He was quiet, alert, and effective, simply because no one expected a man who *looked* like that to be so quick. Gottinger was just the opposite, a tall, thin man with a razor-sharp profile and the absolute and infallible recall of a mnemonist. Before the war he had wanted to be a film director and had since settled disgruntedly for an administrative role in OKH's photographic section. With the two captains was Lieutenant Hummel, a young man with extraordinarily bright blond hair—almost an albino—sharp, aggressive features and the boundless energy that can come only from completely uncritical dedication to an ideal. Hummel had been admitted to the group not because of any special talent he possessed but because of the constantly chastening effect of his presence. How could anyone else falter as long as Hummel continued to believe so fervently, so stridently, so insistently?

"I can see the results written clearly enough on your face, Reinhardt," said Gottinger.

"We should have known better." Schreiber-Hartstein threw the briefcase angrily on the table. The latch sprang open and the papers flew all over the floor. Hummel, eager as ever, leaped to retrieve them.

"No," cried Schreiber-Hartstein, "let them lie there. What good are they? We might as well burn them. Common sense is dead in this good land of ours. There is no cutting edge to truth any longer. It is all dull, dull, dull, and we shall die from it, I promise you. As the words to the old song go, 'stick it in the hunter's horn and blow it in the wind'—truth is dead and honor is no more." He struggled to get a grip on himself, knew that he was behaving badly and that the others were shocked.

"He refused to read it then?" asked Kreppel.

"Oh, no. Not at all. He read it straight through."

"He refused to believe it then?"

"Not that either. He not only believed it but he told me that he had known all of these things for a long time and that they simply didn't matter in the least. Not to him, at any rate. It doesn't matter that the SS are turning the entire Russian countryside against us with their criminal, idiotic behavior? It doesn't matter that their stupidity has cost us at least three full divisions of Russian volunteers already and filled the woods with partisans in the bargain? And all of this while the secret is still kept?"

Beifelder shook his head. "He told Reinhardt to mind his own business."

"As if winning the war isn't our business too," said Schreiber-Hartstein, sitting down at his desk. "The ultimate phrase employed by our elegant general was 'stick it up your ass while you still have one left,' " Schreiber-Hartstein added, his face darkening in fury.

"Well, what next?"

Schreiber-Hartstein sighed. "We have our supporters, even in the SS. We know we are right. Things can't go on like this for much longer. Damn it . . . can't go on? They're getting *worse* every day. Another few months and the SS will have roused the entire country and ruined everything we've been working for. We'll have gone from liberators to savages in their eyes in less than a year. Quite a record, I'd say."

"Then we're going to go ahead in spite of Keitel?"

"I don't see where we have any other choice. Remember all the fine speeches about the 'crusade against bolshevism'? Well, it was true. They were sick of Stalin and his tyranny. They greeted us, from north to south, when we rolled in . . . with flowers—my God, gentlemen, with *flowers.* Can anyone even remember those days now? They held up little children for us to kiss. The women threw themselves on our young men. Instead of taking advantage of the situation, what have we done? I don't even want to talk about it now, it makes me sick to my stomach. But even so, despite all that's happened, we still have over nine hundred thousand Russian prisoners who have already volunteered for our all-Russian army. How can we waste such a gift? We simply *must* organize and equip them. Once they're in the field, with their own commanders, once their own people see them, perhaps then we'll be able to neutralize, at least in part, the damages the cretins in OKH and the SS are doing. The *Ost* policy must and will be changed. In the meantime, we must continue to argue our case. If not before Keitel, then before someone else. I'll go to Reichsminister Rosenberg if it should become necessary. Our court of last resort, apart from Himmler himself. And it may ultimately come to that."

Gottinger had just risen to say something when there was a heavy knocking on the door.

A dispatch rider stood there, his boots and goggles covered with dust, his uniform rumpled. He saluted briskly.

"With the Herr Hauptmann's permission," said the rider, handing Schreiber-Hartstein an envelope.

He tore it open and read it. A strange expression, wary, a trifle sardonic, spread across his face.

"Gentlemen, this could not have arrived at a more opportune time. It is from Major Reiman, at Tempelhof."

"Yes?" said Gottinger and Beifelder at once.

"He wishes to advise us that the plane from Vinnitsa has arrived and that Major General of the Soviet Army Alexander Semyonovitch Golitsyn will shortly be in official residence at number ten Viktoriastrasse. . . ."

Major Gelb held his hands out, palms down, over the tin-can oil lamp—the "rocket" as its type was known, after its propensity for sudden explosion—but he could get neither the chill nor the stiffness out of his fingers. Just why he should feel so cold when the room was actually quite well heated he could not understand. Perhaps it was the all-too-fresh memory of the bitter night in the open the week before during which he had almost frozen to death. He knew he would never be rid of that memory, not in all of what was left of his life. Or perhaps it was really something in the soul, a permanent chill that had settled into him like a slow and insiduous poisoning of the blood. The work he was doing was the cause of it, he understood that well enough. What he could not understand was why it was necessary to do such things. There were so many more important tasks, so many more rewarding, more honest things a man could be doing. He would die of the work long before a German bullet found him; he was certain of that.

Cold or no cold, in the soul or elsewhere, there were orders to be followed. And besides, Pashkov the company clerk, would take all the notes that needed taking. There was no need for Gelb to use his hands at all.

He turned away from the oil lamp, thrust his hands back into his tunic pockets, and looked across the room. The black iron stove in the corner was glowing dangerously and spitting sparks. The windows were covered with a heavy layer of ice through which the outlines of the main street of Pribov could just barely be made out, looking for all the world in its mantled fresh snow like a street in an early Kandinsky painting down which a knight in a pointed silver helmet or an enchanted prince would soon be seen riding.

Gelb wiped off his glasses, replaced them, and tried to make out what Captain Sipyagin the NKVD liaison was doing. He was always trying to understand what Sipyagin was up to and thus far had had such little success that he had almost given up. Either the man was deliberately and perfectly inscrutable or else he himself had no real idea what he was doing or why. Such men, Gelb had concluded, were all too common during wartime. Even men with a normal quotient of integrity and common sense could easily wind up that way.

Sipyagin was a thin, oriental-looking man from Odessa. About thirty-five, ten years younger than Gelb, he seldom spoke about his past life. Someone had said that Sipyagin had studied architecture. Another rumor had to do with doubtful doings during the NEP period. All of it, in any event, was long ago and none of it mattered much at the moment. Certainly, Gelb would never learn the truth from Sipyagin himself. Nor could he read anything in those narrow, slitted eyes in which he could barely see the pupils. He often wondered whether Sipyagin kept his eyes in that perpetual squint so as to avoid anyone's seeing in or simply to avoid having to look out.

Either motive seemed plausible enough, Gelb thought. Sipyagin moved about the table, peered over the nervous Pashkov's shoulder, and finally settled on the edge of a large oil drum, his favorite seat.

Sipyagin lit a cigarette, then changed his mind and pinched it out, putting the charred stub back into the little sardine tin he used for a case. The canvas-covered trucks unloading in the road outside had caught his attention; the Special Purposes units were bringing in more men for interrogation—survivors of the battalions shattered by the Germans west of Kolabyansk and Brinapol, a few men who had fought their way out of encirclements, a few deserters picked up in the forests and on the roads and not shot out of hand.

"It never ceases," said Gelb as though to himself.

"No, it never does," agreed Sipyagin, who always heard everything, no matter how softly it was spoken. "Comrade clerk Pashkov? You have the papers?"

The clerk nodded. There was a shuffling outside and the sound of voices. The door opened, admitting half a dozen bedraggled soldiers, two guards in quilted Siberian long coats, and a draft of freezing, snowy air. Gelb shivered in his plain wool tunic, looked at the exhausted, desperate faces of the men just then pushed into the room, and noted too the even greater despair that appeared on their faces when they saw the bright blue NKVD patches on Sipyagin's collar.

"You . . . your name, your unit," said Sipyagin mechanically.

"Balabanov, Dmitri Yosipovitch—Thirty-ninth Division, Third Regiment, Second Battalion, under Colonel General Grachov."

"The Thirty-ninth Division was encircled a week ago north of Trebsin. You escaped?"

"Yes, comrade Captain."

"Well, here you are, so we must believe *that* story, mustn't we? And, well, there must be a *reason* why you survived, yes? And you will tell us that reason, won't you? Why?"

Gelb was weary and longed for a rest. He could not count on a sense of dedication to keep him going, as in Sipyagin's case. He could not argue with the man and would not, in any event, even if he could have. The orders had come directly from the highest authority. Escaped prisoners, survivors, men who had fought their way out of encirclement, anyone, in fact, who had been even close to the Germans was to be regarded as suspect. And to be suspect in such times was, without more, to be guilty.

The last man had been taken away only a few minutes before. Sipyagin was fighting to stay awake and just barely managing. Ever since the tank battles west of Kolabyansk, neither Gelb nor Sipyagin had had more than three hours' sleep a day. There had simply been too much work to do.

Gelb's eyes slowly closed although he was still standing up. Years ago, when he had been a young artillery lieutenant, he had learned how to sleep on his feet, even with a shell in his arms. A few moments, even a few seconds. It all helped. He thought that if he walked slowly enough he could even manage to sleep between steps.

He was startled out of his standing doze by a pounding on the door of the hut and an angry exchange just outside.

"You must open . . . I insist on seeing . . . at once . . ."

A few words. Then the door flew open with a bang. Sipyagin spun around on his wiry legs, almost dropping the files he had been holding.

"Pashkov . . . who the devil is that?"

Kurenko had dragged himself into the village with his last ounce of strength. Alone.

The sergeant he had picked up near Kolabyansk had collapsed in the snow the day before and had refused to get up. At first Kurenko had tried to carry him but it soon became clear that if he continued to use up what little energy still remained to him there would be two corpses in the snow instead of one. It was that simple. Kurenko was, in the end, astonished that the solid, peasant sergeant should have been the first to fall and that he, a city-bred man, utterly unused to the rigors of the outdoors, should still be standing on his own two feet. His father would have found it all immensely amusing—that the son of a Leningrad watchmaker had outlasted a real peasant in the forest. Eating roots and bark. Surviving. God, what wouldn't he have given for a piece of sausage or a bowl of cabbage soup at that moment? How long had it been since he'd gone walking along Gorki Street eating an ice-cream sandwich from one of the little gray carts that seemed, on sunny days, as ubiquitous as the pigeons and the rooks. How long had it been since he'd strolled with a talkative girl on his arm through the zoo or taken a prostitute up to a room on the far side of the river? A hundred years? Maybe more. Probably it hadn't been him at all who had done such things but only somebody he'd imagined, someone he'd made up. The person in those fantasies had been young, full of energy, strong, and eager. He hadn't stunk like a sewer from his own body odors, he hadn't had a growth of beard so thick that he couldn't even recognize his own reflection, he hadn't felt that every step he took was his last.

Definitely . . . it had been somebody else. Not Vassily Gregorovitch Kurenko.

As he had looked down at the fallen sergeant, lying there slowly freezing to death, Kurenko had thought how pointless it was for him to go on. At best he could survive for a day or two more. If he found a Red army unit the chances were that he'd be thrown into a prison camp. He'd heard stories about what happened to men who'd been too long behind German lines or who'd been captured. He'd never believed them before but now, suddenly, he had experienced a revelation.

Undoubtedly they were true.

Not that he could blame them; it was certainly dangerous to trust anyone these days. The cavalry he'd seen near Kolabyansk had been proof enough of that. He'd have to be very careful. They would have to realize at once just how important he was, that he had vital information for them, that he couldn't just be packed off to a prison camp somewhere.

He took the fallen sergeant's cartridge pouches and a few of the German stick grenades, which were very like the Soviet RGD 33s, and trudged on.

When he had first seen the village, the lines of trucks still under white winter shrouds, and the smouldering cook fires he had been sure that he had come upon the Germans again. At that moment he had almost been ready to give up. It was a hard choice—whether to be killed trying to take a few more of them with him or whether to simply walk in with his hands in the air and hope that they'd at least give him a crust of bread before they shot him. He didn't much care if he died, as long as he had something to eat first.

Then he'd recognized the big T-34 tanks by the roadside and it had all changed. He'd somehow managed to run down the muddy road, shouting like a schoolboy and demanding to be taken at once to the district intelligence officer. The tankers had stared at him in disbelief.

"Kurenko, comrade Captain. Senior Lieutenant Vassily Gregorovitch Kurenko. Headquarters staff, Second Soviet Shock Army."

The guard who had been posted outside the door broke in with a stammered apology.

"Never mind," said Sipyagin calmly. "Let's see what Senior Lieutenant Kurenko wants with us." His eyes narrowed. He was unused, to say the least, to having people seek him out.

Kurenko drew himself up as erectly as three days without sleep would permit and continued his report. The contrast between his appearance and his brisk academy manner was almost too much for Sipyagin. The lieutenant, he thought, looked as though he'd been dipped in mud. He stank. His uniform hung in tatters and his thin, young face was covered with a patchy, leprous growth of dark blond beard. He'd obviously been in the woods for a long time. Sipyagin shook his head. He felt almost sorry for this grimy, bleary-eyed young man, this Kurenko, who had obviously come in on his own and who had no idea what was in store for him. Sipyagin didn't like to see officers handled this way. It was something they could no longer afford, this constant loss of young officers. The Tukaschevsky purges had done enough harm. Ship off the common soldiers if it was absolutely necessary. All right. They could be replaced. But trained officers? How many did they have now, that they could afford to be so wasteful?

He sighed and began his accustomed ritual.

"Where were you found, Kurenko?"

"I wasn't 'found,' comrade Captain. I've been in the woods for two weeks, maybe three. How long has it been since the line broke at Brinapol?"

"It didn't break," said Gelb quietly. "There was a strategic withdrawal."

"Don't tell me about strategic withdrawals, comrade Major. I was *there*. But you can call it whatever you like, it's all right with me. The panzers came through in waves. We had no ammunition. We had no supplies, no reinforcements. There was no way the positions could have been held."

"No one is blaming you, comrade Lieutenant," said Gelb quietly.

"I should make a full report," Kurenko shot back, looking quickly from Sipyagin to Gelb and back again.

"Oh?" Sipyagin's eyebrows inched up. "Why you? What have you to tell us in particular? Why did you ask to be brought here?"

"I was liaison officer between General Golitsyn's headquarters and the front-line positions. The Fourth Division was the last to pull back. I can give you information . . ."

Sipyagin cut him off. "General Golitsyn's personal staff, you say?"

"Yes, yes," Kurenko snapped back, responding to the sudden knife edge of interest in the NKVD man's voice. He began to breathe a little easier.

"Why don't you sit down," suggested Gelb. "Here. Do you want a cigarette? No? Some hot soup? Pashkov, get a tin of soup, will you? Now . . . relax, Kurenko. No one wants to push you. When you're ready, you'll tell us . . ."

"May I see your papers, comrade Captain?" Kurenko said suddenly.

"My *what*?"

"Your papers. I must be certain that I am actually speaking to an authorized NKVD officer."

Gelb held up a hand. "You can be sure, comrade Lieutenant, that this man is exactly what he appears to be. You may speak freely."

Kurenko looked the major up and down. There was something about the sagging, weary face that inspired trust. The major reminded him of his mother's older brother. It was an idiotic reason to trust a man, but it would do. He wasn't too sure about the other one though. The NKVD man looked like a Georgian or even an Armenian. Kurenko had never had any use for Armenians.

"I was on the general's personal staff," he said, emphasizing each word and waiting for them to have their effect. "Since Moscow, comrade Major. I was there too, when he turned back Hoth and Guederian. You remember that? A glorious time."

"I'm sure," said Sipyagin laconically. "But go on, go on. You were close to General Golitsyn?"

"When I was at the Frunze Academy, comrade Major, I was one of his best students. It was just after he'd come back from Canton. I was a guest in his home often," he lied.

"A protégé? How interesting, comrade Senior Lieutenant," said Sipyagin.

"A protégé? No, that would be saying too much, comrade Captain. But he did think highly of me, and I've served well under him." Kurenko was beginning to sweat. Perhaps he had gone a little too far; he wasn't at all sure now that he was making the effect he'd intended.

He drew a deep breath, feeling a little dizzy. By this time, Pashkov had brought the soup, and in order to give himself a breathing spell Kurenko began greedily spooning it down. He hadn't eaten real food in over a week.

When he had finished he wiped his mouth with the back of his hand. Gelb was waiting patiently but Sipyagin was growing annoyed.

Kurenko saw this and began again in a voice that he realized at once was overeager.

"There's more. I didn't insist on seeing you just to make my report. I could have done that with the battalion commander."

"True, true. Very true. But why then *did* you ask to come . . . here? To me?"

"Because of something we saw just west of Kolabyansk, after the panzers had already gone through."

Now. It was time. He could see Sipyagin's eyes suddenly grow brighter, the pupils concentrating.

"And that . . . was?"

Gelb sighed. For a second Kurenko was almost positive that he already knew.

"A German cavalry patrol, Captain. A rear guard. Reconnaissance, I don't know which."

"Nothing unusual in that, Lieutenant," said Gelb, a cautionary note in his voice.

"But they weren't really Germans. They were Russians, Major. With German officers. There was no doubt about it."

"Cossacks?" Sipyagin asked softly.

"Not cossacks. They were riding Kabardian horses."

"You are an expert on horses as well?"

"The sergeant who was with me knew horses. And the men, some of them were clearly Asiatics. The rest, who knows? But they were definitely Russian. Not Germans. The uniforms were a mixture, crazy . . ." He went on, describing what he had seen as best he could, testing, waiting for a reaction.

When he had finished, Gelb leaned back.

"More soup, Pashkov. Perhaps you can find some bread and meat as well. Can't you see? The lieutenant is still hungry," said Sipyagin. "And after that, you must sleep. We will talk further of this later, after you've rested. Your mind must be clear."

"Do you have any word of the general?" Kurenko asked, so as to remind them once again of who he was.

Sipyagin and Gelb exchanged quick, guarded glances. Kurenko, by this time, was too weary to notice, but neither responded directly.

"When you have finished, comrade Senior Lieutenant, Pashkov will take you down to the rest shack. There are a few cots there. We too use them, the major and I, when we get a chance. You'll also find a few bottles of vodka in the locker. Go ahead, help yourself. For officers only. It will make it easier for you to sleep. I know how it is to be as exhausted as you are, believe me I do."

Kurenko stood up.

"Yes, you're right, comrade Captain. I am exhausted. Perhaps this will all make more sense after a few hours' sleep."

"You were absolutely right to come here at once, as you did." Sipyagin hesitated. "You spoke of this cavalry of yours to no one else?"

"You're the first."

"And the other man? The one who was with you?"

"As I said, he's gone. Dead. I left him in the snow two days ago."

"You did very well, comrade Senior Lieutenant. Now go. Rest. You've earned it."

When Kurenko had gone, Sipyagin turned to Pashkov.

"First of all, give me the notes you just took. All right. Now, second . . . you must forget about this man, do you understand? You have not seen him. You know no one by the name of Kurenko."

"I understand, comrade Captain," Pashkov replied hurriedly.

"Good that you do," said Sipyagin. "You know what's to be done about the man who was not here, don't you?"

Again, Pashkov nodded.

Gelb sighed. Sipyagin sank wearily into his chair. He had always felt that if he could avoid actually giving the order himself, then the responsibility somehow wasn't really his.

"Make sure that the lieutenant has actually found the rest shack and is safely asleep. Wait a few hours . . ."

Pashkov shrugged and went out.

Sipyagin looked away, aware all too keenly that Gelb was trying to catch his eye. It was a pity. If the damned fool hadn't mentioned Golitsyn, well, perhaps something might have been done for him. He seemed a decent young man and he'd obviously had a hard time of it.

But then too there was that business about the horsemen. . .

What choice did he have after that?

Sipyagin rose, tore up Pashkov's notes, and thrust the scraps into the crackling stove. The flame leaped up, sending a cheery red glow dancing about the room. Then Sipyagin slammed the door and the light was gone again.

Gelb, by this time, had left the room.

The hut to which the company clerk, Pashkov, had directed him stood at the end of a muddy road beyond which was a low warehouse and a line of light BT-7 tanks, some with their turrets off for repairs, others draped with white canvas covers. Inside the hut were three wooden cots and a number of straw pallets on the floor. Pashkov opened a locker and took out a piece of sausage and a bottle of cherry brandy.

Kurenko wolfed down the sausage and then drank directly from the bottle.

"Good, that's good," said Pashkov mildly. "Now you'll sleep. The company commander will call you if you're needed."

"If there's any news of the general . . ."

"If there's anything, we'll let you know."

Just before throwing himself down on the cot, Kurenko noticed that there were a few bits of equipment hanging on pegs on the wall . . . a coat, two or three *pilotkas,* a few fur caps, a pistol belt, and a single felt boot. A small stove sputtered reassuringly in the corner. There was even a samovar improvised from a 122mm shell casing in which a liter or so of water was bubbling quietly.

Kurenko pulled the blanket up over himself, not even bothering to take off what was left of his boots. He was asleep in a moment.

He slept deeply, bothered only by vague fragments of dreams, which came and went like clouds, never really taking shape. A vision of his student days at the Frunze Academy fled before him, followed by a dark, cloudy landscape, which might have been his home near Mybinsk, and a face that was very much like that of his sister, but even more like that of his dead mother. He saw, too, the face of a dark woman, stern and handsome. It was no one he could remember. He'd never even fallen in love, not even once. What with the academy and then the war, he hadn't had the time.

He saw also, more briefly but with a peculiar vividness, the snowy field outside Kolabyansk and the faces he had glimpsed through his binoculars. The horsemen with their German officers. Then those images vanished too, melting into yet another, a large, vivid, rectangular white space that rammed hard into his consciousness.

It was, in fact, the door of the hut, which had just been flung open. He was aware of this even before he was fully awake.

A bitter cold wind swept into the room, sour and laden with the smell of garbage, oil, and rotting horseflesh. The tin stove sent up a noisy shower of sparks in protest.

Three men stood in the doorway. Kurenko's first horrified impression as he struggled awake was that the town had been silently overrun by Germans while he was asleep.

Then he recognized Pashkov, the clerk, almost hidden behind the other two.

"That's him," said Pashkov.

The other two wore the NKVD crossed-rifles brassard and blue patches and carried heavy Tokarev automatic pistols.

"Senior Lieutenant Vassily Kurenko?" one of them demanded.

"I told you, that's *him*," said Pashkov.

"On your feet. Outside with you."

Kurenko was hardly aware of having gotten up, but all of a sudden he was on his feet, groping for what was left of his padded coat. The wind drilled at him through the doorway, icy and damp, making his teeth chatter uncontrollably. The NKVD men, he saw, were wearing heavy padded coats and fur caps with earflaps down. Past them, out in the dark road, he could see the silhouettes of half a dozen trucks with corrugated tin sides. Their motors were running and the exhaust rose behind them in slow, heavy clouds against a night sky pierced by intensely bright stars.

"Are you deaf? Get on your feet. Outside. Let's get moving."

Finally Kurenko found words. Where were they taking him? Why? Had he been accused of something? If so, what? He demanded to know.

Even as he spoke it seemed to him that the most frightening thing about what was happening was not that he was being arrested, not that he was being dragged off in the middle of the night to God only knew where, but simply that he had always known it was going to happen exactly this way. No matter what he did.

The larger of the two NKVD men gestured with his automatic and held out a paper. Kurenko could not make out entirely what was written on it but it appeared to be an order of some kind, an order of arrest. He'd seen enough of them before. He knew.

At the bottom, in a large, distinct, and almost childish hand, was a signature. The single name—Sipyagin.

3

This is not my defense, it is my self-accusation. I have not said a single word in my defense.

N. I. Bukharin
Trial transcript
March 5, 1938

Serge Petrovitch Budyankov was a habitual pacer; even when there was no need to pace, no reason of any kind, no tension whatever to relieve, he paced like a caged animal. He had, in fact, spent the one real vacation of his life pacing back and forth along the beach at Alupka, while his wife, who had given up trying to get him to relax, had sat despondent and alone on the rocks, gazing longingly up the coast toward Yalta where people were actually enjoying themselves, swimming and talking to one another.

Budyankov simply could not relax. He barely slept and ate little. But to the surprise of everyone who knew him, he neither smoked excessively nor drank tea or coffee in the quantities to be expected from a man of his disposition. He was in his mid-forties and of middle height, a man of totally undistinguished appearance, looking rather like a round-faced rural schoolteacher out of an early Chekhov play. He wore thick glasses, was going bald, and had pronounced liver spots all over his high, domed forehead.

He was also a man of generally benign temperament and had become even more restrained since his release from prison. For two years, following the Tukaschevsky purges, he had sat alone in a damp, cold stone cell in the Lubyanka while the special prosecutor's office labored to find something against him. The slightest something would have sufficed—but being unable to find anything at all that could be used to remotely justify execution or even a trial, they had studiously ignored him in the hopes that neglect and the despair it would breed might cause Budyankov himself to recall something useful. If for no other reason than simply to get out of the dismal cell into which he had been thrown.

In the end, Budyankov's perseverance and his calm, continued silence had had their reward. When the war had started, he had been released, one of the few, and had actually been restored to his full rank of colonel and given important work to do. A few months after his release, someone had gotten the idea, probably from the continued observations to which Budyankov knew he had been secretly subjected, that such a man as he unquestionably was, highly intelligent and learned in the quirks of human behavior, might be particularly useful in intelligence work. Especially as an interrogating officer. After all, Budyankov had been in prison himself; he could be counted on to understand intimately the psychology of those he questioned. He could play upon that knowledge, use it subtly and to good effect. And, then, there was the matter of Budyankov's unusually mild temper, which he was now, in fact, at the point of finally losing, having been awakened while it was still dark, yanked out of a warm bed and away from his wife, and driven without explanation down to the all-too-familiar prison on Lubyanka Street.

There, so he had been told, he was to await a special prisoner who required immediate attention.

Just why this was so no one had bothered to tell him. Thus, for the last three hours, he had stalked impatiently about his shabby, barren office, without a newspaper to read, without even knowing who it was he was to see or what he was supposed to ask. Or, and this was most important, just why it had been necessary to drag him from his bed when the prisoner in question had not even arrived yet. He had considered phoning up to ask Colonel Greenblatt, his immediate superior in the department, but had decided that there was no point in irritating him; if Greenblatt had wanted him to know what was going on, he certainly would have informed him. He would have to grit his teeth, wait, and abide the event. Greenblatt was no fool and there was undoubtedly some sort of method to his behavior.

He shouted for his aide, Gritsky, who could do no more than rub his own bleary eyes and bring in a steaming pot of bitter, undrinkable chicory coffee, which was all that could be found at that hour.

Budyankov had phoned the receiving section of the prison at least half a dozen times in a vain effort to find out at least who it was he was waiting for, who had been brought in during the night, who it *might* be that was shortly to be pushed into his office for questioning. No one had any useful information. There had been many that night. But of all the names they read to him, not one made any impression. The phone did not ring. No new instructions reached him.

Finally, at around seven in the morning—a gray, bitter cold morning filled with the shadowy movement of trucks in the still-dark streets and the fitful blustering of yet more snow in the low sky above the river—there was a perfunctory knock on Budyankov's door.

The door opened. An intelligence captain whose name Budyankov could not recall—Spelter or Schluter or something like that; a Volga German, probably, or a Balt—stood there blinking, obviously as uncomfortable and sleepy as Budyankov was himself. Next to him stood a handsome dark-haired woman wearing a bathrobe.

The expression on the woman's face at once caught Budyankov's attention. A new prisoner's normal reaction was usually either confused fear or, in many cases, an obsequious cheerfulness, as though to signify that everyone really knew what a foolish mistake had been made and what a good joke it all was. The woman who had just been pushed into the room exhibited neither of these customary reactions. Rather, she gazed slowly around, shaking her head, until at last she seemed to take notice of Budyankov, at which point she gave him a look of the purest disdain.

"Colonel Budyankov? This is Nina Andreyeva Golitsyna."

"You have her dossier?" Budyankov answered cautiously, for the moment not having the slightest idea who the woman was or whether he was supposed to know her.

The woman was now staring directly at him. Budyankov's first reaction was to feel himself on her side of things and to be angry at the nervous, bleary-eyed captain who had escorted her.

"I don't think you understand," said the captain. "I said . . . this is Nina Andreyeva Golitsyna."

Suddenly it registered. The captain was talking about General

Golitsyn, Alexander Semyonovitch, the Defender of Moscow, the hero of the December counteroffensive. He had known Golitsyn slightly in the early thirties, after he had first come back from China. When he had gone back the second time, to Canton and Chiang Kai-shek's Wampoa Academy, he, Budyankov, had been in a cell deep in the Lubyanka. But how could one forget such a man? A giant with a broad, impossible face, like a character out of Gogol, incredibly long arms, huge hands. Tall as an oak and ungainly as a stork. As complex and perpetually morose a man as he had ever met. Yet brilliant too. He had never met Golitsyn's wife; she had always stayed well in the background and Budyankov knew little about her. But a sense of outrage nevertheless took hold at once.

"No, no, this is too much. Why is *she* brought here? What possible excuse can there be for a disgrace like this?"

The captain, carefully avoiding Budyankov's direct gaze, thrust a folder at him. While the woman stood silently by, arms folded, he quickly read the papers. After a long silence, Budyankov said, "Why wasn't I informed of this before? What am I supposed to do at this point? I am as surprised by all of this as . . ."

The captain cut him off. "The dispatch only came six hours ago."

"But it was in time enough for you to *arrest* this woman . . . time enough . . . but no time to inform *me*." Budyankov caught himself; was he berating the captain because he was really angry or because he wanted to create confusion in the prisoner's mind, to ensure their being able to start the interrogation easily and with a feeling of mutual understanding?

It was doubtful that the captain understood any of this. He protested, excused himself, and left the room as quickly as he could.

Nina Andreyeva remained where she was. Budyankov realized for the first time that she was a very good-looking woman, with a singularly strong face, very large eyes, and what he was rapidly discovering to be a withering stare. She looked, in fact, rather like Budyankov's own wife when she was angry—a fact that immediately put him at a disadvantage.

After a moment, he said, "Well now, you had better sit down, I think, comrade Golitsyna."

There was only one chair in the room. She took it without a word.

"Would you like some coffee? It's foul but it's hot. . . ."

She nodded, took the cup without thanking him. She should have been ill at ease, if for no other reason than because she was still in her nightclothes. But it seemed to make no difference whatever to her.

She drank the coffee down very slowly and then, after a long pause, which Budyankov was at a loss to punctuate, she said:

"Colonel, how long is this going to go on?"

"How long?"

"I mean, when are you going to tell me what you want of me?"

Budyankov was desperate. He had no idea himself what he was supposed to do. Why didn't the phone ring? Why didn't someone come in with instructions? He felt like a fool, standing there in the empty room, confronting this woman who was sitting comfortably on his only chair. In her nightclothes. And drinking his coffee.

Damn Greenblatt. . . .

His voice became very matter-of-fact. He wondered if she would realize that he was stalling.

"Do you know what's happened?" he asked.

"A rather broad question, don't you think, Colonel? At any rate, I thought you might tell me."

He handed her a copy of the dispatch that the captain had already shown her. Although it carried the highest of security classifications, he could find no sensible reason why the man's wife shouldn't know.

She read it quickly and without any show of surprise.

"Then . . . you knew?" Budyankov asked, somewhat mystified.

"How could I know? I knew only what they told me when I was arrested. But it doesn't surprise me, that's all."

Budyankov continued to study her face. There was still no real reaction, though something, he wasn't quite sure just what, was finally beginning to show through. He sighed.

"Understand, *gospozha* Golitsyna, he has deserted. He is now, officially, a traitor to his country. There's no doubt about it. It isn't just that he's been encircled or captured, though that's been reason enough for coming to the same conclusion in many other cases. He surrendered, voluntarily, all as you see there. He asked to be taken to Berlin. He is *collaborating*. There's no doubt about it. He has offered . . . no, *insisted,* on being given command over all the deserters and malcontents that the fascists have managed to collect these last months. In the midst of this, our great patriotic war, *your* husband . . ."

"You can talk of a patriotic war? Of patriotism of any kind? You could have pushed the Germans all the way back to the Rhine by now if you'd had any officers left. Even I know that. And whose fault is it that we're in such a predicament? You stand there and talk of patriotism to me with the blood of Tukaschevsky on your hands. . . ."

Budyankov took a deep breath and held out his right hand. The fingers were gnarled and twisted; the bones had been broken, every one of them, and had never set properly.

"Not on these hands," he said softly. "Not this Baba Yaga's claw. . . ."

"An accident? A war wound? Should I say I'm sorry? I've seen far worse, Colonel."

"Not a war wound, nor an accident either, *gospozha* Golitsyna. Far from it. I spent two whole years in this very prison, downstairs, along with Tukaschevsky and all the others. Getting my fingers broken one by one. Among other things. Would you like to see the rest?" He made a motion as though to unbutton his jacket.

Nina Andreyeva looked at him coldly.

"And yet you're here, aren't you?" she said. "Which must mean that you too 'collaborated,' as you put it."

"There was no charge brought against me," he said, acutely aware that his tone had become angrily defensive.

"There was none against the others either. No real charge. We all knew that."

"That may or may not be true. I only know that against *me* there was no charge. I had done nothing. But I also know that it was not because of my innocence that I was released."

"Why then?"

"The war, and the fact that they simply hadn't gotten around to me yet. I wasn't very important, you see."

"Assume that is all so . . . why am *I* here? What has all of this got to do with me? And why do you work for them now? How can you? Are you going to break my fingers?"

Budyankov lit a cigarette after first offering one to the general's wife. She refused with a shake of her head.

"There are wrongs and there are greater wrongs, *gospozha* Golitsyna. I *might* have been guilty. They had no way of knowing.

Every system of morality, however rigorously scientific, my dear woman, carries with it the seeds of its own ambiguities."

"Colonel . . . exactly what do you want of me?"

Budyankov did not respond at once. He lit his own cigarette, filled his lungs with smoke, then laid the cigarette in a little cut-glass ashtray on his desk. What was he to say? Just why *had* they arrested the woman? He knew, of course, that anyone connected with anyone who was even suspected of treason was being arrested. And the definition of treason had expanded to an extent unimaginable even two years before. That Nina Andreyeva Golitsyna had been arrested was, under the circumstances, reasonable enough.

But what, exactly, was to be done with her? To what use could she be put? Vague ideas were beginning to form in the back of his mind. He picked up the dossier and leafed through the papers again.

"To cooperate with us, for one thing," he began, slowly, improvising with caution, watching for the slightest reaction.

"What makes you think I'd do that?"

"Your sense of patriotism."

"My sense of morality?"

"That too."

"Which shows how little you know of either myself or Alexander Semyonovitch."

"Surely you aren't going to tell me that you approve of what he's done, are you?"

She shook her head.

"All right then. There is also the question of your own physical safety. You must be aware of what is normally done in cases like this."

"You'll do to me what they did to you, or worse, of course. I have no doubt about that. And you hardly need a reason. No more than they had in your case, Colonel, isn't that right?"

The phone rang. Budyankov held up his hand for silence. He picked up the receiver. For a second he heard only an angry buzzing noise. Connections had not been good for the last week. A German bomb had disrupted the main switching center.

Finally a voice broke through. It was Budyankov's section commander, Greenblatt. Budyankov heaved a sigh of relief.

"You have the woman there now?"

"Yes."

"And matters are progressing?"

Budyankov glanced at the woman. She was not even looking at him; she was busy adjusting the buttons of her robe.

"Progressing . . ." said Budyankov. "You could say that, yes, 'progressing' would be a good way to put it."

"Continue talking to her as long as you like. Take your time. Develop a feeling for the situation. Do you understand? When you're finished, come upstairs."

"As you wish. . . ."

He hung up. There had been something both ominous and relieving in Colonel Greenblatt's tone. He nodded to himself to indicate his satisfaction. Now the woman was looking straight at him. He flushed.

"Instructions, comrade Colonel? Have they told you at last what to do with me?"

"My dear woman . . ."

"They're wasting their own time and yours, you know? What possible help could I give you? Surely, you must know how things stood between Alexander Semyonovitch and myself."

Budyankov was taken off-guard. He blinked into the light. Her voice was hard and accusing. He was being told, he realized, that he was in no small measure a fool.

"Why no, *gospozha* Golitsyna. What do you mean?"

She laughed gratingly.

"Only this, Colonel. Alexander Semyonovitch and I haven't lived together for more than two years. We are divorced. If you hadn't been in prison yourself, perhaps you'd have heard about it. But then perhaps not. Very few people did. My husband was ordered not to make a scandal and, like the good soldier he is, he obeyed his orders to the letter."

"I don't quite understand you, *gospozha* Golitsyna."

"There isn't much to understand, Colonel. It's all quite amusing, really. I mean, that you don't know. You all might have saved yourself the trouble of arresting me . . . if you'd known. It's obvious to me that communications between various sections of our government are not what they might be. Actually, it's rather funny."

"Explain." Budyankov began quite suddenly to feel very foolish and very vulnerable.

"Just this, Colonel. Two years ago, not long after we came back from China, Alexander Semyonovitch was told that he had to divorce me. The order came from Stalin himself, I believe. You see, my parents were *kulaks,* both of them. Decent people, but not appropriate in-laws for a major general of the Soviet army. After Bukharin's trial, class purity had suddenly become very important again, if you recall. Rather like the fascists, wouldn't you say? Like their Jewish policy?" She stopped and licked her lips. It was obviously costing her a good deal of effort. "Do you have a cigarette for me, comrade Colonel? I should not have refused your offer before."

He gave her one. She lit it, took a few puffs, and put it nervously aside.

"I had tainted blood, it seemed, and—so—they ordered him to be rid of me. Apparently the brilliant minds that conceived this idea thought that my husband would refuse and make their own way to the top that much easier. But our good Alexander Semyonovitch did not refuse. His feelings of duty to his country—or possibly to himself, I was never sure which—turned out to be far stronger than any love he bore for me."

"And your feelings, Nina Andreyeva?"

She looked at him, her face briefly flashing indefinable feeling. Then a mask seemed to settle over her features.

"I detest the man. I couldn't care in the least what happens to him and it seems fairly obvious that he cares nothing for me either. So if you had anything of *that* sort in mind . . ."

"No, I assure you . . ." Budyankov heard himself saying. But in that very instant he began to have something else of a very different sort in mind. He would have to speak to certain people. Those who had been close to Golitsyn . . . then . . .

Perhaps nothing would come of it. But perhaps . . . there would be something.

A line of closed-back Studebaker trucks moved north in a slow procession, from Pribov toward Kulya and then into the marshes. In the cab of each truck sat a man from the *Osoby Otdel,* the special department of the NKVD field units. On his lap was a tommy gun, fully loaded. The backs of the trucks were bolted shut from the outside.

In the brief flashes of light that entered now and then through the small wire-covered window at the rear of the truck, Vassily Kurenko could make out some of the unit insignia on what was left of the other prisoners' uniforms. No two were the same, but all of them, he knew, had been in the fighting around Brinapol and Kolabyansk. They were all survivors of Golitsyn's catastrophe.

They stared at each other in the dark, not knowing what to say, where they were going, why, or—worse yet—even who to ask.

One man began to whistle the "Red Sarafan."

A voice from the other end of the truck told him to shut up.

"Why? Are we going to a funeral?"

"Maybe."

"Whose, then, if you know so much?"

There was no answer. The man began to whistle again, the same tune.

Kurenko pulled his ragged coat up around his face. He remembered the tune well enough; the day after he'd graduated from the academy he'd gone to a gypsy place near Arbat Square, just like a character out of Dostoevski, and he'd gotten drunk, really drunk, for the first time in his life.

Now and then they could hear quite distinctly the distant whine of passing aircraft, their engines clearly audible over the grumble of the truck motors because of their intensely higher pitch.

A sadness came over him, not because of what had happened to him but, simply, because of the seeming inevitability of it. He was no different than any of the others after all. It had made no difference that he had been on the general's staff. The general had failed and everyone who had failed with him would have to pay for it. It didn't seem right but he knew that that was the way it was and that it had been only a delusion, his thinking he could avoid it.

"I don't understand, comrade," someone was saying.

Silence.

Then a voice replied. "It doesn't matter whether you understand or not. Who understands?"

Just before dawn the column stopped on the side of the road outside a large village that bordered an ice-choked river. Kurenko had almost fallen asleep when he was awakened by a rough hand on his shoulder. It was the man sitting next to him. He had never seen his face before and they had not spoken but the man pulled at him with the solicitous urgency of an old friend.

"Look out there . . ."

In the gray half-light, through a soft veil of falling snow, they could see a long line of prisoners under guard trudging along the road. They were close to the trucks and it was possible to see them quite clearly.

"Germans?"

"Ours, comrade. Look, you see that man on the end of the line there? I know him. His name's Kislevsky. He was with our artillery regiment. He was captured at Spalnin. Evidently he got away again."

"I was taken at Gorya," said a voice.

"We broke through at Salmask, but we *got away* from the bastards," complained another bitterly, as though to say that the others who had allowed themselves to be captured deserved their fate but he did not.

The line moved on, the faces of the men gradually obscured by the drifting snow and the distance.

The truck motors started up again, refueling completed.

The man sitting next to Kurenko put his arm around Kurenko's shoulder.

It was a gesture, Kurenko knew, that the man would have permitted himself only in a moment of the deepest despair.

Just then, someone at the front end of the truck began to pound on the back of the cab.

"Aren't you bastards even going to let us out to piss?"

She sat on her cot with her head against the wall, wondering how long she would have to wait before they came to take her to her cell. She knew, of course, from what Alexander Semyonovitch had told her once, of the things that had happened during the days of the *Yezhovschina,* that it was possible that they might simply take her down to the cellar and shoot her without a word of explanation or warning, though she could think of no sensible reason why they should do that.

The room was warm, almost too warm. Most likely they kept it that way on purpose, she thought, in order to make her drowsy, to put her off her guard. She heard pipes rattling somewhere in the walls, and the sound of a radio voice, tinny and covered with static, singing "The Blue Kerchief." What a strange thing—in a prison. "The Blue Kerchief"?

Well, it made no real difference. She didn't care now what happened to her. They could do what they liked. The boy was far away, beyond the Urals. What happened to her was of no account.

Once, she thought, it would have mattered very much. Because of him. But she had not seen him for almost three years now. She wondered if what she had told the colonel was entirely true, whether she really detested Alexander Semyonovitch Golitsyn, as she had said, or whether it was something else entirely.

Once, it had been quite different. She remembered all too keenly how it had been once.

When they had met, it had been in the stable of what had been her father's farm near Bolkhov. She had just finished helping the bay mare, Sula, through a difficult foaling. An officer had come suddenly and clumsily through the slatted stable doors, looking like a giant haystack in his peak-topped cloth *budionovka,* a dun-colored greatcoat reaching almost to the tops of his muddy boots. He was all legs, long, dangling arms, and thick, steel-rimmed glasses like an aviator's goggles on a head shapeless as a lump of discarded dough. He looked, in fact, so much like the foal, which was also all legs and big, staring eyes, that she had burst out laughing in spite of herself and in spite of the major's double bars and the chevrons on his coat sleeve.

The officer stood there for a moment, awkward and embarrassed, not knowing what to make of the muddy creature with straw in her black hair and mare's blood up to her elbows who was laughing at him as though she already knew him.

As she subsided, he said softly:

"*Grazhdanka,* I've come for some fodder for the horses, if you please."

Then he explained that he was commandant of the detachment that had come from Bolkhov to help with the collectivization program and to put an end to the peasant riots that had been in progress on and off for the past few weeks.

She had shown him the fodder bins and told him to take as much as he needed. Overcome with generosity, she thought herself like Princess Maria at Bogucharovo, offering the contents of the granary to Nikolai Rostov.

"Just leave enough for Sula," she said, pointing at the hard-breathing mare. "We'll find more for the others somewhere. They can wait. But she, poor creature, she's had a hard time of it. And she's going to be terribly hungry in another hour or so."

The foal nuzzled the officer's leg and whinnied. The officer ran his hand over the creature's head, looked down at her, and smiled.

"Here—I'll give you a receipt for what we take. We're not thieves, you know, even if that's what everyone around here thinks." And he wrote out the amount of fodder he'd taken and signed the paper with his name: Alexander Semyonovitch Golitsyn, Major, Bolkhov District, Third Regiment, Twelfth Division, Infantry.

After a while, Nina Andreyeva led him up to the old main house, which was perched on the hill overlooking the stables and the barn and the few *desyatinas* of land still under cultivation. The major's men had come wearily up the muddy road from the village of Strasneshev and were already bivouacked among the charred stumps of what had once been the apple orchards. There they rested, smoking and eating, a motley collection of exhausted, sullen foot soldiers, horse-drawn wagons, a few machine-gun carts carrying Maxims on stubby tripods, and three decrepit British lorries captured during the days of General Wrangel's offensives in the Ukraine and still in service. To the east, on the far bank of the Oka River, a thin column of smoke trembled in the wind over the village of Strasneshev like the spiral of a tornado.

She took the major into the old log house. There was no furniture left in the big main room. The floor was covered with straw and debris and most of the windows were broken and patched over with oilcloth and heavy waxed paper. Spiders had been busy in the corners and under the eaves. Only the musty storerooms and the corner where she had made her bed, just off the little kitchen, were clean and intact. A few of the junior officers from the detachment came up to the house. They washed in the fenced yard in front of the house, pouring basin after basin of cold water drawn from the well over their naked shoulders, despite the autumn chill.

Afterward, Nina Andreyeva found some cucumbers and dried mushrooms for the officers and a few loaves of black bread for the soldiers who had no food in their own kits. The soldiers ate, squatting in the cold-stiff mud of the yard or sitting on logs. There was something about the skeletal, ruined house that disturbed them.

"Why don't they want to come in? They could eat on the benches there. They don't have to sit in the mud like animals."

"Whose house was this?" asked the major.

"It belonged to the owner of the farm," she said slowly, as though trying to measure the effect of her words on him one at a time. "The owner was transported last year, after the first expropriations. The militia took them all away in trucks, over a hundred from this district alone. Now the house belongs to the village Soviet, I suppose. What's left of it, that is. They didn't leave much. The house was stripped bare. They took everything and left little pieces of paper, receipts like the one you gave me. Most of the livestock went to the *kholkhoz* at Bolkhov. If Strasneshev ever starts a collective of its own, maybe this house will be a part of it. For now, though, only a few people live here. I'm one of them, that's all."

The major nodded gravely.

"Of course, that's why," he said, looking out over his weary troops.

"Why what?"

"Why they don't want to come in. Somehow, they know. Don't ask me how. But it's a way they have. They sense it. It's not such a big house, after all. But they can tell that it was the house of *kulaks* and they don't want to go in. The owner, who was he?"

"My father," she said. "His name was Andrei Pavlovitch Lavrov. He owned the house and the land. All of it. He's gone now. To the Narym district with a railroad work gang."

"And your mother?"

"She died two years ago. Of typhus."

He stared at her and nodded soberly. She had spoken with such a lack of emotion that for a moment he'd been taken aback. Yet he'd known so many cases like hers. All over Russia, ever since the revolution. Sons turning their backs on their fathers, daughters on their mothers. Families simply falling apart, or bursting angrily like grenades going off. There were no regrets. The father was in Narym, the daughter in Bolkhov district. That was the way it was.

"It's hard," he said. "But it has to be done. Stalin is absolutely right, of course. The big farms have to be broken up. And there must be collectives. There isn't any other way. . . ."

"Yes," she agreed. "But, still, it's hard to believe that it's worth all the suffering."

"Your father, you mean?"

"What happened to my father isn't important. He'll manage, wherever he is. He always has. He's strong and he'll feed off his anger if there's nothing else. We fought bitterly. I warned him that his acquisitive ways were going to get him into trouble. He said, what was he doing but what Stalin had told all the middle farmers to do? Sow and grow, he said, and that's what I've done. Only I've done it better than the others, that's all. He had the best harvest in the district year after year and he worked very hard at it. I don't remember a night when he didn't come in from the fields dead tired. Work hard and God will provide, he said. He even started to hire laborers to help him. We had four oxen, six horses, the barn, the stables. When it came time to decide who was a *kulak* and who wasn't, it was the laborers who did it for him. . . . I'd warned him to give the oxen to the collective voluntarily. I told him that the collectives had to be formed, that the old ways weren't going to work anymore. He threw me out of the house for my troubles. If he'd given them the oxen, who knows? The peasants in Strasneshev are decent folk. And now, of course, they're feeling the whip themselves. After they took everything from my father and the others like him, they thought they could keep it all, but now they're being told they have to give it to the collective, and themselves into the bargain. . . ."

"So they let you stay here," the officer said slowly, shaking his head, "because your father threw you out? Because you spoke up for the collectives yourself?"

"No, they let me stay because I'm a doctor. There isn't even a decent *feldsher* in the village. The district committee had no choice. It was either let me stay or go without."

"You're a veterinarian?"

"No, comrade Major. A physician. But if a horse needs help, well, why not?"

She handed him a dipper of water. He drank, then squatted down on the ground in the yard, sifting the rich black soil through his large, pawlike hands.

"And, *grazhdanka* Lavrova, are you a good doctor?"

"With horses, yes. It goes well with people too, and every day, believe me, there's more practice around here."

He stood up again.

"Will you come to Strasneshev with me? You can be of much use there now."

He told her what had happened. She listened, sick at heart, already knowing much of what he was saying. There had been bitter opposition in the Bolkhov district, as elsewhere, to the collectivization decrees. The peasants had refused to join the *kholkhoz* or to turn over their livestock, preferring to kill their cattle first. They had destroyed what little farm machinery they had and burned much of their grain rather than turn it in to meet the government quotas. When the farmers began burning the *kholkhoz* buildings as well as the grain, and murdering the government workers who had been sent to help with the collectivization, the troops had been sent in. The same thing had been going on all over the country since the first decrees in 1929. A real uprising had broken out in Strasneshev the week before, the first time since the middle farmers had been forcibly transported to the camps in the north the previous spring and their property turned over to the collectives. A pitched battle between armed peasants and government troops had been going on since morning, the major said. It made him sick to fire on such people. They weren't really enemies of the state. They just didn't understand. He wanted to help them, not murder them. And that was what it was. Murder. Let there be no mistake about it. But it had to be done. He took the shame on himself willingly. If it would help.

He took her down to the smoking village in one of the old British lorries, together with an escort of cavalry and two machine-gun wagons. The muddy, rutted streets and the marketplace of the village were full of wreckage of every kind: smashed wagons, splintered barrels, a ruined harvesting combine, a few charred trucks. Small fires burned everywhere. Quite a few houses had been gutted.

There were more than fifty wounded laid out on the floor of the old church, with only one harried army doctor and a *feldsher* from Mtsensk to tend to them. The fighting was still going on on the outskirts of the village, behind the chestnut forest. Rifles cracked constantly and now and then Nina Andreyeva heard the brief stutter of a Maxim.

She rolled up her sleeves and did what she could. By late afternoon she thought she'd saved a few. Some had thanked her but a few had cursed her as she bent over them, remembering Andrei Pavlovitch and remembering her as his daughter.

Just before five, the rifle fire had stopped. No more wounded were brought in. A courier handed the major a report that the fighting had ceased at last. The few remaining rioters had fled into the forests. For the time being, there was nothing more for her to do.

"I should go back and see to Sula now," she said wearily, washing the blood off her hands in a tin basin in the churchyard.

Alexander Semyonovitch smiled. "The mare?"

She nodded. "And there's plowing yet to be done. . . ." She smelled of carbolic acid solution and burn ointment.

"Come, let me take you back," he said, squinting through his thick glasses.

And as they were riding back up the road to the farm, he turned to her, "Maybe it's my turn now to help you. You must show me the fields."

The sun was enormous in the sky, spreading a vast stain of orange, like an egg yolk that has broken in the pan. The horizon was nearly obscured by dust and smoke, and a dozen hazy shades of purple and umber settled over the hills and forests in thick layers. A few hawks wheeled high in the sky, puzzled by the smoke and hungrily searching for the smaller birds who had been frightened away by the soldiers and the horse wagons spread out in the ruined orchards around the stable. Even the mice had gone into hiding.

To her astonishment, when they arrived, the officer shucked off his coat, rolled up his sleeves, and asked where the shed was.

"Why, whatever for?"

"I intend to help you with the plowing, what else? There's still an hour or so of good light left. The mare can do without you for a little while longer. She's a good, sturdy animal."

Nina Andreyeva was ashamed; they had nothing but an old wooden harrow that had to be weighted with stones. He picked up the stones easily, as though they weighed nothing at all, then threw the harness over his wide shoulders and hauled the harrow out to the fields beyond the barn.

The exhausted men took little notice. Some were already dozing against their horses. A fire had been lit in the yard. Someone had found a large iron pot and was trying to cook soup. A curl of blue cigarette smoke rose from the orchard's ruin.

The officer said nothing to the men as he led Nina Andreyeva out into the fields.

The soldiers shook their heads and smiled to themselves. Nothing their crazy giant of a commander did was a surprise to them anymore. But, nevertheless, they could not help but take note this time as he padded obediently in the wake of the small, attractive woman and disappeared into the hazy fields.

After they had walked awhile, he stopped and adjusted the harness of the harrow.

"Here?"

"You can see where I started this morning."

He looked down critically at the long black marks in the soil. "Let me tell you . . . I'm from Nizhny Novgorod, and even though my father was a tailor and I was educated by monks in a seminary, I know when a furrow isn't deep enough. Nothing is going to grow in those scratches you've made. Now, let me show you how it's done. You walk behind with the seed . . ."

He leaned into the harness and left a long wake of rich, heavily turned earth. He groaned and swore and struggled against the hard earth and the stones. Sweat poured down his neck like lava in the red sunset.

He was very strong and, she thought, at the same time very gentle. She hadn't had any help from a man in a long while. The district committee wasn't going to drive her off, but they weren't going to do anything for her either. The huge officer was her friend; he understood her situation. He seemed a decent man too, willing to pay her back for her help with his own sweat. And what she'd done hadn't even been for him or his men, but for others, the people he'd been brought in to pacify. Somehow that made it even better.

She liked him for that and for the fact that, unlike so many of her countrymen, he hadn't lost all of the old ways and manners yet.

He stopped to wipe his brow, turning to study her for a long moment. Behind the thick lenses of his glasses, his pale blue eyes were intense and strangely magnified.

"*Grazhdanka* Lavrova . . . the seed please," he said. "Without the seed, nothing will grow." He laughed and pulled the harness of the harrow back into position over his shoulder.

She found no real need for words, dug her hand deep into the seed bag, feeling the warm grain slide around her fingers. The smoky rays of the setting sun caught the first flight of seed as she threw it wide into the furrows.

That evening she sat with the major on the porch of the ruined log house that had once belonged to her father and now belonged to no one. They talked ruefully of the collectives and of Stalin's decrees, and of Nekrasov's poetry and Gorki's novels. It was a way of speaking that she had not experienced in a long time, easy and warm and equal. The other officers kept their distance, smoked and conversed in low voices, their eyes on the black horizon of chestnut and poplar forest in the direction of the Oka.

At the dawn's first gray light, the major rose from the heap of coats and old blankets on which he had bedded down in the back of one of the wagons, and brushed the frost from his boots. Nina Andreyeva brought him a bowl of steaming tea and some groats. He ate in regretful silence, then climbed heavily up onto his mount.

For a second he hesitated, then reached down to touch her hand.

"*Grazhdanka* Lavrova—be careful . . . be well."

She knew by then that she would see him again, no matter what.

Three months later, he came back to Strasneshev and took her away with him. They were married by the clerk in Tula just after New Year's Day, 1931.

Now she leaned back against the cell wall. It had grown even warmer. The voice she had heard before was now singing the mournful "Lonely Accordion." She felt like weeping but her eyes were dry and her head had begun to throb.

There was a small bowl of water on a shelf hanging from the opposite wall. She got up and went over to it, splashed a little water on her forehead, and felt instantly better.

It would do no good to allow herself to become nostalgic and melancholy. She had to keep her wits about her if she was going to have even a chance of surviving.

The corridor outside was silent. The guards moved about in felt boots and one never knew when someone was going to appear at the door. She sat down again on the cot and waited, this time with her eyes wide open and her hands folded peacefully in her lap.

Only her knuckles would give her away; they were bone-white from the pressure.

4

Once there was a soldier
Handsome and daring
But he was only a child's plaything,
For he was a paper soldier.
He wished to change the world
So that all in it would be beautiful.
But he himself could only turn on a string
For he was a paper soldier.
He would have been content to go through fire and smoke
To perish for us twice over.
But all we did was laugh at him
For he was a paper soldier.
We never put our faith in him
Nor trusted him at all.
And why? Because, of course,
He was a paper soldier.
And he—he cursed his fate,
A quiet life was not what he craved.
And so he shouted, "Fire, fire!"
Forgetting that he was paper.
Into the fire? Well, yes, into the fire
He marched, alone and upright,
And there he was lost, gaining nothing for it,
For he was a paper soldier.

Bulat Okudzhava

Budyankov pushed his eyeglasses back up along the bridge of his nose and closed the fat dossier he had been studying. It was all there. Colonel Greenblatt had been remarkably prompt in producing the needed information. But then, considering Golitsyn's rank and importance, it was not surprising that the information was so easy to come by. There were detailed service evaluations going all the way back to the revolution, a sheaf of reports from the China period, and a separate inner folder dealing exclusively with Golitsyn's wife and the aftermath of their divorce.

There were over a dozen studies done by NKVD psychologists who considered in the minutest possible detail the impact of that episode on his service reliability.

One sentence struck Budyankov more forcibly than all the others; it was, in fact, a summation of everything the doctors had written.

"The subject will inevitably act according to his conscience and his sense of duty, but should he be required to injure someone as a result, and although he will do it without hesitation if he believes it to be required of him, his sense of guilt thereafter will be enormous and, ultimately, highly destructive."

Budyankov chewed on the end of a pencil. Greenblatt, an intense, gray-haired man in his late fifties, who had once been a cavalry officer with Budyenny during the Polish campaign, eyed him warily.

"Well, what do you think? Something strikes you?" Greenblatt asked softly.

Budyankov took a sip of the vodka Greenblatt had considerately provided and leaned back, his gnarled right hand splayed on the cover of the folder.

"I see no reason not to proceed," Budyankov said.

"You don't think that the idea is a bit too subtle, Serge Petrovitch? We would be relying very heavily on psychology rather than on direct, controllable action. The plan itself seems sound enough but . . . so complex. . . . Perhaps the stakes are a bit high for such a risk?"

"I knew the man, comrade Greenblatt. Fairly well, as a matter of fact. As you did too, if I recall correctly. And everything here"—he tapped the folder—"confirms my first instinct. What I didn't know was how things were with his wife. I never even met her. It was too long ago. But now that I do know, I see that it is all made to order."

Greenblatt leaned back and ran his hand through his short-cropped gray hair. A curved pipe lay fuming in a green glass ashtray. "Wouldn't an assassination be the simpler way?"

"We would only succeed in making a hero out of a fool," said Budyankov. "And besides, we would then be dealing with only half the problem. And the less important half at that."

"How ironic it is," said Greenblatt. "If we adopt your plan, we may actually have to enlist the cooperation of the Gestapo to carry it off."

"But if we can . . . and if we *do* . . ."

"They'll believe *they've* been the winners and that we're fools."

"And we'll know that exactly the opposite is true, won't we?"

Colonel Greenblatt picked up his pen and signed the authorization order.

"It's settled then. You have full authority to try it your way, Serge Petrovitch. You have my sincere admiration for your ingenuity. If you're successful, not only will you have done a great service for your country but you won't have done badly for yourself either." The colonel smiled in an ambiguous way and stroked his goatee. "You have everything you need?"

"Only one element is missing, and that shouldn't be too hard to find."

"Yes, the escort. One with good credentials. Preferably someone she knows, but only slightly."

"Have you obtained the lists I asked for?"

Greenblatt opened a drawer in his desk and took out a folder.

"The names of all the officers in his classes at the academy before the war. His adjutants, aides-de-camp. Such subordinates as he trusted. There are very few friends. No near relatives. The names marked with a star are men with whom he was particularly close . . . as close as a man like that could ever be. . . ."

"And those marked with an ex?"

"Dead. One way or another. Many of them were lost at the Volkhov and at Brinapol."

Budyankov frowned. "Out of such a large list there are so few left?"

"There will be fewer by tomorrow, no doubt. And fewer still the next day."

"All right then. We begin. Komansky's office will give me the current posting and location for the . . . survivors?"

"To the extent possible, yes. It shouldn't take more than a day or two. When do you think you'll be able to start?"

"Orders for the business at Byeleymostnoy can be sent out at once. There is no impediment."

"And the rest?"

"As soon as I have my man."

Greenblatt nodded, reached across the table for the carafe, and poured out another tumbler of vodka each for Budyankov and himself.

"To a complete success."

"I almost regret having to do this," said Budyankov. "In other times, that man . . ."

Greenblatt cut him off. "These are not 'other times' as you call them."

"To be sure, comrade Greenblatt."

Budyankov swallowed down the vodka and went to the door. There he paused and looked back for a long moment at the gray-haired intelligence officer sitting hunched over his desk.

"What is it, Serge Petrovitch? Why are you staring at me like that?"

"Your goatee, comrade Greenblatt," said Budyankov cheerfully. "Really, if you want my advice, you'd better get rid of it. You look far too much like Trotsky with that goatee."

Sipyagin had spent the evening growing maudlin and more than a little drunk. In Major Gelb's opinion, the distastefulness of his duties was finally beginning to wear him down and in the time-honored Slavic manner he was reacting by feeling sorry for himself rather than for those whom he injured. Gelb was not really critical. He understood, even sympathized, and thought, There but for the grace of whatever God there is go I. But he could not bring himself to join Sipyagin in his broodings, his nostalgia for southern villages or his brandy. Gelb was by nature a very temperate man and thus ideally suited for the kind of administrative intelligence work he did. His way of avoiding participation in Sipyagin's mournful reveries was to excuse himself to do yet another hour's work before trying to catch some much-needed sleep.

He could hear Sipyagin in the next room, singing softly to himself in a reedy, wandering voice. The tune drifted, formed vaguely familiar patterns, dissolved. Sometimes Sipyagin's nasal singing even put Gelb in mind of the synagogue melodies he dimly recalled from his youth.

The front was now far away, one hundred and fifty kilometers at least, and there had been no German planes over all day. The night was clear, full of stars, and infinitely lonely.

Gelb had fixed himself a cup of tea and brought together the records of all the prisoners who had been sent off in convoy during the preceding week. It depressed him to consider the waste; good officers and men who could have been back in the lines fighting the Germans, whose only crime had been to get themselves briefly captured or, even less, to have been cut off for a while behind enemy lines. But the orders were explicit; what right had any man to let himself be captured when his comrades were dying for the motherland?

It was the waste rather than the human misery involved that most upset Major Gelb and, in the end, it was this very self-knowledge that forced him to conclude that he had surpassed even Sipyagin in callousness.

Sipyagin's singing had ceased at last. Perhaps he had gone to sleep. Or finally gotten so drunk that he'd lost consciousness. In the old days it would have been unheard of for an NKVD officer to get drunk where others could see him. But war did odd things to everyone and who was he, Maxim Isayevitch Gelb, to protest? After all, he even liked Sipyagin in a strange sort of way.

Gelb pushed his glasses back up on the bridge of his nose, wiped the steam from the tea from the lenses, and peered at the file in front of him. He'd been reading dispatches all day, some from the front, some from Moscow, highly classified intelligence communiqués, things that not even Sipyagin was supposed to see. All day long he had been correlating information, putting things together like a jigsaw puzzle. He was all too aware of the fact that the answers to almost all questions were lying right there in front of him. They only needed to be assembled in order to be recognized.

All he'd really achieved that day, he admitted sadly, was a sort of superficially neat state of confusion.

He was drowsy now. His gaze passed over a clipped batch of papers in front of him. The dispatch, some twenty pages of it, had been brought in by a motorcycle courier an hour or so earlier. He had paid little attention to it. Experience told him that nothing that long was ever very important.

Suddenly he jumped up, shouting, and ran into the next room.

Sipyagin was asleep on his cot. Gelb shook him awake and thrust the papers under his nose.

"Look here . . . you must read this. At once."

Sipyagin took the sheaf of papers reluctantly. After a moment he tried to sit up, pushed the papers away, and began to shout in frustration and rub his eyes

"Damn it, Maxim Isayevitch, you know perfectly well I've had too much to drink. So tell me, what's in there that's so important?"

Gelb swallowed hard, trying to restrain himself.

"Let me try to explain. Here, listen, pay attention. You see, it's a dispatch concerning General Golitsyn."

"That bastard? Yes? From Moscow?"

Gelb nodded. "It says that there's no doubt about it any longer. He's definitely gone over to the Germans"

"We knew that last week."

"Yes, yes, but there's more Here's a list of men who were closely connected with him in one way or another. His friends, a few relatives, his prize students from the academy, old comrades in arms . . ."

"The usual thing, I suppose. They're to be arrested of course."

"Exactly. But if any of them are found, and this is of the utmost importance—so it says here—they must be sent at once to Moscow. That a Colonel Greenblatt at the Ministry of State Security be notified, and so on. These men, it goes on to say, must under no circumstances be shipped off with any of the special units. We are warned . . ."

Sipyagin yawned and slumped back on the bed.

Gelb was screaming at him now, waving the list of names that had been attached to the dispatch under his nose.

"Don't you realize what we've done? Look, look. *This* name. Don't you remember him? You must . . ."

Sipyagin struggled back up again, again rubbing his eyes.

"Here . . . what's this? Let me see. What's all the fuss about?"

"Last week, the lieutenant who'd seen the turncoat cavalry unit . . ."

"What was his name . . . Kurenko? Here . . . the same . . . Kurenko?"

"Yes, precisely."

"What about him?"

"Why, look here, he's on the list. Don't you understand? *We had him here* and we packed him off like all the others. His name is on the lists we sent into District Headquarters. *Our* records. Think, Sipyagin, what that means."

Sipyagin was far too blowsy with alcohol and fatigue to think clearly about anything, but a cold chill went through him nevertheless.

Gelb drew a breath.

"I only hope that it isn't too late. We should have noticed this at the time we had him arrested."

"How could we possibly know that they'd want him a week later, that he was someone special?" Sipyagin cried.

"No one is blaming you, Sipyagin. I take full responsibility. After all . . ." he hesitated for a second, then went on. "I'm senior to you here. It's my fault. If it can't be rectified, yes, it will be my fault entirely."

"You'd say that? For me?"

"I would."

"Maxim Isayevitch, you're a decent person. There's no doubt about it."

"That's all well and good, but now let's see if we can't make good our mistake."

Sipyagin struggled to his feet, feeling much relieved, and began shouting for Pashkov and the cipher clerk. A message would have to be prepared at once.

By morning, Major Gelb and a full dossier on Senior Lieutenant Vassily Gregorovitch Kurenko were both safely stowed in the open rear cockpit of a PO-2 *Mule* and on their way to Moscow.

The shed had been used as a stable, and not too long ago at that. Wet straw lay in moldering heaps on the floor and the cold stones beneath exuded the pungent ammonia stink of horse urine. There was no heat, not even an old oil drum for a makeshift stove. The air hung in the dark in little frozen semaphores of breath. Kurenko huddled against the man next to him, trying desperately to keep warm. That seemed to him the most important thing a man could do, just try to keep warm. His teeth were chattering violently and now and then he began to shake, the spasms growing so furious at times that he was sure that he would break something. He had already chipped two of his teeth just from the chattering.

The man next to him—whose face he could not see clearly—put his arm around Kurenko's shoulder and pressed him hard to make the shaking stop. Gradually, Kurenko got control of himself again. His breathing became more regular, and the convulsions ceased.

He knew that it was only a matter of time before they started again. He didn't know whether he'd even be able to get on his feet again.

"Ah, so much better," said the man.

"You are very good . . ." said Kurenko with difficulty. "I want you to know that . . . thank you. . . "

"We all do what we can. Sometimes it isn't much."

Kurenko wanted to speak to the man but it was too painful for him. His mouth was full of sores, his lips were cracked and his tongue felt like a brick. Once, he had thought it would be easy to die when the time came but now he saw that dying could be one of the most difficult things in the world. He wondered whether he would be able to manage it with any dignity at all.

That was what bothered him most, the complete lack of dignity in dying this way.

The man next to him stank of onion. Where had he gotten an onion? Kurenko wondered. He could feel himself starting to shake again and made a tremendous effort to hold it in check. The man next to him understood.

"You have a fever?"

"I . . . don't know. Maybe."

"Shansky died of pneumonia yesterday. Is it contagious? Maybe you have pneumonia."

Kurenko felt dizzy. He looked up at the low roof of the stable. A narrow window about a third of a meter wide ran under the eaves, admitting a pale, hallucinatory gray light. Shadows flitted constantly over the walls. Some of the men were weeping openly. How could their own people be doing this to them? Capture by the Germans could not possibly have been worse. They wept with frustration and anger at the unfairness of it all. A few had been able to get to sleep despite the cold and one or two were even snoring. There were fifty or more prisoners jammed into the shed. They had been there for more than two days, with no food, one barrel of water to drink—if they could find something with which to break the ice that constantly formed at the top—and two slop pails for excrement.

Kurenko drew a deep, convulsive breath that cut his lungs like a knife. He wanted to thank the man next to him again, but he hadn't the strength. He hadn't eaten for so long he couldn't remember the last thing he'd had in his mouth. For days they'd been trucked and marched to the north, through increasingly bitter cold, moving mostly in the early morning hours and during the night so that no one in the villages through which they passed would see them. At first they'd seen other convoys going by, just like them, trudging along the roadside. Then nothing. Only the darkness and the snow and the guards and the trucks.

If a man had a coat, he had some hope of life at least. If not, he froze. At first some of the men who'd had coats or padded field jackets tried to share them with those who had none. But after a while it became difficult to get the coats back. There were fights and angry recriminations. Men who had loaned their coats for a while were accused of trying to murder their comrades when they asked for them back. Kurenko could not even remember whether he had started out from Pribov with a coat or not. He certainly had none now.

They were often left at night alone by the roadside in the unheated trucks, locked in. Sometimes they stayed overnight in the forests with only canvas gun-covers for protection. The guards were there with them; that was one thing—the guards had it almost as bad as the prisoners.

Not that it helped much though.

Nothing really helped, Kurenko thought, not even knowing why it had happened, because the reason really didn't make any sense to him. They all knew, but no one could make sense of it. Every one of them had been either a prisoner of the Germans and had escaped or had been behind enemy lines for a week or two.

"What the hell do they think, that half the army has turned traitor? If we wanted to do that, why would we come back at all, tell me?" It was a question they had all asked.

No one could answer.

Kurenko wondered how long he'd last. He wanted to write a letter, at least to let his father and mother know what had happened to him. Once, he thought he'd seen them at a distance, standing in a field, with a stack of valises and an empty parrot cage. It was then he understood that he'd begun hallucinating.

He thought he was hallucinating again when the door of the stable was knocked open by the butt of a submachine gun and two guards bundled in padded coats came in and began shouting.

His name.

"Kurenko? Vassily Gregorovitch Kurenko? Senior Lieutenant?"

No one answered.

"Listen. You'd better come out of there, Kurenko. You're on the list, so don't pretend you're not there."

The man next to him whispered. "Don't say a word if you don't want to. We'll say that this Kurenko died and we buried him. We buried a dozen yesterday. They didn't even take their identity papers."

"You're good . . . a good man," Kurenko said haltingly. His mouth hurt terribly as he stood up.

He didn't see where it made much difference what they did to him or when they did it. If they wanted to shoot him right then and there, just because his commanding officer had lost the battle, well then, let them do it. They were no better than the Germans. If Soviet officers were going to start behaving like Asiatics, then it was time for him to go, and as quickly as they liked.

He took a few shaky steps toward the guards. The sergeant came over. The other prisoners began to mutter. A few stood up in the dark. The straw rustled. One of the guards lowered the barrel of his *Pepesha.*

"It's all right," said Kurenko, not wanting anyone else to get hurt. The sergeant swore, took him by the arm, and pushed him out of the stable.

It was just getting light and, as always, a fine snow was falling. Damp and penetrating. The wind was coming from the south.

"Over there. Don't say a word. You're not to talk to anyone."

The sergeant major gestured toward a small van. The back door was open, the motor running. A soldier in a sheepskin coat stood by the cab holding a bundle. As Kurenko came up to him, the soldier threw him the bundle. In it was a heavy cloth coat and a pair of felt boots.

They shut the door and bolted it from the outside. Kurenko sat in the corner of the truck back, too frightened even to put on the coat. He could feel the heat of the motor coming up through the floor.

Without a word of explanation, they drove him to a nearby airstrip and locked him in a shed next to a hangar.

At four in the afternoon someone came with some food, a

chunk of bread and a tin of scalding tea without sugar. An hour later he was loaded onto a waiting TU-2 and flown north.

A few hours after sunset, the plane winged in over a city that Kurenko was sure must be Moscow. He had never seen Moscow from the air before and it was dark, but he had never seen anyplace so large. The sky above the city was ribboned with a thousand searchlight beams, but there were no German aircraft overhead and no antiaircraft fire.

At the airport he was once again put into a van.

No one had spoken to him other than to order him to get up, to sit down, or to get on the plane. The pilot hadn't said a word to him during the entire flight and the copilot-navigator was too busy with his charts and instruments even to notice him. There had been one good sign though: they'd given him a parachute.

He sat alone in the back of the van as it drove into the dark, sulfurous city, hearing only vague sounds—motors, voices, unidentifiable bangings and thumpings—and seeing blurs of light and shadow flit across the walls of the van.

Had he not been sure that it was impossible—he had had only the tea and the bread at the airport hours before—he would have thought he had somehow been given drugs.

After a drive of almost an hour, the van drew up before a large stone building that stood, as far as he could tell, in an area of old warehouses, low wooden frame buildings and bombed-out factories. Guards appeared, carrying automatic weapons. A gate opened, then closed. Kurenko found himself in a dark, walled courtyard.

All of this had taken place without a single word being spoken to him by any of the people through whose hands he had passed. Not even to offer him a drink, a cigarette, or a chance to urinate.

The door of the van opened.

"Out," said the driver from the cab. A guard looked at him quizzically, nodded, and pointed to another door on the side of the building, near the corner of the yard. The walls were peeling and there was a distinct smell of charred wood in the air.

He had no sooner been prodded into the entryway of the building than he was taken charge of by a man wearing the four bars of full colonel and another officer whose rank he could not make out in the dim light of the warehouse corridor. Papers were exchanged, minutely examined. Kurenko noticed that the older officer, the colonel, seemed to have something wrong with his hand and kept shoving it nervously into his pocket as though to keep it from being seen. The colonel was a short, stocky man of about fifty, with a balding, high-domed head and a face of a certain superficial gentleness, of the kind often found in superior officers who have killed quite enough in their day and can now afford the appearance of humanity.

"You will come this way, comrade Senior Lieutenant, if you please."

The colonel's voice was heavy, a bit harsh, as though he'd recently had a bad cold. Yet his tone was calm enough, even friendly in an odd sort of way. The second officer, a much younger, grave-looking man, wearing a major's tabs and an Order of the Red Banner badge on his breast pocket, nodded sternly and pointed.

For all Kurenko knew, in the next minute someone would put a revolver to the back of his neck and it would all be over. Such things happened, he knew, and in exactly such places. Regularly.

He looked around, intensely curious about the details of the place in which, perhaps, he might be spending the last few moments of his life. Yet, if they were going to kill him, why had they brought him all this way? One more night in the brickyard would have done the job much more efficiently.

Another door opened. He was led into a large, white walled room lit by a single bulb hung in a wire cage from the center of the ceiling.

The room was sparsely furnished. There were three metal folding chairs and a small table in the center of the room. At the rear, by the door, was another table on which stood a large black box. Opposite, on the floor, lay yet another container, long, black, and generally rectangular.

The colonel snapped his fingers.

"Chaikin? Are you prepared?"

An orderly in a gray-brown uniform appeared. Kurenko tensed, not knowing what to do with his hands. He blinked. So far, he had not said a word. No one had asked him anything.

Odd. The colonel was arranging the chairs in a row facing the end of the room. The major was fumbling with the long box. Kurenko realized that it contained a projection screen. The orderly pulled the cover off the box on the table. A motion picture projector, already loaded with a small reel of film, stood waiting.

"Sit, comrade Senior Lieutenant," said the colonel. "Here, between us."

The major lowered himself into his seat and offered Kurenko a cigarette. Kurenko waved it weakly away. "No, it would make me dizzy. . . . I haven't eaten in . . . so long." Besides, he thought, drugged cigarettes were always a possibility. Drugged *anything* was a possibility.

But why? Why such a thing with *him*?

The major grumbled and snapped his fingers.

"Chaikin, get the man something to eat. Can you do that?"

They waited in silence. The screen was raised up. Food was brought. A tray containing a slab of bread, a bowl of kasha, and some cold meat. This, too, Kurenko understood, would be drugged, but he no longer cared. He was starving. He would eat. He could think of no possible reason why he should be drugged. Or why he should be there at all.

The colonel waited patiently, seeming to doze.

"You're finished? Good. Now then. I am Budyankov, and this," he said, indicating the major, a man of about thirty with pale ash-blond hair and a narrow pinched face set with a permanently critical expression, "this is Major Trepov. So . . . now . . . we will begin. Chaikin?"

The lights snapped off. For a second, everything began to spin. The sudden darkness made Kurenko violently dizzy. He lurched against the colonel, almost falling from his seat. Firm hands righted him.

"Chaikin . . . *let us begin.*"

The projector began to hum. Numbers flashed across the screen. The orderly turned the lens to focus the image.

They were watching a lumbering, corrugated Junkers Ju-52 transport come in for a landing at an airfield somewhere near the front. Lines of Heinkel bombers stood in the background, being armed and fueled up. A guard of sorts seemed to have been drawn up alongside the strip. Two dozen steel-helmeted soldiers with submachine guns. Three large black staff cars with OKH bumper tags waited next to a line of sidecar motorcycles. Another fan of soldiers shielded the landing area from the road. Not far off Kurenko could see the silhouette of a big tank, the muzzle of its cannon trained in the direction opposite that from which the transport was coming.

Then the plane was on the ground. A door in the side of the fuselage opened and a ladder was dropped down. Two Wehrmacht officers descended, and after them came a tall, broad-faced man, slightly stoop-shouldered, wearing heavy steel-rimmed glasses and a Soviet army greatcoat from which the insignia of rank had been removed. Behind him came more German officers. The camera moved in closer, catching the receiving party by the staff cars. As the camera focused on the tall Russian's face, a Wehrmacht captain wearing the cuff titles of OKH reached out to shake the big man's hand.

There was another, brief shot of the same tall Russian, now surrounded by the German officers who had been waiting for the plane to land. They all got into the staff cars and drove off, followed by the motorcycles.

Then the screen went white and the lights came up.

Kurenko was aware that both Budyankov and the major were staring directly at him. For a second he didn't know which way to turn.

"So? . . . You recognized him, of course."

Kurenko shook his head. He could not have seen what he was sure he just *had* seen.

"Come now, there's no doubt about it, is there?" said Trepov. "The man you just saw was Golitsyn, your former commanding officer. For your information, and in case it wasn't quite obvious from what we just showed you, he has gone over to the Germans. No, no, don't shake your head like that, and please don't abuse your own intelligence by thinking that he is simply a prisoner. We have reliable, undeniable information from our own agents. Not only did he surrender voluntarily but he has agreed to assist the Germans by leading an army of deserters and criminals to fight against their own countrymen."

"You were on his staff at Brinapol. Also, you were one of his prize students when you were at the academy," Colonel Budyankov said quietly. "Please don't deny it. We have all the records."

Kurenko's mouth was bone-dry. His tongue felt thick as wood and he thought that he might very well throw up. The one thing he could not understand was why they were showing *him* these pictures. Why didn't they just take him out and shoot him?

Major Trepov leaned closer. "More than that, comrade Senior Lieutenant," he said. "He thought very highly of you, Kurenko. He was . . . and we also know this for a fact . . . very fond of you in his own way. As fond of you as a glacier of a man like that could be of anyone. You don't deny it, do you? Have the good grace and intelligence not to lie, please. It's really not important whether you admit it or not."

"What he means, Kurenko," interrupted the colonel, "is that the reason you are here in the first place is that we know all of this to be true and that it is important to us. So there is no reason for you to try to conceal anything. The records, as Trepov has said, are all here."

Kurenko's head was spinning. What was he to say? And what was he to make of their tone, their manner, so conciliatory as to be absolutely menacing?

Budyankov took him by the arm with the gnarled hand, on which, Kurenko now saw clearly, every finger had been broken.

"A few slices of meat and a slab of bread is hardly a sufficient dinner. A hot bath, some decent food. Real food. Then we'll talk again, comrade Kurenko."

In addition to food and a hot bath, Kurenko was given a clean, new uniform and a bottle of vodka. He dressed, stuffed the few belongings he still had into the pockets of his new tunic. Then he ate slowly, a thick soup laden with meat, potatoes, and cabbage, and three cups of steaming hot tea. He knew full well what such rich food would do to his stomach. Perhaps it was part of the plan to make him sick, and thereby to put him off balance, to compromise him in some subtle way. Well, let them. It would be worth it.

He wolfed the food down, alone in a little freshly painted room with green walls. Outside, he could hear the distant pounding of antiaircraft guns and the steady, relentless chunk of German bombs falling somewhere in the city. Now and then, he could actually hear aircraft engines overhead and the *pom-pom-pom* of the peripheral Zenith guns. Through a small window, the first such window in any of the rooms or cells in which he had been held during the past week, he could see the night sky scored by hundreds of searchlight beams. Tracer bullets floated like fireflies between the roving fingers of light. Now and then a puff of black smoke drifted past, high in the sky, and once in a very great while a brief orange and yellow flash lit up the night as a plane was hit thousands of meters up. It was all extremely beautiful in its own way.

After he had rested, an orderly came and led him to another room on the third floor of the building. This room was more like the sitting room of an old-fashioned apartment than an office. There was linoleum on the floor, an intricately decorated Tadzhikistani carpet on the wall, a picture of Stalin and a print of Repin's *Volga Boatman*, a sofa, a small writing desk and a number of upholstered chairs. In one of these chairs sat Colonel Budyankov, smoking his second cigarette of the day in a long holder. Trepov was working on his twenty-sixth. A third, rather rumpled-looking officer, who Kurenko recognized at once as one of the men to whom he'd told his story at Pribov, stood by the desk. Budyankov gestured Kurenko to the sofa.

"Major Trepov you already know. . . . This is . . ."

"I know him too. He's the one who had me arrested."

There was a pained silence. "Yes," said Trepov, "but it's also thanks to him that you're here rather than in a convoy."

"Major Gelb was simply following his orders," said Budyankov placidly. "As I'm sure we all must. Senior Lieutenant Kurenko understands the need for that. He is a good officer."

Kurenko said nothing. It seemed to him that silence was by far the better course for the moment.

Budyankov inhaled, and exhaled like a steam engine. He coughed and seemed for a moment to be looking for something on the ceiling.

"Let us start from the beginning, comrade Kurenko. Where every story should start."

It was all quite simple, he explained. Kurenko had been arrested for two reasons, either of which, alone, would have been sufficient. First, he had been behind German lines for over two weeks, and according to an NKVD field directive, that by itself required his arrest. Second, he had seen the turncoat cavalry unit riding with the Waffen SS. This, too, was enough to have earned him "special treatment."

"The cavalry you saw, Kurenko, were attached to the Fourteenth Waffen SS Grenadier Division, know as the *Galizische* Number One . . . composed, Kurenko, entirely of Soviet nationals."

"There are a large number of other such units formed or being formed," put in Major Gelb. "They are made up of prisoners, deserters, or simply of levies from the captured towns. There already exist veritable legions of these troops—mostly from the nationalities: Volga-Tartar cavalry, Turkomen and Armenian formations, even Georgian separatists and, of course, the Ukrainians who will forever be a plague, one supposes."

"You can imagine, I'm sure," said Trepov, "what a disastrous effect it would have on the morale of our troops if such things were to become general knowledge. Anyone who has contact with these men . . ."

Colonel Budyankov held up his gnarled hand. "What Major Trepov means to say is that the unfortunate truth of the matter is that the German soldier has been welcomed in many parts of our country. He is looked upon as a liberator. The people, perhaps, remember still the 1914 war when it was a choice between the German and the czar."

"They also remember many unfortunate things that have happened during the last decade. They do not understand why a revolution must do what it sometimes must do," said Gelb sadly.

Kurenko fought to stay awake. He was not thinking clearly enough to realize the implications of the question that had already formed on his lips.

"The others? There were two other units. Not only the cavalry."

Gelb and Budyankov exchanged looks. The colonel's mouth began to twitch faintly. Clearly he had been caught by surprise.

"Just exactly what else did you see?"

"This," said Kurenko, reaching into his pocket. He still had one of the little red and blue cockades. "And a third group, comrade Colonel. Russians in German uniforms. The ones with the cockades and the ones in the German uniforms had been at each other."

"You may as well tell him," Gelb said.

"*You* also are aware of this?" Budyankov said, startled.

Gelb nodded. He too had begun to sweat.

Budyankov smiled amicably. "What is the harm, all things considered, eh, comrade Kurenko? You want to know? You shall know." He picked up the little scrap of red and blue cloth. "Russian auxiliaries. Under Waffen SS command, of course. But Russian units nonetheless."

"And the others?"

"Also Russian. But Soviet. *Ours.*"

"In German uniform?"

"Surely you can understand why we must do things like that, Kurenko. As I said before, too often the German has been welcomed by our people. *We* know what he really is. But time does not allow us the luxury of letting him reveal his true character. Sometimes we have to help him along a little bit. The men you saw are special NKVD field units whose particular function is to . . ."

"We're not here to discuss such things," snapped Trepov.

"Nevertheless, if the picture is to be made clear for comrade Kurenko, all these things must be spoken of," said Budyankov. "He must understand that the troops he saw were not an isolated phenomenon. There were thousands of turncoat troops right behind the panzers that smashed Golitsyn's lines at Brinapol, and their numbers grow every day. The fascist is still welcomed, he is thus far regarded by many as the lesser of two evils. And so our own men continue to go over to him, misled, fooled, tricked, thinking that they can trade cooperation for a new Russian regime after the war is over."

Gelb sighed. "This situation may not last much longer. Already the German is showing what he really is. We know that there have been mass killings, deportations, burnings, hundreds of thousands of civilians killed for no reason whatsoever. Jews particularly, and party members. Officers and communists. Wherever the SS goes it is this way. As a result, there is much tension between the SS and the regular army, and who can tell who will win out in the end? The army staff contains men who are not fools and who see exactly where the excesses of the SS are leading. They are determined not to let it happen. Whether they share the criminal SS conception of us as subhuman is not relevant. They know that to act on such an assumption will cost them a crucial advantage. At the moment they are fighting a losing battle. The SS are relentlessly turning the population against them. But in the meantime, the traitor army grows. We cannot afford to wait until the black crows drive our own people back into our arms. We must act, and if what we do seems harsh, how much worse would losing to those beasts be?"

"And General Golitsyn?"

"He . . . and here we have it on the best authority . . . he has undertaken to aid them in organizing all of the prisoners, the deserters, the plain and simple fools, into one vast army of Russians to fight side by side with the Germans. To destroy the Soviet government if they can. Imagine, Kurenko, we will be dealing not with isolated SS divisions under German officers, but an army of a million or more men . . . led by the 'Defender of Moscow.' "

"The Nazi government will actually allow this?"

Trepov scowled. "Thus far they *have* allowed it. There is the usual fighting between factions, of course. It's doubtful that the project has the approval of the very upper levels of government, but that has not stopped the enthusiasts below."

"You know this man, Golitsyn, perhaps better than anyone alive today. General Grech knew him well, but he is dead. Colonel General Kolsky was his best friend but he too is gone. His division was wiped out on the Dnieper. Of the young officers who went through his courses at the academy, we have been able to locate *only you.* Who knows where the others are, whether they are alive or dead? It would be impossible, of course, to use any of the Chinese who were with him at Wampoa. The few others who might help are scattered from Murmansk to Petropavlosk. You are the only one we have been able to bring here so far and we have no time to lose."

Kurenko felt all eyes upon him. He grew cold and began to shake. A trickle of blood wound down from his raw lips. He was beginning to understand why they had brought him there and what they wanted of him.

Gelb leaned forward. "Would he trust you?"

"I could not lift a finger against him, you must understand . . ."

"The man is a traitor," said Trepov. "You have no choice."

"He is *misguided,*" corrected Budyankov. "He does not understand clearly what has happened. He feels himself betrayed and, no doubt, resentment of past . . . indignities and wrongs, real and imagined, play a great part in his present attitude. We must try to understand him, why he thinks as he does, and not be too harsh. Undue severity"—and here Budyankov managed to display his crippled hand without seeming to have done so deliberately—"undue severity is often the cause rather than the result."

"You yourself," Trepov began, "had ample time to think things through. Time that is not given to a man in Golitsyn's position, a man who has gone through what he has gone through. But whatever his motives, he cannot be permitted to go on with this. He could well cost us the war, or, at the very least, make things very, very difficult for us."

There was another painful silence. Trepov's cigarette burned unnoticed down to his fingers.

Finally Kurenko spoke.

"I'll do whatever I can do. Yes. Whatever you ask."

Colonel Budyankov nodded.

"We'll talk further of it in the morning."

"What do you want me to do?" Kurenko insisted.

"In the morning, comrade Lieutenant, we will discuss it further. Now, you will get some more rest. Be assured that what we will ask will be quite simple. You'll be surprised at just how simple a thing it will be."

When Kurenko had been taken from the room, Gelb turned to Budyankov. "And if he refuses?"

"He will have to be shot, of course. Just as each one of us will someday be shot if he should step one centimeter off the line."

"I don't like it at all," Trepov said. "The whole idea is far too subtle. Wouldn't it be much simpler just to arrange to have Golitsyn killed? It could be done easily enough."

"But it would solve only a portion of the problem. This way, however . . ."

"But there are so many ways in which this plan of yours could go wrong."

"Consider . . . if it *does* work," said Budyankov, "consider the magnitude of the achievement."

Trepov lit yet another cigarette. Gelb lifted the little tumbler that had been sitting on the table and quickly drank the clear Georgian vodka down in one fast gulp. Trepov was right. It would be a terribly risky operation. But if it worked . . .

Dimly, Gelb heard Colonel Budyankov instruct Trepov to contact a certain Engineer Captain Babayev and tell him to proceed. Dimly. It made no real impression. He didn't want to hear. He was far too depressed.

But he was now a part of it, inextricably a part.

He should have known better. He really should have.

5

> When they go to their deaths, they sing.
> But before—
> one may weep.
> Semyon Gudzenko

Lake Byeleymostnoy had been well named. For twenty out of every twenty-fours hours during most of the year it was so densely blanketed by fine white mist that it was impossible to see the shoreline for more than a hundred meters. The forest on the opposite side of the lake was invisible. At times, Engineer Captain Babayev was not even sure there was a lake there. In the legends of the people who lived in the region, the lake was the hole that led to the end of the world, the portal through which one could pass into the frozen kingdom of death. There were epic songs about the lake, about the perpetual fog and the bone-splintering winter cold. Babayev could not get those songs out of his head; they stuck there, with their doomful, modal melodies, like guilt. He had carried them with him for years, ever since he'd first come to the region to build railroads.

Once a man had seen the place, Lake Byeleymostnoy—the Lake of White Fog—how could he possibly forget it?

It was the ideal place, then, for a prison camp. The ideal place for many things.

Engineer Captain Babayev pulled the lambswool collar of his sheepskin high up around his cheeks and peered through the slits in the woolen face mask that alone prevented the spit from freezing on his teeth. He felt his own moist breath hot against the wool, and when he touched a portion of it over his nose, little flakes of ice fell away.

He'd been there only a week and already it seemed like an eternity.

He stamped his feet and shuffled down the cinder path the workmen had finished laying only that morning. It would all be solid ice by evening, invisible and lost by the next dawn.

Further down the path he saw the little major from Moscow talking with the construction foreman, sawing the air with his comical hands, gesturing in an angry, insistent way, as though shouting at a Kalmuk was, in anyone's wildest imagination, the way to get things done.

The Kalmuk stared back as though he hadn't even heard.

Babayev shrugged. The whole undertaking was insane. He looked down the road to the compound area where gangs of workmen were struggling with enormous timbers, piling up rocks, hoisting sheets of corrugated tin as big as signboards and as brittle as glass because of the cold. God help the man who touched one of them with his bare fingers.

The Kalmuks kept at it; a full penal battalion, all of them. Convicts, deserters, God only knew what else. They'd probably be the first prisoners in the barracks they were building; if any of them lived through the ordeal of construction.

Babayev walked toward the major, who had just concluded his useless argument with the Kalmuk foreman. Nearby, a guard carrying a Pepesha submachine gun had just started up a bonfire. All the workmen in the area were already headed over to warm themselves. There was no point in chasing them away. If the guards didn't let them warm up every fifteen minutes or so, they'd all die. Babayev thought that perhaps the guards were even worse off than the Kalmuks. After all, at least the workers were able to keep themselves a little warm, while the guards had nothing to do but stand around and freeze. One guard had already taken sick and died. It took a really tough man to stick it out in such a place.

All right—that's why he, Tikhon Porfyrovitch Babayev, had been sent down to take charge. A big bull of a man, he'd worked on every kind of project from hydroelectric plants and dams to cement works, and in every possible kind of rotten climate, hot and cold. He'd been in Mongolia with Zhukov and taught the Japanese a thing or two about combat engineering, and he'd been in Archangel too, freezing his fingers off at the shipyards.

But Byeleymostnoy was the worst, the most miserable place he'd ever been. The perfect spot for a prison, but why not save the effort of building one? Anyone sent here would be dead in a week. It was expensive to build such a place. Bullets were less than a kopeck apiece, and the cold cost nothing at all.

He waved to the wretched Moscow major. It was painful even to look at the man, he was suffering so.

"Babayev?"

"Ah, comrade Major Gelb . . . you're finished with that ox of a foreman? He's still giving you trouble?"

Gelb didn't answer. His eyes were barely visible, his fur cap was pulled down almost to his eyelids. He had spent the last few days telling everyone who would listen that he could not believe he had actually been sent to such a place.

"He says they'll have the framework up by tomorrow, comrade Babayev. Do you believe him?"

"If he says so, then I believe it. Besides, they'd better be finished by tomorrow or they won't get fed."

"You're not serious, are you? You'd let them starve?"

Babayev shrugged. What was the point in arguing with the likes of this Gelb fellow? And why had they thought it necessary to send such a person in the first place? It was engineer's work, that was all . . . no place for an intelligence officer, a desk man, and a Jew in the bargain. It was almost insulting.

Gelb accompanied Babayev back to the foreman's shack. They went inside. Gelb pulled off his heavy fur coat and held his hands out to warm them over the stove. His face was ashen and rimmed with frost. Next to the bearded, massive Babayev, Gelb looked like the corpse of a frozen child.

"How long will it take, all of it?"

"A month, perhaps a little more. It depends on the weather."

"It can get worse than this?" asked Gelb, incredulous.

"It hasn't snowed for two days. Of course it can get worse. But don't worry; you can let them know in Moscow, it will be finished in time. Babayev promises."

"I'll be sure to tell them that."

Gelb cleared a circle on the little window. He could see the workmen below at the frozen lakeside, carrying timbers, pushing barrows full of crushed stone from the batching plant they'd set up where the officers' and guards' barracks were to go. On the shore, the first timber piles for the landing stage had already been driven through the ice. Beyond the skeleton of the dock, clusters of yellow timbers jutted up out of the snow. Gelb could see the outline of the lake itself and perhaps half a kilometer of deep, snow-filled forest fading away into the shadows. And the omnipresent, always shifting mists.

Of the mountains that he knew lay to the north of the lake, he could see not even the dimmest of outlines. He shuddered and took the cup of steaming tea Babayev had just offered him.

"You don't like our forest?" Babayev asked.

"What a dismal place. It's the end of the world."

"So the songs say. They're right, I think. But perhaps it's better here at the end of the world than in some other places . . . where the Germans are, no?"

Gelb did not answer. He touched the inner pocket of his coat, as though to make sure that his papers were still there. His fingers lingered. Slowly he pulled out a little canvas folder. Babayev was busy with his plans now, drawing chalk marks on an elevation pinned to the wall by the door.

Gelb opened the little folder and looked at the photo that Budyankov had given him. He studied the man's features, sad that what was to come would have to come to a man with such a basically decent face. But the uniform was the wrong uniform, and that made all the difference. The sight of the tabs, the boards, the insignia of a lieutenant in the czar's army, these all dulled Major Gelb's sorrow. Finally, he convinced himself that he would not have liked the man, had he ever met him. That seemingly decent face must, after all, mask a deep well of deceit. It could not be otherwise.

He put the photo back.

Engineer Captain Babayev was still chalking away at his plans. At that moment, Gelb thought he heard the sound of distant motors, a plane coming in low from the east, over the mist-shrouded forest.

He listened. Yes, he was sure of it. A plane. *His* plane. Thank God. . . .

To take him back to Moscow, or to wherever else this insane Budyankov person wanted to send him.

Anyplace at all. He didn't care where. There was no place on earth that was not preferable to the frozen hellhole that was Lake Byeleymostnoy.

Because the light had been left on at all times and her watch had been taken away, Nina Andreyeva Golitsyna had no idea of the time or even of how many days she had been in the cell. It was impossible to tell by the frequency of meals, for they came—deliberately, she thought—spaced either much too far apart or too close together. On the whole, though, she had not been treated as badly as she had expected. The cell was more like a small room. There was a cot, a table, even a sink. Every so often a woman guard appeared and asked if she wished to use the toilet, which was in a closet down the corridor.

They had even given her some books to read, some poems of Simonov and some short stories by Alexei Tolstoy.

She had just fallen asleep over one of Tolstoy's historical pieces when Budyankov came quietly into the room.

"I'm sorry, *gospozha* Golitsyna, but I must disturb you. There is unfortunate news. Please prepare yourself."

She sat up suddenly. Trying not to show the chill that shot through her body, she smoothed back the hair from her forehead with a swift, emphatic gesture.

"Unfortunate?" she repeated. "What could be more unfortunate for me than . . . this?"

"Many things," said Budyankov gently. "Many, many things."

"You mean more uncomfortable, perhaps? Yes, that's true. But short of being shot, how much more unfortunate can I be than to be imprisoned because of what . . . *he* . . . has done. It is almost funny, Colonel. A joke."

Budyankov sat on the edge of the cot. He took some chocolates wrapped in foil out of his pocket and offered them to her.

"Here. Do me the honor of sharing my little vice with me. They're quite hard to get, you know."

"Colonel . . ." she said stonily.

"Ah, yes, we talk of misfortune and I offer you chocolates. You find that offensive? Well then, let me come right out with it, *gospozha* Golitsyna. I admit, I've failed. That is to say, I thought something could be worked out in your case. Especially once the circumstances of your relationship with your husband had been confirmed."

"And they were confirmed, of course?"

"Yes."

"But I can see by your expression that, as usual, pure Soviet logic has triumphed. As in all such cases. And it has been found that the facts of this relationship make no difference, yes?"

Budyankov nodded sadly. "*I* understand, of course. *Others* here, sensitive, intelligent men—and yes, there are such men still left, even in times such as these—such men also understand. But there are still others, above even us, who have the power both to propose and to dispose. . . ."

She laughed. "Where are they sending me?"

"To a special camp. It's a place for special people. The relatives of important unreliables, of those who have deserted, and so on. I can't tell you any more. You will not be mistreated or shot, *that* I promise you. You may be of value to us at some future time. But I'm afraid it will be hard for you."

"Life is hard, Colonel. Surely you've noticed." She seized his ruined right hand, causing him to cry out in pain. "Yes," she said, "you *do* notice, don't you? That's good. I'd hate to think that a man of your intelligence had grown insensitive."

He rubbed his hand. "Hardly," he said. "But there are priorities, *gospozha* Golitsyna. Absolute justice does not happen to be high on the list at the moment. First comes . . ."

"Survival?"

"Precisely. Mine, ours, yours too. It would not be good for you to remain here. Already there is much talk about the traitor Golitsyn. The facts are not generally known yet but, in time, how can we keep such things from becoming public knowledge, eh? Who knows what someone might take it into his head to do to you then?"

"And my son?"

"He is a good Pioneer, they tell me. He will not be disturbed. You have my word on that."

"Your word?"

"For whatever good that is to you, yes, my word. It has . . . some value still." He got up to go, leaving the chocolates on the cot. "In about an hour they will come for you. Don't be alarmed.

It will all be as I have said. I'm only sorry that it couldn't have been worked out in . . . another way."

"Thank you at least for your personal concern, Colonel."

Budyankov paused. "You seem to be a decent woman, *gospozha* Golitsyna, and I am genuinely sorry about what happened between you and your husband. But perhaps, in the end, it will turn out to have been best. Who can tell?"

He turned and, without more, went out, closing the cell door firmly behind him.

In four hours, a pair of guards and an officer she had never seen before came to get her, bringing a worn blue uniform, a coat much too large for her, and a pair of frayed felt boots that stank of disinfectant.

Schreiber-Hartstein had taken a light supper at the Cafe Kranzler in the Kurfürstendamm. It really had been too cold to eat outdoors but the tables hadn't been taken in for the winter yet and it pleased him to sit there, absolutely alone, being served by a disgruntled waiter muffled in an overcoat, energetically blowing little puffs of frosty breath and returning the stares of curious passersby with placid equanimity. The food hadn't been as good as he'd remembered it being, the inevitable consequence of wartime conditions, he supposed. The wine had been vaguely sour but he hadn't felt up to complaining. The waiter was annoyed enough as it was.

In his pocket were two tickets for the Philharmonic that Reiman had given him. The *Wunderkind* Von Karajan was conducting. Schreiber-Hartstein didn't care particularly for symphonic music, but he thought he'd give it a try, out of deference to Reiman's enthusiasm. He'd intended to invite someone to go with him but hadn't gotten around to it in time. Now, the idea of sitting there alone, trying to pay attention while a thousand thoughts vied with each other for space in an already crowded brain didn't appeal to him very much. He knew he'd end up sitting there with his eyes closed, rehearsing all the complaints and problems that had plagued him for the past year and hardly hearing the music at all.

He got up, paid, and went to a phone to call Beifelder.

Beifelder was just leaving to pay a visit to a cousin in Potsdam.

"A birthday party for Herbert's little girl," he explained. "I really must go."

"Of course you must," Schreiber-Hartstein said, trying to disguise the disappointment in his voice.

"Go to the concert, Reinhardt. It will do you good."

"Perhaps, perhaps."

"I know. You don't like being alone. I understand that. But listen, the child will be in bed by ten and her father by ten thirty. He's a stodgy fellow, cousin Herbert, and he never lasts long in the evening. Besides, he's sure to drink too much and get sleepy. I'll meet you at the Adlon at, say, half-past eleven."

Schreiber-Hartstein reluctantly agreed.

He walked down the Königgratzerstrasse along the east edge of the Tiergarten until he came to Askanischerplatz and Bernburgerstrasse. A well-dressed crowd was already milling about in front of number 22, the Philharmonie building. He gave the extra ticket to a very young private who was standing forlornly near the entrance. The boy, who could not have been more than nineteen, thanked him effusively.

With the greatest hesitance, Schreiber-Hartstein went in. The posters outside announced a turgid program of Bruckner and early Beethoven. The foyer was crowded with elegantly dressed women and men, most of whom were in formal black uniform. He realized at once that his own workaday *feldgrau* was totally inappropriate for the occasion. Reiman should have warned him to change.

He hovered about the buffet for a time, until the crowd in the foyer had all but emptied into the main hall. Only then did he go in and take his seat next to the young man to whom he'd given his ticket.

"I was afraid you weren't coming, sir," said the boy.

"Why is that? 'Afraid,' I mean?"

"If the Herr Hauptmann pleases, it's such a beautiful program. I wouldn't have wanted you to miss any of it. Not a minute."

Startled by the boy's earnestness, Schreiber-Hartstein replied, "Then I shall certainly try to stay awake."

Von Karajan made his appearance, a somber, Lisztian figure with jet-black hair and deep-set eyes. A hush descended on the audience. Even the high government officials and their wives who sat in the first dozen or so rows fell silent.

But Schreiber-Hartstein's instincts had been correct; the Bruckner was insufferably boring. His mind wandered, he began to think of Beifelder's reports and of the disaster that was rapidly overtaking them. As wave after wave of thick, syrupy sound washed over him, the captain found himself thinking of Golitsyn and their first meeting. It had taken place in a small room on the ground floor of the Viktoriastrasse building. He would never forget that flat, mask-like face, the steel-rimmed glasses, and the pale blue eyes that stared at him from behind the lenses, wary, suspicious.

As he had every right to be.

They had talked, the two of them, for a long time, testing, probing, hunting for the truth. Finally, they had ended by drinking together. Still, the real Golitsyn had not spoken. He had not committed himself. Perhaps he never would.

Perhaps he would never get the chance. If Admiral Canaris was not successful soon in obtaining permission for the formation of a Russian-officered force, then all the understanding in the world would do no good. Golitsyn would wither away, the Russian army would evaporate, and Germany would certainly lose the war.

The symphony went on for what seemed like an eternity. Finally a long-drawn-out chord mercifully brought the piece to a close. Schreiber-Hartstein got up during the applause and left the auditorium.

A street clock on the corner of the Askanischerplatz showed a few minutes past eleven as he turned back up the Königgratzerstrasse, headed toward the foot of the Unter den Linden. The night had grown deceptively calm. The clouds were low and a hint of rain was in the air. A faint fall fragrance still issued from the Tiergarten, the last breath of life before the usual dismal Berlin winter settled in.

A constant stream of automobiles flowed past the canopied entrance to the Adlon Hotel, discharging and picking up passengers just as they had always done during peacetime. The doorman, in his long green coat, bustled back and forth from curb to door like a shuttle in a loom. As Schreiber-Hartstein passed into the building, the doorman gave him a withering look, as though to say that no one, not even an officer, had any right to go into the Adlon looking that shabby.

Schreiber-Hartstein smiled slightly, pleased to have annoyed the man just as he had been pleased to annoy the waiter at the Kranzler. The lobby was crowded. A party of SS functionaries in black formal dinner uniforms was just coming out of the elevator. Schreiber-Hartstein went into the bar without giving them another look, though he thought with some discomfort that he recognized a few of them from OKH headquarters. In the bar, the lights had been lowered and a pianist was quietly playing a medley of the latest Michael Jary tunes in one corner.

Beifelder had already arrived and was sitting at a table near the bar, staring at his glass, a vacant, sleepy look on his face.

"The child had a cold," he announced morosely. "Such a trip, for nothing. I certainly wouldn't have gone all the way out there just for cousin Herbert. I've been here more than an hour now."

Schreiber-Hartstein smiled palely. "So . . . you could have saved me the agony of that impossible church music."

"Don't say that to Reiman, please. You'll hurt his feelings," Beifelder warned. "He loves Bruckner and thought he was doing you a favor."

Schreiber-Hartstein sat down and ordered a bottle of *Pfalzerwein.* There were a few newspapermen at the bar. A reporter from *Das Reich* was holding forth on the necessity of reporting only "encouraging, uplifting news." His companion, a short, bald man with a thick neck straight out of a Grosz drawing, contended that the only acceptable subjects for reportage in such times were sports and cinema.

"It's rather difficult," he said, "to have a politically suspect soccer game."

"Unless," said the other man dourly, "the wrong side loses. And one rarely knows which side that is, does one?"

Schreiber-Hartstein snorted at their foolishness. The Bruckner had sobered as well as bored him. He wanted to talk to Beifelder about the Russian general and Canaris's promise. He could see that the Russian was wavering and that it wouldn't take much to convince him to accept a command. *If* he had a command to offer. Canaris would have to be pushed somehow. Time was precious.

Thus far, Schreiber-Hartstein had held back. He knew all too well the limits of his own authority, the dangerousness of his position. Even if he were to offer, and the Russian were to accept, there was no assurance whatever that they could deliver him an army to command.

More likely they would all end up in a concentration camp. Or worse.

As Schreiber-Hartstein began to unburden himself to his friend he saw out of the corner of his eye that a small, powerfully built man in civilian clothes had gotten up from a nearby table where he had been drinking with a number of Wehrmacht officers and was headed directly toward them, grinning.

"Christ," said Beifelder. "It's Trakl."

"The Gestapo Trakl? You know him?"

"Oh yes, indeed," said Beifelder. "And so do you. Or at least, he knows you. Watch out for that man. Everytime Keitel farts, he sniffs."

Just then, Trakl arrived. He stood by the table, his hands in his pockets, his deceptively cherubic face flushed with drink.

"Ah," he said. "Reinhardt the Red, I see."

"Easy now," said Beifelder, placing a restraining hand on Schreiber-Hartstein's arm.

"No need," the Balt said. "I don't let people like that upset me."

"You should, you know," Trakl went on amiably. " 'People like that' are watching you very closely. 'People like that' are very interested in what you're up to. You didn't know? Well then, it's a good thing I came over to tell you, isn't it?"

"It's nice to know that someone is finally paying attention to us," Schreiber-Hartstein said coolly.

"We're paying attention all right. And you should be too."

"Oh?"

"That's a polite way, Herr Hauptmann, of saying that you'd better watch where you put your feet when you're in a pasture."

"Very artistically phrased," said Beifelder.

"It comes from toadying up to Keitel, Martin. He's got a doctorate in scatology, that one has."

"Careful, careful," said Trakl, his face suddenly darkening.

"Oh," Schreiber-Hartstein shot back, cheerful for the first time in hours, "I thought that such talents were cultivated by our leadership and that competence in the art was highly prized."

"What is he talking about?" Trakl said to Beifelder.

Beifelder looked tranquil and innocent though his heart was pounding wildly.

"He is saying," Beifelder explained, "that he intended a compliment, Inspector. I would have thought so too. Perhaps it's you who are out of step."

"Ever been around Bormann?" Schreiber-Hartstein persisted.

"I have. A master, let me tell you. He makes your field marshal sound like a seminary novice."

"What an odd choice of comparisons."

"I'm an odd man."

"Indeed," said Trakl, grinning without parting his lips. "So we've noticed. And that giant *Untermensch* of yours, he's a bit odd too, isn't he? A real circus freak. A Russian who believes he can think, so I hear. Perhaps we should put you all in a zoo."

The party at Trakl's table had begun to grow boisterous. A full colonel stood up and waved at Trakl to come back.

"You'll excuse me, gentlemen? It seems I'm missed."

Schreiber-Hartstein shrugged and took a sip of his wine.

"*Auf Wiedersehen,* Inspector."

"Oh yes, definitely *auf Wiedersehen,* not *adé,* as they say."

When he had gone, Beifelder leaned close to Schreiber-Hartstein and let out a long, pained breath. He was sweating noticeably.

"You shouldn't let swine like that upset you, Martin."

"He's got sharp teeth for a pig, that one."

"Perhaps, but he's not very smart."

"Oh yes, he is. Don't be misled. You think he's stupid because he lets you know he's watching you? That's all part of it. He wants to make you nervous. If you think he's watching, you'll try to be careful and cover your tracks. That way he may have a clue as to where your tracks actually *are*."

Schreiber-Hartstein looked at his friend soberly; he was silent for a moment.

Then he said, "Yes, yes, you're probably right, Martin. I'll try to be reckless then, yes?"

Beifelder sighed. What was the use?

After a while, they got up to go. Schreiber-Hartstein paid the waiter and in a louder-than-necessary voice, and looking straight across the room to where Trakl sat, he said, "Yes, you're right, let's go. The air isn't as fresh in here as it was before."

"Christ," breathed Beifelder. "You damned fool!"

"Oh? I thought that was the way I was supposed to behave?"

They passed Trakl's table. Everyone turned to stare at them, three colonels, Trakl, two other Gestapo officials, and a brace of red-faced majors who looked like twins.

When they got outside, Beifelder could not even bring himself to look at his friend.

"Suicidal," he muttered. "Simply suicidal."

"Isn't everything we do suicidal?" Schreiber-Hartstein asked briskly. "Isn't just living in this lunatic asylum suicidal?"

As he sat in the back of the van, shivering from the cold, his head aching and his tongue thick with fever, it seemed to Kurenko that the time he had spent with Colonel Budyankov had been nothing but a dream. He had never really left the endless transports, the brickyard prisons, the freezing trucks. All was exactly as it had been before. Only the faces on either side of him were different. And they had been different before too. They had changed every few hours.

He could still hear Budyankov's disquietingly tranquil voice, like the dim, remembered echo of a monastery bell.

"You understand then, Kurenko . . . you will be sent to Lake Byeleymostnoy. A special camp has been set up there. For men who were captured by the Germans and later escaped, for men who were too long behind German lines. A natural place for someone like the general's wife . . . and you . . . to be sent. You will go by convoy with a number of other prisoners, including Golitsyn's wife. During the trip, which will be long and unpleasant, you will ingratiate yourself. When you arrive, you will have further opportunities to . . . develop a relationship. Perhaps she will recognize you. If she does, so much the better. At an appropriate time, there will be an exchange of prisoners. We have our agents in the right places, of course. It will all be arranged. But it is safer that you do not know the details. The two of you will be sent to Berlin where the general is now in residence. That too will be arranged. Once there, you will know what to do. You will convince him that he is wrong, that he must abandon this insane idea. He may listen to you. You will explain to him that we have sent him his wife as a . . . token of our good faith . . . that she was in great danger here because of what *he* had done. Whatever else he may be, Golitsyn is a very moral man. He will do what he thinks is right. For that quality . . ."—and here Budyankov had cast a quick glance at his ruined hand—"I envy him, believe me, I do."

"And if he doesn't agree? If we fail?"

"Why, then, you'll have to kill him, of course. Before he can lead an army in the field and establish himself as a real national leader. That would be disastrous. And, oh, Kurenko, remember this if you please. If any notion of doing as Golitsyn has done should enter your head, please know that our people in Berlin will not hesitate to turn you over to the Gestapo . . . who can be at least as unpleasant as we would be under similar circumstances."

During the early part of the trip, Kurenko had tried not even to look at the general's wife and had sat most of the time with his head in his hands, pretending to sleep. He wondered if she would remember him from that one single evening when he had been invited to the general's flat. There had been a New Year's party for the general's honor students at the academy. That had been more than three years ago. In another century, it seemed.

His manacles were heavy and every now and then he had to rest his hands in his lap because of their weight. The woman sat straight up on the opposite side of the van. A fine, strong-looking woman. There was a wire mesh screen between them, running down the length of the van from the rear door to the cab. And there was almost no light.

The seven other prisioners on the women's side were all asleep. On Kurenko's side of the screen there were nine other men. He had talked with one of them for a while, until the driver had shouted back at them to be silent. The rest, like the women, were asleep.

The truck had picked him up first and then gone on to the Lubyanka for the rest of the prisoners. All of this had been done in the middle of the night. The van was accompanied by two outriders on motorcycles. Kurenko had been given a filthy, ragged uniform and a cosmetic roughing-up.

The convoy had taken the road south out of the city—over the Moskva River and the canal and past the old Simonov monastery. From there they had picked up the long road that led toward Tula. Toward the front, skirting the German-occupied area near Orel.

The night was clear, pale, and suffused with a lingering ghost of twilight. There were no German bombers overhead. The only planes he could hear were the little I-16s, with their unmistakably rackety motors, like angry spring flies, and the old PO-2 light planes that sounded like sewing machines.

He grew hungry. It was a long time since he'd eaten. They could have treated him decently right up to the last but they'd insisted that it would be better if he received the same handling as any other prisoner. So he'd been beaten, starved, and frozen. And he looked it. They were probably right about that—he had never been much of an actor and it was just as well that he was genuinely miserable. He would be far more convincing that way.

The truck droned on down the road. He could see the driver's head through the little front window that opened onto the cab, and a small frame of dim light beyond that—the windshield, all grimy gray-green with what passed for dawn at that time of year. He had no idea how far they'd gone since leaving the city. He could see forests, shadows, now and then the edge of a hill, a ruined house. But no identifiable landmarks.

He could smell the front too, the stink of the war. Ashes, the sweet-sickly stench of dead horses and men, of scorched metal. He wondered if she noticed the smell too.

But she said nothing, sitting there in the far corner, beyond the grating, huddled against the cab. The cab was heated. The front wall was probably the best place to be, the warmest.

He had seen her in the courtyard when the van had stopped at the Lubyanka. They'd brought her out with only one guard, a tall woman in a heavy coat with shoulder boards. The general's wife was not tall, but she gave the impression of height because of the way she held herself. Next to the general, he remembered, she had seemed almost . . . tiny.

There in the yard, she had done an odd thing. She had smiled and taken the woman guard by both shoulders and hugged her hard.

Kurenko could not understand why she had done that.

At first she had tried to doze, lulled by the swaying of the truck and the heavy warmth of the cab wall. But it had been impossible and she had soon given up. No matter how tired she was—and she was past exhaustion—she knew that in the end it would be impossible for her to sleep.

She opened her eyes slowly and straightened up. She could hear the driver humming to himself and the other man in the cab snoring away in a rasping bass, like an out-of-tune cello. In the dark it was impossible to make out any but the nearest of the faces on the men's side of the wire. All she could see clearly were the eyes, which caught the light that now and then flickered through the rear grating, and the flat, somber planes of their faces, etched with shadow.

The man nearest her was an Asiatic. His hands were folded in his lap and his eyes were closed in sleep. He looked positively tranquil, as though he were dozing on a sleepy holiday afternoon.

The longer she stared at the man, the more uneasy she became. It was not that she knew him; she had never laid eyes on him before. Nor did he really look like anyone in particular. Yet his face, which seemed a composite of all the Asiatic faces she had ever seen in her life reminded her—of whom? Of Lin Shai-Pao? Of all the other Chinese cadets at the academy?

She remembered those days so vividly, as though they had passed only a little while before. They had been good days, very good days, and well worth remembering. Even now.

Particularly the last days there, in October of 1938. The last days, which had been full and rich and very fine.

In the large lecture hall of the Wampoa Military Academy four hundred cadets in sand-colored, high-collared uniforms stood up and began to applaud. Alexander Semyonovitch Golitsyn had just completed the last in his series of lectures on infantry tactics. In two days he would be returning to the Soviet Union.

Golitsyn leaned forward on the speaker's rostrum, resting his elbows on the slanting top. Through the windows at the rear of the long hall he could just barely make out a flight of stubby I-153, biplanes wearing the blue and white sun of the Kuomintang, churning the air over the docks of the deep-water harbor. There, he knew, gangs of laborers were feverishly unloading yet another boatload of Russian supplies. It was fall, the air was heavy with rain, and the Japanese had taken Amoy and Foochow. All of the ports north of Canton were under blockade. China needed all the friends she could get.

He lowered his gaze slightly and looked out over the sea of yellow faces before him, overcome with sadness and a bitter self-reproach. Nina Andreyeva, watching him from the first row where she sat between a general of the Twelfth Army Group and a police colonel from Canton, tried not to engage his eyes. If she did, she knew he would read the understanding there and might even weep, which would be unforgivable in front of these stiff, rigidly proper young cadets.

The deputy commandant, Lin Shai-Pao, a reed-slender Chinese who moved with a step like a razor snapping shut, went up to the stage and presented Alexander Semyonovitch with a medal. More applause. Then a rhythmic cheering began. The cadets were truly fond of this huge, gangling Russian, who spoke to them with paternal gentleness and endless patience.

Then the deputy commandant announced that the lecture course was at an end. General Golitsyn was going to leave to join their old friend General Blyukher, the *Ga Lon* of the days of the academy's infancy, who now stood in command of his own divisions in the north, across the border, a bulwark against the Japanese.

Nina Andreyeva's eyes traveled nervously over the rows of expressionless oriental faces, smooth as the pebbles on the river's edge. The commandant of the Twelfth Army Group, Yu-Han-Mou, was sunk in lethargic gloom, his mind on the oncoming Japanese. Only Lin Shai-Pao was smiling.

From the veranda of the deputy commandant's two-story house they took a march-past of the cadets. Regimental and Kuomintang pennants snapped briskly in the late afternoon breeze. The cadets paraded with fixed bayonets, their Sam Browne belts polished to mirror brilliance.

Alexander Semyonovitch remained at rigid attention, arm crooked in salute, until the last of the cadets had goose-stepped by. Lin Shai-Pao was amused but followed suit so as not to embarrass his guest of honor.

The ochre dust settled thickly over the parade ground and the sun began its slow descent into the escarpment above the Pearl River. Afterward, when the commandant's reception, with its endless cups of jasmine tea and British gin in water glasses, was over, Alexander Semyonovitch and Lin Shai-Pao sat alone on the veranda. Lin extracted a *Sobranie* from a silver filigreed cigarette case of Portuguese design, offered one to Golitsyn, and then lit up, leaning back with closed eyes to savor the rich smoke.

A white-jacketed servant brought refreshments. Cool lemonade and gin, and a bowl of steaming towels for the face. Dinner would be served in an hour, Lin said. He hoped that the general and his wife would honor him with their presence. There would probably not be another such occasion, he sighed. The Japanese fleet was cruising close in off Hong Kong while the British continued to play lawn tennis. There was no telling what might happen next.

"You have picked an excellent time to retire, dear Alexander Semyonovitch," Lin smiled. "And it is well for us too that you have had a chance to complete your course. Our cadets, I fear, will soon have a chance to test out your theories. Let us hope they have learned their lessons well."

Alexander Semyonovitch thought it best not to reply. To be drawn into a conversation concerning the Japanese and the Kuomintang cadets would be, inevitably, to display an inexcusable pessimism.

Lin, however, took his silence for doubt rather than diplomatic reticence.

"Perhaps you would prefer to stay with us?"

Alexander Semyonovitch shook his head. "My time here has been a good time, Lin. I would not wish to impose."

"Your time here, as you put it, could easily be extended. And, of course, it would be no imposition at all." Lin leaned forward, toying with a steaming towel. The steam rose and fogged his glasses so that Alexander Semyonovitch could not see his eyes clearly. "Perhaps you do not really wish to return? Who could blame you if that were the case? We could easily find a permanent place for you here if you wished it. After all"—his voice took on a conspiratorial hush though there was no else in the room—"they have shot Bukharin and your great general Tukaschevsky, and so many, many others as well. Who is to say how many more there will be or *who* they will be. It is said that your generals are accused of Bonapartism. Excuse me, dear Alexander Semyonovitch, but what is meant by Bonapartism in a socialist country?"

Golitsyn considered for a long while in silence. There was no point in saying to Lin that none of them there at Wampoa had any more reason to expect to survive the year than any of the present residents of the Lubyanka cellars.

Lin could tell from Golitsyn's expression precisely what the Russian was thinking. He shrugged, his smooth, placid face creased with concern.

"Let me say it directly, dear Alexander Semyonovitch. You may be going back for nothing more than a bullet in the head. Or worse. Who can tell in such times? Nothing is as it should be anymore."

Golitsyn replied at last that he had to go back, that nothing would happen to him as he had done absolutely nothing. There was no reason to fear.

"Ah," sighed Lin, exhaling smoke like a dragon. "That is the worst reason there can be, when the fear is there still and there is no reason for it."

"Nevertheless, I will go back. Things are no better here."

"At least here one knows where the lines are drawn."

"I can't argue with you, you know that. But if I did not go back, I could no longer face myself. I must resolve these contradictions."

"I am afraid, my dear friend, that what you wish is impossible."

"Nevertheless, I must try."

"Sad, sad," Lin whispered. "You would have made a fine Chinese general. Ah, but I could not talk Vassily Konstantinovitch into it either. But, yes, you are probably quite right. We would never have been able to find a uniform large enough for you."

It was still light when dinner was over. Alexander Semyonovitch and Nina Andreyeva walked along the river's edge as the sun settled in a flood of crimson and deep saffron over the bald western hills. The air was filled with the sound of crickets and the long mournful wail of horns from the harbor. A heavy fragrance of rich alluvial mud rose from the riverbank, mixed with the stench of diesel oil, coal, and the million mingled odors of rotting vegetable and animal life that were to be found in any Chinese harbor.

On the rippled breast of the Pearl River flotillas of sampans, junks and barges swarmed like lazy waterbugs, a reminder of the floating islands of roped-together junks that clotted the riverside below at Canton proper. Overhead, wasting precious fuel, the Soviet biplanes buzzed, angry as wasps, their bewildered pilots far happier in the air than on the strange, foreign ground below.

Alexander Semyonovitch held his wife's hand tightly. He was lost in his regrets and in the humid warmth of the evening that seemed a palpable nostalgia for something he had never actually known. Behind them, at some distance, came two cadets. Lin had insisted that Golitsyn always be accompanied when he ventured outside of the academy compounds. One could never be sure of anything. There was a war though no one had declared a war. It was best not to take chances. The guards carried long-barreled Berdan rifles and Mauser pistols with heavy wooden holster stocks.

They followed at a respectful distance, with Lin Shai-Pao a few steps further behind.

"It's going to be all right," Nina Andreyeva said, pressing her husband's hand.

He shook his head.

"It won't be. It can't be. It's all so confused now, don't you see? Lin is right to be cynical. They've shot Tukaschevsky. Yakir's been arrested. Feldman, Primakov, Gamarnik. Who knows how many more?"

Alexander Semyonovitch hung his head. Couldn't Stalin see what he was doing to the country? First Trotsky, then Zinoviev, then General Tukaschevsky and half the officer corps. Now Bukharin, and Yagoda, of all people. Would the trials and executions never end? Even in China, where the solution of political problems by the headsman's axe was an ancient and honored tradition, they thought the Soviets were going mad. And so did Alexander Semyonovitch. Since 1918 it had been one contradiction after another. "This Chinese venture of ours, this is almost the worst contradiction of them all. It makes me fear for my sanity, Ninotchka." At home, the government ruthlessly stamped out the slightest imagined heresy. There, in China, it sent its generals as military advisers to Chiang Kai-shek, supported the Kuomintang, the Whites, and helped them to exterminate the Communist cadres.

Nina Andreyeva had felt his fear and confusion growing for days like a fever, and yet she could say nothing to comfort him. She felt him return the pressure of her hand, but gently, so as not to injure her.

"I'm afraid to go back. I admit it," he continued. "More so for you and for Petya than for myself. But for myself too. I'd be a fool not to admit it. Do you know what I'm most afraid of? That they will *not* arrest me. That I will go on as before, doing what I'm told to do, not what I believe I should do. Still, it's no good staying here either. Here, I feel like a traitor to my own conscience."

"They are good people here," she offered. "No worse than any of the others. Lin is a decent man. Even if you don't agree with his politics."

"Who's to say who is good and who isn't?" he burst out. "Lin? Chiang? Stalin? My God, it's enough to make your head spin." He sucked mournfully on an unlit cigarette. "Who can possibly judge?"

"Sasha . . . Sasha . . . *you* will judge, for yourself, but only when we return and you can see for yourself what's happened instead of relying on what others tell you. Why torment yourself now? You've done nothing wrong and you've nothing to be ashamed of. Perhaps there are reasons for all that's happened. How can we possibly understand what goes on in Moscow when we are in Canton?" She pulled on his sleeve like a child. "You must cheer up, Sasha. Time is so precious. Otherwise, I won't walk with you. I will walk with General Lin and I will cause a fine scandal."

He smiled an ugly, crooked smile. "Then I should have to beat you, no?"

"Like the good, traditional Russian husband you are?" Her chin went up defiantly as if to belie her words.

"Never," he said, softening. "Never that."

She pointed across the harbor. A brilliant lacework of silver and green fireworks printed the dark sky briefly over the quays near the railway spur.

"Oh, look . . . what do you think's the occasion?"

"They're celebrating the arrival of the Vladivostok steamer. They have little enough to celebrate at the moment so I suppose they're entitled at least to that."

"It's beautiful," she said. "I'll miss it very much."

"The fireworks?" His mouth crinkled a bit.

"The people. This place. It's been a good home, Sasha."

He shook his head. "Poor Ninotchka, still believing in fairy tales instead of seeing what's really there. Your beloved Canton is really a foul, wretched sinkhole. It's a wonder there's no plague there now. The government, what there is of it, is a cabal of unbelievably cruel, self-seeking men of no principle whatever. Chiang himself is a fascist swine of the worst kind, and our poor cadets will all be just like him when they're older. They haven't any choice. They won't even be able to stop the Japanese, and the truth is that they don't deserve anyone's help. Certainly not ours."

"Nevertheless," Nina Andreyeva said, "I've lived here with you, Sasha . . . and if I love it for that alone, it is enough."

His pale blue eyes blinked rapidly behind the thick-lensed glasses, as though he had not heard correctly.

Nina Andreyeva looked up at him and laughed.

"I love you, dear Sasha. Is that such an odd thing to say?" She threw her arms around him and held him as tightly as she could.

"Ah, you'll scandalize poor Lin."

But she could see out of the corner of her eye that Lin Shai-Pao had simply turned his back, very discreetly, and so had the two cadets with their long German rifles.

Alexander Semyonovitch and Nina Andreyeva went down the steep embankment to the water's edge. Like children, hand in hand. The river flowed rapidly at that point, dense and gray with mud.

She pulled him after her, and they went scrambling down the last few meters, almost losing their footing, and into the water. He laughed, suddenly and deeply. It was, she thought, as much a sound of pain as of joy.

The devil with them all—the politicians, the ideologues, the military schemers—with all of them who took themselves and their lives so seriously that there was no time to wade in a muddy river.

For a moment he didn't care at all. Standing up to his knees in the swirling gray water he lifted Nina Andreyeva high into the air, almost over his head. Then he kissed her hard and with possessive violence.

"This is the way we should remember China. Always," he said.

It was growing light at last. They were in a dense forest. The tree branches were laden with ice. A sharp wind sent showers of loose snow whirling past the little window at the rear of the van.

Kurenko had just dozed off, his face down into his folded arms—dreaming—it was the convoy from Pribov. . . . He had never been taken to Moscow at all. He had never met Colonel Budankov or Trepov or Gelb. It had all been a nightmare. He was still in that very first truck and they were taking him north, to a camp somewhere. He would die there. He was content to die. If only they'd let him sleep a little first.

At first he hardly heard it, a dull scratching against the mesh. Then a voice.

"You . . . you there . . ."

He looked up. It was the general's wife. Her face was pressed against the screen. She was staring at him.

"You," she said again; her voice was firm, almost musical. His thoughts swirled back to that evening, long ago, at the New Year's party, to the toasts that had been drunk and the strange things he'd felt when he'd had too much to drink.

"Why were you staring at me before?"

He looked up slowly, holding his fingers to his lips and looking meaningfully at the cab.

She laughed and shook her head. "What can he do to us? Talk all you want to. Don't be afraid of *him*."

One of the other prisoners stirred in his sleep, opened one eye, then slumped back again, his teeth chattering from the cold.

"Where are they taking us? Do you know?"

"South, I think."

"But where? Didn't they tell you?"

"A camp," he replied dully. "Let me sleep. It will probably be the last time for a long while that we can sleep. You should sleep too."

"How do you know I haven't been sleeping all this time?"

"I was watching you, don't you remember?"

"Yes, of course. But why?"

"You're a good-looking woman."

She shrugged, taken off balance for an instant.

"Go back to sleep now," she said hastily.

He gripped the wire and brought his face close to hers. She gazed at him intently, with obvious suspicion.

She was, of course, still Alexander Semyonovitch Golitsyn's wife. She was easily ten years older than he was, and she was just as he remembered her from the night of the general's party. There had been a lot to drink that night, though the general himself had hardly touched a drop. He had sat there, huge, ugly, and oddly gentle, beaming while Nina Andreyeva had sung for them, the lullaby from *The Czar's Bride*. Kurenko wondered if she could still sing now.

"You're right," he said at last. "He can't even hear us. And why should I care anyhow? I'll probably never talk to a woman again."

"How old are you?"

"Twenty-four. And you?"

"Older than that. Thirty-seven, if it matters. Tell me, why are you here?"

He breathed a little easier. She hadn't recognized him yet.

"My company was wiped out outside Kolabyansk. I was lost for two weeks. They think I deserted, that's all," he lied.

"In a way we're the same," she said. "How sad . . ."

He opened his hands against the mesh.

"May I touch your fingers?"

"My fingers?"

"Because, also, I will probably never touch a woman's fingers again."

She smiled. Her expression softened fleetingly. He withdrew his hand almost at once.

"I'm sorry. You must think me an idiot. . . ."

She said nothing. Her hand remained where it was, against the mesh.

They slept, talked in whispers, slept again. He tried to study her face when she was dozing but inevitably her eyes would open and she would catch him staring at her. Once, he thought, she smiled again, a wondering, ironic smile.

The van continued on its way through forests, across flat, endless fields, and through shattered villages and towns over which hung palls of smoke so dense that the outlines of the ruined houses could barely be made out. After a while the landscape became bare and featureless, resembling the scarred surface of another planet. By what they judged to be late afternoon, Kurenko began to hear artillery in the distance, the whine of motors, and the faraway scream of dive-bombers. Small arms fire rattled in the hills. They entered a deep forest. Twice they stopped, once to refuel and once so that the prisoners could relieve themselves.

It grew dark again and even colder. The woods were deep, black, and forbidding. The road became a muddy wandering track lined with wrecked vehicles, slab-sided *Gaz* field cars, ruined Studebaker trucks, and here and there the husk of a burned-out BT-7 tank. The smell of scorched metal hung in the air.

Kurenko began to wonder. They had been traveling for almost two days. How much longer was it to continue? Where were they going? He grew morose. How sad to die simply because one had been forgotten.

Suddenly there was an explosion very close by. The van came to a violent halt. The prisoners next to Kurenko were thrown off the narrow seat and fell against the wire. The van lurched, heeled over, and came to rest on its side. Kurenko somehow managed to hold on to the edge of the seat and, so, to remain upright. Golitsyn's wife had kept herself from falling too. He could see her, hanging on to a strut on the side of the van with both hands. He stared at her. For the first time, he saw fright on her face.

He could hear a clear, loud crackling sound; the van was on fire. It would only be a matter of seconds, before the fire hit the gas tank. Then they would be burned alive.

Outside, very close, there was a steady drumming of machine-gun fire and the *pom-pom-pom* of an automatic cannon. Kurenko struggled up and climbed over the men who had been thrown against the wire screen. Through the little rear window he could get only a narrow view of the road behind them.

It was enough.

A wrecked motorcycle jutted up from a drift of smoke-streaked snow, its front wheel spinning slowly. The driver hung over the handlebars, cut almost in half. The dispatch rider lay spread-eagled in the mud some distance away. The other motorcycle was burning like a torch where it stood rammed against a tree, both riders dead, the earth around it churned up by shellfire. German soldiers came running out of the trees, their winter capes flapping behind them. A stutter of machine-guns erupted from the snow-banks alongside the road and a line of tracers moved lazily across the ground toward the truck.

The women prisoners started to scream and beat their fists against the side of the truck. Kurenko could hear Golitsyn's wife shouting at them like a drill instructor to keep calm.

A black shape suddenly blanked out the peephole at the end of the truck. There was a slam of gun butts against the door. It shuddered once, then sprang open. Kurenko crashed to the floor of the truck. He felt a boot stamp down hard on his hand and he howled in pain. As he looked up and around he saw two German soldiers in winter capes standing at the back of the truck, gesturing at him with their machine pistols.

He noticed one thing, even through the smoke and the screaming pain in his hand, something he remembered clearly only later.

The German soldiers did not seem at all surprised by what they saw.

"Raus . . ." The rest of it was lost in the renewed chatter of the machine guns. He could see a solitary man running down the road: the driver. A line of machine-gun bullets moved leisurely along behind him, then touched him lightly across the back. He fell headlong into the tire ruts, sending up a spray of mud.

The nearest of the Germans, a lance corporal with the griffin patch on his shoulder, shouted. The prisoners too were shouting, climbing over one another, trying to get out of the truck. It was hard. The truck was on an angle and they had to jump some distance to get to the ground. Some of them fell, unable to keep their balance with manacled hands.

One man was down on his knees before one of the Germans, shouting over and over again, "I'm from Chernovtsy, for God's sake . . . I'm a Hungarian, I'm an ally. . . . I'm from Chernovtsy . . ."

The German shot him in the face.

The SS with the griffin patches were everywhere, chasing down the rest of the escort. The guard who had ridden in the cab lay with his feet sticking out from under the truck.

"Get behind me . . . behind . . ." Kurenko cried, struggling upright from the snow where he had fallen. He felt Nina Andreyeva's fingers dig hard into his arm, helping him to rise.

Another German struck him across the side of the head with the butt of his machine pistol. It was almost impossible to keep his balance with his hands manacled but, somehow, he managed to stay upright. He could see the road clearly now, despite the ringing in his ears and the purple waves that rippled across his eyes; there, in among the trees, were half a dozen scout vehicles and a large tank or armored car of some kind.

The van had driven almost directly into them.

The lance corporal began to shout orders. The rest of the prisoners were herded toward a ditch by the side of the road, just past the upright motorcycle whose front wheel was still spinning.

"Good-bye," said the general's wife. "What's your name? Before they kill us, tell me."

"Vasya," he said; so, she had not remembered him after all.

"They say it isn't so bad. . . ."

Another man began to plead. One of the Germans hit the man and he fell headlong in the frozen mud. A bullet hit him in the back of the head before he could turn over.

Out of the corner of his eye, Kurenko saw Nina Andreyeva pull herself up erect and stand rooted where she was, defiant, staring straight at the Germans.

Of all the insane bad luck . . .

Then she was almost on top of him, pushed hard so that she had to grab hold of his arm to stay on her feet. They were all being jammed together, so as to make an easier target.

The officers stood up behind the machine guns and shouted something. One of the tankers rose up from a turret and turned a machine gun toward the line. At the same time that the tanker's gun began to fire, the lance corporal pulled the trigger of his Schmeisser, spraying bullets along the opposite end of the line, a dozen or more prisoners away from where they stood.

A soldier nearby, who did not have a machine gun, raised a rifle and pointed it directly at them. The German squinted down the barrel, taking aim slowly, as though he were in a shooting gallery. Nina Andreyeva's fingers dug into Kurenko's arm.

Kurenko swung around as hard as he could, trying to put himself between the woman and the German, pulling her down hard just as the soldier fired. The man was only a few meters away and he could see his face clearly, the red mark on his cheek where he had pressed against the stock of the rifle, the hairs of his eyebrow—each one clear and distinct.

Then the bullet hit him, hard, somewhere in his upper body.

He was not sure just where he had been hit. His breath left him entirely. Still holding on to the general's wife, he pitched over onto one side.

Before his knees had touched the edge of the ditch, he heard another shot, distinct over the machine-gun fire. Nina Andreyeva jerked upright, losing her grip on his arm, stiffened, and fell backward. A vivid red line ran across the side of her head.

Kurenko toppled into the ditch. The trees whirled up around him, lost in the smoke. He saw faces. The Germans, the other dead prisoners who had fallen close by.

The ditch was full of blood and bits of flesh. The machine guns had gotten all the others.

For a few seconds more he clung to consciousness, aware only that the woman, now entirely under his own toppled body, was still moving, her face half buried in the mud.

He twisted, trying to keep his weight off her, to keep from drowning her in the mud.

Then he blacked out, his manacled hands curved over the back of her head, his body still covering hers.

Senior Lieutenant Shelepin, NKVD Special Purposes, Seventh Regiment, Voronezh Sector, shifted the still-smoking Schmeisser to a more comfortable position. He knew he would never get used to the weapon, its noise and its bone-shattering kick. He nodded to Junior Lieutenant Krasmanovitch. Neither said a word. They looked down into the ditch. Only the two on the end were still breathing. Fine. Exactly as it had been ordered. Shelepin had spent hours staring at their photographs, knowing that he would have only a few seconds in which to act and that it would all have to be done without any hesitation at all. Or he would give himself away. Even the man had to be fooled.

Krasmanovitch had performed brilliantly. A crack shot, he could trim the feathers from a kite one at a time at a thousand meters. He could kill anything his weapon could reach. Or hit it exactly where he wanted to hit it.

As was required.

Shelepin gestured to the men who had just come out of the forest and signaled them to blow up the van. It was all very regrettable. But only as far as the driver and the two escort cyclists were concerned. The rest of them, the other prisoners, were all criminals, traitors, or worse. They were no loss. Shelepin had no idea what was involved, only that it was extremely important and that his own head was on the line.

A grenade went off. The van exploded in a great billow of smoke, the flames illuminating the entire forest for a moment, then quickly dying down.

Satisfied, Shelepin jerked his head around and snapped an order in perfect German to the man dressed as a lance corporal—Krasmanovitch.

There was no reason to stay. They had finished what they'd been sent to do.

Within ten minutes the message went out in the clear, on the command channel. Just as had been arranged.

"The cabbage is in the pot." Three times, very slowly.

Then the tank moved off into the deep woods.

6

> There are many elements on all fronts who even run to meet the foe and throw away their weapons on first contact with him. . . .
>
> Joseph Stalin
> Secret Order No. 0019
> July 16, 1941

How long they'd been in the ditch, Kurenko had no idea. But they were both still alive. A point-blank execution and they had survived.

Though he could feel her moving against him, he dared not move himself. At first this was because he was not sure that the Germans had really gone and then it was simply because he was afraid that if he moved he would discover just how badly wounded he was. There was blood in the ditch, running in rivulets down channels in the frozen mud. His arm ached. The sleeve of his shirt was drenched.

He felt Golitsyn's wife stir again.

"You mustn't. Wait. Be still."

"Are you hurt?"

"Not so bad."

But there was no need for silence. He could hear nothing but forest sounds, the soft rustle of underbrush as a small animal passed. And the crackling of the still-burning van.

"Let me look . . ." She began picking at his arm even though her hands were still manacled. Somehow, he managed to hold still and not cry out. "I was a doctor . . . once." She probed for a minute longer, then said, "I think the bullet passed right through. Can you move your arm? Does the bone feel broken?"

He did as she directed; the arm moved and though there was a sharp pain, it was clearly a flesh wound, nothing more. As she turned her face up to him, he saw an angry red line across one side of her head. A thin trickle of blood oozed from the graze. He felt like laughing out loud.

"God protects fools," he said, raising himself cautiously over the edge of the ditch. It was getting dark and slightly warmer. A pale ground haze rose among the trees where the snow had not collected and bare earth still showed. There was no trace of the Germans. Only deep, angry tread marks in the frozen mud.

With difficulty he crawled over to the body of the driver, hauling himself forward on his elbows, waiting tensely for the pain each time he put his weight on the wounded arm. He could move easily enough, and in a moment had reached the body. The keys had to be somewhere. He rolled the corpse over. The man's entrails spilled out of a gaping stomach wound. Kurenko reached hesitatingly out to the blood-soaked belt. The bullet-shredded coat was wet and slimy. He had never touched a man's intestines before. A glaze of ice had already formed over the corpse but there was still a faint warmth there at the stomach where a light stream seemed to hover.

The belt came loose and with it a leather pouch and an empty metal ammunition clip. He reached with both hands into the trouser pocket. The dead man's leg was stiff as wood.

His fingers touched metal; the keys.

He rolled over, the keys in his teeth, and unlocked the heavy manacles, all the while aware that the woman was watching him from the ditch, her head barely visible above a bent human leg that projected up like a root.

He scrambled over to her and undid her cuffs.

She rubbed her wrists together and blew on her hands. She did not thank him but asked, "Do you have any idea where we are?"

"Does it matter?"

She shrugged.

He sucked in his cheeks and took a risk.

"I'm going to find a village. If there are soldiers there, I'm going to turn myself over. . . ."

"To whom?"

"The Germans . . . if I'm lucky."

"They'll kill you."

He swallowed hard. "My own people also tried to kill me." He waited for a response but there was none. "You can come with me or stay here, it's up to you," he said.

"I'll go with you," she said.

He swallowed nervously. He kept seeing the face of the German who had opened the van door, the expressionless, unsurprised face. He remembered the woods outside Kolabyansk and the Russians in German uniforms, the Germans in Russian uniforms . . .

Anything was possible.

Shortly after dark they reached the outskirts of a small village surrounded by low wooden fences and long, foul-smelling ditches. The snow was not heavy. Vast patches of sodden, open ground showed through. Animals fretted and stamped in hidden sheds. A few dozen log houses stood on either side of a rutted and muddy track of a road that ran from the edge of the woods to a low ridge where the forest began again, even heavier and more impenetrable than before. There was no sign of either Germans or Soviet units. Not a single vehicle of any kind stood along the road or by the houses.

Apart from the muted yapping and whining of hungry dogs, the village was still. A few murky yellow smudges of light shone here and there. The silhouettes of the houses were barely distinguishable from the profile of the earth itself.

They moved cautiously along the outer fenceline, keeping well down.

The mud was not frozen there. The snow had not held in many places. Here and there were deep puddles of freezing water and wide patches of marshy ground into which they sank almost up to their knees at times.

Suddenly, a shadow moved nearby at the edge of a mound; a large dog. It sniffed, then growled. They had come to a yard behind a large, low house. It was the dog's yard and he began to snarl, ready to defend his master's property.

Just then, far to the north, a dozen yellow and blue signal rockets sprayed the night sky. A second, identical burst followed, then a solitary flowering of silvery green, high up where the moon, unaccountably absent, should have been. Then the sky went dark again. Even the stars seemed to have been blotted out.

The dog went mad with fear and began barking. More dogs came out of the shadows, at least half a dozen of them, frightened, mangy brutes, all snarling and menace.

Kurenko looked around for a tree limb or a board. His arm hurt abominably and he was having trouble even moving it.

A door opened suddenly and a man came out onto the porch of the house. He was old, bearded, with a wide, leathery face, and wore a sheepskin coat and a coarse woolen hood, like a cossack. Around his waist was a cartridge belt and a heavy holster; a long-barreled shotgun jutted from under his arm.

Kurenko stood where he was, holding his hands well away from his sides to show that he was unarmed and praying that the dogs would not attack. The man squinted, whistled to the dogs, and gestured to Kurenko and the woman to come into the light. The blood-splattered prisoners' uniforms were obviously strange to him. As he motioned them into the house, the dogs began to bark again and he whistled sharply. All at once the dogs were silent and slunk away.

"Listen," said the old man, standing in the overheated kitchen, "you better tell me who you are, or out you go, and the dogs can have the both of you."

"Grandpa, take it easy. We're Russians, just like you."

"Is that so? I never saw uniforms like *those* before."

"We were prisoners," Kurenko explained hurriedly. "They were taking us to a camp of some kind when the Germans bombed the convoy. How we got out alive, I'll never know."

"What kind of prisoners?" the old man demanded. "I don't like that . . . prisoners . . ."

"I was captured by the Germans but I got away, that's all. That wasn't good enough for them, so they were going to put me away again."

"Maybe you did something else," the old man said warily. "How do I know you didn't?"

"I swear. . . ."

"And her?"

"It was because of her husband. You know how these things are. They couldn't get hold of him, so they took her instead."

The old man's expression changed slightly. He nodded. "They did things like that around here in thirty-one. So why not now? It hasn't gotten any better, has it? God's will, you're alive. All right. Come, sit down." He lit a cigarette and poured out some *kvass* from a jug. He put the shotgun down on the table but within easy reach.

"Can you tell us where we are?" asked Kurenko. "We've been in the forest a long time."

The old man sipped his *kvass*. It spilled over his yellowish beard but he made no move to wipe it off. The house was filthy and disordered; it was obvious that he lived there alone. For a moment he remained wary, his eyes narrowed, peering about. Then he started to talk more easily, puffing on his cigarette all the while.

They were in the village of Tversk, not too far from Orel. The Germans were all over the area with their tanks. They'd occupied most of the larger villages and the railheads. In Tversk itself there was a small garrison and a radio station down in the old brick warehouse at the other end of the road. German patrols passed often. It was a wonder they hadn't run into a patrol when they'd come out of the woods. But the Germans didn't like to go out at night now if they could help it, because of the partisans in the woods, so maybe it wasn't so surprising after all.

All the while the old man was explaining the situation to them, he watched intently for any sign of a reaction to his words. Kurenko held back, still unsure of where the old man's loyalties lay. Either way, it could be very dangerous.

The old man lit another cigarette. Smoke curled through his beard. Nina Andreyeva took a deep, longing breath in spite of herself.

"Look, grandpa, can she have a smoke too? She's had a rough time of it."

The old man shrugged and handed Kurenko a cigarette. Before he gave it to Nina Andreyeva, he looked at it quickly and carefully. It wasn't a Russian cigarette. All right. He handed it over.

She lit up with a candle.

"Ah, it makes me dizzy," she said. He helped her to sit down, noticing that the red line across her forehead had started to pale.

The old man wasn't looking at the woman but at Kurenko's arm; blood was dripping down his sleeve and over his hand. Already there was a puddle of it on the floor.

The old man got up and brought some rags and a bowl of water.

"You can wash it off if you want to. There's no doctor here, not even a *feldsher*. But if there's a bullet, I can dig it out for you if you want. . . ."

"Thanks, grandpa. But it went clean through."

The old man went to a cupboard and came back with a bottle of vodka. "You can drink it or put it on the wound, as you like. You'll pay me later. In the morning we'll talk and decide what to do with you."

He pointed to a space by the stove. There was a pile of tarpaulins and some straw, a heavy quilt and some knapsacks. The knapsacks were German. Kurenko saw them but said nothing.

The old man locked the door with a big iron key that hung from his belt. "You'll be safe enough here for the night," he said. Then he went into the passage off the kitchen; there was a small room there, like a closet, with a blanket across the doorway. A paraffin lamp glowed behind the blanket, sending the old man's shadow out into the passageway as he got ready to go to sleep.

Kurenko and the general's wife sat down on the tarpaulins. Then Nina Andreyeva reached over and pulled at Kurenko's sleeve.

"You'd better let me look at that," she said.

"It's nothing," he said. "Yours is far worse. You must have a terrible headache, but you don't say a word."

She ignored him and went on, all concern for his arm.

"The old man is right. You should put some alcohol on it. Even if the bullet went right through there's still a chance of infection."

She bent over his arm, touching the edge of the wound with the point of a knife she'd found on the floor by the stove, but only after first burning the blade in the fire. Then she poured some of the vodka over the wound. He gritted his teeth and whistled. She drank some of the vodka and gave him the bottle.

"I was a doctor . . . once . . . a good doctor, so I know what I'm doing. You think you're all right, but you've lost a lot of blood. You have to rest and get your strength back or you'll pass out. And then, who knows what will happen?" She drew him down onto the canvas and pushed one of the knapsacks under his head.

"I'm ashamed," he said. "You look after me but I haven't done a thing for you. . . ."

"You saved my life. That's a lot, isn't it?"

He didn't answer. He kept remembering the expression on the face of the German who'd kicked open the doors of the van and on the face of the rifleman who'd shot them.

She reached up and turned his face toward her. In the light of the oil lamp by the stove she could see him clearly for the first time. She wiped away some of the dirt with a rag still damp with vodka and blood.

"You're not a bad-looking young man," she said. "Do you have a wife or a sweetheart?"

He blushed. He wasn't used to such talk. "I've never had the time."

She smiled and turned away, stretching out on her back and cradling her head with her hands.

"You're just as big a fool as he was. He never knew what to say when someone complimented him either."

"Who?"

"My husband." She paused. "You knew him, didn't you?"

"Why do you say that?"

"Because I know your face. From somewhere. I don't know exactly where. . . . I've been thinking about it for a long time. At first I thought, no, it's impossible. Your mind is playing tricks on you, Nina Andreyeva. They've given you something. He just looks familiar because when a person is so completely alone, as I am, she wants to see someone she knows. But it *is* true, isn't it? Who are you?"

"My name is Kurenko. Vassily Gregorovitch. Does that mean anything to you?"

"No, but your face does. I never forget faces. Even when we were with the Chinese I could always remember the faces." She took a long drag at the remains of her cigarette. "Do you know who I am?"

He didn't reply but closed his eyes, wondering how he was going to carry it all off.

"I am Nina Andreyeva Golitsyna," she said. "My husband was

Major General Alexander Semyonovitch Golitsyn. They tell me he's turned traitor now. And so, naturally, they arrest me."

"They arrested his students too. And his officers," Kurenko said. "I was both."

"So that's it. What year did you graduate? It wasn't at Wampoa. You're Russian, that's plain enough."

"It was at the Frunze Academy, comrade Nina Andreyeva. Three years ago."

"Just before it happened," she said softly.

"What do you mean?"

"Never mind. It doesn't matter and it can make no possible difference to you." She studied his face again. "I remember a party we gave for that class. There were only a few there. The best. Were you one of them?"

He nodded.

"So that's why you seemed so familiar. Do you remember me?"

"I didn't at first. I was staring just because, well, you're a very handsome woman, that's all. But I got to thinking afterward . . ."

She laughed. "Lie down. You'll need to rest now." She put her head on his shoulder. He winced as a wave of pain ran down his arm again but he clenched his teeth and said nothing.

"You and I, Vasya, he's done for both of us, hasn't he?"

"Who, Nina Andreyeva?"

"Our general. Who else? Alexander Semyonovitch, that's who."

"I remember, you sang that evening," he said, vaguely aware of her warmth and feeling a stirring in spite of himself.

"You remember *that*?" She thought for a moment. "Yes, you're right. I remember too. Was it this one?" She began to sing to him, very softly.

He nodded again. There was a faint movement behind the blanket in the passage. The shadow cast by the paraffin lamp shifted. The old man hadn't gone to sleep yet.

He closed his eyes. She did the same, and pressed closer to him for warmth, pulling the canvas up over them both.

It was impossible to sleep. He dozed fitfully, tormented by nightmares. His arm began to throb and he could not get the memory of the ditch out of his mind. He could hear the dogs whining in the freezing yard outside. Once he heard the sounds of a motor lorry passing somewhere not far off. But mostly there was a thick stillness from which the slow crackling of the fire in the stove, the hiss of the lamp, and Nina Andreyeva's slow, labored breathing were the only relief. The light still burned behind the blanket. The old man had not moved.

"Nina Andreyeva?" he whispered. She was asleep and did not stir.

Gently, he moved her head away from his stiff shoulder and got up. He didn't trust the old man and was afraid of what he might do. There had been too many accidents already.

He went into the passage and pulled the blanket back a little. The old man was sitting on a wooden bed, loading a brand-new Mauser pistol. He jerked around, a look of fear on his face. It was obvious that he hadn't heard Kurenko come up on him.

"Don't worry," Kurenko said. "It's all right."

The old man flattened back against the wall. The chamber of the pistol was open and the shotgun lay at the foot of the bed, beyond reach. He was vulnerable and he knew it.

"What d'you mean? Why should I worry? You're Russian, just like me. Or are you?"

"We're Russians all right, grandpa. But whether we're just like you, I don't know." He paused. The old man didn't dare move. It was worth a try. He said, "Let me tell you, I've had enough. They don't seem to have treated you badly, have they, the Germans? No? All right, I'll take the chance then. Who's in charge in this place?"

"Dyachuk is mayor, yes. So?"

"Can you go to him? Then . . . the two of you go to the German officers at the garrison."

"What d'you want with them?" The old man seemed relieved. His fingers dropped away from the pistol. It was clear that he'd been intending to turn them in all along.

"We want to give ourselves up," Kurenko said. "But I don't want to get shot down in the street either. Will you get them and bring them here? You can take the credit."

The old man shrugged and got up, pulling on his sheepskin and his hood and taking both guns with him.

"God wills," he said softly, and went out, locking the door again behind him.

He touched her gently on the face. It was dawn. A gray watery light was leaking in through the mica windows, making everything look harsh and far uglier than it had by lamplight. Her face was puffy with fatigue, the graze-wound livid.

He had heard the sounds outside only a few seconds before.

"Nina Andreyeva . . . we have visitors. You must wake up."

She sat up straight, her eyes wide open, then got to her feet just as the door opened.

The old man stood there, next to him a stocky, gray-bearded man in a padded coat. Behind them were two German soldiers and a young officer holding an automatic pistol.

Before the startled officer had a chance to say anything, Nina Andreyeva stepped forward, as though she'd known exactly what was going to happen.

"I am the wife of General of the Soviet army Alexander Semyonovitch Golitsyn. This man with me is a staff officer. You will tell your commandant that we wish to surrender to him and then to be taken at once to my husband."

Oberleutnant Konigsberg was growing angry. Had the Russian woman's manner not been so aggressively indifferent and so superior, he would have ordered her shot at once, along with the man they'd brought in with her. Although he hadn't the slightest idea who General Golitsyn was, the calm manner in which the woman insisted that he advise his superiors of her presence made him suspicious that she was actually entitled to her arrogant manner. He was not entirely sure—but doubtful enough so that he was afraid not to believe her. He had learned *that* particular lesson the hard way, and too many times over already.

They sat in a large room in a building that had earlier been used both as the district agricultural committee headquarters and a grain warehouse and was now used as the Germans' local command post for the town of Kolvo.

Oberleutnant Konigsberg was talking to his sergeant, a burly, pleasant-enough-looking man with the ruddy face of a baker. It was obvious that the young officer did not know what to do and in the time-honored way was looking to the older noncom for advice.

Outside, motorcycles with sidecars churned up the muddy, fly-ridden streets. Goats bleated in the fenced-in yards and now and then a group of surly villagers with shovels over their shoulders could be seen passing along the road under German escort.

The sergeant regarded Kurenko and the woman critically.

"If the Herr Oberleutnant pleases, the clothes . . . they aren't uniforms, but . . ."

"I've told you twice already," said Nina Andreyeva. "These are prison uniforms. You see these numbers? What do you *think* they're for?"

The lieutenant wavered. "What she says could be true, of course, but even if it is, it still doesn't tell us what should be done."

"We must be taken to your division headquarters. They'll know what should be done with us if you don't."

The lieutenant leaned forward. His pinched, pale face drained of such color as still remained to it. The woman's tone had just passed over the thin dividing line between arrogance and insolence. He was not going to stand for any more. He had heard, only the day before, of what had happened at Rostov, and the defeat weighed heavily on him. For the first time in his young life, he was beginning to have doubts.

He took a sip of coffee and waited. He wanted the woman to become impatient, to give him an excuse to hit her. There was something about her expression that was eating away at him.

"Prison uniforms," he repeated dully. "And you would care to tell us just why, if you are the wife of a Soviet general, you should be wearing such a uniform?"

"Ask your superiors if you don't believe me. My husband is in Berlin at the moment, with your General Staff. Is that reason enough?"

"And you, on the other hand, are in a peasant's hut in this god-forsaken ruin of a place? You really expect me to believe such shit?"

"We were being taken to a transfer point," Kurenko broke in. "We were to be exchanged . . ." He stopped short. Budyankov had not told him for whom they were being exchanged and it was clear from the expression on Nina Andreyeva's face that Budyankov had told her nothing at all.

Oberleutnant Konigsberg smiled meanly, seeing Kurenko's confusion.

"Yes, yes. Suppose you tell us. Just who were you to be exchanged for?"

"I can't. Of course I can't. How could I possibly know?"

"Naturally you don't know, since you're both spies and since none of this fairy tale of yours is true. You're wearing aviator's uniforms, that's what. You were parachuted in here, weren't you? Come, tell the truth."

"These are prison uniforms," said Nina Andreyeva. "We were being transported south when one of your units caught us in the forest and destroyed the truck and the escort. Everyone else was killed."

"How convenient."

"Nevertheless, it's true. Do you think he put a bullet through his own arm? Do you think I did this to myself?" She pointed to the livid crease on the side of her head.

The sergeant went over to her and prodded the wound.

"It's true, Herr Oberleutnant. It's a bullet graze all right."

The lieutenant appeared disappointed. He half rose and pushed a map across the table.

"Suppose you show us just where all of this occurred, *gnädige Frau.*"

She hesitated. Kurenko gave her a questioning look. She seemed so sure of herself that he felt ashamed.

She thrust a finger at the map. "I would say, here, in this area. Just below Kromy. They were Waffen SS, the patch had a griffin and three crowns on it. I'm positive."

Kurenko swallowed twice, quickly. The damned griffin patch. He stared at the officer, aghast, overcome by a sudden if inexplicable feeling that the general's wife had just sentenced them both to death.

The lieutenant's expression hardened. "You will wait right here," he snapped, stalking out of the room with the sergeant right behind him. The two lance corporals who had been left in the map room drew their PKs. Kurenko and the general's wife stood where they were, their backs to the wall . . . a position, Kurenko thought, which was stunningly appropriate.

Oberleutnant Konigsberg went immediately to the radio shack and directed his communications sergeant to put in a call at once to the Fourteenth Waffen SS Grenadier field headquarters.

When contact had been made, he snatched away the field telephone and spoke directly to the wireman at the other end. After a moment, his exhausted face brightened. He nodded, handed the phone back to the operator, and left the building.

In the roadway outside the shack, Konigsberg spoke hastily to his sergeant.

"You will see to it that Hauptstürmführer Harz is notified at once."

"The SS Einsatz Kommando Regiment?" The sergeant looked puzzled. It was clear that he shared the common soldier's prejudices; to him, the Waffen SS were madmen at best and homicidal maniacs at the very least. Particularly the Einsatz Kommando groups.

"Hauptstürmführer Harz is the ranking intelligence officer in this sector. Those people are to be turned over to him at once."

"The Oberleutnant is sure that he knows what he's doing?"

"The Oberleutnant is indeed sure, Emil. They are clearly spies, the two of them. She gave it away, the whore with the big mouth. You see, there isn't a company of the Fourteenth Waffen SS anywhere near that forest. And there hasn't been in over a month. So what do you make of the *gnädige Frau*'s story now, eh, sergeant? Tell me that. . . ."

In a burrow more than a meter below the surface of the snow, an NKVD wireman wriggled slowly on his back below a tangle of wires and cables. It was hard to breathe in the gravelike enclosure. He had been there for over eight hours. The air pipe that projected above the snow crust had clogged twice, nearly suffocating him. But he remained there stoically, the earphones clamped on his head, his thickly gloved hand on the intercept cable that connected just below the surface of the ground with the German field-net wires. All night he had been listening to routine, unimportant messages. He was growing drowsy. Only hunger kept him at least partially alert. He was down to his last hard ration and wished desperately for a cigarette.

Melting snow dripped steadily down the plank shoring inside his narrow burrow. It was far too warm, but he had no room even to take off his jacket.

He listened.

Finally, it came, the message he had been waiting for.

He rolled a half turn and found the phone pack—an American unit of the latest manufacture. Lend-lease. He rang. The line was clear. He heard a click at the other end, at Senior Lieutenant Shelepin's post. From there, the message would go out in the clear, by radio.

He spoke quickly, and distinctly, repeating the words only twice, sure that he had been heard. A prearranged phrase. Shelepin would know exactly what to do.

"The cabbage is now cooking. Repeat, the cabbage is now cooking."

Then he hung up.

At 11:45 that morning, the cipher officer in the communications center at Army Group D headquarters in Bryansk received for retransmission to Waffen SS Grenadier Division Fourteenth, a message that caused him to wrench off his headphones and go running for his superiors.

For a moment, the others in the room thought that the cipher officer had just decoded news of another Soviet breakthrough. Had Timoshenko's tanks cracked the ring at Orel? Were five thousand T-34s hurtling down on them from the Kromy forest? They had all lost the arrogance bred by their first easy victories the year before. Winter and the implacable vastness of the land had already taught them a painful lesson in humility. Now they were beginning to learn fear as well.

The cipher officer, one Oberleutnant Gruber, went directly to his immediate superior, a graying German Balt named Schlussel, who was too old to have been still a captain but was one nevertheless, thanks mostly to his national origin. On cold winter evenings when there was no fighting and an advance or a withdrawal had been held up by the weather, Gruber often joined Captain Schlussel in a glass of whiskey and listened to him complain about the stupidity of the OKH staff in Berlin and the obtuseness of Reichsminister Rosenberg in particular. Gruber had quickly become convinced, more by Schlussel's tone and professional air than by his logic, that Operation Barbarossa would have long since been successfully concluded had the SS not insisted on alienating the entire population by trying to murder half of it.

During one of those nights, often more than twelve hours long at certain times of the year, Gruber had met another officer, a chubby young captain named Beifelder, who had come over to army group as liaison from OKH field headquarters. It was Beifelder and his remarks about his coterie in Berlin and their plans that now sent Oberleutnant Gruber crunching rapidly down the snowy main street of Bryansk in search of Captain Schlussel.

"You should read this at once, Captain," he exclaimed, having at last found Schlussel near the ammunition depot. Trucks laden with artillery shells were coming and going and making so much noise that Gruber felt no hesitation about speaking his mind.

"You sent this on to the Fourteenth?"

"To Hauptstürmführer Harz, as directed, sir. I could hardly stop it from being sent on, but I thought you should see it at once."

"This is the only copy of the transmission?"

Gruber nodded. Schlussel tore up the tissue.

"You were absolutely right to show this to me, Gruber. My God, what incredible stupidity. One could expect such things from the SS, but from a regular army officer? He certainly should have known better. How long ago was this sent on?"

"Ten minutes, no more."

Schlussel stared down at the shreds of paper at his feet; the wind had already carried most of them away. Two spies had been apprehended; one of them, a woman, claimed to be the wife of a Soviet general named Golitsyn. If the Einsatz Kommando would be kind enough to come and collect them, the sender would be most pleased to be rid of them. Or if the authorities would just as soon that they were hung at once, the sender would also be glad to oblige.

"Do you know if this is true, Gruber? About the woman?"

"I have no way of knowing, sir."

"Of course you don't. But *if* it is . . ." Schlussel's voice trailed off into a painful silence.

Then: "This fellow Konigsberg . . . do you know him? What a damned fool to be in charge at such a moment."

"So many have been killed, sir. The choices for command are very limited."

"And many more will be killed—unnecessarily—if this kind of idiocy continues. Here . . . Gruber . . . do whatever you have to, but see to it that Harz's people don't get their hands on the two Russians, particularly the woman. If you need help, call Major Baum, who is the Abwehr operations officer in Orel. He has authority from OKH in Berlin as well as from his own superiors in cases like this. I want the two of them here by tonight . . . this Frau Golitsyn and the other one."

"And you, sir?"

"I am going to try to get in touch with Schreiber-Hartstein in Berlin. Assuming the radios are still working. Tell the communications operator to set up the network at once."

Kurenko and Nina Andreyeva were bound and thrown into the back of a staff car equipped with special cleated tires and a low-temperature engine. The weather was threatening and although there was still little snow on the roads much was expected within the next twenty-four hours. It was necessary that the prisoners be taken to a nearby rail junction where the Fourteenth Waffen SS, composed of Ukrainians with German officers, was located. Even the driver of the car and the guard who rode with a machine gun across his lap seemed unhappy. Oberleutnant Konigsberg had declined to accompany his prisoners. He had heard what the *Einsatzgruppen* had been doing in the villages near Bryansk and doubted that he had the stomach to confront any of their handiwork. He knew of one case where an officer had gotten sick and vomited at the sight of one of the *Einsatzgruppen* massacres and had been promptly sent to a penal battalion for his squeamishness.

Kurenko had been told to keep silent. It was to him that all orders were now addressed. No one, it seemed, cared to talk to the woman. There was something about her flinty self-confidence and the vaguely bemused look she bestowed on her captors that made them all distinctly uneasy. She had not been raped or even manhandled. Oberleutnant Konigsberg had given strict orders that no one was to touch her. He wanted her intact, he explained, for the SS interrogators to work on.

Kurenko was frightened and was trying desperately not to show it before the general's wife. It seemed to him that everything that could possibly have gone wrong had gone wrong. And yet, he had a nagging feeling that almost everything that had happened was exactly as Colonel Budyankov had planned it.

Nina Andreyeva seemed unperturbed. Her calm, her acceptance of everything that had happened thus far, and her unshakable superiority simply made matters worse. If only she would show some slight sign of fear, perhaps there might be some hope. Kurenko admired her for her strength but at the same time felt that it demeaned him.

It made little difference in the long run, for he doubted now whether they would live out the night. Budyankov might have taken many things into account, but how could he have anticipated an arrogant ignoramus like Oberleutnant Konigsberg?

The front was not far off. As the staff car pressed on along the muddy, rutted road, they could hear the boom of guns and the high, distant whine of aircraft engines. The guards looked up, every bit as nervous as their prisoners. It was late afternoon and it was imperative that they reach the railhead before dark. The woods, so Konigsberg had warned his driver, were full of partisans at night.

Suddenly, the driver gave a shout and slammed on the brakes. The car almost skidded onto the shoulder of the road. A heavy ice-slick had already formed over the mud and the new cleated tires had not held.

A *Kübelwagen* with two officers standing in the back had been drawn across the road about one hundred meters ahead. On either side stood half a dozen infantrymen.

The staff car came to a stop and the confused driver got out.

One of the two officers, a stocky captain wearing a heavy winter coat of the newest kind, clambered down from the *Kübelwagen* and came forward waving an envelope.

The driver read the orders and handed the envelope back.

"If the Herr Hauptmann pleases, my orders are to take the two prisoners to Hauptstürmführer Harz, Galizische Division, SS."

"You now have new orders, sergeant."

"But, Herr Hauptmann . . ."

"You *can* read, can't you? Do I have to remind you that I am your superior officer?"

"Oberleutnant Konigsberg is also my superior, Herr Hauptmann."

"And I am *his* superior. You will also note that the order carries General Weigl's endorsement as well as that of the Abwehr. Which should answer any questions you may have. Now . . . *the prisoners.* At once. Do I make myself clear?" The captain's hand dropped to his holster.

The driver gestured to the guards, who pushed the two Russians out of the car. Nina Andreyeva stumbled and fell.

"Pick her up at once, Oberjäger," the stocky Wehrmacht captain snapped. The flustered driver did as he was told.

"You will excuse him, Frau Golitsyn. He does not understand who you are." The captain paused and allowed himself the briefest play of a hopeful smile. "Such things will not, I trust, happen again." To the baffled driver and the two guards, he said, "You may advise this Oberleutnant Konigsberg of yours, whoever he may be, that no charges will be brought against him for his criminal stupidity. Here . . . here is your receipt. Everything is in order? Good. All is as it should be."

The captain turned toward his prisoners. "You will come with us now . . . if you please. . . ."

It was still pitch-dark when the pilots of Attack Bomber Squadron Sixteen came out of the corrugated metal sheds in which they slept between missions.

The white, sharklike Stormoviks were already on line by the end of the runway, surrounded by mechanics blowing plumes of frosty breath into the predawn air, swarming over the heavily armored planes like lemmings, loading the underwing racks, handing up ammunition for the cannon, fixing the rockets in position, making sure that the machine guns were operative in the bitter cold.

Squadron Commander Azarkhin stood by the operations shack, a low, heavily camouflaged building that looked more like a snow-covered hummock than a man-made structure. His feet were cold in his dog-fur boots, and he was angry. Why did it have to be in the middle of the night? Couldn't they have let him sleep for a few more hours? He'd gotten no more than four hours' sleep in the last three days. Not much of a recommendation for combat flying.

A few lights winked on along the runway, blue pinpoints where the takeoff guide flares were set.

Azarkhin moved slowly toward his own plane. Belov, his mechanic, was standing under the port wing. His gunner, Erdenko, was already in the rear seat, checking out the lethal twin VYas.

Azarkhin did not even look at the chart he had carried out of the briefing shed with him. He knew the terrain around Kolvo as well as he knew the body of his own wife. He'd been born not far from there, less than fifty kilometers away, and he'd visited Kolvo many times. By the time they were ten minutes out of the airfield, it would start to grow light. The ground was only partially covered with snow and it would be easy to spot landmarks, roads, rivers, a village here and there. He would have no trouble leading his attack group straight into Kolvo.

He climbed silently into the cockpit, still wondering whether they would meet any opposition. Probably not, they had told him. There was nothing to worry about. And certainly not from the ground. The few Flak towers the Germans had in the Kolvo sector boasted nothing that could even put a dent in one of Ilyushin's "flying tanks," much less bring it down.

The powerful AM-42 turned over and began to hum. Azarkhin turned in the cramped seat and leaned as far back as he could, clapping his gunner, Erdenko, on the shoulder. For luck. Around him, two dozen dull red wing lights winked on.

Then the Stormovik was rolling down the hard, frozen runway. He felt the plane strain against its heavy load of bombs and rockets, trying to get airborne. Then came the blessed feeling of lift building under the wings. He eased back on the stick, just slightly, the Ilyushin heaved into the air and began a steep, graceful climb.

Kolvo, he thought, remembering its muddy, rutted streets and the dozen or so brick warehouses around the marketplace. Had it changed much since he'd last seen it? Why the devil would anyone want such a place leveled? It was absolutely worthless even when completely intact. To the Germans, to anyone.

He glanced over his shoulder. Behind him, the rest of the squadron was already airborne, and had taken up its arranged flight pattern, a long arrowhead, low to the ground, skimming over the snowy treetops, black against the gradually lightening sky.

Why Kolvo? he wondered again, and turned back, staring straight ahead to the east.

Herbert Harz, Hauptstürmführer SS, pushed the peasant woman he had been sleeping with roughly aside and swung his legs over the edge of the bed.

What the devil was that hammering? He'd have his orderly, Corporal Feustel, shot if it was he. But whoever it was, it had better be damned important to warrant waking him up at such an hour.

Hurriedly, he pulled on his trousers, slipped his suspenders over his shoulders, picked up his tunic, and went to the door.

"Stay there," he told the woman. "I'll be right back." As long as he was awake, he thought, why not? There was no rule that said early morning wasn't as good as the middle of the night.

He pulled the door open. A bitter-cold, snowy predawn grayness struck him in the face. Rottenführer Feustel stood there shivering in his greatcoat and rubbing his mittened hands together.

"You'd better come quickly, Hauptstürmführer."

"What the hell is bothering you?"

"It's very odd, Herr Hauptstürmführer. You'd better come and see for yourself."

Harz went back and got his boots and his coat. He threw the coat on over his underwear without bothering to put on his tunic first. The cold be damned. If the Russians could live with it, so could he.

Feustel hurried him down the rutted road to a point about a dozen meters from the house where he'd quartered himself. From there they could both see the few log and stone houses that were Bryansk all lumped together like heaps of coal not far off. Beyond them, on the low ridge, clearly visible against the dawn sky just then going dove gray, something could be seen moving toward them.

"You idiot," Harz exclaimed. "Those are Panzer IIIs." He squinted into the half-light. He could see what looked like a straggling line of infantry coming up behind the tanks. The silhouettes of the helmets, the long, flapping coats, were familiar enough.

"What unit is that?" Harz demanded. "What's the matter with you, Feustel? Are you good for nothing?" He could see other men of his company coming out of their houses, wakened by the slow rumbling of the armor. "Feustel, find out who the hell they are and what they're doing here."

Harz stood there, his coat open, the wind pushing at his chest. He rubbed his eyes, trying to figure out what division it could possibly be. There were no tanks in Kolvo. The nearest panzers, as far as he knew, were at Myaslov, eighty kilometers to the west. He'd had no information about an armored movement of any kind. What the devil, exactly, was going on?

Just then, Feustel let out a scream. Harz's head whipped around.

He saw it come whooshing up from somewhere behind the oncoming tank formation—five long, rapidly moving fingers of white smoke, rushing across the gray sky right at them.

He had no time to even open his mouth. The rockets struck all around him. The explosions were deafening. The ground rose up on all sides, carrying the flimsy buildings with them, logs, masonry, wattles, and brick. Harz and Feustel together went flying through the air, born by the explosion, both dead before their feet had left the ground.

The tanks opened fire as another brace of Katyushas let loose from the eastern edge of the town. The infantry had by now fanned out and was advancing in a wide semicircle that enclosed Bryansk like the hook of a scythe.

By the time the firing had stopped, the captured tanks of Senior Lieutenant Shelepin's Special Purposes Regiment were drawn up in a solid ring around what remained of the town. Major Trepov, distinctly uncomfortable in his German field grays, stood in the snow a dozen meters from the burning radio shack.

It was Shelepin who first emerged from the smoking building. His face was blackened by smoke and he was coughing, but in his hand he held a sheaf of papers. He stood for a moment in front of the waiting Trepov, trying to catch his breath. As he bent almost double with coughing, his men drove the radio operator out of the burning shed and shot him.

All over the village came the sharp snap of rifle fire. Orders were being carried out. Surprise had been complete. Most of the dead Germans scattered around the streets of the town and crumpled in the snow were still in their underwear. They had caught almost the entire garrison asleep.

Finally Shelepin straightened up and handed the papers over.

"This is what you're looking for, Major," he said.

Trepov took the charred signal tissues and glanced quickly through them.

"Exactly," he said. "Now you can do whatever you want with the rest of them. It's of no concern to me."

A light, absolutely vertical rain that left no discernible dark marks on the shoulders and sleeves of Schreiber-Hartstein's coat was slowly turning the fabric to lead.

Few aircraft had dared try to land in such weather. Despite the rain, a low fog still hung over the entire field. The lights on the runways and the control towers winked fitfully in the shifting, cloud-blown darkness, barely more than cat's eyes and invisible at a distance greater than one hundred meters.

Schreiber-Hartstein stood by the east runway, next to his car, his face upturned, as though he could actually see something. The rain was hard and cold on his face; it reminded him painfully of the splash of the sea against the coastal rocks above Riga where he had been born. He strained to listen. There had been no enemy aircraft over Berlin that night; the fog and the rain had prevented that at least. There were no motors of any kind now, only a deathly silence in which shadowy, pterodactyloid shapes glided silent as the rain itself about the periphery of his vision. The evening before—and he had been there then too, waiting out his second day—the field had been a mass of smoldering wrecks, shell holes pitted with fire above which long lancets of light scraped the sky. The British bombers had come over, high and with infuriating swiftness; gone before the searchlights could find them. The radio in the operations room had blared forth *"Wir fahren gegen England"* ceaselessly, in celebration of the fact that although the Stirlings had leveled large parts of Berlin the night before, the Luftwaffe had managed to down six of them and the flak installations another three. If we go on like that, Schreiber-Hartstein had wondered bitterly, we will run out of city long before the British run out of bombing planes.

Tonight, though, there was only a chill, suffocating darkness. It was like being at the bottom of a pool of black water in which not even blind fish could live. He shuddered, wishing he had something warm to drink.

He could just as easily have waited in the car. His driver was in the front seat, reading a copy of *Die Brennessel.* Beifelder was asleep in the back, under a camel's hair lap robe.

Only Schreiber-Hartstein waited in the open. It was fitting. He *was* exposed, in everything he did. Exposed and misunderstood by almost everyone.

They had gotten to Golitsyn's wife and her companion just ahead of the SS. To his astonishment, he had not yet received the usual lilac-penciled memo from Keitel demanding an explanation. A pall of silence had settled over the whole episode. The very fact that no one had been raising hell about it made him extremely nervous.

He tried without success to light a cigarette, regretted the loss of his pipe, tried and failed again. He consulted his watch. It was just after midnight.

The plane was thirty minutes overdue, according to the last report. But who could tell? There had been a dozen such reports and he had been there at the airport for almost thirty-six hours now. Each new report had proven false. Why should this latest be any different?

But then, suddenly, he saw the landing lights and heard the sound of the motors. The big, bullet-nosed Heinkel III dropped down through the fog like a shadow.

He reached through the partly open car window and tugged at Beifelder's shoulder.

"Martin . . . wake up. I think they've come at last."

The twin-engined Heinkel dropped onto the runway and came to a rolling stop not far from the car.

"How can they possibly see in such weather?" Beifelder breathed.

"The will of God," said Schreiber-Hartstein. "Seeing has nothing to do with it."

Beifelder looked surprised and would have been even more so had he not been so fatigued. Such a remark was unlike the usually phlegmatic, always intensely matter-of-fact Balt. But the closeness of death, he knew, had an odd way of shading a man's personality. He shrugged and turned to watch the hatch on the side of the Heinkel swing open. A number of indistinct figures clambered down. In single file, leaning hard against a sharp, brooming wind, they made their way across the rain-slicked tarmac. There were four of them. Two German officers in leather greatcoats. Between them walked a woman, shapeless and bundled in an officer's cloth coat, and a bare-headed young man wearing an odd bluish coverall of some sort.

The light from the nearby marker was just strong enough for Schreiber-Hartstein to make out the woman's features. He knew the face well enough. He had been staring at her photograph for days. Before she had time to adjust her eyes to the light—he was standing in silhouette against the rotating amber beacon on the main control tower—he stepped forward.

"Welcome, Frau Golitsyn. We welcome you to Berlin," he said.

Part II

7

Once a prisoner, he began to deliberate on what he should do. He was politically educated, he admired Stalin, but he had no convictions of his own, only ambitions. He realized that his military career was at an end. If the Soviet Union was victorious, the best he could hope for was demotion. There remained only one solution: to accept the German's offer and do everything to bring about a German victory. Then he would become Commander-in-Chief or Minister of War in a truncated Russia under the aegis of a victorious Hitler. Naturally he never said anything of the kind to anyone. In his broadcasts he declared that he had long hated the Soviet regime, that he was eager "to free Russia from the Bolsheviks" but had he not also quoted to me the saying, "Every jack uses his own excuses"?

Ilya Ehrenburg,
The War: 1941–1945

Number 10 Viktoriastrasse was a building of little distinction on a street of even less. Four stories of gray stone, clumsily designed and badly built, it was not even really ugly by the standards of the neighborhood, but simply shabby. Seen from the street, it seemed no different from the other buildings in the neighborhood, but from the air it gave the impression of a *caserma*, or police barracks, being a hollow square with a large courtyard at its center, overlooked on two sides by four stories of iron railed balconies.

It was for this reason, as well as for its location, that it had been chosen by Schreiber-Hartstein's group to house the Soviet turncoats who were to make up the cadres of the proposed Russian Liberation Army.

Shortly before four in the afternoon, with the previous night's fog and slowly settling rain showing no signs of letting up, two black Daimlers and a Mercedes-Benz painted dark green pulled up in front of the building's single glass-doored entrance. Schreiber-Hartstein was the first to get out, followed by General Golitsyn's wife and Lieutenant Kurenko, who was now wearing an ill-fitting suit of civilian clothes and a shapeless felt hat.

Schreiber-Hartstein pointed and they went quickly up the three stone steps and into the vestibule. The passengers in the first and third cars, all officers of Schreiber-Hartstein's group, remained where they were. They would sit and wait until the new guests had been installed.

For four hours that morning, both Kurenko and the general's wife had been subjected to a restrained but thorough interrogation. Kurenko had told Schreiber-Hartstein who he was, and described his arrest, giving as the reason his "closeness" to the defected general. He told of the transport to the camp at Lake Byeleymostnoy, so far as he had understood it from Colonel Budyankov, and of all that had happened after that. Nina Andreyeva had apparently told an almost identical story.

For the moment, the Germans were satisfied.

Still puzzled by all that had happened but more convinced than ever that everything was proceeding according to Colonel Budyankov's plan, Kurenko allowed himself to be bathed, fed, and reclothed. After all, what difference could it possibly make that they had reached Berlin by way of a near disaster in the Kromy forest and a vicious young Oberleutnant in Kolvo rather than via a prisoner exchange? They were *in* Berlin, and that was what mattered.

Kurenko had joined Golitsyn's wife in the captain's office and was astonished to see the transformation that a plain dress, stockings, and some soap had wrought. She had struck him before as a woman commanding respect. Now he saw her as almost beautiful. For a moment, he could not contain his embarrassment and flushed. She noticed this, laughed fleetingly, but said nothing.

All of the Germans of Schreiber-Hartstein's group spoke Russian fluently and it would hardly do to be indiscreet.

They had ridden to Viktoriastrasse in relative silence, listening to Schreiber-Hartstein rattle off facts, figures, troop strengths, and unit designations. Kurenko was at once dumbfounded and depressed. If all that the German officer said was true, then it was hard to see how merely neutralizing General Golitsyn was going to change anything. So much had been done thus far without him that it seemed impossible that it could not also be completed without him. In a few month's time, an army of almost a million Russians would be ready to march into the Soviet Union. The consequences of such an undertaking were almost impossible to foresee. No wonder Budyankov had spoken so bitterly of Golitsyn's betrayal.

Kurenko was brought back to the reality of the moment by the slamming of doors behind him.

"Follow me," Schreiber-Hartstein snapped, going buoyantly up the stairs. They halted on the second landing before a massive oak door fitted with a buzzer and a peephole.

A sallow, gray-faced man in his late fifties answered. Kurenko knew he had seen him somewhere before.

"Dushkin . . . is the general here?"

"Where else would he be, unless you knew about it?"

Schreiber-Hartstein looked disappointed.

"He is not a prisoner. He knows that."

"But does your police?" asked Dushkin sourly. "Never mind . . . who are all these people?" He strained to see into the shadowy hall.

Just then a voice sounded within the apartment, calling Dushkin in a soft, sonorous bass.

"Dushkin? Who is it?"

"That's what I'm trying to find out, your excellency."

An unusually tall, stoop-shouldered man in a shapeless gray uniform of gray wool appeared at the end of the hallway. Alexander Semyonovitch Golitsyn still wore his heavy, steel-rimmed eyeglasses. His coarse, iron-gray hair was cut short above a high, broad forehead, which dropped like the wall of a cliff to his sad, deep-set eyes. His mouth opened fleetingly in a gasp of astonishment.

He stared at the woman, then at Schreiber-Hartstein. Nina Andreyeva said nothing but fastened on him an intense, unwavering stare. Schreiber-Hartstein glanced from one to the other of them, expecting at the very least some small sign of emotion. But there was nothing; neither husband nor wife moved a centimeter from where they stood.

Dushkin, the orderly, looked perplexed and embarrassed. It was clear that he did not recognize the general's wife and had no idea what had occurred.

At last the general broke the strained silence and took Nina Andreyeva by both shoulders and, with a sudden, unexpected violence, pressed her to him. Though his face was turned away from the Germans, Kurenko could see that his features were contorted. He was struggling hard to keep control of himself. On Nina Andreyeva's face, however, was the same impassive expression that inevitably seemed to mask her feelings at precisely those moments when she should have been expected to show them most openly.

Schreiber-Hartstein realized at once that the woman's arrival had not made the impression he had anticipated.

Something was wrong, but he had no idea what it was.

"How did this . . . happen?" The voice was Golitsyn's, but not as Kurenko remembered it, brisk and sure, but throaty and wavering.

"How . . . did this happen?" he repeated.

"She will tell you herself, General. I won't be boor enough to interfere. She's tired but unharmed, as you see, and all things considered, she hasn't had too bad a time of it. We've done our best."

"That's right," said Nina Andreyeva. "They've done their best, you can be sure of that."

Golitsyn gave her a sad, reproving look.

"And look, Alexander Semyonovitch, we are even rebuilding your staff for you. We've brought you Kurenko."

The general took a deep breath. "God is good," he said. "I thought you were dead, Vassily Gregorovitch."

"I thought the same of you."

"And so," the general said, "we were both wrong, it seems. So very wrong." He hesitated, then threw both arms around Kurenko in a brief, hard embrace.

"We will talk this evening, General," said Schreiber-Hartstein. "In the meantime, we leave you all to become reacquainted. It's been quite a while, I know." He smiled in a hesitant sort of way. Even that slight attempt at a smile did not sit well on his sober face.

"At Stalkov's party," the general said. "Of course. You are invited?"

"Of course," said the captain. "We shall certainly be there, Beifelder and myself."

With that, Schreiber-Hartstein turned and left, closing the heavy oak door with a sharp slam.

Kurenko stood in the hallway a few paces from Dushkin. The general waited for a few seconds, his hands on Nina Andreyeva's shoulders. Then, as Schreiber-Hartstein's footsteps faded down the stairs, he stepped forward and embraced Kurenko once again.

"You see, God *is* good," he cried. "And he chooses strange ways to show us his goodness. Vassily Gregorovitch, how wonderful it is to see you again, even here, in this place."

Kurenko, despite himself, felt the tears come to his eyes.

"Come, come . . . Dushkin will get some vodka. Some tea, some cookies. Whatever you want. Amazing, ah, God is good, is he not, Vassily Gregorovitch? If anyone had asked me, I would have said without hesitation, no, I will never see Lieutenant Kurenko alive again."

Nina Andreyeva, who was standing against the wall at that moment, began to laugh. Golitsyn turned to her with a look so pained and sorrowful that Kurenko felt his breath catch in his throat.

"Tell him, Sasha . . . tell him. Poor young man, he doesn't understand any of this. You embrace him. You ignore me. He's a sensitive young man. He sees and yet he doesn't understand."

Golitsyn shook his head.

"You said nothing to him?"

"Why should I have said anything? What difference would it have made? They apparently arrested him because he'd been caught in a German encirclement. It was only afterward that they realized who he was. As for me, they arrested me simply because they thought I was still your wife. Can you imagine . . . because of *that*?"

"Nina . . ." the general cried, stepping forward. He stopped himself, short of touching her, as though he was desperately afraid. "Ah . . . we will talk. But not here."

"As you wish, Sasha. It's always been that way, so why should it be different now?"

There was a long silence. Finally Golitsyn spread his enormous arms as though to gather them all in, his wife, Kurenko, and Dushkin as well.

"The vodka, the tea. And then there is Stalkov's birthday celebration. We shall all drink too much and, perhaps, we shall all talk too much as well."

By nine that evening the birthday celebration for Boris Stalkov was in full swing. Altogether there were about twenty people present, all Russians, all men. They wore their German clothing poorly and looked out of place, even with each other. Most of the more important residents of 10 Viktoriastrasse were there, gathered in the shabbily ornate sitting room of Golitsyn's quarters. The window shades had been drawn according to regulation, but with the permission of the German authorities not only had the lights been turned on. A string quartet had been brought in and was busy playing one of the Rasumovsky quartets . . . Schreiber-Hartstein's idea . . . "the union of two cultures" as he had hopefully put it.

A samovar gurgled on the sideboard, ignored by most of those present in favor of the bar that had ben set up by the piano. Whiskey had been provided by OKH.

"That gloomy bear over there," said Golitsyn, now slightly flushed with drink, "that great mammoth of a man is Boris Stalkov. It is for his sake that we celebrate. And just look at him. How he scowls, as though he were to be shot within the hour."

Kurenko had already been introduced to most of the others. A few of them, only a few, made him really take notice. The rest seemed uniformly dull, frightened, and unsure of themselves, just as Kurenko had imagined such people would be. But there were two or three who stood out. One was a man named Zhilinsky. He had caught only that much, neither Christian name nor patronymic. A man to be wary of. A rapid talker, intense, with deep, piercing eyes staring out of a handsome, vaguely cruel face that looked as though it had been carved out of ivory. Delicate hands . . . the man was a fine pianist, Golitsyn had said . . . small and compact, with a crackling energy that made everyone else in the room seem almost somnolent. Zhilinsky was generally referred to as "the idealist," though no one had as yet told Kurenko just why.

Across the room, leaning on the piano and within comfortable range of the bar, was a chunky, distinctly un-Russian-looking man who went by the name of Obriyan. Dushkin had already explained the origin of the odd name—his great-great-grandfather had been an Irish mercenary who had come to Russia with Napoleon's army and had been left behind to die of his wounds. He had not died but had survived instead to marry a woman from Smolensk and found a line, the most recent addition to which was the red-haired, urbane Pyotr Antonovitch Obriyan.

It was, however, to Boris Stalkov that the general enthusiastically guided Kurenko. Behind them, at the same cautious distance that she had maintained all evening, came Nina Andreyeva.

The enormous Stalkov rose. He was fully as tall as Golitsyn and much broader in the shoulders. Framed by a corona of wild black hair, stiff as wire, his massive head seemed more a continuation of his shoulders than a separate, discrete part of his body. His eyes were small but searching, his mouth so thin that in the wrong light it almost disappeared altogether. There was thick black hair on the backs of his hands, one of which he now thrust out in Kurenko's direction.

"We have only two alternatives, young man," he said. "Each day we either grow older or we die. I prefer to grow older but I have not yet found a way to prevent others from embarrassing me over it. So . . . welcome, welcome. Have a drink and then tell me, how it is you come to be in such a place as this?"

The man was obviously more than a little drunk, but then so was almost everyone else in the room.

Nina Andreyeva took Kurenko by the arm.

"You're not going to drink too, are you?"

The general looked at her unhappily.

"Nina, Nina . . . for once, let up, eh? We all have such a little time on this earth. . . ."

The string quartet continued to play, somewhat faster than before. Stalkov brightened.

"So you are the young man whom the general has to thank for bringing Nina Andreyeva to him? God, what a story. Already it has gone up and down this wretched building like the plague. Our life here is very dull, you see. We do a great deal of waiting and little else. I would like to hear all of your story . . . all of it, eh?"

Golitsyn put his hand on Nina Andreyeva's arm. "We have things to discuss. You will excuse us, Boris Trifomovitch?"

"Who can deny you anything, General?"

Before Kurenko could object, the general had left him alone with Stalkov.

As soon as Golitsyn was out of earshot, Stalkov's expression changed. He lost his vaguely inebriated look. His eyes became bright, their focus hard.

"Come now. I want to know everything," he said quickly.

There was something almost hypnotic in Stalkov's gaze. In spite of himself, Kurenko began to retell the story. He had told it so many times during the past few days that the words came out as woodenly as though he were reading them.

After a long and attentive silence, Stalkov said, "Lake Byeleymostnoy? There is a camp there?"

"For unreliables, yes. Officers who allowed themselves to be captured by the Germans, relatives of collaborators. Men who have been exposed . . ."

"To uncertain influences, yes? Ah, what fools, what damned fools. But then, if they were not such hateful fools, none of us would be here, would we?"

Kurenko thought it wiser not to answer. To break the tension he looked toward the musicians and at Nina Andreyeva, who was now talking to Zhilinsky near the piano.

But Stalkov would not let go.

"Tell me more of this camp at Byeleymostnoy. Is it a big place?"

"We never got there, so how am I to know?"

"Surely someone must have mentioned it. You were interrogated?"

"When I was arrested, yes. Or, rather, just before they arrested me." Rapidly, he told Stalkov what he had seen at Kolabyansk. Budyankov had said nothing about keeping *that* a secret and at the moment he saw no reason to do so.

Stalkov began to laugh. He threw one massive arm around Kurenko's shoulders.

"You should get drunk tonight, *malchik*. . . . You *must* get drunk tonight. Do you know why you were arrested, really? You've told me, but I don't think you really understand. . . ."

"Because I was behind German lines for two weeks."

"No, and you don't believe that either."

"If not that, then because of what I saw."

"And what exactly do you think you saw?"

"First a troop of cavalry, Russian all right, but with German officers. Then, later, in the forest, the corpses of many men wearing odd uniforms. They were also Russian, I'm sure of it. The insignia they wore . . ." He reached into his pocket and took out one of the red and blue cockades.

Stalkov snorted.

"Kromiadi's men . . . what's left of them."

"Kromiadi?"

"Colonel Konstantin Kromiadi. Ah, *malchik,* what an innocent you are. You don't know about Kromiadi? No, of course you don't. No one's ever told you, have they? They've kept it from all of you."

Kurenko stared at Stalkov with a confused, anguished expression that was far more eloquent than any words could have been.

Stalkov lit a cigarette and smiled.

"It wasn't the first time, but it may be the last," he said enigmatically. "Listen. Since the war began there have been many, *many* of us fighting on the German side. For many reasons, some of them good, some not so good. The separatists like Melnik and Bandera in the Ukraine, the Estonians and the Latvians, the Circassians and the Georgians, all living in the nineteenth century with their antiquated notions of national independence. Then the cossacks, of course, and the Kalmuk levies—complete with tents, women and children, and goats. Hundreds of thousands have served as auxiliaries to the Germans, *Hilfswillige*, 'Hiwis,' they call them. But they have all been officered by the Germans and used by the Germans for their own purposes. They are very pleased to let them do their dirty work, of course. First in the attack, last in retreat. Kromiadi's brigade was the first to have Russian officers. They set up a model unit at Osintorf, very secretly at first. Four battalions and artillery, Russian uniforms and the cockades you saw. They went out on a few small-scale raids while the unit built up. Then, just when they were getting strong enough to accomplish something, General von Kluge saw how strong they looked, got frightened, and disarmed them. He only got away with it by tricking the officers. Believe me, they'd have all turned on the Germans if they'd realized what Von Kluge was up to. But the general had his way. The men were parceled out to the Waffen SS. Some of the officers deserted to the partisans. The rest . . . well, you saw what's happened to them. An awful stew . . ."

Kurenko was stunned. Budyankov hadn't told him even half the story then. Perhaps he hadn't even known himself.

"And the cavalry?"

"Who knows? Kalmuks, cossacks. They don't mean anything.

For it to mean anything, there must be a real Russian army with Russian officers fighting for Russian goals. There must be a real Russian leader whom the men and the world will respect. It is our last chance now, with this man . . ."

"Golitsyn?"

"Who else? And who could play the part more perfectly? The Defender of Moscow. Oh yes, they'll all listen to *him*. If he's given a chance. . . ."

At that moment, Schreiber-Hartstein entered the room with Captain Beifelder and two other officers. No one turned. No one even seemed to notice him.

"Boris Trifomovitch? My congratulations," said Schreiber-Hartstein, coming over.

"Your excellency . . . is it you that I have to thank for the brandy on which I'm becoming so pleasantly drunk?"

"A small thing, Boris Trifomovitch."

"Things are small or large depending on the circumstances. At such a time and place, a real bottle of Courvoisier is a gift from the gods."

"We try our best."

"But not," said a voice, "always with success." It was Golitsyn.

"By which you mean what?" Beifelder asked unhappily.

"You know exactly what I mean. When is our army to be formed? When will we be allowed to fight under our own officers, as an independent unit?"

Schreiber-Hartstein grew sober and thoughtful.

"I wish I could answer you, General. You know how much I wish it." He shook his head. "Eventually, common sense will win out. I promise you, soon you will lead your troops straight on to Moscow."

"You honestly believe that, Captain?" Golitsyn asked gently. "Yes—you do believe it—and we respect you for your belief. But you must forgive us our doubts. Uniforms and flags and pronouncements mean very little without guns."

"They will never arm us under our own commanders," said Zhilinsky, who had just come over. "That's as plain as the nose on your face. Although it's the only way it can be carried off, as we all know, they are simply too stupid to face up to it. General Golitsyn must lead his troops *in the field*. His face must be seen. Everyone must know."

"It *will* happen," Schreiber-Hartstein said.

"Even if they do allow it, it won't last. There will be a double-cross. As with Kromiadi. You can count on it."

"And then?" asked Schreiber-Hartstein, looking very pained.

"And then," said Stalkov, "we will all take to the forests and fight as partisans."

"In which case," Schreiber-Hartstein replied, "it will be my duty to hunt you in that forest and kill you, just as you would kill me."

For a second, the thin, scholarly-looking German officer stood there with an expression of deep sadness on his face. Then, just as suddenly, he brightened and began to speak in an abnormally loud voice.

"But why talk this way? I haven't come here tonight for such talk. Gentlemen . . . gather round, please. . . ." And he began to rap for attention on the table.

All conversation stopped at once. Even Stalkov looked surprised.

"Our friend Stepan Abramovitch says that you will never receive arms and the right to your own command. Well, gentlemen, I have come here tonight to give our friend Stalkov a present, to give all of us a present. Good news, gentlemen. We have made important progress."

Schreiber-Hartstein stopped for breath. Stalkov looked puzzled, as though he were astonished that the captain could be about to tell them all something that he did not already know. Golitsyn looked merely confused.

Schreiber-Hartstein went on. "This afternoon, gentlemen, my office received a communiqué from Admiral Canaris. He has succeeded, on our behalf, in obtaining permission for the formal organization of your forces. Under your own commanders, gentlemen. Not ours. You will be armed, you will choose your own staff. There will be four regiments of infantry, one of artillery, and an engineer unit as well. The Russian Liberation Army will be a reality within a few days' time. General Golitsyn will see to the staff organization and, of course, will be your commander. In a few days' time, gentlemen, all this will come to pass. And, God willing, there will soon be an appropriate opportunity for you all to prove yourselves. Once that has been done, a new day will dawn. One division will become a hundred. We will be together again, as we were fifteen years ago. The Russian and the German will stand as allies just as they did in those dark days when we were forbidden by the Versailles Treaty to . . ."

"Who is this 'we'?" came a voice. It was Zhilinsky again. "When all of that charming cooperation was going on, Herr Hauptmann, were you a Russian or a German?"

There was a stunned silence. Then Stalkov jumped up.

"You damned cosmopolitan, you perpetual doomsayer, shut your mouth. Never mind him, Captain . . . what man here knows what he really is? If there's one who does, let him speak up. Otherwise keep quiet, you blockheads."

Schreiber-Hartstein said not a word. Stalkov climbed up onto a table and held up his glass.

"A toast to Reinhardt Gavrilovitch Schreiber-Hartstein," he exclaimed. "To a man who is, at least, no worse than anyone here."

And in silence they all drank. Not once but in solemn ritual three times in a row, glasses full each time.

All, that is, but Nina Andreyeva, who continued to nurse the single glass of wine she had been holding for the past half hour.

The party went on well into the small hours of the morning. Schreiber-Hartstein, heartsick and unable to fend off the insistent Zhilinsky, departed early. As Beifelder too left, he took Zhilinsky angrily by the arm.

"You shouldn't torment him like that. Don't you realize how hard he's worked for you?"

"Don't make me laugh. Every drop he sweats is to expiate the guilt he feels for wearing that uniform."

Beifelder left hurriedly after that.

Kurenko excused himself. He was tired. He had only just arrived. The trip had been a long one. He needed some sleep.

On the second-floor landing, a shadow detached itself from the corridor and came quickly over to him. It was Obriyan. Kurenko tensed, then relaxed as he realized that the man was drunk and could barely stand. Obriyan threw both arms around him.

"My God, he will get us all killed."

"Who?"

"Zhilinsky . . . you heard him. It's always the same story with him. Ever since Alexander Semyonovich arrived. *Golitsyn* must lead us. *Golitsyn* must do this, *Golitsyn* must do that. They say you were his favorite. What a blessing. For God's sake, talk to him. Make him see what a deadly fool this Zhilinsky is."

"And what do you propose?"

"That we die in our beds like decent men."

"Well then, go to your bed and start dying. . . ."

"Oh yes, to bed, to bed. But you'll have to show me the way, Lieutenant. You will do that, won't you?"

Alexander Semyonovitch Golitsyn was exhausted. He had allowed himself to drink too much, something he had never done before coming to Berlin, and he had made a bad job of it. Yet he was not really drunk, only depressed and enervated. He was sure that a man must feel this way when dying. A total exhaustion, not so much physical as mental. In the past it had always been his body that had given out first. He had not had to concern himself, in those days, with moral problems. Everything had seemed quite clear. His duty. His politics.

Even when they had ordered him to leave his wife it had all seemed quite clear.

Then he had been betrayed and left to die in the marshes beyond Leningrad. Everything had once again seemed quite clear. But in a completely different way.

He could recall with numbing clarity the nights he had wandered through the shattered forests, half frozen to death, suffering from a painful leg wound, with only an adjutant and the faithful Dushkin, a fierce thirst for justice growing in him. At that moment, his notion of justice had been clear enough. Justice meant the destruction of everyone and everything that had led him to that place. He had eaten bark and roots. He had defecated in the mud like an animal. He had become an animal. Any system, any leader who could reduce Alexander Semyonovitch Golitsyn to such a condition must be wrong, no matter what he had thought before.

He reviewed his grievances. He thought long and hard about the purges that had destroyed so many of his friends but had left him unscathed. He had thought of all the good men who had been murdered in dark, unknown basements. This had brought him, in turn, to a review of the events of the last twenty years and, just as inevitably, to add to that long list of names compiled in one year, 1938, an even longer list that stretched back to the days of the October Revolution. He had passed safely through it all. But why? What had it been that had protected him from persecution and had armored him so against the schemings and paranoias of little men?

On the night before he had decided to surrender, he had finally realized what it had been. Standing alone at the edge of a birch forest, gazing out over the endless, dreary marsh, above which an incredibly starry night had spread, it had come to him.

It was, simply, that during all those years he had lacked a sense of guilt.

He had not yet fully thought through the implications of this startling discovery. But to have discovered the cause seemed sufficient for the moment. He would unravel the complexities of his new understanding later. It would be enough, now, to act in the only way that seemed possible for him.

Weary, his mind full of recollections of his terrible days in the marshes along the Volkhov, confused by old confusions and troubled by new doubts, he slumped in a shabby armchair, his uniform coat still on, perspiring heavily and going over once again all that had happened to him since that night.

One thing was certain. He had cured his ailment. Guilt he now felt, in abundance.

There were so many times when he should have felt guilt, when, had he understood more clearly the implications of his own acts, he should have felt a full weight of moral responsibility instead of merely a passing and self-indulgent sorrow.

The years in China had been just such a time. But at the end of that time he had felt only regret, not real guilt. He had *thought* that he had understood. He had *thought* that he had measured and weighed the priorities of his life.

But he had been wrong.

As he had been wrong so many times before and since.

He had answered the questions put to him that morning at Wampoa too quickly and too easily. There had been other answers possible, answers he had not even considered then.

He remembered it all so clearly—particularly that last morning when Nina Andreyeva's voice had shattered his sleep like a hammer's blow on a tocsin, calling him to a confrontation with his conscience that he had deftly avoided by a blind resort to his concept of duty.

But there was no such thing as duty, except *to* one's own conscience. He knew that now. The trick was to hear and understand the voice of that conscience, to be able to interpret its often incomprehensible cries.

As he had heard her cry that morning.

"Sasha—wake up—you must wake up."

He had opened his eyes and sat up on his cot with a start. Through the yellowish white mosquito netting he could see Nina Andreyeva, already dressed, leaning over him, her face partly obscured by the deep folds of the netting. Across the room, by the door, stood two Chinese cadets carrying Mauser automatic pistols.

He struggled awake, stung by the urgency in her voice. He tried to clear his head. All night he had been a prey to nightmares of dank cellars, shadowy courtrooms, and open graves. Now the dawn was streaming warm and rose tinted into his bedroom through the slatted bamboo shades.

"Here—you must get dressed at once," Nina Andreyeva urged, parting the netting and handing her husband his clothes.

"Tell them to leave."

She gestured; the cadets nodded and went outside. Alexander Semyonovitch got up, poured water over his head from a bowl on the washstand while she watched him. There was no need to ask questions. He could hear the dull booming of naval guns in the far distance, up the river, beyond Canton, toward Taya Bay.

He pulled on his tunic and searched in the drawer of his bureau for his service revolver.

"There isn't time," Nina Andreyeva said flatly. "Lin is waiting outside for us. We must go."

"Petya? Where's Petya?"

"For God's sake, Sasha—do you think I'd leave the child?" She gestured toward the door. The cadets had left it open a crack. In the hallway stood the old *amma,* holding the boy by the hand. He was dressed in a blue sailor suit and carried a little cardboard valise tied with string. He stood there, rubbing the sleep from his eyes and smiling; it was all a great adventure to him.

A big Mercedes staff car was waiting for them on the road in front of General Golitsyn's quarters. The car had come from the British concession on Shameen Island. The sky over the academy compound and as far as they could see toward the Pearl River was streaked with a fragile silvery light, like the delicate wash of a Chinese brush painting. The eastern horizon, however, glowed like a red-hot stove top.

Lin was standing by the rear door of the car, waiting for them. For the first time that Alexander Semyonovitch could remember, he was wearing sidearms, a big wooden holster holding a Luger *parabellum* and a smaller but no less formidable leather holster out of which protruded the butt end of a British Webley.

"It has started somewhat earlier than we had anticipated," he said languidly.

"So I see—or, rather, hear."

"Yes," said Lin. "They have come up the river with gunboats as well as by land. The Humen fortress is under attack at the moment." He pointed languidly to the east. Above the hills in the far distance rose a smudgy wash of smoke. The air seemed to be in constant motion. As the dawn light intensified, it was possible to make out the little black specks darting to and fro like angry insects; the Japanese attack planes.

Lin nodded. "General Yu will hold them, I believe. If necessary, we shall commit our cadets." He stopped short and turned an expectant stare on Alexander Semyonovitch. There was no need for him to say anything; the general knew exactly what was in Lin's mind.

He looked again toward the eastern horizon. What real difference would it make if he did stay?

Nina Andreyeva read it in his eyes. "If you think it's right, Sasha . . . here or with Vassily Konstantinovitch, there will be the same Japanese to fight. And think . . . if you can stop them *here*. . . ."

He considered for a moment The *amma* came down the gravel walkway with Petya and his little valise. Their own luggage had already been strapped to the back of the Mercedes.

She was right, he thought. There *was* a perfectly good reason to stay. Not just for fear of what might be waiting for him in Russia. If he stayed, it would be to fight together with the very men he'd been sent to train. They had sent him there. How then could they question his motives?

And how better to prove his dedication and absolute loyalty

than by following to the letter orders in which he personally did not believe?

A series of low flashes lit up the eastern horizon just above the hill line. The flashes were followed a moment later by the long rumble of artillery blasts in barrage, rolling one into the other.

Lin remained absolutely still. The driver did not turn. They could hear the distant buzz of the Russian biplanes taking off from the field near the harbor. The Japanese aircraft, barely visible over the fortress of Humen, were soundless.

"Aren't we going, father?" Petya started to pull away from the *amma*. He wanted to explore the inside of the Mercedes and play with the instruments as he was always allowed to do.

Alexander Semyonovitch didn't answer him. His gaze was fixed on the hills before Humen. Nina Andreyeva knew better than to break the silence. He was hanging by a thread at that moment; she knew the look in his eyes well enough. She'd seen that same look the very first day they'd met, in the old barn outside Strasneshev.

Lin seemed to be holding his breath, but his fingers were white from pressure. He would not urge or argue. It was not Lin's way to do that.

Then it passed.

The Chinese sighed.

Alexander Semyonovitch reached for the car door.

"Petya, in front with the driver, yes? There's a good lad. If you go. . . ."

He shook Lin's hand.

"Will you go with Yu-Han-mou?"

A file of helmeted cadets in full battle gear, gas mask canisters swinging from their Sam Brownes, and carrying Manlicher rifles and packs, moved by at the far end of the parade ground. A truck engine grumbled in a shed nearby.

"Of course," said Lin. "You must do as you think best. Goodbye, dear Alexander Semyonovitch. It saddens me to see you go, particularly at this moment. But you are a man of principle. I respect that, above all things. May you always remain true to your principles."

The general and his wife got into the car. As the Mercedes moved out along the dirt road that led to the airfield and the waiting trimotor, a formation of the Soviet biplanes dipped low over the field, the rising sun glancing from their wing tips.

Alexander Semyonovitch felt as though his heart would break.

Now the sorrow was far deeper, far more acute, a black carcinoma of the soul. He had already traveled far beyond tears.

Suffocating, he began to pull at his high stiff collar, finally managing to unbutton it a little. The pressure in his head eased. He fumbled with the shoulder straps and with his belt but was unable to undo the buckles. His fingers would not obey him.

For a few seconds he considered calling for Dushkin but then thought better of it.

He could not bear to have anyone see him as he was then, not even dear, loyal Osip Vissarionovitch.

Gradually, the visions of China faded and the sweating abated.

Now he saw a multitude of familiar faces. Russian faces. His men. The long, long files of his soldiers, all staring up at him. He could hear their voices and they would not be still. They asked questions, demanded answers, and he had none to give.

He groped along the bureau for the bottle which Dushkin now always kept full; a decanter intended for cologne but now full of vodka. He had not the heart to tell Schreiber-Hartstein that he preferred Scotch whiskey.

As he stared at his own face in the ornate wall mirror he saw that Nina Andreyeva had come into the room behind him. She stood there, wearing a plain gray sweater buttoned down the front, like an Englishwoman, her hair pulled back severely from her forehead.

He felt a sudden pressure in his chest. He had not really realized until just that moment when she appeared at the threshold of his room, how much he still loved her.

He watched her for a moment in the mirror. She stopped just inside the doorway and leaned against the frame, her shoulders sagging. She took out a cigarette.

"Do you want one, Sasha? They're Leningrad . . . the ones with the brown paper tips. Or have you forgotten?"

"That isn't necessary, Nina. . . ."

"I'm sorry," she said in a flat, weary voice. "I don't mean to be sarcastic. It's just that there's so little to be charitable about these days."

Finally he turned. There was sweat on his forehead, a beaded line of it just under his hairline. His face was gray and expressionless. In the past there had been something almost magisterial in his homeliness but now he looked simply worn out, almost ugly. He shuddered; he deserved anything she might say to him, but he was not sure that he could bear it.

She crossed the room and sat down on the edge of his bed, her legs crossed, letting the hand holding the cigarette hang over her knee.

"You look like Dietrich in that . . . film . . ." he began.

"Not at all, Sasha. But thank you for the compliment anyway. Do you remember, there was a time we went to films? Was that one of the ones we saw together? Or was it before . . . ?"

"It was in Chungking, of all places."

She laughed without humor and let a trickle of smoke wind up toward the ceiling. He looked down at the floor, clasping his hands between his knees.

"Nina . . ."

"It isn't necessary for you to say anything, Sasha. I realize that the situation here is . . . very awkward for you. It is for me too. I only came up here because I thought I should. You understand about such things, don't you? Duty . . . ?"

"Nina . . . how is it that you're here? . . . I can't . . ."

"You mean your new masters haven't told you yet?"

He flushed, turned on her angrily, and then caught himself.

"Ah, that's good, Sasha. You've become human enough to get angry at me. That's an improvement. Too bad the timing is so poor." She sat back, dangling her legs like a schoolgirl.

"All right," she said. "I'll tell you the whole thing. . . ."

He sat, eyes downcast, listening listlessly. What mattered was not so much how she had come to be there but that she *was* there and that he, in a way, was freer now than he had ever been in his life.

When she had finished, she added, "So . . . you see? I lost you because of your damned sense of conscience, of duty, or whatever you choose to call it. And now you have me back precisely because you've thrown it all out the window. It's very funny, don't you think?"

"A man must act according to his conscience, Nina."

"And the demands of conscience always come before love, don't they? You've said that so many times, Sasha. Please don't say it again."

"I did love you, Nina." His expression was so genuinely tragic at that moment that she was almost moved to pity him.

"You picked a strange way to show it," she said.

"There was no choice. Surely you understand that. If I hadn't obeyed they would have sacked me, or worse, and done God only knows what to you and your father."

"Oh, yes, we are to thank you for our lives, is that it? It's comforting for you to believe that, I'm sure. But you must realize what a lie it is. The only one who would have suffered if you'd stood up to them would have been Alexander Semyonovitch Golitsyn."

"That isn't true," he cried. "You *know* that isn't true."

"It is, Sasha. Don't abuse your honesty by pretending otherwise. You did what was expedient and called it patriotism. The 'revolution demands' this, the 'revolution demands' that, etcetera, etcetera."

"My God," he breathed, holding his head in his hands. There was a long silence. Then, as he lowered his hands and returned them to his lap, he said, "Your father, at least . . . is he well? Nothing has happened to him? And Petya? They haven't touched him, have they?"

She shook her head.

"God be praised," he said and reached for the carafe on the table, his hand trembling visibly.

"You never used to do *that* before," she said acidly. "Is that what these fine Germans of yours have reduced you to, a Marmeladov?"

He could not answer her; to argue would be to admit his weakness, to put the carafe back worse still. He poured a tumblerful for himself and then another for her.

"To our reunion. The occasion could have been happier but . . ."

She poured the vodka on the floor.

"You must be mad, Sasha."

"It's hopeless then? Truly hopeless?"

She was silent.

He stood up and spoke in a low, terrible voice. "Then why in the name of God did you come? Why did they send you, Nina?"

"They didn't *send* me. Didn't you hear what I said? It happened just as I told you it did."

"You talk about lies. Maybe you believe that lie. I don't. Well, perhaps it did happen that way. Who knows? But didn't they ask you to try and talk me out of going ahead with this . . . thing?"

"Do you have doubts?"

"How could I possibly not have doubts? No one but a priest or an utter fool can even be absolutely sure of *anything*. But I am reasonably sure and that's enough. Besides, I have no choice. If I don't go ahead with it, the Germans will certainly kill both of us. And if I do, our own countrymen will try their best to do the same."

"Would you blame them?"

"Some of them, no. Not the ones whose hands already reek of Russian blood. They too have their imperatives."

She shook her head. "And what's yours, Sasha? Your imperative?"

"To see justice done. Can you believe that, Nina? Justice has become an obsession with me. A military man should never allow himself to become concerned with questions of justice. It's the shortest road to insanity that I know of. And look, Nina, I'm halfway there already."

"If you were to find a way to withdraw . . ."

"Not while there is a chance of success."

"What kind of success? Do you really believe that the Germans will allow you any kind of freedom?"

"Schreiber-Hartstein is an honorable man. He and many others far more powerful have given their word. . . ."

"And they could all be lined up against a wall and shot tomorrow morning."

"Yes, and us with them." He reached out and took her by the shoulders. "At least we will be together in that, Nina, if it happens that way. Whether you want it or not."

"You're not only a fool, Sasha, but a romantic as well. I never suspected that of you."

"Nina, forgive me, for God's sake . . . *forgive me,*" he shouted, his fingers digging into her shoulders as though he could wrench what he wanted from her by force. He swayed, like some great oak tree ready to fall.

Her eyes narrowed; she took a sudden step backward. His hands fell from her shoulders.

"For what you did to me? Never. Do you understand? Never."

8

> The ROA is first of all a Russian army, that is, one which is national in nature, aim, and spirit. The prime goal of its struggle is the creation of a national Russian state. It is a liberation army which seeks to free the people from the present regime. However, it does not seek to restore the pre-Revolutionary state of affairs, but to build a new Russia based on new principles. It is not only an instrument of struggle but a political force as well, a part of the liberation movement of the peoples of Russia.
>
> ROA Propaganda Office Press, 1943

Shortly after ten on that same, crisp, cold morning, Colonel Budyankov walked into the Moscow office of the deputy minister of transportation, Arkady Narishkin. Narishkin had only just arrived and was caught unaware, still in his coat and snow-crusted boots.

Budyankov brushed the snow from his shoulders, stamped, and said, "Don't let me rush you, comrade Narishkin. Take your time. By all means, take all the time you wish."

"And who the devil are you?" cried Deputy Minister Narishkin angrily. He was not used to such a tone nor to being spoken to in such a manner in his own office.

Budyankov completed his brushing with infuriating deliberateness. The last bit of snow fell from his shoulders, finally revealing his rank and department. Narishkin's florid, pudgy face went white when he saw the blue tabs and NKVD markings.

He began to stammer excuses. He had been delayed by a detour—the road he normally took had been bombed out the day before. He had, he admitted, started out late, but there was a good reason. . . .

"I can assure you, comrade Colonel, I do not normally arrive at this hour. No one is more attentive to his duty than I am."

"I don't doubt that, comrade Narishkin. Please . . . have I said something to disturb you? No? Good. I certainly wouldn't want to upset you. On the contrary . . ." and at this point he sat himself down on a small sofa directly below a portrait of Stalin. "Quite the contrary. I want your full attention, your maximum effort."

"You want something . . . from me?"

"You were contacted yesterday, by a certain Major Trepov of my department?"

"Trepov? *Trepov?* Oh . . . yes. Something about a special train—to where . . . where was it?"

"Kursk," said Budyankov.

"Yes, of course. Kursk."

"And what have you done about it? Since yesterday?"

"Why . . . nothing. As I told this Major Trepov, it's simply impossible. The necessary cars can't be diverted. Perhaps next month."

"Perhaps next week."

"Really, comrade Colonel . . ."

"Perhaps tomorrow."

Budyankov smiled and lit his first cigarette of the day. From his tunic he drew a small envelope. He handed it to Narishkin without a word.

The deputy minister tore the envelope open and blanched as he saw the letterhead and signature. The order came directly from Beria.

"Is there any question in your mind now?" Budyankov inquired politely. "You will notice that it is also signed by Colonel Greenblatt, with whom I'm sure you're acquainted."

Narishkin went gray and fell back into his desk chair.

"Now, as Major Trepov told you . . ."

"Yes, yes. Cars enough for two hundred men."

"Two hundred *prisoners,*" corrected Budyankov.

"Yes, that too. . . ."

"As long as they're alive when they get there, comrade Narishkin. We don't need the *Orient Express,* you understand."

Narishkin was silent for a moment. "There *is* a possibility. Yes, let me see . . ." He began to make calculations. "There are some ammunition cars at Trudlo . . ."

"—which will do quite nicely, provided they can be gotten to the proper places in time." He took out another fold of paper and thrust it in front of the perspiring deputy minister.

"How are we to do *this*?" Narishkin cried when he saw the points on the map where the train was expected to pick up its passengers.

"There will be trucks from the prisons to the depots. That is our worry, not yours."

"Even so—"

"Even so? You can and *will* do it, won't you? This is a part of an extremely complex and very sensitive operation, comrade Narishkin. It cannot be allowed to fail just because a few cattle cars don't reach the right junction at the right time. Do you understand?"

"The orders will go out this morning, comrade Colonel. When will your prisoners be ready to go?"

"They are at the depots now, waiting. A day or two at most, that's all they can wait. Then the food will run out."

"The crews," began Narishkin, "are there any special requirements?"

"We will have our own guards, of course, and none of the prisoners speak Russian so there should be no problem. Just see to it that there are no Kalmuk engineers on the trains and everything should go very well."

"Of course. At once."

"I will tell Major Trepov. He will be very pleased that you've found that you can accommodate him. . . ."

The convoy followed the rail line south out of Berlin toward Zossen, which lay some forty kilometers away. By noon they arrived at Dabendorf camp, formerly an assembly point for French prisoners of war.

From a distance, the place looked almost like a concentration camp; the site was desolate and barren. A peatworks spread dun and dark to the east, and beyond that were long, low sheds with tarpaper roofs and a railway spur that swung in from the west. On the southern flank of the camp lay an area of low ground that appeared to be a marsh of some kind.

The camp was surrounded by high barbed-wire fences capped here and there with blue glass electrodes and tall timber guard towers spaced more or less equally along the perimeter. But that was where the resemblance to the concentration camps ended. As they drew closer, Kurenko could see that the buildings were decently constructed wooden barracks. Smoke rose from a number of chimneys and there were many vehicles parked along the dirt roads that crisscrossed the interior of the camp. Trucks, *Kübelwagens,* open-back VW staff cars, and motorcycles with sidecars stood all around.

The convoy turned through a high iron gate. Kurenko saw with some astonishment that the guards were not wearing regulation Wehrmacht uniforms but a strange hybrid, odder even than the uniforms he had seen on the corpses outside Kolabyansk. The tunics were Soviet, the old style known as the "French" without shoulder boards, crisscrossed by leather straps. On the collar and the sleeves of their tunics the men wore the familiar red and blue cockades.

Most of the men carried heavy, deadly-looking submachine guns of a kind Kurenko had never seen before.

The convoy proceeded down the dirt road between the lines of barracks. Schreiber-Hartstein stood up in the open back of the head car, then sat down again. He turned to General Golitsyn, who had been sitting in the back between Stalkov and Kurenko.

"If you please, General . . . stand up, so that your men can see you. They've been waiting quite a while."

The cars swung down a wide road and came suddenly onto what was obviously a drill field. There, to Kurenko's astonishment, what looked like three battalions, well over two thousand men, had been drawn up. The uniformed ranks stood in perfect order, trimmed and precise, under a pale yellow sun barely visible through the haze that rose from the peatworks. The front ranks brought their rifles to present arms as the convoy slowed and the touring car carrying the now-erect General Golitsyn began a slow passage along the formation front.

Stalkov leaned across and with a sour expression on his ursine face said, "Ah, yes, but you can rest assured, the rifles aren't loaded."

Kurenko nodded noncommittally. He had not yet been able to figure Stalkov out. He knew the man's background—fifty-two years old, born in Minsk, in service for a year under the czar as a military engineer. Then a revolutionary until the Tukaschevsky purges, when he had been imprisoned and brutally treated. According to Obriyan, Stalkov's two brothers and his mother had both died in prison. Stalkov's public utterances were bitterly anti-Soviet; in that, at least, he was consistent. But Kurenko sensed a dark, ambiguous current running through the man, as though there were two sides of his personality in a constant, unrelenting struggle with each other.

Russian commands snapped through the air, but they were neither the specific words to which Kurenko was accustomed nor the old commands of prerevolutionary days. The words seemed to be direct translations of the forms of command used by the Germans.

Dust rose. The sun burned its way out from behind the haze and streamed onto the pennants that were being hoisted and dipped in salute, banners of red, blue, and white, the old colors, but in a different configuration: a blue St. Andrew's cross on a white field edged with red.

Golitsyn's arm remained locked in a rigid salute, his fingers glued to the visor of his cap, and his long face utterly without expression. He might as well have been at a siding watching a long freight train going by. His eyes were invisible behind the thick lenses of his spectacles, against which the sun now glinted with infuriating persistence.

Suddenly, the front rank swung their rifles to their shoulders and a twenty-gun salute cracked through the air.

"You see," said Schreiber-Hartstein as the smoke drifted up into the gray sky, "the rifles *are* loaded, Boris Trifomovitch."

"Yes, yes, but where are the machine guns, Captain? Will you send us against tanks with lances, like Poles?"

"In time, in time, there will be machine guns, Boris Trifomovitch, and tanks and planes as well," Schreiber-Hartstein replied and turned away, nettled and frustrated. It was clear that what the man wanted most was a little encouragement, a few words of thanks for what he'd done. But all he got was Stalkov's carping and General Keitel's lilac-colored threats.

For a split second, Golitsyn lowered his gaze. He had not been staring off into space at all; he had been listening.

"Be quiet," he hissed at Stalkov, "you blockhead, keep your

mouth shut." Then he quickly raised his head again as the open car passed along the front of what was clearly intended to be an engineers' company.

Finally the review was over. They had passed not two but closer to three thousand troops all drawn up on the field in perfect order. Well fed, enthusiastic, alert. Kurenko's heart sank. For the first time he had some real idea of what Budyankov had been talking about. The sight of all these men, every one of them but lately a Soviet soldier, healthy and aggressive, caused him a thrill of intense fear.

All of a sudden a band started playing. The tune was familiar but Kurenko could not place it. That it was Russian, not German, there was no doubt.

When at last he climbed down from the car, along with the general, Stalkov and the German officers, he was shaking. In spite of himself, he realized, he had been moved by the sight of all these men.

But moved by what? Pity or fury? It was impossible to tell. Or could it have been something else entirely? The very thought that such a thing might be possible had him in a frenzy.

"And now, you see that it *is* a reality," said Schreiber-Hartstein, addressing the general. "We have done this much and we will do more. Come, I'll show you your new headquarters. You'll have all the necessary equipment. You will choose your own staff, acquaint yourself with what we have done already. Then we will discuss the next phase."

Golitsyn's voice was husky and the words emerged slowly.

"And what is that, Herr Hauptmann?"

"A proving operation, General. The Russian Liberation Army must and *will* go into action. But the time and place must be well chosen. Everything will depend on the success of the first engagement."

Golitsyn said nothing but signaled the others to fall in behind him. He strode behind the captain down a gravel path that led to a low building roofed with black tar paper in front of which there had been arranged—insanely—successive banks of flowers, red, blue, and white, so as to form a huge duplicate of the shoulder badges worn by the troops on the field.

Much later, Kurenko recalled having seen Stalkov smile at that moment and thinking him amused by the absurdity of the flower beds. As for Kurenko, he had said nothing. Schreiber-Hartstein's words echoed in his mind, gradually losing their shape and focus. A sure sign to Vassily Kurenko that they had a meaning and a resonance that was, at that moment, beyond his ability to perceive.

"A proving operation. Time and place. Well chosen. Everything may depend on it."

He remembered, at that moment, what Budyankov had told him.

He had, it seemed, even less time left than he had thought.

The stubby little I-16 fighter drifted down through the clouds at less than half power. Little more than a flying engine, it could function quite nicely on even less power than that. Lieutenant Pashayev would not have traded the little *Rata* for one of the sleek new MIGs or even one of the "wooden-wonder" Lavochkins that his comrades all insisted were the nimblest things that ever flew. He liked the beer-barreled I-16 and had been flying one ever since Spain. He liked the feel of the slipstream in his face and had steadfastly refused to have anything to do with the newer, enclosed-cockpit versions. When he'd finally had to take one, he'd gotten his flight mechanic to remove the canopy and bring the craft back to its original configuration, even though to do so was a violation of the rules and could get both pilot and mechanic into serious trouble.

But what worse trouble could he be in than he was in just then, flying around in circles around Kursk, looking for German observation planes, but under orders not to shoot them down if he found any?

He had been in the air for almost an hour and his fuel was getting low. He had enough for perhaps another thirty minutes. His wingmen were invisible, but they were there, he knew, spread out in a wide "net" formation, two on either side, high up, over a thousand feet above him and well back. Radio contact was forbidden.

He might as well have been flying in a cave.

The clouds were heavy. Below, a layer of ground mist blended imperceptibly into the puffy snow-bellies that hugged the mountains to the north of the lakes.

He leaned out over the open side of the cockpit and looked down past the leading edge of his wing.

There was a shadow far below and to his left front, about ten o'clock. He let the I-16 drop another five hundred feet. The shadow grew more distinct against the lower clouds.

To Pashayev's practiced eye there was no mistaking the configuration of that shadow. It was a Focke-Wulf observation craft. The twin booms and heavy central greenhouse were unmistakable.

There was no alternative but to follow orders. He checked his bearings, read his instruments quickly, and dropped down again. Now he could see the German plane quite clearly. He had to come in almost parallel to it so as to avoid fire from the machine guns at the rear of the center pod. There was a blind spot, just to the side of the plane, and he would have to exploit that blindness with all the skill at his command. To shoot the Focke-Wulf down would have been the simplest thing in the world, particularly with the element of surprise he now held. But to shepherd it some fifty kilometers to the south and make sure that it passed over the installation at Byeleymostnoy was another thing entirely.

Pashayev glanced quickly to his right and high. Just barely visible within an opaline cloud formation was the first of his wingmen. A glance to the left told the same story.

He was almost on top of the Focke-Wulf now. There was nothing to do but get on with it and try to stay clear of that tail stinger while he was at it.

He fired a clearing burst from the two 7-62mm ShKAS in his wings and a second from the twins mounted on the top fuselage decking. Then he wheeled sharply to his left and down. The relative airspeeds of the two craft made it seem as though the German plane was standing still.

A stream of tracers went over the rear pod, just behind the antenna. The Focke-Wulf dipped, swung down into a cloud bank, and for a moment was completely lost. Pashayev pulled back on the stick and the *Rata* lifted clear and soared up in a wide arc. Out of the corner of his eye he could see the first of his wingmen coming down straight for the spot where the German plane had disappeared. That had to be Weinberg. Only he would be foolish enough to do such a thing. The man flew like a lunatic. He'd been bad enough before, but since he'd learned that his entire family had been killed he'd been like a madman.

Pashayev could see the tracers spit out of Weinberg's wing guns, then watched—horrified—as the *Rata* vanished into the same hole in the clouds that had received the Focke-Wulf. Had the man gone completely crazy? Pashayev knew Weinberg's technique; the man was going for a kill.

Just then he saw the Focke-Wulf drop below the lowest of the cloud banks and skim out along the upper edge of the ground-mist cover. Tall firs, laden with new snow, jutted up through the mist. The land rose, climbing into a low range of hills beyond which lay the lakes.

Pashayev barely had time to bring the *Rata* around for another pass when he saw Weinberg's plane turn and dive straight at the German, all guns firing. The clouds had parted both above and below. A great wash of cold winter sun poured down, catching the Focke-Wulf and the *Rata* both in its full light.

Without thinking, Pashayev brought his plane around and went plummeting down to interpose himself between the German and his own wingman. The Focke-Wulf must not be brought down. It must be pushed just a little farther south, out over the edge of the forest to a point where it could not fail to see the installation at the far end of the lake. The weather was perfect. The sun had broken through at just the right moment. The clouds had thinned out and the mists were gone. The lake sparkled like a blue mirror in the distance. Already Pashayev could make out the buildings at the far end of the lake and the long brown lines that cut the shore. He could see clearly the walls, the towers. The German observer could not fail to see them either.

Then Pashayev saw Weinberg coming straight at him. He rolled over, at the same time flicking the radio switch; the *Ratas* had flown for years without radios, but the latest models had them. Orders or no orders, Pashayev felt he had no alternative. There were perhaps sixty seconds left. If only Weinberg held his fire.

"Sokol six, Sokol six . . . you idiot, pull off. What are you doing?"

He heard Weinberg's voice come back at him, close, hard, and clear.

"Get out of the way."

"Orders . . ." Pashayev screamed.

Weinberg fired. The tracers cut a wide swathe just in front of Pashayev's nose. He rolled. Too late. The bullets caught a section of wing and tore it away. Pashayev saw the wood and cloth go floating away like pieces of a kite through the sparkling air.

They were dead center over the lake now.

At that moment, Pashayev became aware of just how close to the Focke-Wulf he was. He saw the rear gunner bring his twin MG-81s directly to bear on him.

Throwing himself forward against the stick, he nosed the *Rata* over into a desperate dive. He still had the advantage of speed but the surface of the lake was far too close for comfort.

Bullets from the Focke-Wulf tore away the tip of his rudder and chewed a chunk out of his windshield. Glass spattered all over the cockpit. A ragged piece tore across his cheek and he felt the blood spurt. The lake rushed up at him. Somehow, he had managed to drop below the German just a little too fast for the rear gunner to track him.

He turned hard and his left wing tip almost grazed the water. The *Rata* leveled out less than ten meters from the surface. Streaming blood, the cold air sawing at him, he managed to bring the plane out in a full circle, coming up once again behind the Focke-Wulf.

Without another thought, he began to climb, as hard and as fast as he could. High up, heading for the clouds, he saw Weinberg's plane, retreating to his assigned position as though nothing had happened. The son of a bitch, he'd almost gotten him killed. And for what? A family that couldn't be brought back to life no matter what he did. Did the man think he was the only one?

"Sokol six, Sokol six . . . come in."

There was no response. Pashayev gritted his teeth in anger and in pain. He wanted to curse Weinberg out, to tell him what he thought of him. He looked up. The other *Rata* had ceased climbing and was now heeling over in a slow roll. Pashayev watched in horror, knowing exactly what was going to happen next.

Weinberg's plane flopped over and started to come down in a slow spin, a trail of heavy black smoke winding out from the tail. There was no parachute. The plane fell lazily, almost beautifully, until it vanished into the forest mists.

There was a brief flash, then only smoke.

Pashayev wiped the blood away from his mouth and turned. The Focke-Wulf was out of sight now. It had passed across the southern end of the lake, straight over the camp.

He wondered whether Weinberg had been killed by bullets or had died in the crash. It seemed to make a difference.

The kitchen at 10 Viktoriastrasse was a huge white-tiled affair, large as a hospital operating room and twice as high. An enormous black iron stove was kept going day and night so that coffee would always be available. Dushkin had just brought a bucket of coal up from the basement. Nina Andreyeva, muffled in a heavy woolen sweater, was brooding over a tin cup full of coffee, waiting for it to cool enough to drink. The coffee was bitter, mostly chicory or whatever it was that the Germans used; but it filled a need for warmth, for something comforting in a body that had not felt so empty since the birth of her child.

Steam curled up toward the high ceiling, leaving a splotch of moisture where it touched the tile. She pushed her hand absently through her hair. Upstairs someone was playing the radio . . . *"Auf den Flügeln bunter Träumen* . . . on the wings of colored dreams . . ." The reedy, sexless voice was eerie and unreal. It suited her mood.

She thought about Alexander Semyonovitch incessantly, though she had thus far avoided him as much as possible. There was still hate there for what he had done to her, but slowly, in spite of herself, she was coming at least to understand why he had done it. The cruelty still repelled and angered her, but there was now at least a grudging respect for his honesty.

He had stopped trying to talk to her and had left her to herself as much as he could. When they were with the others, she masked her feelings and did the correct thing. But she still slept alone.

She touched the cup, lifted it, inhaling the bitter steam.

"*Gospozha* Golitsyna?" It was a deep, oddly gentle voice from somewhere behind her. He had come in through the service entrance; Stalkov.

He pointed at the coffeepot. "Is there enough left for me?"

"There's enough for an army, so why not for you as well?" She went over to the stove to pour him a cup. "So . . . there. If you can actually drink it, more power to you. Tell me, Boris Trifomovitch, why are you here? I thought you'd all gone out to the camp. The general left before it was even light."

"To Dabendorf, yes. Very early this morning. But I have work here too, preparing propaganda materials. There will have to be leaflets explaining what we are doing, explaining our program, our plans. . . ."

"I thought you were a field officer, not a *politruk*."

"We must all sometimes be what we are not and, even sometimes, what we would rather not be."

She laughed. "I find that rather difficult."

"To understand?"

"To do."

"So it would seem, Nina Andreyeva." He moved closer and leaned across the table. His eyes were deep and penetrating and for a second she felt a little afraid of him. "Really," he went on, his voice very low, "he is a good man. Perhaps even a great man, who knows?"

"Who do you mean?" she asked, taken aback.

"Why, Alexander Semyonovitch, of course."

"A great man? A great coward, perhaps."

"He's no coward, Nina Andreyeva. He obeys his conscience in everything. Surely you, of all people, must know that. Conscience can be a cruel master sometimes. And sometimes it is difficult at first to understand the choices it forces on us. For example, Nina Andreyeva, could you sacrifice even one human life if all that it took to save it was for you to deny yourself something dear to you?"

"If it meant injuring someone I loved? Never."

"Don't say that, Nina Andreyeva. You don't really believe it and you can't make me believe that you do."

She sat back, her hands gripping the edges of the chair. The kitchen was still empty. If only Dushkin would reappear, or the German cook . . . someone.

But no one came.

"What do you want of me, Boris Trifomovitch?"

"That you stop this terrible game you are playing with him. He loves you, Nina Andreyeva. That's perfectly clear. What he did, he had to do."

"You know?" she said, aghast. She had had no idea that Stalkov understood how things really were.

"I know, Nina Andreyeva. But you needn't worry. I'm the only one here who does. He took me into his confidence some while back. He talks to me. I'm the only one he really talks to. I'm sorry if my knowing offends you, but that's the way it is. You must understand, Nina Andreyeva, he is a very unhappy man. For many reasons, but not the least among them because of what happened between you two. You must understand that, please try to understand. . . ."

She grew angry, cold. "This is none of your affair."

"It's the affair of every one of us here. You are destroying that man. He was sure of himself before you came, he knew what he was doing. Now it has all changed. If it continues you will not only destroy him but you will destroy every one of us."

"I didn't ask to come here."

"Do you deny that we are doing the right thing? That no matter what else, that monster who sits in the Kremlin must be rooted out? You have seen for yourself what he can do. Before. For the last decade, and now, worse than ever. You must have seen the transports. Men whose only crime was to have lost a battle, or to have been encircled and to have escaped. Do you know how many camps there are? You yourself were on your way to a camp. The Arctic Circle is full of such places. They send men there whose only life is to build more such places for more men who will come and in their turn build yet more, and more. . . ." Stalkov was shouting now. He had half risen from the table. The coffee cup fell to the floor with a clatter. "Do you reject the idea of a free Russia, of a true constitution with real rights for our citizens? Can you deny . . . ?"

"And all this is to be obtained by siding with the Germans?"

"Which is no more than what Stalin himself did when he thought he could benefit by it," Stalkov cried.

There was a sudden stillness in the white-tiled room. Only the slow whisper of the coal fire could be heard.

"I'll think about what you've said. I must have time. Perhaps . . . if I am given time."

"There is very little time left," said Stalkov in a voice so low and so suddenly controlled that for a moment she thought that perhaps he had been acting before. "Think, but don't take too long."

"You seem to know how it will all come out."

"You're an intelligent woman, Nina Andreyeva."

With that he turned and went to the door leading to the corridor. There he paused, turned, and with a sudden smile on his face, said:

"Egg shells in the coffee, Nina Andreyeva. They will take some of the sourness out of that sawdust they use. Eggshells. Remember that."

Martin Beifelder looked both downcast and relieved. He pushed the yellow signal carbon across Schreiber-Hartstein's desk and waited nervously for a reaction.

There was no rage, no explosion; he had not really expected that there would be. In all the years he had known the soft-spoken Balt he had never once heard him raise his voice. Not when he was angry, not when he had had too much to drink, not even when his wife had died of cancer.

Schreiber-Harstein simply shook his head and drew a deep breath.

"When did this come?"

"This morning. Gottinger was afraid to show it to you. Naturally we've already started trying to get it reversed. Kreppel has phoned Colonel Gruner at Abwehr to advise him, in case they haven't gotten a copy yet. And Hummel's gone over to Keitel's office to see if anything can be done at that level."

Schreiber-Hartstein turned the little yellow tissue in his hand. It was from Field Marshal von Kluge's office; an order that the just-formed RONA be broken up at once and assigned in battalion strength to existing Wehrmacht and SS divisions.

"Do you think Gruner will be able to do anything?"

"I doubt it. As much as Canaris is against the *Ost* policy, it isn't a particularly good time for him to set himself up against Von Kluge. We need a few victories before you can expect anyone to worry about the way the SS are behaving themselves."

"And of course it hasn't occurred to any of those blockheads that one of the main reasons we haven't been having many victories recently is precisely *because* of the way the SS are behaving themselves?" He looked down at the signal carbon again. "This must be rescinded, of course. Otherwise the whole thing goes up in smoke and we along with it."

"What's to be done?"

Schreiber-Hartstein looked vaguely amused, though Beifelder had not the slightest idea why.

"Did you know, Martin, that's the title of an excellent novel on the genesis of the Soviet revolution? *What's to Be Done* by Chernyshevsky. All of us should read it, particularly Von Kluge. It might give him a little insight."

Beifelder said nothing. He poured himself some cold coffee from the thermos on Schreiber-Hartstein's desk.

"Actually, there's only one thing to be done now," Schreiber-Hartstein said. "We must take the bit in our teeth and go straight on ahead, right to the finish."

"Excuse me, Reinhardt. What the devil are you talking about?"

Schreiber-Hartstein leaned back in his chair, knit his hands together, and smiled a pale smile of recognition.

"Please ask Hummel to initiate a request for an interview on my behalf, at once."

"With whom, for God's sake? Surely not with Von Kluge."

"Better than that, or worse, possibly. And as inevitable as the sunrise, Martin. We shall have to speak to Reichsminister Rosenberg. No one else will do at this point."

"You can't be serious. He won't see you, surely . . ."

"If he doesn't, it's all over. If he does, it may be all over too. In either case, get Hummel to do it at once, will you?"

At precisely six the next morning, Stalkov began hammering on the door of Kurenko's room. When Kurenko struggled to his feet and flung open the door he found Stalkov standing there not in the shapeless gray suit he'd been wearing for the past few days, but in a neatly pressed uniform. He wore the two red bars of a major on his shoulder straps and collar patch. The red and blue cockade was in evidence both on the shoulders and on the cuffs. Stalkov's face was flushed, his mass of black hair brushed oddly back. Over his left arm he was carrying another uniform; from his right hand dangled a pair of field boots like the ones he was wearing.

"There's a transport waiting downstairs. Put these on as quickly as you can."

Kurenko barely had time to pull himself together. He had not eaten. He had a slight hangover.

"I don't understand, Boris Trifomovitch. . . ."

"You may have forgotten, but you're still in service."

Kurenko dressed sullenly while Stalkov watched from the doorway and then followed him down to the vestibule. Zhilinsky, Obriyan, and a dozen others were waiting on the front steps. Three trucks and a field car stood at the curb. From the radiator of the field car fluttered the little OKH pennant.

Kurenko looked around, confused. "Where's Golitsyn?"

"He'll be along in a while. We're going out to Dabendorf. Something special."

In the car, Kurenko noticed for the first time the insignia on the uniform he had donned.

"What's this?" he asked, pointing to the two pips on the collar.

"Weren't you told? Congratulations . . . you've been promoted to captain." Stalkov's eyes sparkled maliciously. "A tribute to your talent for survival, it would seem. The general insisted on it."

9

> Since the beginning of the eastern campaign numerous members of the Russian people have volunteered to take part as soldiers, farmers or mechanics in the liberation of their native land from Sovietism. The Russians, who had been cut off from the rest of the Continent by the wall of Bolshevism, have thus joined in the fight for the liberation of Europe. Their conception of Germany, derived from more than twenty-five years of Bolshevist propaganda, is undergoing a complete revision.
>
> *Signal*, 1943

She had brooded for a long time over what Stalkov had said. It was hardly the first time she had considered such things. But she was no closer to an answer now than she had ever been.

In the beginning, during the time of the collectivization drive, she had honestly believed that it would all turn out to be for the best. Suffering could not be avoided. In reality, the civil war had never really ended and the revolution still had a long way to go. She had even accepted what they had done to her father. He had deserved everything that had happened to him; she had tried to warn him but he wouldn't listen. And so, she understood and accepted. In the end, they promised, things would be better.

But the better days had never come.

After China, there had been Finland and the dreary, fear-ridden winter after the Bukharin trials. It had been during that winter that Alexander Semyonovitch had invited a number of the young officers from the academy to his apartment for New Year's. Kurenko had been there, the only time she had ever seen him before the van in the Lubyanka yard. It had also been during that winter that she had finally realized that things were not going to get better. Not ever. No matter what anyone said.

She stared up at the ceiling, her eyes half closed, as though she could see there images of those days projected by some wonderful, unsuspected mechanism of her mind.

New Year's Eve, 1939.

Winter had seized Moscow by the throat and left her gasping for breath. The streets were piled so high with snow that the contours of the buildings had all but vanished and the outlines of the streets and walks were nowhere to be seen. The days were fierce and short, providing no more than an uncertain glimmer of pale, grimy light for a few hours. Then darkness would return again, with a brittle, freezing night against which even the most valiant stove was no protection. The sky was mocking, clear, and bright with icy stars. It was the kind of night, as Gogol had once observed, on which "the crunch of snow under a boot could be heard a mile away."

Nina Andreyeva had done her best to decorate their apartment on Chapayev Street for the party. She knew how important it was to Alexander Semyonovitch, even though he would not say so in so many words.

It was important for a number of reasons; the young men who were to be the guests were his best class at the Frunze Academy so far and he was very proud of them. Poland had fallen to the Germans, and Stalin, protected by his new pact with Hitler, had first helped himself to large chunks of eastern Poland and then ordered the army into Finland. Almost since the first day of the invasion, the news had been bad. The Finns had been mauling the Russians with increasing ferocity. With two thirds of its officer corps wiped out during the purges that had followed Marshal Tukaschevsky's execution, the Soviet army had found itself without effective leadership in the Finnish forests and near helpless before the unorthodox tactics of the elusive enemy ski troops. Stalin's error was clearly written in blood on the snows before Khumo, Leikaa, and Tolvajarvi. It would not do, Alexander Semyonovitch had said, to bemoan what was past. There had undoubtedly been good reasons for what Stalin had done and, someday, they would all understand them. For the time being they must concentrate on the immediate goal; if the Finns were to be defeated, fresh, well-trained young officers would be required. Alexander Semyonovitch had done his best to produce what was needed and he was proud of what he had accomplished.

The drawing room of the apartment was brightly lit. A trestle table loaded with *zakuski* ran along one wall under the inscribed photos of Chiang Kai-shek and the framed prints of Repin landscapes that Nina Andreyeva had cut from magazines and collected until they formed a miniature gallery of her own.

She was exhausted and flushed. She had managed all the preparations without losing so much as an hour from her duties at the hospital. Now she felt exhausted. Petya had been put to bed an hour before but she knew perfectly well that if she were to suddenly open the hall door he would come tumbling out, all boyish excuses and tousled blond hair.

Alexander Semyonovitch was already ensconced in his favorite chair, like a great, gangling Buddha, looking uncomfortable in his brand-new uniform with its old-fashioned shoulder boards and general's stars. He had given up cigarettes in favor of his old pipe and was just then exhaling so great a mouthful of smoke that he looked more than anything else like some sulfureously fuming *chernobog* of Slavic myth.

"They make me feel so old," he'd complained. "After all, Ninotchka, I'm only forty-four. . . ."

"But they're *half* your age, Sasha. That does make a difference, doesn't it?"

Now, he looked as though it did.

A number of the young men had already arrived. There was the stolid Junior Lieutenant Luchenok, whose flat Tartar face with its little slits for eyes was as impenetrable as ever Lin Shai-Pao's had been, and Timofeyev, slender and faintly effeminate, whom Alexander Semyonovitch had spoken of as having potentially the finest military mind he had ever encountered. Voronov, the son of a czarist officer of the Preobrazhensky Guards who had served with Budyenny after the outbreak of the revolution, was a small, nervous, large-headed young man with a big nose, big ears, and a stare that would have shattered Perseus's shield. In the vestibule, Junior Lieutenant Kurenko, looking intense as usual, stamped the snow from his boots and tried not to drip water on the Persian mat. Captain Polovinkin, the oldest of the group, had brought his waxed mustache and his guitar and announced his determination to play until dawn or as long as the militia would let him.

Already the air of the drawing room was dense with cigarette smoke, which the humid heat seemed to transform into something almost solid. Only one of the officers had brought his wife—a stocky factory girl from Kharkov—while two others had come with young women they were seeing. One was a nurse from the same hospital where Nina Andreyeva herself worked, the other a plump, pretty blond engineer from the Ilyushin Design Bureau.

As there were only three other women at the party and none of them nearly as handsome as Nina Andreyeva, even in her exhausted state, she found herself the center of much attention. There was a curious camaraderie between her husband and these much younger men, which she had never fully perceived before. She had expected him to be somewhat paternal—and he was—but she had also expected to see a certain distance maintained—which she did not. He seemed to her rather like an overgrown puppy, trying to romp with the older dogs. An odd reversal, certainly, but endearing.

The table was heavily freighted with bottles, flavored vodkas of all kinds, some good Caucasian wines, which no one had touched yet, and a few bottles of American Scotch whiskey. The elegant Yarsky samovar, the only heirloom Nina Andreyeva had managed to save from her parents' home, bubbled from the corner of the room like a hot spring about to gush.

The conversation, stimulated by the free-flowing alcohol, was not as cheerful.

"We're getting the devil kicked out of us, comrade General," Voronov was complaining with much sawing of the air. "And we all know why. . . ."

"The bastards . . ." exclaimed Luchenok darkly.

"Who? The Finns or those who are responsible for . . . ?"

"Are you drunk already? You'd better be still," cautioned Timofeyev.

"Here?" Voronov shot back with a scathing expression in his voice.

"One never knows, does one?" said Timofeyev quietly.

Alexander Semyonovitch remained stubbornly placid throughout this exchange. Tonight he was not going to let even the acid-tongued Voronov upset him. Yet he could not help but be annoyed by Timofeyev's remark; it was, in a way, an insult to him, direct and pointed.

The tile stove glowed. The heat in the room had become almost overwhelming. The young officers tugged at their high stand-up collars. Polovinkin, without waiting for the general to set the style, had already unbuttoned his tunic a bit. The owlish Timofeyev leaned toward Nina Andreyeva, his Scotch already low.

"He talks a great deal, that one, doesn't he?" he said, as though he were sharing a confidence.

"Why, who do you mean?" she replied, helping him to some cold dumplings that she had made the night before.

"Why, Voronov, of course."

Nina Andreyeva's face clouded for a moment. Then she laughed. "It's hard to know what to say anymore. So it's safest not to say anything, don't you think?"

Timofeyev nodded, not quite sure whether his hostess was agreeing with him or mocking him.

Just then she felt, rather than actually saw, that Junior Lieutenant Kurenko was staring at her. She moved away quickly, embarrassed and a little annoyed by the frankness of the young man's gaze. She should have felt flattered, she knew, but actually she resented it because she knew that if Alexander Semyonovitch noticed he would be angry with Kurenko and she did not want anything at all to spoil her husband's pride in his students.

She went over to the little Ilyushin engineer and offered her some cookies. Somehow, the lieutenant's stare disturbed her. Kurenko was fragile. Alexander Semyonovitch had said so more than once. "He's too intense, that one. He doesn't know when to let up. He won't ever admit to being confused, even a little, and he would never doubt anything I told him. That's what worries me."

It worried her too. They were all so like children, clumsy, unsure of themselves, and therefore too outwardly self-confident. Who could blame them? It was difficult to be sure of anything in such times.

Polovinkin had taken his guitar out of its case and was tuning it, a pitch pipe stuck comically between his teeth like a round of cucumber. By spring, she thought with a shiver, he too could be dead in the forests before Helsinki.

Alexander Semyonovitch came over to her and took her arm. "They're quite a troop, aren't they?" he said, almost sadly. "Am I wrong to be so proud of them? I love them, Ninotchka, every one of them."

She laughed lightly, trying to soften his intensity. "To me they are reflections of their teacher, Sasha. . . ."

Just then Captain Polovinkin began to strum his guitar and to sing "The White Acacia" in a ready, penetrating baritone. The plump blond girl from the Ilyushin bureau joined in and soon everyone was singing. The cramped apartment vibrated with the sound of young voices. Only Alexander Semyonovitch, who could not have carried a tune, as they say, with a wheelbarrow, did not sing, but there were tears of joy in the corners of his eyes.

Nina Andreyeva stood by the samovar, full of foreboding. She remembered keenly the day Alexander Semyonovitch had knelt in her father's fields at Straneshev and let the rich black soil sift through his fingers. As long as he loved only the land he was safe. The land, at least, would never betray him. To love the men of that land was another thing entirely. She feared for her husband. He was a brilliant man but there were many things he could not and would not understand. He did not understand people, wily a strategist as he was. He was a fool when it came to judging men. He was a fundamentalist, a true Manichaean. For him there was only good and evil and nothing in between. When confronted with the idea that there was indeed much between, he became confused and resentful.

Looking around her, she feared much for the future.

They drank heavily throughout the night. A kind of ferocious gaiety took hold. The chubby Luchenok shook the floor with his stamping boots. Guitar strings slipped out of tune but Polovinkin continued playing anyhow. Twice little Petya came into the room and twice he had to be taken back and tucked firmly into bed.

Nina Andreyeva had never seen anything like it before, not since she had married Alexander Semyonovitch. It was a barracks-room scene out of Andreyev, strained, bitter, and violent.

To save herself, she too began to sing. Alexander Semyonovitch's arm slipped around her shoulder in an open and affectionate manner she would never have expected him to display in public.

Captain Polovinkin's E string snapped.

"Damn . . . look what it's done. Who's got another?"

They all laughed while Polovinkin came over to Nina Andreyeva carrying his now useless guitar.

"Sing for us, *grazhdanka,*" he said.

"Sing. Me?"

"The general's always saying what a fine voice you have, comrade Nina Andreyeva. God help us, you do. I heard you myself a minute ago."

"Oh yes, do," echoed the nurse from Nina Andreyeva's hospital.

She glanced at her husband. It was hard to make out the expression in the eyes behind the heavy glasses.

"Well then, why not?" she said. As a girl she had always wanted to sing, to be like Boronat or Kouznetsof. She often sang for her son, lullabies her mother had sung for her, and strange songs she had learned in China.

There was a little spinet almost invisible under a thick purple Persian shawl heavy with fringes. No, she did not wish anyone to play. If they wanted her to sing, she would sing, but without piano or guitar. As she sang for her son.

She sat in a corner of the room. All at once the young officers grew silent. Alexander Semyonovitch leaned forward apprehensively, his chin cupped in his hands. He had not really heard his wife sing for years and wondered now why she had suddenly agreed to do so.

The silence isolated her and restored her control over those in the room. She leaned back in the straight wooden chair she had chosen and began to sing. Her voice was strong and unexpectedly deep, as dark and glossy as her hair.

Lyubasha's song from *The Czar's Bride*. It seemed an appropriate song, she thought—and more than one of the young men understood what made her choose it. Lyubasha, the soon-to-be-abandoned mistress of the Oprichniki leader, Gryaznoi, sings to entertain the assembled men, the Praetorian Guard of Ivan the Terrible. . . .

Hurry, dearest mother, help your daughter don her bridal gown
I promise not to grieve you any longer
for I have renounced my true love . . .

There was an absolute silence in the room as she sang, and through half-closed eyes she could see a bewildering variety of expressions on the faces of her husband's guests.

She had reestablished by her voice alone a kind of primacy in the room that her husband had almost let slip entirely. No one moved. The wind threw clouds of snow against the window panes. The lights wavered; a momentary power fluctuation. Such things had happened frequently that winter.

Light waxen tapers at my head,
Then call the old bridegroom
Let him come and stand in awe . . .

Lieutenant Kurenko rubbed the side of his nose and Polovinkin sighed deeply.

"What a song, Nina Andreyeva, what a song," said Voronov when she had finished. All was calm, subdued, with faces flushed from the heat of the tile stove. Alexander Semyonovitch sat silently, with a strange, distant look on his owlish face.

After that they all spoke in low, confidential tones. Even when Polovinkin discovered another E string in his tunic pocket, he did not restring his instrument but, rather, continued to discuss with Junior Lieutenant Kurenko the tactics of the Finnish ski patrols.

The young men now sat, cross-legged and sober, talking of the Mannerheim line. It had been the song, of course, not just the way she had sung it, but the song itself. They all knew it, and the story from which it came. The shadow of Ivan the Terrible had suddenly fallen on the little room on Chapayev Street. Were they themselves the new Oprichniki? Was Helsinki to be their Pskov?

Everyone thought of Tukashevsky but no one dared speak the name.

At length, Alexander Semyonovitch took his wife aside and poured her a glass of cherry vodka.

"What a strange thing to do," he said. "And look what a change you've wrought."

She hesitated, the faint note of criticism and disappointment in his voice cutting her more harshly than he could possibly have intended.

"Have I spoiled it for you?" she asked. "They were behaving like unruly children. . . ."

"No, you haven't spoiled anything, Ninotchka. I was deceiving myself, that was all."

"How, Sasha?"

"Because of *their* innocence, I managed to believe in my own for a moment."

She did not wait for any further response. Instead, she handed him back the tumbler of vodka. He drank it down quickly, at one swallow, and without a word. His eyes swam behind the thick lenses.

She held his hand. He sighed again, deeply and harshly, and looked at her with longing.

One by one, the young officers excused themselves and went off into the early morning dark, through which, now, a little snow was once again drifting down.

At last only Alexander Semyonovitch and his wife were left in the room.

The front door banged shut at the end of the hall. Junior Lieutenant Kurenko had just gone out, the last to leave.

Alexander Semyonovitch went off for a moment and then reappeared with a small bottle of French champagne wrapped in a towel.

"Look, Ninotchka . . . Klabin at the Supply Ministry got this for us."

She was touched. The heart was still there, as always, and that was what mattered.

The cork popped, leaving a black mark on the ceiling, and a trail of foam on the floor. Alexander Semyonovitch turned on the wireless. Utesov's dance band was playing a "Boston."

The champagne was flat. They drank it anyway and then, holding hands, went slowly down the corridor to bed.

The day was cold and coming up gray with rain. A sullen drizzle fell over Viktoriastrasse as the convoy began its move out of Berlin. Kurenko sat silently next to Stalkov.

No matter where Kurenko moved, Stalkov was there. And always with the same grim, critical stare, as though the man could see right through his skin and bone.

The ride was long and silent. There was much traffic on the streets. Mostly trucks and motorcyclists. Overhead, aircraft droned low in the rainswept sky. Along the streets and in the alleys, hundreds of fires still smouldered, mementos of the week's bombings. Here and there, in a row of undamaged buildings a great heap of masonry with stairwells, railings, and window frames jutted up out of the tumble like so many broken bones out of a fracture. A huge poster in front of a cinema advertised a film called *The Great Love.*

Stalkov kept silent, but a faint murmur now and then escaped Zhilinsky's lips. That he was going to fight on the same side as the Germans was irrelevant; he approved of the destruction that the bombs had wrought. The Germans were getting paid back now, at last. They drove through the gates at Dabendorf without slowing down. On the broad, muddy fields behind the barracks, the soldiers were doing calisthenics in the slow, gray drizzle. An obstacle course had been set up at the north end of the drill field and men were climbing along railings, up ropes, and dropping off twenty feet or more in the air with full packs on their backs. The rattle of small arms fire, greatly muffled by the heavy weather, could be heard.

Beifelder and two other Wehrmacht officers were waiting for them in the low headquarters building at the north end of the compound. They were led through a corridor and into a large map room. An oak table three meters long sat in the middle of the room. On the walls were a number of brightly colored charts and maps.

An orderly brought a tray of rolls and coffee. The men ate in stoney silence. Only Stalkov seemed animated; he was waiting for something, his gaze constantly darting about the room, settling first on one object, one person, then another. When the officers had finished, Beifelder lit a cigarette and began talking in a distant, subdued tone.

"Let me tell you this at once, gentlemen. Hauptmann Schreiber-Hartstein has high hopes. . . . It may be possible, very shortly . . . for the RONA to go into action as a unit. All of this is in motion now. It only remains to secure final approval, but we expect . . ."

"And if approval is not given, what then?"

"We'll worry about that in the same way we worry about all other possibilities . . . when the time comes and not before. We will proceed as though permission had been given and it was up to us to exploit that permission to best advantage."

"And that's why we've been hauled out here this morning?" asked Zhilinsky.

"Exactly, Major. The question then is, assuming that permission is given, what type of operation would be most to our advantage?"

"*Our* advantage?" said Zhilinsky.

"I consider myself one of you, gentlemen," said Beifelder, removing his glasses. "Just, I trust, as you now consider yourselves my comrades. We all work toward a common goal, I think."

There was silence. No one was about to ask just what that common goal might be.

At length Beifelder said, "Well, have any of you any ideas? Nothing specific, of course, that's not expected. You couldn't possibly be aware of the details of the strategic situation at the moment. But you will be *made* aware shortly. For now, may we have some general ideas? Bearing in mind that something of stunning theatrical impact is required. I hate to put it that way, but the truth is the truth."

"Do you consider the propaganda value more important than the tactical?" asked Obriyan soberly.

"I must say, yes, I do. Though I know that such an answer may not be the most popular with you gentlemen."

"We appreciate your honesty," said Obriyan, satisfied.

Beifelder, however, felt it necessary to continue the defense. "If the RONA is to succeed as a *force* as well as an idea, it must prove itself not only in action but in the minds of those who oppose it. We must show the SS and those on the General Staff who think us insane that it *can* be brought off and that it *can* have meaningful results. With less than a division, nothing tactically important can be achieved at this time. What we need, therefore, is a *coup de théâtre* and, preferably, one that will bring still more men into our ranks."

Stalkov stood up, his vast bulk throwing a shadow across the table.

"May I ask Captain Kurenko a question?"

"Of course."

Stalkov cleared his throat. "When your convoy was attacked, you were on your way to a prison camp, yes?"

"That's correct."

"A special kind of prison camp, wasn't it?"

"So I was told." Kurenko's mouth was rapidly going dry. He felt himself wither under Stalkov's gaze. He had to be very, very careful.

"For the benefit of the rest of us, will you repeat what you told me, Vasya?"

"I was told that it was a camp for people such as myself. . . ."

"Yes, go on."

"For men who had been behind German lines, men who had been held captive for any length of time."

Stalkov extended his arms as though to embrace the world. For the first time since Kurenko had met him, he saw a really broad smile on the man's face.

"You see, gentlemen? *There* is your answer. If it is possible tactically, then it could be a magnificent enterprise. The perfect project. What do you say, Hauptmann?"

Beifelder looked confused. He had not been thinking in such terms, but as the idea sank in, he too began to smile.

"A strike against this . . . prison camp? Is that what you're suggesting?"

"Not a strike, but the liberation of the camp and all its inmates. The propaganda value would be immense."

Beifelder considered for a moment. The idea was so obvious yet at the same time so astonishingly right he could find almost nothing to say. Finally he got his thoughts together.

"Such a gesture might be misinterpreted . . . as though to say that the RONA must depend entirely on turncoats and traitors. . . ."

"Not only do you know better than that but so does every citizen of the Soviet Union. To rise up against a despotism that destroys its bravest citizens for the sole reason that they have been captured or cut off by the enemy is the clearest kind of patriotism imaginable."

Kurenko looked around in astonishment. The idea had never occurred to him and now he felt horribly guilty; it was all his fault. There had been no need for him to mention the camp at Byeleymostnoy to Stalkov. No, that wasn't true either. It *had* been necessary in order for him to corroborate his story. Budyankov would have said something if he'd wanted him not to mention it. Besides, wasn't the plan to arrange an exchange of prisoners? Certainly the Germans would have known . . .

Beifelder was speaking. "I will pass on your suggestion to Captain Schreiber-Hartstein. In the meanwhile"—he cleared his throat and reached for his coffee cup—"and though I hardly think it necessary, does anyone have any other ideas?"

Between Pribalsk and Ushakov there was nothing but an expanse of frozen forests and what, during milder weather, might have been charitably called a marsh. Broken only here and there by thickets the height of a man and tangles of low, twisted trees sheathed in ice, it appeared as a vast track of pale blue glass.

To the south, Golikov's Fortieth Army was trying to drive the Germans out of Kharkov with a thousand T-34s and wave after wave of Stormovik attack bombers. Sometimes, in the silence of the forest, Gelb thought he could actually hear the distant drone of planes and the thud of heavy guns.

"No such thing, comrade Major," said old Kourbash, the partisan officer who had accompanied them on horseback from the village of Pulya. "It's much too far. Even for my good ears. What are you hearing? Who knows? Maybe it's your own heart."

Budyankov had arranged everything neatly and efficiently. If only he had sent someone else, Gelb thought, then everything would have been perfect. He could feel Trepov's eyes on him and hear the soft crunching of snow under the hooves of Trepov's bay. Trepov was a far better horseman than Gelb; his long, lean body infinitely more compatible with saddle and mount than Gelb's short, heavy frame. But Trepov could not stand the cold of the forest nearly as well. There was Gelb's consolation; Trepov, who seemed to be freezing to death all the time, had been out weeks longer than he had. After the trip to Byeleymostnoy, Gelb had gotten back to Moscow, while Trepov had been stranded out in the field with an NKVD Special Purposes unit.

Gelb considered the question: why didn't he mind the cold? Perhaps it was all those years he had spent as a child almost frozen to death during the long winters, with never enough food in his belly or warm enough clothes on his back or enough wood in the stove. Trepov had lived in the city. It hadn't been nearly so bad for him. Besides, Trepov wasn't a Jew.

Old Kourbash leaned forward in the saddle and signaled for silence. He was at least sixty-five, maybe seventy, but was in magnificent physical condition, straight as a rod, with enormous strength in his hands and a vast white beard that looked like an avalanche.

"I hear something . . . rein in . . . hush, be quiet now," he whispered.

Trepov pulled back. The three of them waited on the snowy forest trail. Gelb could hear nothing but the whistling of the wind in the ice-laden trees. The wind cut like a razor. If only the sound that

Kourbash thought he heard was the NKVD battalion they had been sent to meet and take south with them to Byeleymostnoy. . . .

Kourbash remained immobile for another long moment. Then a smile spread across his wrinkled face. "Yes, yes. We go forward now."

"I don't hear a damned thing," said Trepov.

"But *I* do, comrade Major, so we go."

Gelb had traveled by car, by rail, by air for part of the trip, also by cart and now, finally, on horseback. It was impossible to reach Major Chekarin's battalion by the usual means. Because of the nature of their operations, they had been working, up to then, under strict radio silence. A courier would have to go into the area each time new orders were to be transmitted. No, better, two men this time. Gelb and Trepov. To inform Major Chekarin that his men were now under Colonel Budyankov's direct orders and were to present themselves as soon as possible at the Starsk railroad junction. The trains carrying the Kalmuk prisoners were already on their way.

Gelb also knew that the trains would not wait at Starsk indefinitely. He was already two days behind schedule because it had thus far proven impossible to locate Chekarin's men. The threat of German panzers to the west grew daily; at any moment there might be a breakthrough, and if the armored train carrying Chekarin's unit had not left by then, the entire operation would be ruined.

When Kourbash and his squadron of partisan cavalry had turned up at Firopova, where Gelb and Trepov had spent the night, he had laughed uproariously, drunk an entire bottle of vodka, and told the two men that, of course, *he* knew where the "damned policeman" was. *Any* fool would know, they left such obvious tracks in the snow. Even though *they* thought they were being very clever and hiding themselves so well. Anyone could find them, except the Germans, of course, with whom Chekarin's men had been playing cat and mouse for weeks. They might understand skiing, the Germans, but the Russian forests in winter? Never.

And so, reluctantly, but seeing no other alternative, Gelb and Trepov had taken off into the snowy woods on horseback with the partisan, Kourbash, as a guide. They had been riding for over four hours when the distant sounds, still unheard by either Gelb or Trepov, had caused the old man to come to a sudden halt.

Gelb pulled the hood of his quilted coat tight over his *shapka.* His left hand dropped to the butt of his Tokarev automatic.

"On foot from here," Kourbash said, his beard blowing out in the icy wind. The snow powdered down from the overhead branches, for a moment obscuring everything.

Once off the trail, Gelb found himself knee-deep in snow. It was hard going. Trepov grunted and swore.

Suddenly Kourbash stopped.

"Come out of there, you rabbit. You think you're well hidden, do you?"

There was a rustling and a snow-covered thicket began to fall apart. A man covered with a white camouflage cape and holding a *Pepesha* submachine gun stood up, shedding huge chunks of snow and branches.

"Hey, it's you again, is it, grandpa? What the devil do you want here?"

Gelb stepped forward, at the same time pulling out the oilskin packet in which the signed unit orders were folded.

"Where's your commander?"

"You'd like to know, wouldn't you?" said the man, raising the snout of the submachine gun. "Well, who the devil are you?"

"My name is Gelb. Here are my papers. We are looking for the commander of the Seventh Special Purposes Regiment."

"You've found him, comrade Major," came a voice. Trepov spun around. Another snowbank started to disintegrate. A tall, round-faced man wearing ski goggles stood where a moment before there had been only a pile of snow-covered bushes.

"Not bad at all," said Kourbash. "There's hope for you people yet."

"Major Chekarin?"

"You're a little hard to find," Trepov said nervously.

"For the Germans too," said Chekarin, pushing up his ski goggles. His eyes were almost as narrow as the slits in the wooden slats. "That's the point, isn't it? Now, may I see your orders?" He looked around. Gelb suddenly became aware that the woods were full of men, all perfectly camouflaged, absolutely invisible in the snow. They rose, one by one, until Gelb, Trepov, and Kourbash were completely ringed by them. Fifty or more men, all draped with white snow-capes and all carrying submachine guns.

"Everything seems in order, Major. It's a good thing you had this old billy goat with you. He's well known around here. Otherwise we might have started shooting first and looked at your papers later. The woods are full of Germans, or haven't you noticed?"

"No, not a one. We haven't seen a thing."

"Well, they're there all right," Chekarin said. "All over the place. You've just been lucky, that's all."

"You won't have to worry about them for a while," said Trepov. "We've got to leave at once. There's a transport waiting."

Chekarin smiled grimly. "It won't hurt any of us to get out of the woods for a while."

"How long will it take to get your full unit together and be ready to move out?"

"Together? Why, Major . . . they're all here, or haven't you noticed?"

Gelb felt his stomach fill with ice. "How many? I don't see more than . . . what is it . . . fifty? Seventy at most."

"You count well, and fast," said Chekarin. "For a city man, that is. But you're quite right, unfortunately. We've lost quite a few in the last month."

"Doing punitive work?"

"Fighting for our lives, comrade. We've been cut off six times."

"How many are left?"

"Sixty-three, plus myself, plus Senior Lieutenant Stepanov and Doctor Zmeykov, our medical technician."

Trepov whistled, his pale face flaming. "We may as well turn around and . . ."

"The devil we will. What we've got, we've got," said Gelb. "And the train at Starsk won't wait forever."

"At Starsk?" exclaimed Chekarin. "There's not a chance in the world of getting through to Starsk."

"Why do you say that?"

"Because," put in Kourbash, "there are Germans all the way from Gorbal to Stepyanko. You'll never get through without a fight. Which means you'll never get through at all, because there are a hundred times more of them than of you. The game's up, boys. Even my lads can't help you here."

"All right. Show us," Gelb snapped.

Kourbash shrugged, squatted in the snow, and began drawing a diagram of their positions with a tree branch.

"There, at Gorbal . . . what kind of unit?" asked Gelb, aware that Chekarin was watching him with a look of amusement and contempt.

"Panzers," said Kourbash. "No chance of getting through there."

"And here, west of Stepyanko?"

"Infantry. The One Hundred Twenty-eighth, and thick as fleas. All fresh troops, too."

Gelb's heart sank. He looked to Trepov for support but the pale headquarters man was no source of strength in a situation like this.

Gelb pointed in desperation to an area between the towns of Tul and Nyekov, just north of the rail line and less than twenty kilometers from the Starsk junction.

"And here?"

Kourbash was silent for a few seconds. Then he spat into the snow. "Punishment battalion," he whispered. "Murderers."

"*Einsaztsgruppen,* comrade Major," Chekarin said. They stared at each other for a moment.

"We go through there, then," Gelb said.

"I think not," replied Chekarin. "We have only sixty-three men. . . ."

"Which should be more than enough, even if we have to fight our way through. You know what those units are. They're not soldiers, they're butchers. The worst kind of scum."

"Even so . . ."

Gelb jumped up. "Comrade Major, you will read the orders again, please, and note the signature on the bottom. This isn't a matter of field discretion. When comrade Beria directs a thing to be done . . ."

Chekarin's face went gray. He snapped the ski goggles down again, hiding his eyes.

"Stepanov, get over here. We move out in half an hour."

Gelb said nothing, but stood with his arms folded, watching the sudden activity deep within the forest.

Nor did he make the slightest move when Chekarin stalked away muttering under his breath.

". . . and you'll be the first, you son of a bitch."

By late afternoon, what was left of the NKVD Seventh Special Purposes Regiment had made its way as far as the forests ten kilometers east of Tul. Scouts had been sent out to check the German positions and to make sure that there were no armored units in the area. If luck was with them, it might be possible to slip by along the gully to the north of the village under cover of dark without being noticed.

Kourbash had gone off to see if he could find any of his partisans to assist Chekarin's passage. His men were mostly villagers, "popular volunteers" as they were called, but there were many old cossacks among them and they were good fighters, even at their age, and excellent horsemen.

Gelb, Chekarin, and Trepov waited in a deep copse almost barren of snow cover. The scouts rode up excited, their white *bashliks* shrouding their heads.

"Well, Galkin? What did you find?"

"It's very strange, comrade Major. The German's aren't in Tul."

"Where then?"

"In the woods, just to the south, and not too many. There can't be more than two hundred of them. They went into the woods while we were watching from the hills outside the village. A whole convoy of trucks."

"Trucks?" said Gelb. His mouth went dry at the sound of that word. "What kind of trucks?"

"Big, black trucks. Not army trucks, but more like vans. With special snow tires. A lot of them are just sitting there right now, with their motors running."

"Closed-back?"

"As best as we could see, yes."

Gelb turned to Chekarin. "Have your men ready their weapons." His face was flushed. Even the normally phlegmatic Trepov was alarmed. "We're going through now."

"To the north?"

"I said *through*. Not around."

Chekarin's face grew dark. "What the hell do you mean, comrade Major? You heard what Galkin said, didn't you? The way is clear to the north. A piece of luck."

"The 'way' is clear all right, Major. We go to the south, right through the swine, and we don't leave a single one of those swine alive, do you understand? That's an order, by the authority given me . . ."

"Your orders are to get us through to Starsk."

"My orders are that I am in absolute command, Major. Don't force me to put you under arrest."

Chekarin swallowed whatever it was he was going to say and stomped off angrily. Trepov seized Gelb by the arm.

"Have you gone crazy?"

"No more so than you. . . . Now leave me alone and let's get on our way."

Within fifteen minutes, Chekarin's unit had fanned out through the woods and was swinging down on the woods south of Tul in a broad, sicklelike movement, pivoting from a road position just to the north of a heavy forest of poplar and birch. There was only one road cleared, and that was the road up which the truck convoy had just gone.

Gelb went with the advance party, forcing Chekarin to go along with him. His bare hand sweated around the grip of his tommy gun, even though the cold was still numbing. Chekarin had not said a word other than to convey Gelb's orders to his men. Whatever else he might be, the NKVD major was strictly obedient. He was too acutely aware of the consequences of disobedience not to be.

Gelb crouched in the snow-laden bushes from where he could see a part of the dirt road that wound up from Tul. All of a sudden he became aware of the low grumbling of motors coming from somewhere deep in the woods.

The truck convoy.

"Hold your fire. Wait until they're almost past," said Gelb.

"Listen to me," said Chekarin harshly. "You may have the authority to tell me *what* to do at the moment but you don't have to tell me *how* to do it. We know our business."

Gelb held a hand to his mouth. He wasn't going to argue with Chekarin. The first of the German trucks had just come into view. There was a long line of them—twenty or more—heavy black vans with large, square bodies of the kind that police use to carry prisoners. Only the last three were different—these were ordinary open-backed personnel carriers, crammed with SS troops.

Then, as the trucks lumbered by, spinning up a powdery cloud of dry snow, and moving so slowly that Gelb could even see the drivers' faces quite clearly, an officer in a black winter coat climbed out onto the running board of the lead truck and signaled a halt. The trucks stopped in a line on the forest road.

Out of the corner of his eye, Gelb could just barely see Senior

Lieutenant Stepanov and a rocket launcher team crawling into position on his right. Far to his left, in line with the rear truck, Gelb saw a second assault launcher going into position.

Gelb's mouth was bone dry. He had given orders not to fire on the trucks themselves; would Chekarin's men listen? Below, the SS troops were climbing down from the last three trucks. Officers shouted orders. The men began to run around toward the vans.

Chekarin suddenly stood up. "First unit . . . fire . . ."

A flash, and a brace of rockets flew into the last truck of the line. It went up in a huge mushroom of flame, flinging the bodies of the men who had just dismounted for many meters in all directions.

"Unit the second, fire . . ."

There was another blast, a sharp whooshing sound like a hundred gas ranges catching at once, and the front truck was engulfed in flame.

Gelb screamed in anguish, "I told you not to . . ."

Chekarin turned his head slightly and threw him a steely look. He said nothing, unhitched a string of grenades from his belt, and ran down the slope. A shower of stick grenades hurtled through the air. Chekarin's men followed after him, firing their tommy guns from the hip.

At that moment, a loud shouting was heard. From the forest to the west burst a line of horsemen swinging sabers and scythes. The Germans shouted in terror as they fell under the rushing hooves.

The NKVD men were on the road now, firing in all directions at the scrambling SS trapped along the truck line. Gelb walked slowly among them, firing his tommy gun until the drum was empty, then taking up a Schmeisser from a dead SS man and continuing to fire until that too was empty. He knelt and retrieved yet another. There was no shortage.

In front of one van, he cornered a wild-eyed officer trying desperately to get out of the way. The man had no weapon. He had lost his helmet and Gelb could see the handsome young face contorted and ugly with fear.

He raised the Schmeisser and fired right into the German's face, throwing him back against the fender of the truck, his head torn almost completely off.

The sabers of Kourbash's partisans chopped up and down. The

muddy roadway was littered with bloody corpses. A few of the horsemen pursued fleeing Germans into the woods, spearing them against trees, cleaving them down like animals.

At last it was over. Through the smoke, Gelb could see Chekarin standing by the third truck, a tommy gun in his arms. Lieutenant Stepanov was on his knees, holding a wounded arm, the blood running through his fingers. Chekarin saw Gelb, looked around him, and came over very unsteadily. His face was ashen, his normally slitted eyes wide, and though he was not wounded, he looked as though he would fall at any moment.

"Look, look . . . you madman. Another twenty men gone. And for what? We could have gone *around* them. There was no need for this. . . ."

Gelb grabbed Chekarin by the arm, hard.

"Wasn't there? Wasn't there any need? Just pray we weren't too late. Don't you know what these are? These are gas vans, you fool. Look here . . ." He fired the last of his magazine at the rear door of the nearest van, taking off the lock. The doors fell open. A rush of carbon monoxide billowed out into the cold forest air. Gelb pulled Chekarin around, pushing him to the door. He could see, even as he did this, that Kourbash and some of his horsemen had come around in a circle behind him.

"Look, look. Now tell me it wasn't necessary."

Chekarin turned slowly, his round face as white as the snow.

"Forgive me," he muttered, "I'd never seen . . ."

He knelt in the snow, holding himself up with one hand, and vomited.

The van was filled with corpses. The naked blue bodies of men, women, and children, old and young. From the back of the van came the overpowering stench of urine, feces, and vomit.

The horses of Kourbash's irregulars whinnied and shied. Old Kourbash's seamed face was suddenly wet with tears.

Gelb turned toward the NKVD men who had come up behind him.

"Get the other vans open. Do what you can. There may be some still alive. And if there's one of these fascist scum still breathing, blow his brains out at once."

He waited until Chekarin had finished throwing up.

"*Now,* comrade Major . . . we go on to Starsk."

10

And what did the soldier's wife receive
from the vast Russian land?
From Russia she received her widow's veil,
For the funeral rites, a widow's veil.
That's what she received from the Russian land.
Bertolt Brecht
From "*Und was bekam des Soldaten Weib?*"

Schreiber-Hartstein had spent a bad night tossing and turning on his narrow bed. Dreams of his youth in Riga, of his days as a cadet at the St. Petersburg Academy, tormented him without letup. He awoke time and time again bathed in a hot sweat, groping out of his dreams like a swimmer who must reach the surface before his air gives out.

By dawn, he was exhausted. He got up, washed and dressed, and sat for a while on the edge of the bed in his small, spartan quarters. He wondered whether he would have strength enough to face the day. There had been no air raid that night. Everyone else would have slept well. It would, therefore, be a dangerous day for him and it would take an extraordinary effort to keep from committing some terrible blunder.

He arrived at the OKH building shortly after seven. The guards at the gate let him pass without a word, though he felt sure they had all noticed his pallor, his hollow eyes, and his unsteady walk.

By the time he had made his way to his office, he had used up all of his energy and slumped helplessly in the chair normally occupied by his orderly. He felt sure that he was coming down with something. That would be good. He could take to his bed for a few days and try to sort things out. No one would bother him if he had a fever.

He had no sooner gotten up the stairs and begun to move uncertainly toward his own office when the iron door behind him opened and the landing guard, one Corporal Schmidt, stuck his head in.

"Hauptmann, is that you?"

"What is it, Schmidt?"

"There's a messenger to see you, Hauptmann."

"A messenger?" Schreiber-Hartstein could not remember having done anything that could bring a messenger to his office at such an hour. Was he getting feverish already? He felt his forehead.

"Shall I bring him up, Hauptmann?"

There was something in Schmidt's tone that mandated an immediate yes. Schreiber-Hartstein gave it. The corporal disappeared down the corridor at a dead run.

Now what the devil can it be that makes him run like a rabbit so early in the morning? thought Schreiber-Hartstein, wondering if he really cared. Perhaps it was the Gestapo or the SD, come to take him in.

The answer came almost at once. There was a clicking of boot soles on the corridor floor and a helmeted SS Stürmscharfführer clattered into the room. The young man's expression was wooden, his eyes glued to the wall opposite as he brought his heels together and saluted with a stiff outthrust arm, exclaimed his *"Heil Hitler,"* and waited for a response.

Schreiber-Hartstein was at least awake enough to be discreet. He got to his feet, gave the appropriate salute, and asked what the man wanted.

"Hauptmann Reinhardt Schreiber-Hartstein?"

"Yes, yes . . ."

"A message, sir. Will there be a response?"

"Let me see it, Stürmscharfführer."

"At once." The man handed him a pale blue envelope. It was obvious from the size of it that the message within was brief.

As he ripped open the envelope, Schreiber-Hartstein caught the imprint on the left corner. His hand began to shake. Inside was a single slip of the same blue-colored paper. Across the top ran the mark and office insignia of Reichsminister Alfred Rosenberg.

The note read: "The Reichsminister will see Hauptmann Schreiber-Hartstein at 1400 hours, date as above. The interview will last no more than fifteen minutes."

Schreiber-Hartstein looked up at the messenger. He could hardly catch his breath. He did not know whether to rejoice or to despair. The way was open. It was entirely up to him now. He had a little more than six hours to prepare himself.

"Will there be a reply?" the SS man asked again.

"Yes, yes. You may say that, of course, I am at the Reichsminister's disposal. I will obey the summons punctually. And without fail."

The "Nodding Ass," as Field Marshal Keitel was known, for his ready acquiescence to everything that Hitler said, looked up from his cluttered desk. He had just heard the private entrance to his office begin to creak open. He put down the pencil he'd been toying with and lit a cigarette. For a moment, he avoided looking up at the Gestapo inspector who had just entered the room and now stood waiting patiently by the door, briefcase in hand.

It was just as well that he did not look up at that moment or he would have seen the look of faintly veiled amusement on Inspector Trakl's face. Keitel was not well liked. His equals referred to him as *Laikaitel,* a play on the German word for flunky. His subordinates considered him pompous, crude, and stupid—and often said so. It all showed on Trakl's pudgy, boyish face.

As Keitel slowly began to raise his head, the expression of contempt disappeared from Trakl's face to be replaced by a studied simulation of respect.

Keitel nudged his monocle into position.

"You've read the reports, Trakl?"

"Yes, Feldmarschall."

"You understand what a pack of scoundrels we're dealing with?"

"Yes, Feldmarschall."

"Stop that shit, Trakl. Sit down and have a cigarette. Don't pretend with me. I know exactly what's going on in that pig's brain of yours. Act naturally with me, I warn you, or I'll call Mueller and have you sent to Smolensk."

Trakl blanched. He sat down opposite the field marshal and lit a cigarette as he had been directed to do. He liked to think of himself as an acute observer, clever, with a penetrating insight and naturally superior to most of the people with whom he came in contact. He had been a lawyer in Salzburg for two years before joining the police, a fact that did not diminish his sense of superiority and self-importance one iota.

He was twenty-nine, very sure of himself, and just then on the borderline of insolence. Keitel understood this; many people behaved that way behind his back. It was rather refreshing to have someone behave that way to his face so he pretended not to notice.

"Is the ox in residence yet?" Keitel asked.

"Golitsyn?"

Keitel nodded.

"According to the reports . . ."

"Up the ass with the reports, Trakl. Do you know or don't you?"

Trakl swallowed hard. "Yes, Feldmarschall. It can be reliably stated that the . . . that Major General Golitsyn is in residence."

"And that monumental bag of shit who keeps sending me these reports about how unfairly we are dealing with the poor Russians?"

"Schreiber-Hartstein?"

"Yes, Trakl. Exactly. Who else?"

"He is under close observation."

"And the others? That whole gang of degenerate Ivan-lickers?"

"They're all under observation, Feldmarschall."

"Good. Good. I don't want any more of these damned reports, do you understand? See to it, Trakl, if you know what's good for you."

"If I may make the suggestion, Feldmarschall . . . though I'm sure it must have occurred to you already . . . why not simply have them all packed off to a concentration camp. Or to Smolensk? I think you mentioned Smolensk a minute ago, Feldmarschall?"

"Because, you *drecksack*, they're under Canaris's protection, that's why." He sat back and smiled, letting the monocle drop out of his eye; he began polishing it against his cuff. "Not exactly his protection, Inspector. The good admiral is too diplomatic for that. Let us simply say that the situation is very complicated and the obvious answer to the problem isn't the best answer at the moment. At any rate, we don't want to upset the good admiral, do we? He has his ways of getting even, Trakl. He'll come in here to complain with those damned dachshunds of his and the dogs will piss all over my carpet. They do it on purpose. He's trained them, I swear. But what can I say, eh, Trakl? Do we have concentration camps for dogs who wet the carpets in field marshal's offices?"

"After a fashion, Feldmarschall," Trakl replied, suppressing a giggle.

"Ah then, you just do as you're told. Keep an eye on them. Tickle them a little. Keep them worried."

Trakl studied the field marshal's face, hunting for some sign of intelligence. No, he decided, it wouldn't be at all wise to tell him that the Gestapo had already taken steps, that there was a new temporary "cooperation" with the Russians in the offing. The Ruskies didn't want Golitsyn taking charge of an army anymore than Hitler or Keitel did. They'd already hinted, through an agent with whom Trakl had maintained a discreet and cautious contact, that they'd be more than willing to help get rid of the "ox," as Keitel persisted in calling him. And in a way that the Ivan-lickers' supporters couldn't do a thing about.

But if the field marshal knew that Trakl was even considering cooperating with the Russians—for *any* reason—he'd have a *blutspurtz* right then and there. Trakl had his eye on the rewards of success all right, but he was also going to be very careful where he put his feet. The new "cooperation" would have to be managed very delicately indeed.

"So," said Keitel at length, "what are you standing there for, Trakl? Out, out. If you're finished go, get out."

"Are *you* finished, Feldmarschall?"

Keitel replaced his monocle, screwed it into his eye, glared, and said:

"For the moment, you *drecksack*. Only for the moment."

Nina Andreyeva had not gone near Alexander Semyonovitch since he had returned from Dabendorf that afternoon nor tried in any way to communicate with him.

All day she had waited for him, finally sure in her mind of just what she must do and waiting only for the opportunity. But when he had come clattering up the stairs, muffled in a long gray coat that reached almost to his ankles, his cap visor down to the tops of his eyeglasses, and his pale blue eyes gazing distractedly off into the distance, she had not known even how to approach him.

She fell back before that gaze, suddenly haunted by terrible memories.

She understood that look. She had seen it too many times before—a gaze that bored straight ahead, fixed on a distant goal which no one else could see. The man could walk through fire without even noticing it when he was like that.

He did not even see her standing there on the landing, so obviously waiting for him. When he had that look on his face, he seemed not even to be breathing.

Schreiber-Hartstein and Stalkov had seen her standing there, and for a moment she thought that the German was going to call to her. But they went on by in silence, up to the third floor, the German officer and his entourage of Russians, all with flushed faces and distant, fixed expressions.

Just like Alexander Semyonovitch's expression. Exactly like that.

She went back to her room and sat by the window looking out into the courtyard. But all she could see was Alexander Semyonovitch's face, the two pale blue eyes staring from behind the thick lenses.

Just as they had stared at her that day almost four years before as they stood together before the clerk's desk in the *Zags* office.

The frost had come early to Moscow in the fall of 1940, ringing in the ears like the breaking of giant panes of glass and touching the flat walls of its low buildings with a heavy sheen of hoarfrost. There was not enough fuel in the boilers of the four-story house on Chapayev Street where Alexander Semyonovitch had his apartment, and the rooms, in consequence, were cold and clammy. An oppressive damp had risen from the river and had seeped into every crevice and crack in the city. The sky was low and unrelentingly dismal. In the restaurants and cafes of Gorki Street, in the Metropole Hotel, and in the Cocktail Hall, people—in uniform and out—stared at each other apprehensively and drank with a tense ferocity, trying to pretend that they did not know what was coming.

It was over a year now since the Germans had rolled over Poland. In the wake of the German invasion, the Soviet army had been ordered into the eastern marches, falling upon the shattered remains of the Polish army and butchering the country. The Finnish war was over but the victory, such as it was, had been dearly bought and, in the end, hollow, a cause for shame not satisfaction. The British had suffered a disaster at Dunkirk and the French had been defeated. Hitler and Stalin acknowledged each other with guarded smiles. Russian opera was enjoying a vogue in Berlin and *Die Walküre* was produced at the Bolshoi.

Alexander Semyonovitch had begun to have severe headaches. In the evenings, when he returned from lecturing at the Frunze Military Academy, he would eat, take some medication or other, and retire sullenly and sometimes angrily to bed. Often he would not even speak to his son.

Nina Andreyeva did her best to minister to him but the more she tried to help him, it seemed, the more he resented her. It was as though he were seeking a refuge from the madness of the times behind a barricade of imagined bodily ills. She tried to understand and tried to deal with him very gently. Her long experience in the hospital was a help, but the strain on her was overwhelming.

Her workdays had grown longer and more exhausting each week. A promised promotion to section chief for internal medicine had not come through. Instead, and inexplicably, she had been moved to an insignificant position in the wards. She had bitten her lip and said nothing. But she also noticed that during the past few weeks superiors who had previously been very friendly had begun to avoid her.

She had no idea why.

Under such circumstances, it was very hard to deal with Alexander Semyonovitch's moods. Many evenings, after the staff car had brought him home to Chapayev Street, she found herself sitting alone at the dining room table, drinking cup after cup of scalding tea and reading Nekrasov's bitter poems.

> I am in fact nothing, useless . . .
> wasting day after ruined day.

Alexander Semyonovitch would lie on his side on the sofa in the drawing room, still wearing his uniform, an alcohol compress on his head.

Often he lay with his face to the wall, as though he were an old man preparing for death. Petya was puzzled and sulked about the apartment, frequently bursting into fits of uncontrollable sobbing at the slightest provocation.

Alexander Semyonovitch's periods of intense depression would alternate with bouts of boisterous enthusiasm so violent that he seemed drunk. He would pick up his wife and toss her in the air as though she were a schoolgirl. Little Petya, completely forgetting the days when his father would not even speak to him, clapped his hands in delight, unaware of the terror in his mother's eyes.

And then, one day, the envelope came.

A courier from the War Ministry arrived just after a silent evening meal in late October. Alexander Semyonovitch's food lay uneaten on his plate. The only thing he'd touched had been the wine bottle, and that he had almost completely drained.

The courier, a tall Georgian junior lieutenant, stood in the vestibule in his stiff boots, his mustache frosted, the visor of his cap pulled down over his eyebrows.

Alexander Semyonovitch held the letter in his hand. His tunic was unbuttoned. He had been listening to a phonograph record and drinking tea. Nina Andreyeva was in the kitchen making soup. The apartment smelled of onions.

Alexander Semyonovitch stared at the courier; he flushed with confusion.

"Thank you, comrade," he said at last. "There's no reason for you to stay. You don't need an answer *now,* do you? Of course not. Good night then, comrade Lieutenant. . . ."

"Who's that, Sasha?" came Nina Andreyeva's voice from the cramped confines of the kitchen. "Tell him to be quiet. We don't want to wake Petya."

The courier stamped out, leaving a trail of little black puddles on the floor where the snow had melted from his boots.

Outside, in Chapayev Street, it was all a white swirl, a cloud of light fall flakes driven by a wind that could not make up its mind in which direction to blow. An open pharmacy glowed like an oven at the corner of the street, its windows all crimson and yellow. Otherwise the street was already dark and empty, but for the snow.

"News?" asked Nina Andreyeva hesitatingly, poking her head out of the little kitchen, a pot of soup held between towel-wrapped hands. A strand of hair hung damply down over her forehead. She was flushed and somehow was feeling happy.

Alexander Semyonovitch held out the letter.

"They want me to divorce you," he said in a dull, flat voice, as though he'd just received a letter telling him that a new uniform was ready to be picked up at the tailor's.

She put the tureen down on the table where it immediately began raising blisters on the varnished surface.

"Sasha . . ." she began. "You're joking?"

"Look here. It's from the War Ministry. Four signatures. Just like that. Look for yourself."

He was shaking all over.

She took the letter. It was as he had said. The message was in terse, mechanical language, brief and to the point. It had been determined that under present conditions, and considering the attitude of the great Soviet people following the disgraceful Tukaschevsky affair and its aftermath, it could no longer be considered appropriate for a trusted general of the Soviet army to be married to the daughter of kulaks. A divorce would have to be obtained as rapidly as possible.

She had not even time to finish. He pulled her into his arms and held her tightly to him. She felt his hot tears on her cheek and neck. The letter drifted almost unnoticed to the floor as they stood there holding each other in silence.

"You will have to do as they say, Sasha . . ." she whispered at last.

He shook his head dumbly, picked up the letter, and crumpled it into a ball.

"No," he said. "No."

It was what she wanted him to say. But even as he said it, she knew what would happen. She had, after all, married a man in whose life love of country was the most overpowering emotion of all.

Later, when she looked back on it, she realized that it was at that moment—exactly—that she had first begun to hate him.

Three days later, no more, no less, early on a gray, drizzling Saturday morning, they walked to the nearest offices of the *Zags,* the Registry Bureau.

The streets were empty of people and full of slush. Turgid, muddy streams ran bubbling in the gutters and between the cobblestones, washing away the exposed earth. The walls of the low brick and wood buildings on either side of the street were streaked with rain, and the air had become unnaturally warm again, melting the week's earlier snow even before the drizzle had begun.

Alexander Semyonovitch had not worn his uniform. He was ashamed and wanted no one to recognize him. He had declined an offer of a staff car to take them to the registry. If it had to be done, he would do it himself, without anyone else being involved.

Just before they had put on their galoshes and gone out, she had asked: "I suppose once there is a divorce, they'll have no objection if we go on living together?"

"They won't agree," he replied soberly. "Besides, how could I do that to you? You must be free . . ."

"Free?" She had laughed. "What about Petya? Think of him."

"They will provide. They've assured me . . ."

"Will you see Petya?"

"In time, yes. For the present, they say that I should . . ."

" 'They say' . . . Sasha, why is it always 'they say'? Why isn't it 'I want' or 'I will do'?"

He didn't answer and walked on in silence, a little ahead of her, his hands thrust into the pockets of his overcoat, bareheaded, the drizzle running down over his eyes and streaking his glasses.

A torn half of a newspaper drifted by in the gutter on a stream of black, slushy water. The headlines told of the introduction of tuition fees for higher education in the Soviet schools and the signing of a pact between Italy, Japan, and Germany.

When they arrived at the *Zags* building for the hearing, they went at once to the chief clerk's office, a bare, cheerless room occupied by a few tables, a large black German typewriter, a few wooden filing cabinets with hundreds of little drawers in them, like the ones that house a library's filing card system, and one large picture of Stalin high on the wall and tilted forward in old Russian style, as though ready to fall.

The clerk, a wan, emaciated type straight out of Gogol, looking rather the way Alexander Semyonovitch had always imagined Bashmachkin to look, at first asked all the routine questions. Could the citizens not compose their differences? Now was not an ideal time to disrupt family life. The Soviet family must close ranks in the face of coming adversity, he said. The Soviet family must stand together. The clerk repeated his catechism wearily and without enthusiasm.

No, Alexander Semyonovitch said, it was impossible to compose their differences, as there were no differences to begin with.

How was it, then, that they were seeking a divorce?

Nina Andreyeva did not answer. Alexander Semyonovitch remained silent. His face was distorted and puffy. He could barely keep back his rage and his tears. He pressed Nina Andreyeva's hands so hard that she winced.

"Sasha," she whispered. "It's not necessary for you to say anything."

"I know. I know, God help me. . . ."

The clerk droned on. It was for the good of society, for the good of the children. Ah, yes, there were children, were there not? Certainly with a couple their age there must be children.

There was one child, Nina Andreyeva answered calmly. A boy, six years old. He would be well looked after. He would stay with his mother, of course.

"One-fourth of your earnings, citizen," said the clerk, looking levelly at Alexander Semyonovitch. "Deducted at the source, citizen. Which is . . . ?"

Alexander Semyonovitch handed the clerk his documents. The man blanched and looked nervously about the room. It was, apart from the three of them, quite empty still.

"One-fourth, citizen," the clerk repeated dully, staining Alexander Semyonovitch's identity papers with his greasy fingers.

The general stared at the clerk blankly. "No more questions, please, comrade clerk. . . ."

"Of course, of course. Pardon me. It's my duty, you understand. I must ask certain things. I mean no offense. . . ."

Nina Andreyeva grew impatient with the man, though she knew it was not his fault. She nodded hastily. "Please, just do it as quickly as you can."

The clerk said that he understood and began filling out the necessary forms.

Alexander Semyonovitch paid the fifty-ruble fee. As they left the room they could hear the typewriter begin to clack.

In front of the *Zags* building they stepped aside to let an angrily quarreling young couple rush through the doors. The man was in uniform, red-faced and gesticulating, the girl was in tears. They disappeared inside and slammed up the stairs.

Nina Andreyeva looked at the man who, up until a few moments before, had been her husband. Why had he agreed to do what they'd demanded of him? Surely a way might have been found . . .

A trolley went by, trailing sparks from its overhead wires and sending up a fan of dark, slushy spray below. They could hear a heavy multiengined aircraft droning away somewhere high above the gray blanket of rainclouds.

Neither of them was able to speak. It seemed quite superfluous, in any event, to say anything at all.

The silence continued for the three agonizing days that they remained together. Neither of them knew what to do. Then, without saying a word—for in all that time he had been unable to find so much as a single sentence even remotely adequate to explain to her what he could not possibly explain even to himself—Alexander Semyonovitch packed a valise, kissed his son, and moved to a room in the Moskva Hotel.

In four days he had left the city entirely.

She did not try to find out where he had gone. It was quite enough that he had gone and that there was nothing whatever she could do about it.

Two months later she managed to obtain a small room of her own, with the help of the hospital director. Two of her new neighbors helped her to move.

The gray Opel staff car carrying Reinhardt Schreiber-Hartstein and Martin Beifelder crossed the river at the old Cornelius Bridge and sped the short distance up Friedrich Wilhelm to Rauchstrasse where the office of the Ministry for Occupied Eastern Territories was located. The building, which had once housed the Yugoslav embassy, gleamed in the late fall sunlight, its polished stone flanks as smooth as mirrors. Beifelder turned away, pretending to be blinded.

"One needs sunglasses here," he muttered.

"Or a gas mask," Schreiber-Hartstein said gloomily.

Beifelder gave him a surprised look. "I hope you're not going to talk that way once you're inside. They tell me Rosenberg is very sensitive to criticism . . . quite moody."

"Have you ever met him?"

"No."

"Neither have I. We shall have to hope for the best, that's all."

The Opel drew up before the entrance. The steel-helmeted guards looked bored and hardly noticed as the two captains trotted up the steps and into the splendid vestibule to confront the receptionist. The girl glanced quickly at her appointment book, then at the pale blue tissue Schreiber-Hartstein had handed her. She was a good-looking girl, well scrubbed, with a snub nose and a pleasant manner. Schreiber-Hartstein wondered what she was doing in a place like that.

"Herr Hauptmann . . . I'm sorry," the receptionist said.

Schreiber-Hartstein froze. "The Reichsminister cannot . . . ?"

"Oh yes, Herr Hauptmann, but the appointment is only for one."

"But we have both come on the same business. Surely—"

"The Reichsminister is most insistent on seeing only one at a time. The signal clearly says one only. Which of you is . . . Hauptmann Schreiber-Hartstein, please? Your papers?"

Schreiber-Hartstein sighed. Beifelder, who had had no real desire to be in the room during the meeting and had only come along at his friend's insistence, shrugged and retired. Schreiber-Hartstein gave the girl his papers. A buzzer sounded and a page, an old man in a brown tailcoat and a mustardy expression, came out of a side door.

"You will follow him, please," the receptionist said. "You will be shown directly to the Reichminister's rooms. Oh, yes, and one other thing. Please . . . your sidearms?"

Schreiber-Hartstein unbuckled his holster belt and handed it over to be stowed in a drawer and locked up.

"Good luck, Reinhardt. . . ."

"Let us hope luck plays no part in this."

Beifelder settled himself on a sofa on the far side of the room, under a large red and blue map of the Ukraine, and picked up a copy of *Signal* to read.

Rosenberg's office was very large and well furnished. A spacious desk occupied one end of the room. A number of tufted yellow armchairs were laid out in a circle around the desk. A large globe on a floor stand, a few pieces of sculpture, and a large bronze eagle perched on a wreathed swastika completed the decorations. A tapestry hung behind the desk and more than half of the marble floor was covered by an enormous Persian carpet. The room appeared rather like a copy of the Führer's study as it had appeared in countless magazine pictures. The imitation was almost pathetic, Schreiber-Hartstein thought, but then, by all accounts Alfred Rosenberg was a rather pathetic man. Not a single person of his acquaintance who had met the Reichsminister for the East had a kind word to say about him. He was considered weak, muddle-headed, insecure, and some even thought him mad. He could not control the butcher-boy Gauleiters who had been assigned to govern the conquered eastern territories nominally under his control; he could not even approach Hitler anymore. His theories of a chain of independent Slavic states ran head-on into Hitler's concepts of Pan-Slavic serfdom. The only thing that kept him where he was was his authorship of the *Myth of the Twentieth Century*, which still retained a place second only to *Mein Kampf* in the National Socialist literary pantheon.

Of such things are rulers of empires made, Schreiber-Hartstein thought ruefully as he was ushered into the room.

Before he even saw Reichsminister Rosenberg, who was seated low behind his mahogany desk, Schreiber-Hartstein found himself confronted by a wary Alsatian whose low growl gave ample warning that he was not to be trifled with.

Rosenberg rose, with some difficulty. He was not a well man and suffered from tubercular bone malformation. With a soft, incomprehensible command he brought the dog back to the side of the desk.

"What is it you want to tell me?" Rosenberg began at once, his head slightly lowered, his dark eyes peering from under furrowed brows. The impression conveyed by his peculiar stance and expression was of a man at once suspicious and fearful, which, considering his position and power, was odd indeed. Schreiber-Hartstein stopped where he was and saluted. The Alsatian growled softly. Rosenberg nodded but did not return the salute. In his yellow-tan uniform, he gave the impression of a throw-back to the thirties when uniforms of such color had been far more commonplace.

"How is it I've never seen you before?" Rosenberg asked in his heavy Baltic accent.

"I beg your pardon, Reichsminister?"

"You're an Estonian, aren't you?"

"I'm from Riga, Reichsminister."

"I was born in Tallinn or as we used to call it, Reval. Did you know that, Captain?"

"I'd heard, sir."

"Do sit down. . . ."

The dog relaxed at last, thrust out its paws, and put its head down. The eyes closed almost entirely; but not quite.

"Now . . ." said Rosenberg, glancing at his watch.

"Concerning General Golitsyn and the RONA units, Reichsminister . . ."

Rosenberg nodded. He seemed extremely nervous. His sallow face set off deep, staring eyes. For a moment, Schreiber-Hartstein thought, The man is actually . . . afraid of *me*. . . .

"I've read the memorandum you've sent me. If I hadn't read it, I never would have consented to an interview. Understand?"

"Sir . . ." Schreiber-Hartstein replied.

"A man like you would never be here, you'd not be wearing that uniform, if it wasn't for me," Rosenberg said sharply.

Schreiber-Hartstein found himself caught off balance. He had no idea what Rosenberg was talking about and cast about desperately for a way to steer back to the topic he had come to discuss.

Then, abruptly, Rosenberg seemed to relax. He sank back in the deep desk chair and knit his fingers together over his chest.

"I, like you," he said, "am an engineer. Did you know I have a diploma in architecture from the University of Moscow? Did you know that when I volunteered for service in the German army, I was turned down because they said I was a 'Russian'? Did you know that for two years I have been trying to get Himmler to change his idiotic policies in the east . . . *my* east?" His voice had now grown highly charged, almost pleading, the pitch considerably elevated. Then, suddenly again, he seemed to collapse, his voice reduced to a sigh. "Now, tell me about your General Golitsyn. . . ."

"Reichsminister, it is all in the memorandum. . . ."

"Yes, of course it is. And you expect me to do an about-face of such severity, is that it? To support this person with his manic Pan-Slavism . . . ?"

"He is not a Pan-Slav," Schreiber-Hartstein ventured. "He is simply a Russian patroit. . . ."

"All Russian patriots are Pan-Slavs, just as all German patriots are Pan-German. How could it be otherwise? Nevertheless, and assuming he is what you say, the army you propose is a Pan-Slavic force, isn't it?"

Schreiber-Hartstein swallowed hard. He knew exactly where Rosenberg was going and there was nothing he could do about it. He had hoped against hope that today's realities would triumph over yesterday's theories but it seemed as though he had been too optimistic.

"What has all this to do with a Ukrainian free state? What has it all to do with a free Georgia? What has it . . ."

Schreiber-Hartstein leaned forward and, with due regard for the possible consequences, interrupted the Reichsminister.

"It has as much to do with all of those ideas, Reichsminister, as Himmler's notions of the Slavic *Untermensch* and Gauleiter Koch's *Einsatzkommandos*. The fact is, that with Golitsyn and an active RONA there is a chance to salvage something out there. Without him . . . if I may speak frankly, Herr Reichsminister, there will be nothing but disaster."

Rosenberg sank back in his chair. His knuckles were white and there was an almost pitifully confused look on his face. He seemed on the verge of tears. Again Schreiber-Hartstein found himself caught completely off by the Reichsminister's mood swings. He was not sure what to say next, or whether he should say anything at all.

"Captain, you must understand . . . that I have been trying for the last two years to make them change their ways. I fought with Keitel over the treatment of the prisoners of war and the civilians. I proposed to the Führer the establishment of a new Eastern church. I have tried to stop the SS from driving the populace into the arms of the Bolsheviks. All this has come to nothing. What makes you think that your general and his band of malcontents is going to accomplish anything that I have not been able to accomplish?"

"It is well known, Reichsminister, that your vision of the East policy is . . . different than that which has been in effect thus far. . . ."

"Different?" Rosenberg for the first time uttered what sounded like a laugh. "How could anything be more different?"

"And so," Schreiber-Hartstein went on, "up till now, nothing has been accomplished. But the times are different. Talk to the generals now. Talk to Keitel again. Talk to anyone who's been out there. They'll all tell each other what you and I, Reichsminister, don't have to be told because we know firsthand. Those men that Himmler persists in calling subhuman are fighting as well or better than our men, they're building bigger and stronger tanks, they're flying rings around our Luftwaffe. They're surviving and fighting under conditions that have our best troops running for warm cover with their tails between their legs. . . ."

"Captain!"

"It's true, Reichsminister. Those 'subhumans' are beating us. And we've been helping them do it. Even the Kochs and the Keitels must see that by now. They can think what they like, they can believe whatever theories they care to believe, but there is a *truth* out there that can't be denied."

"And you honestly believe that letting your Russian divisions loose can change all that?"

"With Golitsyn at their head, yes, Reichsminister, I do. And all I want is a chance to prove it."

Rosenberg pushed a button on his desk and spoke into a little intercom box.

"Fraülein Hoff? Yes . . . we will not be disturbed. Is that clear? Tell my next appointment, whoever it is, that he must wait. Only if there is an emergency, then you may ring, not otherwise. Is that understood?"

He flicked off the switch.

"Now, if you wish, Captain . . . smoke if it pleases you. And tell me about this Russian colossus of yours and the miracles he will make for us. . . ."

By nine in the evening most of the newly created RONA division staff had been assembled in the map room of the headquarters shed at Dabendorf. General Golitsyn, looking wan and nervous, occupied the high-backed chair at the end of the table. To his right sat Kurenko, now captain, to his left Major Stalkov. Obriyan, Zhilinsky, and half a dozen others of the upper echelon were there too, summoned from their own or other people's beds: Kruzhno, the engineers' chief, a former fighter pilot named Nikiforov, the cavalry officers Zakutny and Vayner, and a few others whom Kurenko had seen around Viktoriastrasse but whose names he did not know.

For over half an hour, they waited, hardly speaking to one another. No one knew why they had been brought together at such an hour. Golitsyn sat there, stony-faced, smoking one cigarette after another. Obriyan got up and paced back and forth, pausing now and then to examine the many maps that had been pinned to the walls. Kurenko noted that a small projection screen stood in one corner. A slide projector in a case sat near the door. An orderly brought in tea and coffee. No one drank it. The room gradually began to fill with smoke until it resembled a Chinese opium den.

At 9:46 the door opened and Schreiber-Hartstein entered, accompanied by Captain Gottinger and Lieutenant Hummel. The almost-always-present Beifelder was nowhere to be seen. Schreiber-Hartstein was obviously excited; his face was flushed and he was sweating. His eyes darted from side to side, as though he could not quite control himself. Kurenko saw too that his hands were shaking slightly. A hushed expectancy filled the room. Stalkov coughed, as he always did when nervous.

Schreiber-Hartstein's heightened nervous state was contagious. He slammed his briefcase down on the table.

"Gentlemen," he exclaimed, "momentous news. This afternoon, I met with Reichsminister Rosenberg. What we said to each other is not important. He listened to me, far more attentively than I had dared hope for. He understood, he agreed. I have obtained the temporary rescission, on the Reichsminister's authority, of Keitel's order disbanding and parceling out the RONA. He has agreed to allow the deployment of the First RONA Division. In full strength, with its own officers."

There was an audible murmur of surprised approval around the table. Only Golitsyn himself remained silent and wary.

Schreiber-Hartstein went on, "We will be allowed *one* proving operation. A test, gentlemen. All eyes will be on us. We may choose the operation, according to our best judgment, and subject only to a veto from Abwehr if the current state of tactical intelligence should dictate. We will be permitted to deploy up to full strength if appropriate. The choice is ours. But we must bring off a stunning victory, nothing less. We are being given a chance, gentlemen, only a chance, not full approval. Reichsminister Rosenberg made that absolutely clear. As you certainly know, there is much opposition to the idea, particularly from important elements of the SS and the SD in particular. Even the Reichsminister is running a serious risk in allowing us to go forward. We will have only one opportunity. If we bring it off, there's no limit to what may be accomplished. If we fail, it will be the end of the RONA as an independent entity."

Obriyan jumped to his feet and cried "Hurrah." In a second, everyone else in the room was up and cheering. All, that is, except Golitsyn, who, though he too had risen, stood back, apart and still silent.

There were tears in Schreiber-Hartstein's eyes.

Stalkov's voice was the first to be heard after the shouting had died down.

"And what will we be called on to do? A parachute attack on the Kremlin might be good for a start."

"You yourself gave us the idea," said Schreiber-Hartstein. "Lieutenant Hummel, will you set up the screen and the projector? You will see, Major Stalkov, how quickly and effectively we can move once the fetters are off. After you've viewed the films, you can decide . . . Stalkov's idea or something else. But in my opinion, as it was in yours, Major, the idea is a grand one. And so, we have taken the liberty of developing it a little."

The lights went out. Lieutenant Hummel turned on the projector. A slide of an aerial photo leaped onto the screen.

"Lake Byeleymostnoy, gentlemen. The Lake of White Mist. These pictures were taken by a Luftwaffe reconnaissance aircraft a week ago on a routine flight. Military intelligence provided them at our request. By the way, I'm told they will be only too glad to lend their assistance to our venture."

"Major Stalkov," said Gottinger, "don't lean so far forward, if you please. You're in the way."

A gruff laugh. Stalkov pulled back.

"Brilliant, brilliant," Zhilinsky muttered.

The slides flipped by, clear photos of a large, fenced-in barracks complex. All in all there were more than two dozen long, shedlike buildings within the enclosure. The shadows of the guard towers were clearly visible on the snow. The whole thing appeared almost like an architect's plān view.

The camp lay at the southern end of a long, tear-shaped lake. Just to the northeast a hump of land jutted out, creating a small bay and sheltering the camp. To the south, perhaps one hundred meters away, was another group of buildings, which must have been the guards' and officers' quarters. A cookhouse and a landing stage at the edge of the lake were also visible. A railroad spur line wound in from the northeast and ended just outside the barracks compound.

"How many prisoners does it hold?" Stalkov asked.

"It's hard to say. We have some intelligence on train movements in the area but not much. Abwehr estimates between five and seven hundred, perhaps more. Possibly as many as a thousand."

"It would be a fantastic gesture," said Zhilinsky from somewhere in the darkened room. "General Golitsyn would lead us in the liberation of the very men whom that butcher in the Kremlin has betrayed most horribly . . . those who tried to fight for their country and . . ."

"Don't make speeches," said Stalkov. "And whether the general's place is in the field or right here is something we'll have to discuss later."

"I can speak for myself, Major Stalkov."

"I'm sure you will, General. And at the proper moment."

"Gentlemen," Schreiber-Hartstein snapped, "all of this in due course. Tell me first, what do you think of the idea?"

"It's certainly a possibility," said Obriyan.

"It's more than that. It's a stroke of genius," said Zhilinsky.

"But can it be done?"

Schreiber-Hartstein grew calm, almost transfigured. "Lights on, Hummel." When the room was lit again, he opened his briefcase and took out a sheaf of papers and a number of maps. Grasping these in one hand and a wooden pointer in the other, he went quickly to the wall.

"There are high mountain ridges directly to the north. We can't approach from that direction. And to the south, presently, at a distance of about sixty-five kilometers, is General Strukachev's tank army. On the west bank of the lake there is a heavy forest that runs all the way up to Kursk. An approach from *that* direction is possible but it could not be managed without our being seen."

"What you're saying, then, is that it really can't be done?"

"Not at all, Captain Obriyan. I'm certainly saying that it will be difficult. But if it is carried out successfully, it will be all the more brilliant for its daring method of execution."

"How then?"

Captain Gottinger got to his feet.

"By air," he said.

Obriyan shook his head. "Into those woods? And at this time of year? It's out of the question."

"In one week's time," said Gottinger, "the lake will still be frozen solid, won't it?"

Zhilinsky nodded, puzzled. "Without a doubt. I know the area quite well. These are treacherous times . . . the ice isn't always firm at this time of year but . . . with the cold we've been having, yes . . . yes. You're correct on that point."

"So, don't you see?"

"No, I don't see. You can't drop parachute troops onto a frozen lake. Everyone of them would break a leg or worse."

"We didn't have paratroops in mind," Gottinger said softly.

"What then?"

"Gliders," said Gottinger.

"You're insane."

"It could be done," said Schreiber-Hartstein. "You see the peninsula that protects the camp, the one that forms the enclosure of the bay? If we brought the gliders down *here,* in the center of the lake and under cover of the mist—and silently, gentlemen, without a sound other than the whisper of the wind—if we could land *here*, behind that peninsula, and then bring our troops across the ice, up onto shore—here—and over the land projection under cover of the forest, then we would be hidden until we're almost on top of them. As you can see from the map and the location of the forest, there's enough cover for a full battalion, perhaps more."

There was a stunned silence in the room. Then Stalkov began to grin. He clapped his hands. Golitsyn winced. The pilot, Nikiforov, who had not spoken up until then, leaned forward.

"What he says is true, General. It *is* possible. It could be done."

"Bravo," cried Stalkov. "Bravo, Nikiforov."

"Yes, yes," repeated Golitsyn dully. "It could be done. Even a fool can see that."

Schreiber-Hartstein rapped his pointer against the wall.

"Then unless there's some objection, gentlemen, we may consider the question settled. With our thanks to Major Stalkov, of course. And, God willing, we will succeed."

Part III

11

> I don't estimate our personal chances to be very good, even though I believe the Stalin regime will fall; thirty percent that the Germans liquidate us; thirty percent that we fall into Stalin's hands; thirty percent that the Americans and English hang us, despite our respect for them. I allow only a ten percent chance that we come out of this with a whole skin.
>
> Mileti A. Zykov
> Member of the RONA

The last lion left in the Berlin zoo was roaring with hunger. There had been no meat for three, perhaps four, days. The beast was near starvation and bellowing his outrage without letup.

Inspector Trakl shuddered. The sound was too much like a human voice, like some he remembered, like—in fact—all the roars of pain and outrage he had ever heard all rolled up into one. He wondered whether he would continue to hear that lion bellowing in his dreams just as he heard so many other sounds of pain and outrage and saw so many other sights he would just as soon have forgotten.

He probably would. Life was like that.

Most of the animals had either died or been taken out to the country. Only a few of the large, carnivorous beasts were left. They would either survive or not, as fate decreed. Trakl often wondered what would happen if the zoo suffered a few bomb hits and the animals escaped. The idea of a ravenous lion loose in the streets of Berlin seemed to him particularly appropriate.

He passed along a concrete walkway between a line of empty,

foul-smelling cages. At the end of the walk was the polar bear's cage, a large, iron-barred enclosure within which was an artificial cliff complete with a honeycomb of caves. In the center was the bear's pool, now empty, a cistern about six feet deep. A small, scummy puddle of water lay at the bottom.

Trakl took out his identity disc. He could feel the little embossed eagle with his fingertip. He traced its outline with his thumb, then ran his finger over the raised letters on the back that spelled his name, and the words *Secret State Police.*

He had first dealt with the man called Lensky back in 1928, when the Russians had been secretly helping the new German army to train in violation of the Versailles treaty. He had come close to meeting the man face to face twice after that, but each time the contact had been made without his actually getting a glimpse of him. Since then there had been other moments of "cooperation," moments when the objectives of both the Gestapo and the GPU or the NKVD or whatever it was called at the time had coincided. Infrequent but, when they occurred, absolutely reliable. The Tukaschevsky affair, that had been another such time. And the period of the nonaggression pact. Now, even during the war, there were still such times. It was odd, Trakl thought, but somehow he trusted this Lensky far more than he would have trusted his own colleagues in the SD and certainly more than the men of the Abwehr.

He halted before the empty polar bear cage. The huge iron gate was open. The lion continued to roar in the echoing, empty recesses of the lion house.

Trakl stepped into the cage and slammed the door shut. He moved to the far side of the pit, took out his identity disc, and flung it as hard as he could over the bars and into the darkness.

Then he waited. Just as he had promised to do.

There was an understanding between them, between Trakl and Lensky and others like them. One had to act with honor when one gave one's word to the enemy. To do otherwise could have lethal results. At other times, there were no restraints whatever. Someday, Trakl vowed, he would catch up with Lensky. But not when he had given his word, as he had now.

There was information he wanted. Lensky, for his own reasons, was prepared to give it to him.

The minutes went by. Trakl thought he saw a furtive movement a ways down the path near the empty lion house. No, he was wrong. It was nothing.

Where was the man? Had something happened to him? Trakl could not see the spot where his disc had landed. It was pitch-dark there. An elephant could have walked by unnoticed.

Then, suddenly, something came hurtling over the bars and into the cage. It landed with a dull plop just on the other side of the empty pit. Trakl instinctively flinched.

Nothing happened. There was no explosion.

No, of course there wasn't. Lensky was as scrupulous as he was. They had made an arrangement. It would be honored.

He waited for a moment and then went over and picked up the package. It was a small oilskin-wrapped bundle. His identity disc was fixed to the top by a piece of black electric tape.

He opened the package. Inside were a number of folded papers, a sheaf of typewritten questions and answers, and a signal tissue, charred around one edge.

The light was bad, almost nonexistent. But Trakl knew at once that he held in his hands exactly what Lensky had promised him.

Now it was up to him to keep his part of the bargain.

The general had risen before dawn, dressed in his brand-new uniform, and was downstairs waiting for Schreiber-Hartstein's car to come by and pick him up before a single light had appeared in any of the windows on Viktoriastrasse. From the bakery next door came the odor of freshly baked bread and the muted voices of the bakers sweating and grunting at the ovens. The night had been calm. There had been no English bombers and the inhabitants of Berlin had slept a deep and exhausted sleep. A low bank of dense rain clouds hung uncertainly over the city.

A chill wind swept down the gray-dark street, chasing scraps of newspaper and bits of charred debris before it. The general pulled at the collar of his coat, wishing he could turn it up around his neck. He knew, however, that he had to set an example even if there was no one there to see him. At all times, and even in small things. So he straightened himself up, clasped his hands behind his back, and waited. The others, those who had not remained at Dabendorf the night before, had not yet risen. Dushkin was still snoring and Kurenko, who was usually up and prowling the halls by that hour, was nowhere to be seen.

The general would be the first to arrive, which was only proper.

A solitary gray automobile bearing Wehrmacht plates turned into the head of Viktoriastrasse. As it drew up to the curb, the general saw Schreiber-Hartstein in the backseat, a briefcase in his lap, freshly shaven and looking alert. The general sighed; what endless enthusiasm the Balt had. How he wished he could feel even a hundredth of the man's energy.

"Good morning, Alexander Semyonovitch. Don't let the clouds deceive you. We have the latest weather reports from Signal. It will be a beautiful day. A perfect day for the formation, for the announcement, don't you think?"

Golitsyn bent and with some difficulty crammed himself into the backseat. The Germans had obviously not built their cars with men of Golitsyn's size in mind. Schreiber-Hartstein opened his briefcase and, as the car moved back into the middle of the street and took the road south for Dabendorf, he produced not the draft of the announcement to the troops that Golitsyn had expected to see but a parcel wrapped in grease-stained brown butcher's paper and a thermos.

"Real coffee, Alexander Semyonovitch. Fresh rolls and the best Westphalian ham I have ever tasted. Courtesy of the Reichsminister's office, believe it or not. Rosenberg is trying to bribe us to behave, I think," he said with a wink. "At least we shall start the day with a good breakfast, you and I."

By the time they had reached the entrance to the Dabendorf camp, the sun had begun to force its way out from behind the clouds far to the east, sending down misty bars of light that spiked the far end of the muddy drill fields like a giant fence. The rest of Dabendorf camp lay hidden in a gray dawn darkness, as though a great shadow had settled over it.

Golitsyn got out of the car, stretched his cramped legs, and strode across the field with Schreiber-Hartstein struggling to keep up. He would at least manage a counterfeit of energy, for the sake of the men; he owed them that. But the depression that had been with him for weeks, ever since Nina Andreyeva and Kurenko had appeared, clung to him like a ground mist, implacable and inescapable.

A light shone in the headquarters hut. Who had gotten there ahead of him? Perhaps some of the officers who had stayed over for the night. Obriyan? Nikiforov? Across the field he could see lights in the barracks buildings and the distant, imprecise shapes of formations gathering in the semidarkness.

"Reinhardt Gavrilovitch . . . who gets up earlier than we do? Who is there already in the hut?"

Schreiber-Hartstein strained his eyes, wiped his glasses, and shook his head. A small Opel was parked on the shadowed west side of the building. Schreiber-Hartstein did not recognize it. His heart almost stopped but he struggled not to let his alarm show. He glanced at the general . . . a giant but so vulnerable figure, all trust and moral certainty.

"You didn't answer, Reinhardt Gavrilovitch."

"Whoever it is, we'll see soon enough."

The Opel had Wehrmacht plates. Signal Division. Beifelder? Or a liaison from Von Kluge's office? There was no way of telling. Schreiber-Hartstein's hand fell involuntarily to the flap of his holster.

The general pushed open the door.

Nina Andreyeva sat at the map table, wreathed in cigarette smoke. She was dressed in the best, cleanest clothes she had and she had even made an attempt at makeup.

"Nina Andreyeva, how did you get out here?" the general blurted out, dumbstruck. "And why . . . ?"

"As to the first question, Sasha, your Major Stalkov was good enough to provide transportation. He and Captain Beifelder brought out a stack of leaflets. And me." She paused. "As to the second question, why, I'm here to be with you when you face your men."

Golitsyn stood there like a stone, not at all sure he had understood what she had said.

Schreiber-Hartstein smiled tentatively.

"You will excuse me, Alexander Semyonovitch? I must see Martin about the leaflets."

The door opened. A gust of wind swept into the room, rattling the maps pinned to the walls. Then it closed. Silence.

Golitsyn had not moved an inch.

"Sasha . . . I *know* about the announcement."

"And so?" he said in almost a whisper.

"I want to be here when you tell the men. A wife should do that. Particularly your wife."

"My wife?"

"Yes . . . after all, a piece of paper . . . what is a piece of paper, a form?"

"You would do that . . . in spite of . . . ?"

"There's no reason to say 'in spite of' any longer. That's all done with."

"Nina, please . . . I don't understand any of this."

"Neither do I. Who knows why we do what we do? But it should be this way, that I *do* know. I thought I would never change my mind about you, that it could never be as it was. Well, it can't, but it can be different than it has been. If you still want it." She put her cigarette down. "Dushkin has moved all my things to your apartment by now. You can throw me out again if you like."

"I'm not going to throw you out. My God, how can you say such a thing?"

"We have both been very cruel to each other," she said.

He took one lurching step toward her and enfolded her in his arms. The flaps of his coat opened and she was gone. His glasses slipped off and fell to the floor, the lenses unbroken. He did not stoop to retrieve them. On his homely face there was an expression impossible to interpret, part joy, part unbearable suffering.

He found her mouth. For the first time in almost three years.

Kurenko was standing next to the pilot, Nikiforov, when the open-backed car carrying the general moved out of the headquarters compound toward the waiting lines of troops on the drill field. The sun had edged a little further out from behind the clouds and a pale wintry light now bathed the entire field. The wind, bitter and chill from the east, took hold of the guidons and snapped them out full length with a sound like little firecrackers going off.

Kurenko's mood was black. He gritted his teeth and looked up despairingly. He was at an absolute loss to know what to do. He hadn't had enough time even to make an approach much less begin to convince the general to give it up. No one had contacted him. No one had given him any instructions. Surely Budyankov had not intended for things to come to this pass. What was he expected to do now? For all he knew, he was once again considered an enemy of the state.

He could see the general standing up straight in the back of the slowly moving car as it swung into a position from which Golitsyn could troop the line. Schreiber-Hartstein sat in front, next to the driver. Then Kurenko saw that the general was not alone. There was someone else there, sitting at first, then rising as the car made a sharp turn and began to move across the brigade front.

It was Nina Andreyeva.

As she rose and her hair caught the wind and billowed out behind her, Nikiforov uttered a gasp of astonishment.

"Well, who would have believed it . . . the *bitch*. . . ."

The troops began to cheer. Discipline vanished and a loud, utterly Russian "Hurrah" split the air.

They had all known, down to the last man. There were no secrets at Dabendorf and least of all were there any secrets about General Golitsyn.

Kurenko could barely restrain himself. Some of the soldiers nearest him, flat-faced peasants who could not possibly understand the complexity of what was happening just then, had tears in their eyes.

"Hurrah . . ." A second time. The cry rang out again. A hundred caps sailed into the air.

Kurenko's heart sank; it was the end. What could possibly be accomplished now? Budyankov, in spite of himself, had given Golitsyn the one real anchor he needed. And he, Vassily Gregorovitch Kurenko, had failed utterly to stop it.

If he had ever had any chance at all, it was surely gone now.

The cry rang out a third time. The caps fell, dotting the field.

The general smiled, then rubbed at his eyes, overcome.

Schreiber-Hartstein rose and held both arms over his head. The soldiers shouted again.

Then the Balt turned sideways to the general, who, in a gesture totally uncharacteristic of him, had actually put his arm around his wife's shoulder. With his free hand, Golitsyn brandished the paper upon which he had written his address and began to speak.

"Friends . . . brothers . . . Russians . . ."

Once again the troops gave way to their emotions and shouted their lungs out.

When silence had at last returned to Dabendorf field, Golitsyn went on in a voice shaken with passion.

"Friends and brothers . . . shall I stand here before you and tell you that which you already know all too well? Yet it must be said again and again and again. Bolshevism is the enemy of all the Russian peoples. It has brought incalculable misery to our country and has plunged the Russian people into a bloody war for reasons that may never be clear to us. Millions have died, millions will yet die, all in the service of Stalin's criminal attempt to dominate the world. Old men, children, women, have died from hunger and disease, from cold, from unbearable overwork. Millions of your comrades in arms have perished in defeats unparalleled in our history. One battle after another has been lost. Not because your comrades lacked valor, not because they were not ready to sacrifice their lives for their land, but because their leaders have betrayed them time after time. . . ."

And Vassily Gregorovitch Kurenko, despite himself, felt a catch in his throat, an emotion almost as powerful as the black, absolute certainty of doom that had taken hold of his heart.

12

As a loyal son of my native land, I voluntarily enter the ranks of the Russian Liberation Army and solemnly swear that I will fight sincerely against Bolshevism and for the welfare of my people. In this struggle, which is being waged on the side of the German and allied armies against the common foe, I pledge Adolf Hitler, as Leader and Commander in Chief of the Liberation Armies, fidelity and unconditional obedience. I am prepared at all times to risk my life for this oath.

Oath for Auxiliaries
Regulation 5000

It was the second anniversary of the death of Schreiber-Hartstein's wife. Just two years before, she had lost her long battle against cancer in a small room in the Charité Hospital. He could remember that room so clearly, the cold, antiseptic smells, the sharp odor of vomit that hung over the bed. He tried to put it out of his mind as he watched the Russians go through their exercises on the drill field. It was no good. There were days when the thought of death was with him always. He could smell it, feel it in the dampness of the air. Sooner or later, he knew, he would have to give in to it.

The engineer officers were training a company in the erection of portable bridges under fire. Zhilinsky, a captain's stripe on his shoulder tabs, was shouting orders and waving his riding crop in the air. His shrill voice carried like an air-raid siren through the dark, wintry air. From the east came a cold, sour wind, bringing with it a faint smell of late snow.

Schreiber-Hartstein pulled his coat more tightly about his chest. He thought he smelled vomit in the air.

Nearby, Kreppel was reading a map he had spread out on the

hood of the command car that had brought the OKH contingent out from Berlin. In the shed, Obriyan and Nikiforov, the pilot, were beginning to work out a rough plan for the glider assault. A dozen others were busy with the support planning, the equipment lists, the radio gear that would be required, the special firearms needed for a quick, devastating attack. They were like new men; suddenly they were flooded with energy. Ukrainsky, the de facto quartermaster, and Sakonchik, the radio chief, had been working without sleep since midafternoon of the day before. Schreiber-Hartstein had never seen such enthusiasm and so violent a change in men before. He could understand it, intellectually, but somehow could not feel it. His spirit was buoyed, but his body was tired. He felt his age, in his arms, in the back of his neck. . . .

And, more and more, he thought of his dead wife.

What would she have said if she could have seen him at that moment? Certainly, she would have approved. She might even have pushed him farther in the direction of real opposition than he'd already gone. When he considered his actions, now, he felt almost ashamed of himself. He'd taken the easy way out. It had all been clever but superficial. He'd really done nothing but soothe his conscience. Not once had he really exposed himself to danger.

He shuddered. Perhaps that was all he'd ever be able to do.

Just then, he heard someone calling his name. It was Stalkov, at the door of the shed.

"What is it, Boris Trifomovitch?"

"A problem, Captain."

"Problems can be solved. Most of them, at least. Let's see what it is this time."

Schreiber-Hartstein went into the shed. The long, low room was full of smoke and the pungent aroma of ersatz coffee. The map table was littered with papers. As Schreiber-Hartstein came into the room, Nikiforov, stocky and red-faced, looked up and shook his head.

"Well?" said Schreiber-Hartstein. "What is it?"

"These," Stalkov replied, handing him a sheaf of closely typed papers on the Abwehr letterhead. "They came about an hour ago, by courier. We've been asking for them all day."

"Weather reports?"

"Exactly. Read them and you'll see at once what the problem is."

Schreiber-Hartstein frowned. He glanced up and down the lines of numbers. Wind speeds, degrees, averages, altitudes. What did it all mean? He sat down at the table and spread the papers out in front of him.

"Boris Trifomovitch . . . I don't understand all this."

"It's the ice," said Nikiforov. "Zhilinsky was wrong. We might have guessed. Either that or they're having a freak period of weather. It's clear, the operation will have to be put off."

"How long?"

"Permanently, or until next winter. Look at those figures."

"I'm looking at them. What am I supposed to see?"

Stalkov sighed, drew in a deep breath, and began to speak. His tone was that of an adult explaining something quite obvious to an especially stupid child.

"As you know, Captain, the gliders must land on the ice under cover of the mist. On the *ice*. That's the point. Behind the peninsula."

"Yes?"

"The question is, can the ice take the landing impact? If the lake is frozen over, solid, the answer is, yes. Marginally. At this time of year, Zhilinsky assured us, the lake would still be frozen. But here, look at these readings. Do they suggest to you that the ice at Byeleymostnoy will be strong enough in a week? In two weeks?"

"It's impossible to consider putting off the operation," said Schreiber-Hartstein. "Any day, permission could be rescinded. . . ."

"Are you willing to take a chance with five hundred, perhaps a thousand men? Would it be better to lose them all before a shot could be fired?"

"But these reports, Boris Trifomovitch . . . they don't apply at all. I hadn't noticed. They show unusually warm weather, yes. But not at the lake itself. Here, look where the readings were taken. Am I right, this is at least two hundred kilometers to the west? The elevations are vastly different. There are mountains between the lake and the weather station. . . ."

"I know that," Stalkov said.

"It would be suicidal," put in Nikiforov.

For a moment, there was absolute silence. Only the hiss of oil lamps could be heard. Schreiber-Hartstein felt sick. Stalkov was right, of course. How could he take such a chance? Even if he ordered them to go, would they obey? And if they mutinied? What a disaster that would be.

Stalkov put a hand on Schreiber-Hartstein's shoulder.

"There's one way, Captain."

"And that is?"

"Someone must go in. Perhaps the ice is thick enough. Perhaps these reports aren't good enough. We must have reliable information. We haven't got it. It's as simple as that. . . . We have to go and get what we need. There, in the middle of the lake. And nowhere else."

"That's insane, Boris Trifomovitch."

"No more insane than risking a landing without knowing how thick the ice really is. Are you ready to do that?"

"No, no. You're right, of course. Wait, let me think a moment. Send someone in? Who? . . . It would have to be by parachute. Abwehr might . . ."

"If you want my advice, you won't breathe a word of this to anyone. And certainly not to Abwehr. If your opponents get wind of the problem . . ."

Schreiber-Hartstein nodded. Stalkov was right there too. One word in the wrong place could ruin everything. Generally speaking, the Abwehr people were on his side, Admiral Canaris in particular. But one couldn't be sure. There was no such thing as real security.

"So what do you suggest?"

"One of us," Stalkov said slowly.

Schreiber-Hartstein stared at him. "You, I suppose? Is that what you're suggesting?"

"If you wish."

Schreiber-Hartstein laughed gratingly, an exhausted, desperate, grinding sound that shook everyone in the room by its harshness.

"Drop you in there? Talk of risks . . . with all you know?"

"You think I'd go back over?"

"It's possible, isn't it?"

"All right. If you don't trust me. . . ."

"No, no . . . damn it." Schreiber-Hartstein flushed. "How can I not trust you? I've asked you to trust *me* all this while, to put yourselves in my hands. And you've done so. How can I say, now . . ."

"Think about it. But not for too long."

Schreiber-Hartstein nodded. He crumpled the offending weather reports into a ball and threw them on the floor.

"I'll speak to you in the morning. It can wait until then. I'm too tired to think clearly now."

"In the morning then."

"If you decide, yes, there will have to be two men. One should be an engineer or an artillery officer. Someone who can use instruments."

Schreiber-Hartstein was silent for a long while. Then he got up and went over to the window of the shed. He looked out across the field to where the men were drilling, bolting iron trestles together, hurtling over barricades, shouting, swinging from ropes

"In the morning, Boris Trifomovitch. You'll have my answer then."

With a shy, hesitant expression on his face, the bulky newspaper-wrapped package he had carried into the room still under his arm, Schreiber-Hartstein sat down at the end of the shabby sofa in Alexander Semyonovitch's front room and lit a cigarette.

Then, with embarrassed afterthought, for his mind was obviously elsewhere, he offered the pack to the general.

Golitsyn shook his head and extracted his pipe from the pocket of his tunic.

"Well, Reinhardt Gavrilovitch . . . what's on your mind?"

Schreiber-Hartstein studied his boots and shifted the package nervously.

"Don't take this amiss, Alexander Semyonovitch, but we thought, that is—*I* thought, actually—that perhaps all of this was becoming too heavy a strain on you and that . . ."

Golitsyn allowed himself a rueful smile.

"To say that it is all a strain, Reinhardt Gavrilovitch, is putting it very diplomatically. What else could it possibly be? To you and to you only can I speak the truth, and the truth is that what I am doing now I do only with the greatest hesitation. Of course it creates a great strain. It is not easy to know that two hundred million people consider you a traitor. . . ."

"I understand," Schreiber-Hartstein said in a barely audible voice.

"Perhaps you do, perhaps you don't. I think, though, that you do, which is why I consider you a friend. Nevertheless, it is very hard for me. I no longer know what is right. Only what is wrong."

Schreiber-Hartstein sighed. "You need to take your mind off all of this, Alexander Semyonovitch. Even if only for a few hours. If you wish, consider it a night out. To celebrate."

Without further ado, Schreiber-Hartstein reached into the pocket of his tunic and, resting one elbow on the arm of the sofa, he extracted a small yellow envelope and held it out to Golitsyn.

"What's this, Reinhardt Gavrilovitch?"

"You may think me foolish, but I hope, at least, that you will understand my motives."

Puzzled, Alexander Semyonovitch opened the envelope and took out two small white slips of paper covered with printing.

"Tickets? But tickets for what?"

"For the variety at the Plaza. I thought it might take your mind off our—problems—for a while."

Alexander Semyonovitch's gray face widened into a broad grin; the idea was so absurd and unexpected that he could not help but be delighted.

"But," he said, "even so . . . how can I possibly go?" He indicated his threadbare Soviet uniform. "After all, a Russian general attending a Berlin circus is bound to cause a commotion, wouldn't you agree?"

Schreiber-Hartstein pointed to the package.

"I am embarrassed, Alexander Semyonovitch. I did the best that I could, and believe me, it was not an easy thing to find something . . . *anything* in your size."

Alexander Semyonovitch undid the string and turned back the newspaper revealing a neatly folded suit of civilian clothes, shabby and worn from too much cleaning.

Schreiber-Hartstein looked away; he knew exactly what Golitsyn was thinking: This man wishes me to lead a Russian army of a million men against Stalin and he cannot provide me with a proper suit of clothes. God help us all.

Schreiber-Hartstein said, "I've had a few dresses sent to Nina Andreyeva's room and . . . a few cosmetics too. . . . I hope I've picked out the right things. I'm not too expert in such matters, you understand."

Alexander Semyonovitch began to laugh—a booming, mirthful explosion that went on until the tears were streaming down his cheeks. Schreiber-Hartstein was startled. There was a harsh edge to the laughter that caused a chill to travel down his back.

Dushkin, alarmed, stuck his head in through the doorway to see what was going on.

"Osip, Osip . . . see if you can find Nina Andreyeva, will you?" the general exclaimed. "We're going . . ." He stopped short.

"Yes, comrade General?"

"To the circus, Osip. The circus."

And he began laughing again, uncontrollably, as though he would never stop.

The posters on the walls outside the Plaza Variety showed a woman in a green tunic and red calf-length stockings doing a handstand on the back of a prancing horse. Underneath were written the words *"Kraft durch Freude"*—Strength through Joy.

"The circus, Sasha?" exclaimed Nina Andreyeva, holding tight to her husband's arm; he had not told her up until then where they were going. He had only mentioned that Schreiber-Hartstein had arranged for an evening out, the first since they had arrived in Berlin.

"How could I refuse? After all the trouble that poor Reinhardt Gavrilovitch went to?"

She looked around warily at the Berliners streaming by into the crowded foyer of the theater. There was a uniformity of feature and coloring about them that she found instantly repellent, in a way that had nothing to do with the fact that they were the enemy. The same pale white faces, the same consistently slack, lusterless hair. Even the women, with their sharp scarlet mouths and rouged cheeks, looked like lifeless mannequins. Perhaps that very lifeless quality was what accounted for the ferocity of their behavior. It was as if they sensed that they had to make up for the way they were, to convince themselves that they were really alive, in a way that a Russian would never find necessary.

From within the auditorium they could hear the pit orchestra playing some kind of a march, not a heavy military march but a jaunty circus tune, very much like the "Parade of the Gladiators." The posters in the foyer announced a dizzying profusion of acts: singers, comedians, jugglers, acrobats.

They went inside, unaccompanied. They had taken the underground from a station near the head of Viktoriastrasse. The tunnels and platforms were littered with mattresses and blankets, where many people slept regularly because of the air raids. The tunnels were far better than the shelters. A bunker on the Alexanderplatz had taken a direct hit the week before and everyone in it had been killed.

When Golitsyn had asked Schreiber-Hartstein how it was that he was being allowed to go out without an escort, Schreiber-Hartstein had appeared injured.

"You *must* understand, Alexander Semyonovitch—you are our guest. Our ally. You are not a prisoner."

"No," Golitsyn had replied. "No more than you are, I suppose."

The theater was crowded. No raid was expected that evening. The seven o'clock news broadcast had announced that the cowardly English had thought better of it, having lost more than twenty bombers to the brave pilots of the Luftwaffe the night before over Kassel. And there was no sign of the Americans whatsoever. The announcer had then played *"Wir fahren gegen England"* and signed off, giving way to a program of song requests from servicemen.

The variety show was already in progress. Members of the audience came and went up and down the aisles. It was, in fact, more like a real circus than a theatrical performance. The lights were only partly dimmed, permitting Alexander Semyonovitch a good look at the Berliners sitting all around him. The white spotlights that lanced down from the rear of the theater, high above the balcony, etched deep shadows into the faces of the people on either side of him, illuminating the flat planes of their foreheads, the cheekbones, the powdered noses of the women, and giving them all a spectral, otherworldly look. How desperately they all seemed to be trying to look as though the war were not going on at all, as though everything was as it had been five years before, or ten.

On stage, a quartet of young girls was just finishing a musical number. It was a familiar song, one that Alexander Semyonovitch had heard on the Berlin radio many times since he had been there. The master of ceremonies stood to one side, a short, stocky man with a face that shaded off from geniality into obsequiousness. As the girls, identified by a signboard on a tripod at the side of the stage as the Bachmann sisters, concluded their song, the master of ceremonies signaled the audience for applause. The audience responded with what seemed excessive enthusiasm. Everyone around the general seemed flushed with sudden pleasure, whereas a moment before they had been uniformly apathetic.

Nina Andreyeva pressed her elbow into her husband's side. "Please, Sasha . . . applaud too. . . . They'll notice you otherwise."

Already the elderly man occupying the seat next to Golitsyn was giving him odd sideways glances.

Notice him? thought Alexander Semyonovitch. . . . What an odd thing to say. Of course they would notice him. He was a head taller, at least, than anyone else in the theater. And the geography of his face was so different from that of the Berliners around him that he might as well have been a Martian. Already he felt that some of them were staring at him—soldiers in uniform on leave from the *Ostfront,* who knew perfectly well what a Russian face looked like.

A magician came out on stage, decked out in traditional top hat and evening clothes, and began a running patter that was so fast that Alexander Semyonovitch was able to pick out only a few isolated phrases. The audience responded to almost everything the man said with staccato bursts of laughter.

When they laughed, Alexander Semyonovitch thought, the pretense to normalcy deserted them at once. The reality was there in the laughter, which was at its sharpest, as best as he could tell, when the comedian-magician said something cruel.

How am I deceiving myself? he thought. Is it possible to deal with these people? Or is it only because Reinhardt Gavrilovitch is really a Russian in his soul—yes, a Russian by birth too—that I am able to believe in him? But the others are like *these* people, only worse. How can I deceive myself that it is any different than it has ever been with these people, these Germans?

A cold chill of foreboding took hold of him and he began to shiver faintly, which, in a man of his size, was instantly noticeable.

"Sasha," Nina Andreyeva whispered, "are you sick? Let me touch your forehead."

"No, no, it's all right," he said. The elderly gentleman with the thick mustache sitting next to him turned more than he had before and glared. A young woman with bobbed blond hair, sitting directly in front of them, turned and hissed at them to be quiet.

The magician performed his tricks, making balls disappear in midair and a flock of pigeons fly from his handkerchief. The audience applauded enthusiastically again.

It was like that, Alexander Semyonovitch thought. Things were made to vanish and they were really still there. Things were made to appear and they were not there. It was all illusion. The magician knew that it was all a trick; the others convinced themselves that it was real. They believed in the illusions, and they applauded.

The pit orchestra began to play a march of the kind the general had heard when entering the theater. The rear curtains were hauled up and away to enlarge the stage area. The master of ceremonies, still standing on the side of the stage apron, said something, and the audience began to applaud again.

The spotlights crisscrossed on center stage and grew even brighter while the orchestra drummed out its march.

Then a slender young woman pranced out onto the stage, high stepping, dressed in a red top adorned with rows of bright brass buttons which left her arms and part of her breasts bare. She wore a short black skirt and high red leather boots and carried a long whip with a loop at the end of it.

The music boomed. The master of ceremonies urged the audience to applaud even more loudly. The young woman bowed, snapped her whip, and from the opposite side of the stage lumbered an enormous brown bear with a leather muzzle over its mouth.

The bear walked on its hind legs over to the woman in the red boots. She snapped her whip again and the bear began to dance.

Alexander Semyonovitch looked away. Why, he could not tell. Surely he had seen trained bears often enough in his life. Every provincial circus in Russia had its own trained bears. Yet he felt a chill again and his hands began to sweat.

The trainer beat her whip on the ground and the bear lumbered forward, fell to all fours, and then executed a slow, painful stand on its forelegs. The animal remained in that position for some seconds while the audience howled with laughter.

Alexander Semyonovitch looked not at the woman, whose mouth was set hard in a thin crimson line, but at the animal's eyes. He could see them clearly enough from where they sat. They glinted like fire in the spotlights. The bear was not looking down but out toward the audience.

Then the trainer rapped the animal on the back of its head with the end of the whip and the bear dropped its hindquarters. An assistant came out with a tray of bottles, one of which the trainer picked up with the loop on the end of her whip and held out to the animal.

The look of hatred in the bear's eyes had not diminished. The muzzle alone would never have stopped an animal of that size from tearing the taunting woman limb from limb. His paws, with their long, razor-sharp claws, were all the weapon he needed. And his weight. Yet there was something that did stop him, and he stood up again on his hind legs and waved his paws, then clapped them together, begging for the bottle dangling in front of him.

Alexander Semyonovitch looked away, suffocated. He could not stand to feel the animal's yellow eyes boring into him as though they were searchlights. He could not delude himself any longer. They both responded, performed, willingly . . . though both had the strength to refuse.

"This is . . . impossible," he exclaimed in a stifled voice and jumped to his feet. People turned and stared. Nina Andreyeva pulled at his arm.

"No, no, let go of me," he protested, trying to force his way past and into the aisle.

The bear began to caper about on the stage and the woman in the red boots slapped her whip against the stage floor. The orchestra continued to play merrily.

The look on Alexander Semyonovitch's face was so terrifying that almost none of those who turned to stare at him were able to say a word. Only one woman snapped at him as he pushed by her, causing her to drop some of the sweets she had been eating.

Alexander Semyonovitch rushed up the aisle, his wife directly behind him. If he did not reach the exit, if he could not gain the outside air in another few seconds, he knew he would be sick.

"A madman . . ." someone said.

He slipped and fell to his knees just at the head of the aisle. Nina Andreyeva, a stricken look on her face, helped him to his feet. An usher, in some sort of a brown uniform with gold piping like an admiral's, started over.

"No, no, it's all right. . . ."

They pushed through the doors at the rear of the auditorium and into the empty foyer. The ticket windows were closed, the gratings down. Alexander Semyonovitch pulled at his collar. Sweat was pouring down his face.

"The bear, Nina . . ." he whispered.

She nodded. Poor Reinhardt Gavrilovitch, she thought. No matter what else he was, he had tried to be a decent man. He must not know what had happened. He would feel so guilty if he knew.

The street was thick with pedestrians. A movie palace was doing heavy business just down the street. The hoardings in front of the theater were covered with huge stills of women in operetta ball gowns.

Alexander Semyonovitch stood there, watching the crowds go in, seeing nothing. Slowly, his breathing returned to normal, the pallor in his face replaced by his normal ruddy coloring.

Finally, he tried to smile, took Nina Andreyeva by the hand, and without a word they walked back through the streets, very slowly, to Viktoriastrasse.

Beifelder burst into Schreiber-Hartstein's office without even knocking.

"Reinhardt, you'd better come downstairs. There's something you should see. At once."

Schreiber-Hartstein stood up, startled, apprehensive.

"No, no," Beifelder reassured him. "I think it's going to be very helpful."

Schreiber-Hartstein followed Beifelder downstairs to the map room. Gottinger was waiting for them by a large horizontal map board. He held a small packet of signal tissues in his right hand.

"It's exactly as it seemed at first," Gottinger said as the two men entered the room.

Beifelder said, "Reichminister Rosenberg has given his permission for the attack, correct?"

"Correct," agreed Schreiber-Hartstein, puzzled.

"But there are reservations nevertheless?"

"Also correct. Which is why we must move quickly. Keitel's office is still very resistant. I understand that the Feldmarschall is furious. He hasn't done anything yet but I'm told he's been swearing at me nonstop for days—for going over his head. He'd like to sack me, or worse, I'm sure. But now he doesn't dare."

"Do you want to change all that?" asked Beifelder with a sly smile.

"What do you mean, Martin?"

"Look here—and then tell me if you don't agree. You can have Keitel's support on a silver platter. He'll do anything to curry favor with Himmler, won't he? Well, I think we've just been handed a perfect set of circumstances. . . ."

As the three of them bent over the map table, and Schreiber-Hartstein followed the tip of Gottinger's pointer, he began to grin, his normally sober face lit by an expression just this side of malicious.

"I see exactly what you mean," he said quietly.

"I thought you would."

Field Marshal Keitel jumped up from behind his desk, his face flaming with indignation.

"You dare show yourself in here, Hauptmann? Before *me*?"

Schreiber-Hartstein saluted briskly. "The appointment was arranged properly, Feldmarschall. Naturally, I assumed that if the Feldmarschall did not wish to see me, then . . ."

"What I wish to do is to send you to Flossenberg, that's what I wish. You and your whole damned crew."

Schreiber-Hartstein maintained a tranquil impervious facade. "If the Feldmarschall wishes, I shall withdraw."

"What the devil did you come in here for in the first place, Hartstein? I admit that under the circumstances it takes a certain amount of gall, and I suppose I've got to respect you for that at least. So, speak up. Why aren't you off with that degenerate Slav rabble of yours, disobeying my explicit orders?"

"The Feldmarschall may perhaps reconsider his opinion if . . ."

"The devil I will—"

"—if the Feldmarschall cares to look at this map."

Without waiting for Keitel to signal him to proceed, Schreiber-Hartstein spread out a small map of the Byeleymostnoy area on the field marshal's desk and pointed to a small blue cross about sixty kilometers to the southwest of the Russian camp.

"If the Feldmarschall will note—"

"What's that? The blue cross?" Keitel asked suspiciously.

"That cross is a unit of the Sixteenth Panzer Grenadier, Waffen SS. They've been cut off without ammunition or supplies in the woods there for more than three weeks. With no hope, I might add, of their getting out, considering their present strength and the level of their supplies."

"The Sixteenth?" A glimmer of understanding flickered across the field marshal's flinty face.

"The Sixteenth, sir. I can see that the Feldmarschall recalls the

Sixteenth. The most decorated unit in the Waffen SS, I believe. Knight's Crosses by the barrelful."

"Major Dietrich?" suggested Keitel hesitantly.

"Precisely, Feldmarschall. The very same Major Dietrich who was decorated by Reichführer SS Himmler's own hand two months ago. Oak clusters. The same Major Dietrich whom the Führer himself . . ."

"All right, enough."

"—the very same," Schreiber-Hartstein went on. "One can be quite sure that the Reichführer SS would be very grateful to anyone who could rescue Major Dietrich and his men from their present predicament."

"And you propose?" Keitel's eyes had narrowed until the pupils had almost vanished. The crafty expression that had taken hold of his features was close to comical in its lack of subtlety.

"To bring him out, Feldmarschall. Once we've released the prisoners at the Byeleymostnoy installation, we'll be more than strong enough to do the job. A little extra equipment and ammunition should be no problem. My Slavs have strong backs."

"Are you blackmailing me, by any chance, Hartstein?"

"I am merely suggesting an extension of our operation. One that could have the most significant consequences."

"For me—" Keitel said quickly. "You bastard, you're smart, aren't you? Smarter than I ever would have guessed, Hartstein."

Schreiber-Hartstein bit his lip. The two men understood each other perfectly. There was no need for any further discussion. The deal had already been made.

Keitel sat back heavily, his face split by a wide, malicious grin. "All right, you win, Hartstein. You win. You will have my complete support. Whatever you need. You may tell Reichminister Rosenberg that he need have no fear that I'll do anything to upset your plans. I may even put in a good word for you with Himmler, who knows?" He reached into a desk drawer and pulled out a bottle. "A little *Schnaps,* Hauptmann? You've earned it, I'd say."

Finally, and only over his muttered protest, she turned on a single lamp. The general had been standing in the dark by the window ever since they had returned. She thought that she was going crazy.

"I must have light, Sasha, I simply must."

"Isn't that what Goethe said just before he died? I must have light?"

"Sasha, for God's sake, calm yourself," Nina Andreyeva cried. It seemed as though it had been at least an hour since Alexander Semyonovitch had come stumbling up the stairs back into his apartment, but he had not yet stopped shaking. Thank God none of the others had seen him.

"How am I to be calm, tell me? I *know* what I am. I know what has happened to me. Oh, Ninotchka, what am I to do? I can see no right way. There is not one single road open to me."

Her voice was low and choked, her speech very rapid. She was deathly afraid of him now. In all the years she had known him, since that day in the stables at Strasneshev, she had never seen him behave this way. Morose, yes, depressed, often. But never once as close to the brink of hysteria as he was at that moment. It was a terrible thing to see a man as physically large as Alexander Semyonovitch lose control of himself in such a way.

"Some tea, Sasha? Tea or hot milk? You always liked hot milk before going to bed. With a lot of sugar, yes? Lots of sugar. I'll find some sugar, I swear I will."

Then she was gone from the room, as fast as she could go, not because it was important to fetch the milk quickly, which it was not, of course, but because she could not stand to remain there a second longer.

The moment she had gone, he slumped against the window, the cold pane against his forehead. His temples were pounding. He felt like a condemned man waiting for the bullets of the firing squad. There was absolutely no way out. Nothing he could possibly do now could make any difference.

He had been wrong all of his life, in everything. Wrong to have believed in the revolution and the men who had made it, wrong to have believed in Stalin, wrong to have believed in the rational, gentle Balt with the schoolteacher's face. Worst of all, wrong to believe in himself.

What was he to do? Which way was he to turn?

He heard footsteps outside the door. How had Nina Andreyeva managed to return so quickly? He shut his eyes. Whoever it was would find their way in.

The door opened, closed.

"General?"

It was Kurenko's voice. What was he to do with Kurenko? He shuddered, opened his eyes, and dropped his hands from his face, trying to compose himself.

"*Bozhe moy*," breathed Kurenko, catching sight of Alexander Semyonovitch's face in the dim, covered lamplight. "Are you ill—what's the matter with you?"

"What do you want here?" Alexander Semyonovitch said hollowly.

"Let me help you. . . ."

Before he could do anything to prevent it, Alexander Semyonovitch found himself being led from the wall to the sofa. Gently, Kurenko helped him to sit.

"Shall I call a doctor? You look . . ."

"Never mind about doctors," Alexander Semyonovitch said.

"Nina Andreyeva, then?"

"She's gone down for milk. Isn't that amusing, Vassily Gregorovitch? Hot milk, with sugar in it. For me."

"General . . . if you please . . ." Kurenko's face was ashen. He had been caught completely unaware by the general's condition and had no idea what to do.

Suddenly Alexander Semyonovitch smiled. The smile, as he saw it reflected back at him in the cracked mirror over the spinet, seemed touched with a faint insanity that he thought entirely appropriate.

He reached out and took Kurenko's arm in a sudden, reassuringly firm grip. The expression on the young man's face was that of a child who has just seen his father go mad; he had seen such a child once, and just such a look, on the streets of Canton. The old man had been dancing and banging his forehead with a wooden clapper while the child stood by, horrified, realizing that he had suddenly been cast adrift, that he had nothing to hold on to any longer.

He could not let that happen.

With a tremendous effort he managed to control himself. As his breath began to come more easily and he ceased to tremble, he realized how strange it was that he had been able to make the effort for Kurenko whereas he had not been able to do so for Nina Andreyeva.

His voice, when he spoke, was firm.

"So, tell me . . . why are you here?"

Kurenko was not so easily put off. "Are you sure you're all right, General? Perhaps a doctor should be summoned. Dushkin can call, or we could have Obriyan look at you. He has some medical knowledge. If it's nothing . . ."

"It *is* nothing. Nothing, that is, that can be cured. And nothing, I suppose, that I will die of either." The general reached out for a carafe on the table. "Will you join me? Reinhardt Gavrilovitch was good enough to find me some Scotch whiskey. Excellent stuff. English, I think."

Kurenko nodded dully. What else could he do?

"I came to talk to you," he said. "But it seems that I picked the wrong time."

"No time is the right time, no time is the wrong time. Whatever you have to say, Vassily Gregorovitch, please to say it now."

He handed Kurenko a tumbler of whiskey, took one himself, and drained it with a shudder.

Kurenko looked away. He had no idea how to begin. Though he had rehearsed his opening words a thousand times in the past weeks, he found now that he had forgotten everything.

"Comrade General . . ." he stammered, at once aware that he had not used that form of address since arriving at Viktoriastrasse.

"Ah," said Alexander Semyonovitch. "So it's *that,* is it?"

Kurenko averted his eyes. "I meant nothing by . . ."

"Yes, you did. I can hear it in your voice. Oh yes, I can hear it, Vassily Gregorovitch."

Just then the door opened again and Nina Andreyeva came in with a tray and a jug of steaming milk.

"What is *he* doing here?" she exclaimed, realizing at once that a tremendous change had taken place since she had left, that Alexander Semyonovitch had somehow retreated from the edge of hysteria and was now sitting with Kurenko, calm, self-possessed, as if nothing at all had happened. Drinking whiskey.

She felt as though she'd been made a fool of.

"I believe that Vassily Gregorovitch has come to try and talk me out of what I have so foolishly agreed to do, isn't that right, Vassily Gregorovitch?"

"General, I haven't said a word yet . . ." Kurenko protested. "How can you know?"

"You see, Nina? I was right, wasn't I? I can still see a few things clearly. A few, a very few. But those things that I *can* see, I see very clearly. Yes, quite clearly." He reached out and took the cup of hot milk that she held out to him. "Sit, Nina. There are no secrets here. It is a relief to know where Vassily Gregorovitch stands, isn't it? I was concerned, very concerned, for him."

Alexander Semyonovitch turned to Kurenko and held up a cautionary hand. "You are young. Very young, if I may say so. The war has not aged you even as much as it has most others like you. I'm not an old man, but there are some things I can understand still." He leaned back against the threadbare violet pillows of the sofa. "So, tell me what you've come to tell me, Vassily Gregorovitch. Or shall I tell you not to bother?"

"Not to bother? I don't understand. What does that mean, not to bother?"

"Don't play the fool," Nina Andreyeva snapped. "You know exactly what he means."

"Perhaps he doesn't," said Alexander Semyonovitch. "Perhaps I don't myself." His voice was distant, hollow. Nina Andreyeva began to grow alarmed again.

"I simply wish to ask you to consider what you're doing," said Kurenko, very quietly. "Here, in this house, I know how things must seem to you. But . . . if you knew . . ." He lowered his head. "What are we to do? What can I possibly say that would mean anything? I will tell you about the deportations. You will already know. I will tell you about the massacres, the burnings, the destruction. All of this you already know far better than I do. For every argument I make, you will have an answer. How could it be otherwise, comrade General? I *know* what you have seen. I know what you've been through yourself. The trouble is that there is no lesser of two evils here. There is simply no choice." He let out a long, anguished groan. "How could they possibly have expected me to . . ."

"They?"

Nina Andreyeva turned angrily on Kurenko, her fists clenched. Suddenly the general began to laugh.

"They? Of course, *they*. Who else would it have been? Are we all children, to believe in such providential accidents as your finding your way clear across two countries to this wretched place?

'They' . . . why, of course, '*they*.' " The general's face had gone gray. "You too, Ninotchka? Did *they* send you as well?"

"Sasha, I swear . . ."

"Well, why not? We should all swear, shouldn't we? Swearing is good for the soul. One should have something to swear on, though, shouldn't one? The Bible, a mother's life, one's honor? Without something to swear *on,* it is meaningless to swear." He turned suddenly on Kurenko, rising up from the sofa and almost upsetting the tray. "Tell me, Vassily Gregorovitch, on what should *I* swear? What is left to me on which I could honestly swear, tell me that?"

Two A.M. The doorbell of Schreiber-Hartstein's apartment rang shrilly and insistently. He rolled over in bed, cursing, hoping that it would stop.

Whoever it was had no intention of going away.

He switched on the light and glanced at the clock. He'd been asleep less than three hours. His head ached and his mouth was dry and sour. Finally he gave in, put on his slippers, and went to the door.

It was Beifelder.

"I'm sorry to do this to you, Reinhardt, but I have to speak to you at once."

Schreiber-Hartstein ushered Beifelder into the sitting room of his apartment. Automatically he went to turn on the gas jet under the kettle. Tea, coffee, whatever there was in the cupboard, he had to have something to drink.

"Do you want a whiskey, Martin?"

"Yes, and you'll want one too."

It was at that moment that Schreiber-Hartstein recalled the problem about the ice. Had Beifelder come about that? He poured a whiskey and stood by the range, waiting for the water to boil.

"Come now, it can't be so bad. . . . We've got permission. We have our operation underway and it will be a good one. The SS doesn't dare go against Rosenberg, so what can it be?"

"The Gestapo, I'm afraid. I just got word from our man in Mueller's office."

Schreiber-Hartstein grimaced. He hadn't been prepared for *that.* Suddenly he felt chilled and realized that he was standing there in his pajamas. It was March and there was no heat in the building.

"Something's turned up," Beifelder said, pausing to down his whiskey in one gulp. "It's got to do with that fellow Kurenko, the one who came here with Golitsyn's wife.

"They suspect him of something?"

"I don't know just what it is, Reinhardt, but it's got them jumping about like monkeys on a rock down there."

"What the devil can it be? You're sure you don't know?"

"Wouldn't I tell you if I did? Besides, they probably don't know themselves. It's enough that something's put the scent in their nostrils."

"And we don't know what that 'something' is? No, of course we don't . . . but, damn it, we can't afford a problem like that, not now."

"Suppose they're right? Suppose there *is* something? Shouldn't we try to find out first?"

"And if there was? If he was an agent, a plant? What a pack of fools we'd look like then. That would be the end of everything, I can assure you. Everyone would be suspect, right up to Golitsyn himself. They'd never let us move. Of all the damned times for something like this to happen. . . ."

He turned and without another word stalked into his bedroom. When he returned he was fully dressed. Beifelder could not believe that anyone could have gotten his clothes on so quickly.

"Where are you going?"

"To see that this whole business doesn't blow up in our faces. While I'm at it, see if you can get hold of Major Reiman. I want a plane standing by at Gatow. And call Nikiforov when that's done."

"Nikiforov?"

"Yes, damn it, Nikiforov. Have him get together all the tools and instruments he thinks are needed to check on the problem we were talking about this afternoon. He'll know what I mean." Schreiber-Hartstein paused by the door. "And it's just as well that you don't, at least for the moment."

The sirens had been sounding for more than half an hour but no planes had yet appeared. The city was silent and dark but overhead a hundred searchlight beams scoured the underbellies of the clouds. Somewhere, high above the uppermost reach of the beams, the night fighters circled, waiting for the attack.

Schreiber-Hartstein pulled a handkerchief from his pocket and blew his nose. There was no doubt about it. He was getting a cold. He eased the car cautiously up to the curb in front of number 10 Viktoriastrasse.

The face of the building was dark. Here and there one could detect a faint smudge of light. Some of the inmates had stayed in their rooms, waiting for the first bombs to fall before going down to the cellar.

From somewhere across the street drifted the sound of singing. It was Zarah Leander's throaty voice.

He wondered if Beifelder had succeeded in getting hold of Reiman and if he had been able to do as he'd been asked. Probably not, not with a raid expected at any moment. He stood there for a few seconds, half hoping that a bomb would drop suddenly and definitively. He was sick of worrying, of trying.

Then he went into the building, carefully fitting the keys into the succession of iron locks, opening grates and gates and prowling down familiar vestibules and corridors. The building stank from stale cooking odors. Strange, he had never noticed them before. A radio crackled somewhere, mostly static. Footsteps echoed in the stone corridors and mice scampered through forgotten accumulations of trash.

He found his way to the second-floor room where Kurenko should have been. He was not there. All right; he was probably in the cellar with the others.

He stopped for a moment on the landing, attracted by the sound of voices coming from somewhere upstairs.

He climbed to the next floor. A rat ran by him on the stairs. He kicked at it angrily.

He found himself standing before the large oak door behind which lay Golitsyn's apartment. A smudge of light showed under the door. He fitted a key cautiously to the lock. He had keys for every room in the building, though this was the first time he had ever used any of them.

Voices. In the sitting room at the end of the hallway. He had been right after all. He recognized Golitsyn's somber basso. Nina Andreyeva was there. And a third voice. He listened. It was Kurenko.

He unbuttoned his coat, let his right hand fall on the butt of his Walther, and quickly pushed open the door to the room.

Golitsyn was standing by the window, looking strange and awkward in the suit of civilian clothes that had been brought him earlier that day. He was barely recognizable. His face was contorted, and his eyes were blinking rapidly behind his glasses. Nina Andreyeva sat on the sofa, twisting her hands between her knees. She looked up as Schreiber-Hartstein came into the room and gasped. Kurenko, who was standing near the general, gave a start and began to back away, then checked himself and stood very still.

"Please . . ." Schreiber-Hartstein said, "don't get up, Nina Andreyeva. General. You, Kurenko, stay where you are, if you please. In fact, I would prefer it if you would put both hands out where I can see them."

"What does the captain mean?" Golitsyn protested. Though Schreiber-Hartstein had said nothing specific as yet, his tone conveyed much.

Kurenko, as though he had not heard, started to move away again, his hands for a second obscured by the open fold of his tunic. Schreiber-Hartstein yanked the Walther from its holster and leveled it at him.

"I have no wish to shoot you but I'll do it without hesitation if it's necessary. Now sit down, and keep your hands where I can see them, please."

Outside, the first bomb fell, a dull, drumming sound that might have come from another dimension.

No one seemed to notice.

Golitsyn's face was gray, like the face of a man about to have a heart attack. For a second, Schreiber-Hartstein thought that the man had fallen deathly ill. But he could see clearly enough from the firmness of his movements that there was nothing physically wrong with him. It was equally clear to him, from the expression on Kurenko's face and Nina Andreyeva's high state of agitation, that the two men had been arguing violently when he had burst into the room.

"My apologies," Schreiber-Hartstein said. "It appears that I've interrupted something."

"Nothing nearly as important as whatever it was you came to say to me," Golitsyn replied, his eyes now fixed on the Walther.

"I've never seen you with one of those in your hand before, Reinhardt Gavrilovitch. Why now?"

Schreiber-Hartstein shook his head and holstered the automatic. "There. You see? I trust you both. Both of you. Perhaps I'm a fool. Perhaps we're all fools. At any rate, there's a matter I must discuss with you, at once. Shall I sit down?"

"By all means. And take off your coat. The bombs pose no real danger at the moment, so we may as well be comfortable. Vasya, will you give the captain a cup of hot milk? Or a whiskey, Reinhardt Gavrilovitch?"

"What is it he wants?" Kurenko snapped in Russian.

"Why don't you ask me? I'll tell you quickly enough, Kurenko. It's you I've come to see."

Nina Andreyeva stared and began to say something. The general gestured at her to be silent and she obeyed.

"Am I under arrest?" Kurenko asked quietly.

"Pass me the sugar, will you, General? Please . . . look up, Kurenko. Please look at me when I'm talking to you. That's better now. Yes, you were asking—are you under arrest? Let me ask you, is there any reason that you should be?"

"There is none," said Golitsyn. "Absolutely none."

"The Gestapo seem to think that there is. Can you think why?"

Kurenko was silent. Golitsyn avoided his gaze, looked away. Nina Andreyeva knit her fingers together. Outside, the bombs were falling more frequently now and the antiaircraft guns had begun hammering away.

Schreiber-Hartstein broke the long silence.

"Never mind, Kurenko. It hardly makes any difference. And if there was a reason, how could I expect you to tell me? You're not that much of a fool. No, on the contrary, you strike me as a very clever young man. But something must be done, you realize that, don't you? The very fact that you're suspected could bring down all of our plans. . . ."

Golitsyn leaned forward. "I must warn you, Reinhardt Gavrilovitch, if any harm comes to Vasya I will be forced to reconsider my position here. I will have no alternative but . . ."

"Enough," Schreiber-Hartstein cried. "You talk of alternatives? What are our alternatives? Not to commit ourselves without thinking things through? Do we have any choice but that? To pray that we think clearly and do the right thing? Why do you think I've acted as I have? To help win this insane war? Perhaps, but to win it with some trace of honor left. I will not be a victor in the kind of a war that is being waged now. But if I can be a victor in a war that liberates Russia from a pack of butchers every bit as bad as those who rule *this* country at the moment, then I'll have accomplished something. . . . We'll all have accomplished something if we can do that. But we all must recognize that it's not a simple Manichaean exercise. It's damned complicated. Now sit down, both of you."

His face was almost dead white. The bombs were falling nearer now. They could all hear the steady *pom-pom-pom* of the flak guns.

"I refuse to let this entire operation be ruined because of you, Kurenko. Understand, under no circumstances will I turn you over to those Gestapo thugs. But I have very little room left in which to maneuver. I must remove you. You're under suspicion, God knows why. But that's enough. A storm will gather. It always does when it's possible to put a storm to good use, to get rid of an embarrassment and a threat and, believe me, we are exactly that to those people. There's nothing Keitel or Müller or any of the others down there would like better than to have ten Viktoriastrasse hit by a bomb. The SS would be delighted to turn Dabendorf into a concentration camp. All of this we must prevent."

"What do you propose?" asked Golitsyn cautiously.

"I haven't thought this through. . . . I haven't had time. My head aches, and under other circumstances I would refuse even to try to tell the hour much less to make such a decision, but time is precisely what we don't have." Schreiber-Hartstein drew a deep breath. He was about to take a desperate gamble, a chance like none he had ever taken before in his life. "I'm going to send Kurenko on an important mission. Not alone. He will go with Stalkov, whom I trust implicitly. If he does what he is required to do, he will be a hero by the time the operation is over. If not, he will be dead. It's as simple as that. In the meantime, the integrity of the RONA will be maintained. No one will be able to accuse us of deliberately harboring spies. It will be too late to do anything."

"And what is it you want me to do?" Kurenko asked quietly.

"You already know the outlines of the proposed strike on the camp at Byeleymostnoy. The gliders must land under cover of the mist. On the ice, behind the peninsula. . . ."

"Yes?"

"The question is whether the ice can take the landing impact. It is critical that we know how thick the ice is. We have no information to go on. It must be gathered there, in the middle of the lake and nowhere else. You will go with Stalkov. It's already arranged. The plane should be ready now. You will be taken to the airfield at Nezhin. Then you will be flown to a point just north of the lake. There's an open area there that is ideal for a parachute landing."

"I've never jumped in my life," said Kurenko, horrified.

"Then you'll learn. Very quickly. If you don't kill yourself, you'll go on with Stalkov to the lake. You're an engineer . . . the equipment for calibrating ice thickness should be familiar to you. If not, you can learn to use it in a few hours. Come now. The important thing right now is that you leave."

"At this moment? Now? And if I refuse?"

"You'll go, all right," said Schreiber-Hartstein. "There's no question of that."

Lieutenant Hummel's face was almost completely obscured in darkness; the only light came from the tip of the cigarette he held clenched betwen his teeth. The streets were stygian. There was not a single light on anywhere. It was as if, in one instant, Berlin had ceased to exist. Sirens were wailing from every rooftop. Hummel had switched off the car lights the moment the first siren had sounded. There was no point in being stopped by an Orpo unit or by the military police. People were shot on the spot for showing lights after the sirens had started up.

Hummel had driven in the dark many times before. He was a born Berliner and knew every twist and turn of the city's streets by heart. He could do it blindfolded. And there was no reason to slow down just because the British were coming over again for another night of bombing.

In the backseat of the car, on either side of Schreiber-Hartstein, sat Kurenko and Stalkov, both dressed in regulation army jackets and fur-lined boots. In the trunk of the Mercedes was a haversack full of instruments, auger bits and an odd object that looked to Hummel like a miniature windwill with wires trailing out of its base.

Kurenko sat there motionless, sure that at any moment Hummel was going to drive the car into a wall. He was almost as terrified of Hummel's blind driving as he was by the fact that he had never made a parachute jump before in his life.

Gatow airfield was dark except for the scattered lights from the searchlight batteries that surrounded it. The sky was thick with flak. The first wave of bombers was expected over the city at any moment. The "running commentary" radio had been tracking a huge fleet of Stirlings and Lancasters all the way from Belgium. Over the city, high above the uppermost reach of the searchlights, a swarm of Me-110s and single-engined fighters hovered, waiting to drop down in a *wilde Sau* attack the moment the bombers appeared over the city.

The car drew up before a hangar at the north end of the field, by the farthest gates. The area was pocked with bomb craters from earlier raids. A wrecked Ju-52 stood, nose down, tail up, in skeletal prominence, a blackened hulk not yet removed.

Hummel blew the horn three times. The hangar doors groaned open. They drove inside. Shaded blue lamps flooded the interior with a pale light. A tangle of wires, spare wheels and tires, radio parts, a long workbench, and racks of parachutes and pilots' overalls.

Schreiber-Hartstein could just make out Kreppel and Gottinger standing by the port wing of a twin-engined Junkers Ju-88 bomber, talking to a man in coveralls.

Kreppel called out to him in greeting.

"No trouble?"

"Not so far. Is everything ready here?"

"As ready as can be, considering the circumstances," said Gottinger. "There's no chance of a takeoff for at least an hour. Until our visitors decide to go home."

"We can't chance it. We have to go now."

The pilot shook his head.

"Excuse me, gentlemen," said Kreppel. "This is Lieutenant Bauer, your pilot. You'll be in his capable hands for the next few hours, so you really should be introduced properly. Major Stalkov . . . Captain Kurenko. The rest of us you already know . . . all right, what do you say?"

"It's possible to go now. Risky. But it can be done."

"With the British overhead?"

"Unless they decide on Gatow as a target, there's no reason why not," said Bauer with a grin. "There's light enough from the searchlight batteries for me to see, and no other planes on the runways. Our flak is firing at 14,500 feet and our radar is high level. We should be able to get out under both our own antiaircraft and radar without too much trouble."

"Well then . . . you heard him, gentlemen," said Schreiber-Hartstein. "Let's get on board. You're ready to go, Lieutenant Bauer?"

"We've been waiting for you for an hour, Captain."

Kurenko glanced at Stalkov. He seemed even larger than usual in the blue shadows of the hangar. He was already wearing flyer's boots and a heavy leather jacket and had strapped on an old Mauser machine pistol.

"So, Vassily Gregorovitch, we go back to the motherland a little sooner than we anticipated. Don't worry. It will be a good trip." He smiled, but there was nothing comforting to Kurenko in that smile; it seemed to him, rather, the smile of a bear who is relishing a good meal.

In a moment they had clambered through the hatch. Bauer stayed below for a while longer, poring over a map board with Schreiber-Hartstein, by the light of an electric torch. Then he too climbed in and strapped himself into the pilot's seat.

Suddenly, the Junkers was being rolled out onto the runway. Above, the sky was alive with lights, an aurora borealis of searchlight beams dotted with the constant puffballs of the flak exploding high above.

The two big Jumo engines turned over, a steady, high-pitched whine. The lights in the greenhouse front cabin of the Junkers glowed mysteriously, like a bottle of fireflies. Through the overhead canopy, Kurenko could see the searchlights, the flak, the moon, the endless sky. He could not believe he was where he was, that it had happened, and so rapidly. He had not even had time to take a coat and now realized that his teeth were chattering. He realized, suddenly, that when the plane gained altitude, he would begin to freeze to death. Slowly.

Stalkov turned, saw him hugging his arms around his body, and produced a flight jacket from under the pilot's seat.

Then they were moving along the dark runway, gaining speed. The whine of the motors grew louder, rising in pitch. Kurenko could feel the wings starting to buck against the pressure below them as the plane strained into the air. Then the sound of the landing gear rolling against the runway ceased and the craft lifted, suddenly nosing upward.

"Up we go, gentlemen," cried Bauer cheerfully. Kurenko looked past him, over the forward instrument panel and into the night sky. And in that second, he froze in horror.

An enormous, fiery pinwheel was whirling down almost directly in front of them. At the rate of speed they were going, they would reach it at almost the same instant that it struck the runway. They had no altitude; there was no room to maneuver, to bank out of the way. He heard Bauer shout, saw him lean far back against the seat, swearing, the sweat pouring from his forehead, his face dead white.

Kurenko realized instantly what had happened: One of the British bombers had been hit and was about to crash in flames almost directly on top of them.

The Junkers lunged up into the air, tail down at a forty-five-degree angle. There was a tremendous, slamming explosion. A stream of flaming debris engulfed the cockpit enclosure. It was as though the plane had been thrust into a smelting furnace. Kurenko was thrown across the cabin and rammed into the radio equipment.

Then, suddenly, the flame and the wheeling, fiery debris were gone. The Junkers leveled out, rose gently like a feather into the sky. Around them there was nothing but blackness and—high above—a delicate web of searchlight beams and puffballs.

"Not bad, this crate," came Lieutenant Bauer's voice. "It seems they got the bugs out of her at last."

The plane banked gracefully, and as it began a turn that would put it on course to the east, Kurenko caught one fleeting glimpse of the field far below and the flaming wreck that had nearly carried them with it.

"One in a million," called Bauer. "It should be smooth from here on out, at least as far as I'm going." He turned in his seat, the autopilot already set. "We're going back to Mother Russia, gentlemen. Why don't you smile?"

13

"Get a move on, coachman . . ."
"I can't—the horses, sir, are having heavy going. The snow is sticking to my eyes, and all the roads have vanished. Look for yourself, the trail is gone. We're lost, sir. What shall we do?"

Alexander Pushkin
From *Evil Spirits*

It was bitter cold. The temperature had plummeted again. The mercury was now hovering just below the zero mark. Snow had swept in and covered everything. Not deep, but enough to impede movement and make every kilometer a torture.

Below the low mountains that guarded Lake Byeleymostnoy to the north, a thick pine forest spread out, dropping level by level until it came to the eroded stone cliffs that bordered the lake. The pines grew right up to the edge of the lake so that an unsuspecting traveler on a day when the mist was rising white and thick from the frozen surface of Byeleymostnoy might easily step from the forest straight into the lake itself. And by then, if the ice had not yet firmed, it would be too late. Not until almost fifty meters out from the shore had the wind broomed away enough of the dry, powdery snow so that the ice below could be felt and seen. There were ballads in the villages to the south that told of hunters who had ventured out onto Byeleymostnoy's frozen surface and been dragged under its black waters by the ice demons and the witches that dwelt in the depths.

The Ju-88 had taken Stalkov and Kurenko as far as the airdrome at Minsk. From there they had been flown by a trimotor transport to a temporary airfield near Kharkov where they were left standing by the hangar in a light snow while Lieutenant Bauer, who continued to accompany them, went into the *Gruppe* headquarters building to check the final transport arrangements.

"The bastards might at least have taken us inside for some coffee."

Stalkov grinned. He seemed to like the snow. He stood there, breathing the frigid air in deep, hungry gulps. "They think that we Russians are at home in the snow, that we love this weather."

"They leave their horses out in it too," said Kurenko.

The door of the shed opened and Bauer whistled to them to come in. "A humanitarian," said Kurenko.

Kurenko had never worn a parachute in his life much less jumped, and he had never flown in an open-cockpit plane. Now he was doing both for the first time. He craned his neck. Behind, at a slightly lower elevation, he could see the second of the two Henschel biplanes that were to drop them in the mountains north of the lake. It had been Bauer's idea. The Henschel 123s were being used for routine observation work and low-level support. A few had been modified to a two-seater configuration. They were lightly armed, with only two machine guns mounted to fire through the airscrew, and so obsolete that the Russian patrols usually left them alone. There was little they could do except frighten the unknowing with the terrible noise of their engines. Bauer had radioed ahead from Kharkov and found that the Ninth *Gruppe* at Lebyovka had a full complement of the old planes, including three that had been fitted out with a second seat for photographic use. Perfect. They would fly over the forests in the old biplanes, hugging the trees, almost hidden by the mists that had for days cloaked the woods in a mantle of deep, impenetrable white. When over the target area they would gain just enough altitude to enable their passengers to jump, then drop down again and continue on their way. Undetected.

Kurenko and Stalkov had been given white jump suits that approximated the usual Russian winter coveralls that Kurenko had been wearing up until the episode of Kolabyansk. Skis were out of the question, although they would have made the descent to the lake much easier. Each man had been given a pack, a pair of snowshoes, two days' worth of dried rations, and the necessary weapons. But whereas Stalkov carried a Schmeisser machine pistol, Kurenko had been given only a service revolver and no ammunition. The bullets were in a pouch at Stalkov's waist. The rest of the equipment had been divided up. Stalkov was to carry the radio, the thermometers, and the weighted lines, while Kurenko was laden down with the heavy auger and the rest of the drilling apparatus.

Much to Kurenko's annoyance, they had been treated decently enough by the fliers of the Ninth *Gruppe,* had been given a hot meal, the same as everyone else was eating, and even some whiskey before being loaded into the Henschels for takeoff. As they were getting ready to go, Bauer had turned in his seat and handed Kurenko a flask filled with brandy.

"Good French stuff, Captain. Smooth as a woman's ass. Save it for later."

Just before four in the afternoon, they had taken off. By the time they reached the drop area, it would be almost dark.

The Henschels skimmed over the forest, their wheels almost touching the treetops. The mountains drifted in and out of the freezing mists. It was hard to realize that the landscape below was the same through which Kurenko had been conveyed by truck only a few months before. Here and there, on the side of a road, a dark black patch announced a ruined vehicle, though it was impossible to tell whether it was German or Soviet. Dark trails rose in the far distance, over a horizon almost impossible to discern; a burning village. Flashes of light filtered through the mists; cannons firing somewhere, though without sound. Nothing could be heard over the frightening whine of the Henschels' engines. Kurenko recalled stories of how these same planes had dispersed whole divisions of Poles during their retreat from Warsaw without firing a shot. By the terrifying sound of their engines alone.

The light dimmed, the mists gained depth and shadow. The black tops of the firs below began to grope up out of the fog. Suddenly Bauer's plane began to climb. The wind whistled against the struts, whining fearfully. Kurenko adjusted the straps of his parachute as he had been told to do and checked the auxiliary chute, which was to take the pack down ahead of him. Tatters of mist swam over the wing tips. He felt dizzy, revived only by a sudden rush of arctic air against his face as the Henschel swung around and began its approach.

Bauer spoke quickly into the intercom.

"You can see the place up ahead, where the trees thin out. There's a field. It was used for transport when we were here last year. Now, nothing. We'll be back. You're our calling card." Bauer laughed in a cheerful sort of way that was difficult to dislike. "Get ready, now. . . ."

Kurenko looked behind him. The second plane seemed so close. What if he jumped and was borne back into the propeller of Stalkov's aircraft? His stomach began to churn. Then he looked down.

Bauer's voice crackled over the head set. "Out with the pack, now. . . ."

Kurenko did as he was told.

"Now, you . . . quickly. Good luck. . . ."

Somehow, amazingly, he was out, dropping free. The second Henschel whirled by him, only a few meters away. He saw Stalkov come hurtling down, the chute already streaming out behind him. He wrenched at the rip cord and felt the snap and tug of the lines flowing out. He knew that they had barely enough altitude for the chutes to open before they would be down. Perhaps he had waited too long already. The ground spun up under him. The field, which had looked so large from above, now seemed no bigger than an unfolded newspaper. He had visions of being hung up in the trees, of dangling there until he froze to death.

The chute opened, caught the air, billowed. The lines pulled hard and up, yanking him so violently that he thought his back was broken. Then he was down, rolling in the snow, tangled in the chute lines, snow in his mouth, in his boots, up his sleeves.

When he recovered his breath, he sat up, draped in the silk, and began to laugh hysterically. He had actually made it down. Alive. And the pack had come down less than ten meters from him. Now, for the first time, he realized what a skillful pilot Bauer was.

Before he had time to regain his composure, he found himself looking up at Stalkov. The man had not only unhooked himself and already buried his chute but had recovered his pack and was standing over him, adjusting the harness. Stalkov had on a fur *ushanka* with the earflaps pulled down so that his beard was all bunched up and jutted out in absurd, comical clumps. But the eyes were still fierce, unrelenting. Kurenko was all too aware of the empty revolver in his holster and of Schreiber-Hartstein's words. Stalkov had his instructions.

"Well, are you going to sit there all day or are we going to get along?"

"Here, help me up. . . ."

"You're hurt? No? Then help yourself. Make the effort. It will be good for you. I thought you were a soldier. What kind of soldier sits in the snow like a stone when there's work to be done?"

It was at that moment that Kurenko realized that his greatest problem was going to be simply keeping up with Stalkov. Everything else would be secondary. He read in the man's eyes the kind of almost sadistic pleasure that a good woodsman often takes in the inability of a lesser man to keep up. He shuddered, hauled himself up, and went looking for his pack.

The Henschels were long gone. The mists had closed in over the field, blurring the edges of the forest and shutting out what little of the sky had been visible before.

Stalkov had his compass out, a small map on his knee. He pointed, and set off. Kurenko struggled with his snowshoes and found that Stalkov had already made it into the woods before he even had the straps adjusted.

The pack pulling deep into his shoulders, Kurenko pushed forward through the snow. It was not deep, just deep enough to make movement without the shoes difficult. The ground below already seemed a little soft. Kurenko was sweating. What the devil did they want of him? He was an engineers officer, not an olympic skier.

He found Stalkov leaning against a tree, waiting for him.

"How far," said Kurenko, already out of breath. In all his time at the front, he had never had to do this. He doubted that he would make it to Lake Byeleymostnoy. Let Stalkov go on without him. He would stay there and freeze to death.

"Five kilometers, perhaps six. A brisk walk for a holiday afternoon. Don't look so glum, you'll make it."

"You think so? That's comforting to hear." He glanced at the huge Mauser hanging from the belt around Stalkov's ample waist. "And when do I get a bullet or two from that in the back of my neck?"

"Listen, *malchik,* I don't know what the problem is between you and the good Hauptmann, and I don't much care. He said I should look after you. I'll do that, and that's all, you understand? We have work to do, so let's get on with it."

"With this?" Kurenko held up his empty revolver. "What if we run into . . ." He didn't finish. Who was it, exactly, that he was afraid of running into?

Stalkov looked thoughtful. For a second, his eyes clouded, then he reached down to his belt, pulled loose the ammunition pouch, and flung it to Kurenko.

"See, I trust you. Load up. But remember—if you shoot me in the back, you'll never get out of here alive."

Kurenko was silent. He took the pouch, loaded the revolver, and stuck it back in his holster.

Now what was he supposed to do?

Under normal circumstances, it should have taken no more than three hours, even through heavy snow, to make the five kilometers down to the headwaters of the lake. But the terrain was monstrously difficult, full of gullies, ravines, and knolls, which made the going twice as difficult as it should have been, particularly with the heavy packs that both men carried. Night had fallen and the cold had intensified. With it came a thick, freezing white mist through which, by a freak of nature, now and then fell a faint powdering of new snow.

Twice they stopped to rest and to eat something. The second time Kurenko remembered the flask Bauer had given him. He took it out of his quilted coat, drank some, and offered the rest to Stalkov. The man looked puzzled, then smiled in a guarded sort of way and took the flask. He handed it back empty.

There was no sound at all in the forest other than the sighing of the wind through the trees and the soft whisper of snow falling from overweighted boughs. Once, shortly after they had come out of the trees for a brief while and onto a high knoll overlooking a long, shallow hillside, they saw in the far distance a horizon briefly lit by the flash of artillery firing from some unseen defilade. But there was no sound. Kurenko waited, but the boom of the guns had been swallowed whole by the distance, the cold, and the wind.

They struggled on again. The trees closed over them, lacing the sky with icy branches through which, when the mist drifted away for a moment, a starry sky could be seen. Kurenko was drenched with sweat. He could feel it running down his body under the heavy coat. His shoulders ached. But he was damned if he was going to give Stalkov the satisfaction of seeing him lag behind.

Then the ground started to slope down a little. Stalkov's walk became a crouch. They were getting near.

"Take off the shoes. By the tree, there . . ." Stalkov whispered. "You can't use the shoes on the ice."

"Are we there?"

"Another ten meters and you'll fall in. Can't you hear the wind?"

Stalkov was right. He could hear it, a definite change in the sound of the wind. It was now a high, open whine. Just a little ahead of him the forest ceased and gave way to open ice.

They took off their snowshoes and moved forward at a crawl, pulling their packs behind them. There was no telling what they might find once they were actually at the lake.

Then Kurenko saw it, just ahead: a last row of trees, a drift of dry snow blown up like a barricade, and beyond that a wide space of dazzling blue-white—the lake.

They came out through the treeline and up to the edge of the palisades. Ten meters down was the frozen surface of the lake. The snow had mounded up high and deep against the rocks so that it was easy enough for them to descend. They had come out of the forest just behind a hook of land that jutted far out into the lake. Kurenko recalled the shape of the shoreline from the map at Dabendorf.

"Follow me, but slowly, *malchik*. Don't make a sound. . . . There may be guards." Stalkov moved silently and with a grace incredible for a man of his size. He had left his pack in the snow and Kurenko, without being told, did the same.

In a moment, they had arrived at the tip of the peninsula. Tall firs, heavily weighted with snow, loomed above them. To the right, the open surface of the lake. Cautiously, they looked around the last obstacle at the end of the finger of land.

The camp was not far away, perhaps a kilometer at most. A long line of dull lights glowed through the mist, and behind them, shadows. The guard towers, the barracks, the high wire and log walls, all just as he had visualized them from the reconnaissance photos.

Stalkov nodded. "We're in the right place, that's certain. Now let's go back and get to work."

Retrieving their packs, they headed back along the shore, going north until, some twenty minutes later, Stalkov signaled a halt. By that time the lights of the camp had almost vanished in the mist. The surface of the lake could barely be seen. A stiff, arctic wind was scything the ice just above the surface but despite its velocity the mist remained unthinned.

"Here . . . this will be about right," Stalkov said. "Let's get to work."

Kurenko opened the pack, took out the auger bits, the brace, and the measuring cords. The ice was thick enough to hold him, he had no doubt about that, but how much thicker than that it was there was no telling.

"Move along. I'll get the wind device set." He attached a long cord to Kurenko's waist and pushed him out.

Kurenko moved slowly, testing the ice with his foot, waiting to see if it gave. He had to rely as much on sound as on feel, for he could see almost nothing. The freezing mist blinded him; his eyes were raw and he could barely keep them open. He pushed his face down into the collar of his heavy coat, wishing desperately that he had a woolen face mask. The perspiration soaked through the thin cloth gloves he wore and the moisture froze and caused the auger bit to stick to the cloth.

He was out perhaps fifteen meters. Still nothing. The ice seemed solid as the earth. There was a thin powdering of snow on the surface and he had no difficulty keeping his footing.

Another fifteen meters. He counted footsteps. Forty-five, ninety, one hundred and fifteen . . . one hundred and sixty.

He pulled on the cord. For a moment, nothing, then an answering jerk. Stalkov was still there.

Relieved and feeling foolish, he moved forward again, now thrusting the long auger bit and brace out before him, probing. The ice was still solid. There was not the slightest sign of weakness.

Far enough, he thought. The peninsula jutted out into the lake some eight hundred meters. The gliders would have to come in behind it, so there was no point in going out to the geographic center of the lake. It was enough to have reached the farthest point at which the gliders could possibly land and still not be seen from the camp.

He got down on his knees, brushing the snow away until he found the smooth surface of the ice. He fitted the bit to the long wooden auger and began, very slowly, to drill. He had read stories of Laplanders and Eskimos cutting holes in the ice in order to fish or to spear seals. They did it as a matter of course, every day of their lives. Was this any different?

As he drilled, the thought of the black waters directly below him turned his blood to ice. One wrong judgment and the ice might crack, rear up, and in an instant he would be gone. It was said that the shock of immersion in such water killed a man at once. Perhaps so. But if not, what a horror. . . .

He went on turning the drill. It bit into the ice smoothly and easily. The feel of it was important. Stalkov had said that he would know when he had penetrated the bottom of the ice cover by the way the drill turned, a sudden easing, a loss of pressure. That sounded reasonable enough. But would he be able to tell?

He continued drilling. The bit went in, down to the brace. He would have to screw in the next extension. Before doing so, he dropped the weighted line down the hole. He could feel the jar as the plumb hit bottom, still in the ice.

He hauled the line up and fitted an extension to the auger.

The bit turned cleanly, just as before. The ice was dense and tight, without soft spots.

Keep going, keep going, he thought. Every turn meant another few centimeters of depth. Good, good. But for what? For the gliders? Had he gone entirely mad?

Then he had reached the end of the second extension. He fitted a third. There was only one more left.

Ten turns, fifteen, twenty. Keep the pressure steady and even. Twenty-one. Twenty-two. . . .

Suddenly he felt the auger brace slip in his hand. The point had gone through. It was all he could do to keep from scrambling back, as though the water would come jetting out of the hole and drown him. He listened. Nothing. Only a very faint rushing sound; the lake beneath him, the whisper of the freezing water far under the ice.

He droped in the line, feeding it slowly, hand over hand, very carefully. He would have to tell from the way it felt when it had gone into the water. His hands were almost numb. How was he supposed to manage such a perception? Wasn't the depth of the bit itself enough, the length, the number of extensions?

Then he felt it. He marked the spot on the cord where his hand was and carefully hauled the line out again.

The bottom was wet and froze at once to his glove. He counted the knots in the line. They tallied almost exactly with what he had estimated the depth to have been from the number of auger extensions and the number of turns on the last length.

The ice was still almost two meters thick.

Slowly, he backed away from the hole. There was a little water around it now. He could feel it with the toe of his boot. He tugged on the line, felt the answer, and started back.

Five meters, then ten, then fifteen. He moved as slowly as he had before. Stalkov hauled in the line after him, keeping it taut so that he could maintain the proper direction.

Then he could see the dark shadows of the trees through the mist, the shore. He felt the dry crunch of snow under his boots. Then he could hear Stalkov breathing. He was back.

In the ghostly starlight that filtered down through the white mist he could see Stalkov working at some kind of mechanism he had rigged high in the trees directly over the palisade. It looked like a propeller of some sort, and from it ran a thin wire, which ended in a small black box that Stalkov was already burying in the snow.

"How did it measure?"

"Two meters," Kurenko said.

"Good, good. I'm just about done here too. It didn't take long, did it?"

"What is that contraption?"

"For the wind, *malchik*. You don't think knowing the depth of ice alone is enough, do you? Everything has to be done with good German thoroughness. They're not like us, the Germans. Science, *malchik*. Wind velocity and direction and temperature. The little propeller measures both the direction and the velocity and the little black box sends it all back to whomever wants to know. A series of beeps. Even if it's overheard, no one can possibly tell what it means."

"Is it running?"

"Not only is it running, but the signal it's sending out means we have exactly five hours to make our rendezvous."

"Are you insane? Rendezvous? With whom and where? There are no German troops within two hundred kilometers of this godforsaken place."

Stalkov allowed himself a laugh. "Come along and you'll see. You wouldn't want me to tell you how we're going to do it, would you? That would spoil everything. . . ."

"We're not going to walk out of here, are we?"

"Not entirely. But come along, *malchik*. You'll see. Just keep your mouth closed and don't let the wind in. You'll freeze your teeth if you keep talking."

And with that, Stalkov turned and trudged back up the mounded palisade and into the trees.

They had been struggling through the woods for three hours. The cold had not let up and the way had been steep. Though it was mid-March, there was not a trace of thaw in the air; the woods were as deep with snow as though it had been midwinter. It seemed to Kurenko that they had come on a fool's errand; of course the ice would hold. With the temperature as it was now, the ice would probably be firm for another six weeks, at least.

Kurenko was almost at the point of collapse. Ahead of him, with seemingly limitless energy, Stalkov stalked on, like a great, shambling bear, not uttering a sound. It was impossible even to hear the man's breathing.

Finally, Kurenko could stand it no longer. He had to rest. He called ahead. Stalkov stopped and turned.

"You can't, *malchik,*" he said, his voice soft and concerned. "Listen to me. . . . It's no good if you stop. You'll freeze to death. You should know that. You've been through all this before. You're soaked through and through. These German coats aren't like our own; they're too thin. We won't last out the night."

"You go then. I can't take another step." As he spoke, Kurenko recalled with horror the sergeant he had left to freeze to death in the forests beyond Kolabyansk. It was his turn now.

"You'll make it. It shouldn't be much farther now. . . ."

"You sound as if you know where you're going."

"Oh, I do, I do. I was here a year or so ago. Just before I went over. Our last battle wasn't far from here. During the big fall push. That's when I was captured. But come on now, we haven't got that much time." He reached out and pulled Kurenko up from his knees. "If I have to, I'll drag you. . . ."

"I'll try, Boris Trifomovitch, I'll try. . . ."

"Good lad, that's it. . . ." But he did not release his grasp. They moved forward, but almost all of Kurenko's weight was on the bigger man.

How long this went on, Kurenko had no idea. Every step was an agony, even though he was almost being carried along. His head hung, he could barely lift his feet. Stalkov dragged him along like a sack of grain. Somehow he found at least the minimal energy needed to stay upright.

The forest grew lighter. At first, a dull, sear gray, like ice seen below the water's surface. Then a pale, whitish glow through the trees.

They came out on a wide plateau, below which the snowy forest continued its interminable sprawl. In the dim light of approaching dawn, Kurenko could see that there were odd shapes scattered around the field. Large mounds, the outlines of whatever lay beneath blurred by the snow. The field itself ran perhaps two hundred meters until the next treeline. Not far off was a large, low shack of some sort, almost entirely covered with snow.

Stalkov stepped out into the clearing. Above was a clear, steel gray sky. He looked at his watch and nodded.

"*Malchik,* you're going to have to find the strength. I can't manage this by myself."

Kurenko dragged himself up, rejuvenated by the sight of the open sky and the feel of the wind in his face. It was still freezing cold, but in the open, the deep arctic blackness of the night had dissipated and the dawn had brought with it at least an illusion of renewed energy.

As he watched, Stalkov went over to the shed, shook the snow from the doors, and went inside. In a moment he emerged, dragging a long cable.

"Now," Stalkov called, "see if you can find a big pole, like a telegraph upright. It should be in the snow just . . . ah, keep going . . . a little to the right. Look around."

"It's here. . . . what am I to do with it?"

"Why, stand it up, of course. But first . . . hook this cable to the ring at the top. Come, I'll help you."

Together, they rigged the pole and raised it. A second pole lay under the snow some ten meters away. To this they hooked the other end of the cable and, as they had with the first, hoisted it up and jammed it firmly into the frozen ground. Stalkov wedged rocks around the base of both poles for added strength and then turned to survey his handiwork.

From the center of the cable dangled another length of wire with a hook on the end of it. Stalkov looked at his watch again.

"Not much time. They'll be here in fifteen or twenty minutes. Come along. One last effort."

"You've gone mad. . . . What is this, erecting goal posts in the middle of a snowfield. . . . How is this going to get us out of here?"

"You'll see. Just be patient. . . ."

He beckoned him back to the shed and this time pulled the doors wide open. There was something inside, a big, dark shape that spread out from one side of the long shed to the other.

"Come on, help me with this. It isn't heavy, but we haven't much time."

Then Kurenko understood. As Stalkov handed him the cable, he knew what the thing was: a small glider, of the kind he had seen many times at sporting meets. Of the kind the Nazis had used when the building of an airforce had been prohibited by the Versailles treaty. So *that* was how they were going to get out. He broke out in a heavy sweat and a grin at the same time. The devil with thinking it through, with resolving the questions that had been whirling about in his head for days. The devil with it all. They had a chance, they were going to get out after all and he would live to worry for a few more days.

They hauled the little glider out onto the field and hooked the nose line to the dangling cable between the uprights. And while they did so, Stalkov explained: The place to which they had come had once been an airfield for a German reconnaissance squadron. The gliders had been sent there as an experiment. Because of the successful use of attack gliders in Belgium, every Luftwaffe officer worth his salt was trying to think up a new use for the silent, soaring craft. When the Russians had pushed the Germans out of the area months before, the field had been abandoned. The mounds of snow to the sides of the field were wrecked planes, now snowed over and frozen in. Some still had their pilots in them, dead at the controls. There were many such fields all over the area. It was luck that this one, so close to Lake Byeleymostnoy, had had gliders as part of its equipment. There were at least five others similarly equipped and similarly ruined within twenty kilometers.

"Shall we get in, *malchik*? We don't want to be standing around when Lieutenant Bauer comes over to pick up the mail, do we?"

Stalkov bent and pulled open the canopy. There was just room for two men inside, one behind the other.

"Do you know how to fly one of these things?" Kurenko asked.

"I'm told they come down like a feather. In the snow, there should be no problem. And if there is, at least it's a clean way to be killed. Now, *in,* please. And do you have any more of Bauer's good cognac on you by any chance?"

"You drank it all," Kurenko reminded him.

Just then they heard the distant whine of an engine. Kurenko looked up. There was no doubt—it was one of the Henschels. The sound was unmistakable.

Stalkov pulled the glider canopy down and latched it. They stared up through the frosted glass. Out of the gray, western sky a single black speck came drifting, grew, and became a biplane, its engines growing louder and more raucous every second.

The plane swooped down low over the field, shot up, turned, banked, and came in again, this time trailing a long hook.

"Brace yourself. . . ."

There was a sudden impact. The hook snagged the line, the uprights flew into the air, and for one long moment Kurenko watched with a combination of horror and fascination as the line trailing from the Henschel grew taut.

Then the glider jolted free of the snow and was yanked into the air. Stalkov gripped the single control lever that jutted up between his legs. The wings wobbled for a moment, then caught the lift, and the craft rose slowly and smoothly behind the biplane.

Kurenko leaned back and closed his eyes, and in the deep silence that followed, dreamed of ice cream and young girls in Gorki Park.

In the radio room at Dabendorf, Schreiber-Hartstein leaned so close over the back of the operator that he almost fell. He could see the man's hands flitting over the dials, while the needles on the board flicked back and forth like cow's tails on a hot day. The room was dimly lit, the black tar-paper shades pulled down over the windows. In the distance, north of Berlin, the English bombers were at work again, methodically pulverizing a ball-bearings plant.

Finally, the operator turned and pulled off his earphones.

Schreiber-Hartstein licked his lips. "Well, have you made contact?"

"It's difficult, sir. Even with the new antenna."

"But have you made contact?"

"Yes, sir. We've picked them up. Shall I send in code or clear?"

"As arranged. Just ask the one question. We must know. . . . I can't hold the transport for much longer."

The operator spoke rapidly into the open microphone. A burst of static answered him. He turned a dial, flicked another switch. The static dwindled to a rushing noise. Then, gradually, a voice cut through the rushing sound, clear and sharp.

Schreiber-Hartstein smiled.

Almost eight hundred miles away, at the airfield near Taraganskaya, the radioman was sending the two words he most wanted to hear. Over and over again, so there could be no mistake.

"*Wasserfogel* . . . waterbird. Affirmative. *Wasserfogel.* Do you hear me, Dabendorf? Affirmative. *Wasserfogel.*"

Schreiber-Hartstein turned to Captain Gottinger, who had been waiting at the door to the room, his face obscured by cigarette smoke.

"Tell Beifelder that we go. The windmill is working. By the time we reach Taraganskaya airfield, we should have all the information we need."

Gottinger nodded and went out.

At Gatow a line of Junkers Ju-52s was waiting, fully fueled for flight to Taraganskaya. An escort of Me-109s was ready to assure their safe passage as far as the fighter's range would allow. Gottinger crossed the open field between the radio shed and the road where the OKH command car was parked. In the distance he could see the men stamping about out in the open, their field packs piled up on the ground, their weapons stacked. Seven hundred of them, smoking quietly, talking. Watching the distant fireworks as the bombers drove through a floodlit sky over the ball-bearing works.

He paused. It was like a scene out of another century. The night before the battle of Austerlitz, or Jena. . . . He saw fixed bayonets. They would have to be unfixed, of course, before they boarded the Junkers. How odd . . . yet how perfectly right. Someone was singing, a thin, piercing tenor, but very soft. Gottinger could not understand the words, but he understood clearly enough the message of the melody.

He shivered, hurried his pace, and got into the car, taking care not to slam the door too hard.

"Viktoriastrasse," he told the driver. "Then to Gatow."

Inspector Trakl was at the window of his Prinz Albrechtstrasse office, watching the bombing raid on the ball-bearing works as though it were a fireworks display, when his desk phone rang.

Irritated, he snapped up the receiver.

"Trakl here. What the devil is it?"

"A message for you, Inspector," came a softly accented voice on the other end. A voice Trakl did not recognize.

"Obviously, or you would not have called. *Who is this?*"

"It's not important who I am. The message is from Lensky."

Trakl's breath caught in his throat. Of all the damned times . . . with an air raid going on. The lights wavered, went out. A temporary power failure.

"Go ahead," Trakl snapped, swearing under his breath.

"The message is, 'Now' . . . Inspector."

"You're positive?"

"Absolutely. They're getting ready to leave at this very moment. The troops have moved out from Dabendorf already. You have less than an hour."

There was a click at the other end. Trakl shouted violently across the darkened office. The room was lit only by the distant bomb flashes and the reflected beams of the searchlight batteries; a blackout was in effect throughout the city.

"Get Glantz down here at once. You, Bachstein, I want a full squad and a troop unit, two dozen, fully armed. Have vehicles ready in ten minutes. *Make it fast. . . .*"

Shadows jumped up from behind desks and darted across the room. Doors slammed. Trakl shouted more orders into the telephone.

"I don't give a damn whether there's a raid going on or not. I can *see* there's a raid going on, you idiot. Get moving or you're on your way to Kharkov in the morning."

He snatched up his coat, slapped his holster to make sure that his Walther was there, and then stamped out of his office into the pitch-black corridor.

A third wave of Stirlings was just then going over the Helmstauffer works.

She stared down at the kit laid out on his cot, the folded tunic, the belt and holster, the map packet wrapped in oilskin, all the absurd paraphernalia of soldiery that she had come to detest.

"I don't understand you anymore, Sasha," she said. "The other night you saw everything so clearly. You wept. You were even indignant that Vassily Gregorovitch presumed to instruct you. Yet now it's all back the way it was." She shook her head and could not bring herself to look at him. "You're really going to go, aren't you? In spite of everything. You're going to let them do this thing to you. . . ."

"If word comes that the ice will hold," he whispered, "yes, I will go. I must. I have no choice."

"I suppose you're going to tell me that the men depend on you or something like that. . . ."

"Do you have a better answer?"

"They'll go with you or without you, Sasha. Let them. Don't be a part of it. You've always followed your conscience before, even when it led you astray. Follow it now."

"But how can I do that—to *them*?" Alexander Semyonovitch's eyes were clouded, perhaps with tears. He pushed his hand hard over his sparse, brush-cut hair in a gesture of terminal weariness. "*I* may have a choice of sorts, but what choice do *they* have? Do you think the Germans will say, Oh, so you've changed your mind, have you?—Well, that's perfectly all right with us, just go back to your warm barracks? To make matters worse, there is a unit of Waffen SS trapped in a pocket not far from the camp. It is now part of the operation that after liberating the prisoners, we are to link up with them and bring them out. A double rescue operation. The propaganda value is enormous, so there is no question of going or not going. They *must* go, and they will be *made* to go whether they want to or not. But they will say, Golitsyn is not there. And they will begin to doubt. Some of them will think and they will know the truth. Can I let them die without the solace of some small illusion to ease their consciences? Without me they will go to their deaths in shame, like condemned men who die knowing they have committed a terrible crime." He took off his glasses and stared at her, the pupils of his pale blue eyes growing large and hazy. "How can I desert them? How can I let them die that way?"

"What difference does it make how they die? Either way it will be a criminal waste. Must you sacrifice yourself for that?"

"But at least if I am there, perhaps they will die believing."

"In a lie?"

"But a lie that will allow them to die at peace with themselves. Surely that's worth something."

"It is not worth your sacrificing yourself. Stay. Stay for your own sake and for mine. I love you, Sasha. I love you."

"That you should say that to me . . . *now*."

"It's no lie, Sasha. I love you, believe me . . . I . . ."

"When you came to me at the camp, I was grateful. I said, she has understood a little, at last. But I thought that you were doing it for me because you thought it would help me, that you were pretending—that it was no more than that."

"Whatever it was then—and I'm not even sure myself—it's no pretending now. It's not duty, it's not out of a sense of obligation. Understand. *I forgive you everything.* I love you. Can't you allow me to say that? It's all as it was before, for me—if it is with you."

"How strange are the ways in which God moves us about," he said in a low, subdued voice. He looked toward the bed, which was loaded with the gear Dushkin had laid out for him: a knife, a compass, weatherproof matches, gloves, snow glasses. "But why did it have to be now? Just at this moment?"

"If it hadn't been now, it wouldn't have been at all."

He held her tightly. "And, so, we should be thankful, is that it? Yes, I am thankful, Nina. For an hour, a minute, of knowing that you want to be with me, in spite of everything that has happened, and that it might have been possible to have things as they once were."

She sat down on the edge of the bed, her head in her hands. Tears sluiced through her fingers. She knew it was useless.

"Don't go with them, Sasha . . . please, don't go."

He took a long look at her. She was shaking, as though she were freezing to death. He reached out, then drew back. She continued to weep. Finally she took her hands away and revealed her face. Red and swollen. Ugly.

"There's really no choice," he said dully. "If God wills it, we'll have more years together. At least that's a possibility now. . . ."

He sat down next to her, a strange tranquility stealing over him. The tremors had stopped. His hand was steady again.

Was there anything in life more important to him than this woman? None of the rest mattered. Yet if it had not been for the rest of it, as she had said, they would never have come together again, no matter how fervently he had wished it.

He spoke to her, so softly that he barely heard his own voice.

"Understand, there is no choice," he said. "None at all. For us, who knows, perhaps there never was."

14

No,
The war took my soul
and forgot it midway.
Margarita Aliger
From *The Kazan Notebook*

Nina Andreyeva remained seated on the edge of the bed while the general finished putting on his uniform. An empty whiskey bottle stood on the disordered bureau next to his cap. His pistol was unloaded but he had put it in the holster nevertheless. Schreiber-Hartstein had promised to give him ammunition once they were on-board the plane.

It was hard to see; the double canvas shades were drawn tight because of the air raid and the room was lit only by an old-fashioned globe lamp, the brightest illumination allowed during an attack.

Golitsyn looked at himself in the mirror. A tired gray face stared back at him, the eyes dull and unfamiliar, the shape of the head strange, as though it had been made of wax and had melted a little. On the shoulder boards were three gold stars; they had given him a full general's insignia of rank and he felt ashamed.

Nina Andreyeva smoked in silence, her face a mask of despair. Golitsyn adjusted his glasses, studying her reflection in the cracked mirror and wishing that he had some adhesive tape to hold the glasses in place. His eyesight had grown steadily worse during the past few years and without his glasses he could hardly see at all. If he lost them during the attack he would be worse than useless.

As he wearily buckled the Sam Browne over his shoulder, Dushkin came into the room carrying the carafe, which, for the last month, had been kept full not of vodka but of the good Scotch whiskey that Golitsyn preferred.

Dushkin hesitated, seeing the general's wife and noting her grim expression.

The general smiled. "Come, come, Osip. You arrive at just the right moment. How many glasses do you have? Two? Three?"

"Excellency," Dushkin began. "Perhaps it would be better . . ."

"No time could be better than right now. Three glasses? Excellent. You'll join us, Osip, won't you?"

"Sasha . . . no!"

"What difference can one drink make before I go. Perhaps we can even think of an appropriate toast. Nina?"

"To the end of the world, then," she said, waving toward the window.

"To the end of the world," he repeated, pouring three tumblers full and handing them around.

He swallowed the whiskey at a gulp. Tears came to his eyes. He hurled the glass against the wall, smashing it to bits. Dushkin, coughing weakly and red in the face, followed suit.

As he placed the carafe on the table before him, Golitsyn heard an odd sound—the rapid slamming of boot soles in the stairwell outside. He knew the sound of Schreiber-Hartstein's boots, the rhythm of Beifelder's slight limp, he knew Kurenko's quick, nervous run and Zhilinsky's ponderous tread; it was none of these.

"Ninotchka?" he said in a suddenly suffocated voice. Something was very wrong and he knew it.

She shrugged, hearing what he heard. "They're hurrying back because they've forgotten something." She tossed off the whiskey. "Perhaps it's their courage."

The boots were coming closer now, up the stairs and onto the landing. They were right outside the door to his apartment. He could hear the unmistakable clank of weapons too; no one was allowed to carry weapons inside number 10 Viktoriastrasse.

Then there was a rapid pounding.

"Open the door. At once. *Open!*"

"Dushkin, see who it is, will you?"

The orderly went out hurriedly.

The voice outside the door came again, harsh and, like the footsteps, unfamiliar.

Golitsyn's hand fell instinctively to his holster.

"It's not loaded, Sasha."

The pounding continued. Golitsyn went gray in the face. He stood rooted to the spot, his greatcoat over his shoulder, his general's stars catching the wavering lamplight.

Then someone kicked in the door.

Five men in civilian clothes rushed into the vestibule. In the hall, on the landing were half a dozen steel-helmeted SS, carrying submachine guns.

She knew those faces, though she had never seen these particular men before; policemen all looked the same, Soviet or German.

"*Gostyi* . . . it's the same all over again. We should have known."

"You, get out of the way," cried a stocky man in a leather overcoat. He pointed at Nina Andreyeva. "That's her. There she is."

The general stepped between the stocky man and his wife.

"This is an outrage. How dare you burst in here like this?"

The stocky man spat at him, held up an oval metal disc.

"Trakl. Gestapo. Now, get out of the way. I warn you, you better not interfere. We have no business with you. Only with her."

Nina Andreyeva uttered a wild, piercing laugh that made the two men standing directly behind the Gestapo officer start back for a second.

"Don't you understand, Sasha? They've come for me. It's *me* they want, not you."

"You have no authority here," Golitsyn boomed. He reached out to seize the Gestapo man who was at least a head shorter than he was. Trakl batted his arm aside.

"Didn't you hear me, you great Slavic imbecile? This isn't your concern. You're drunk. My God, what a stink. You're a disgrace, that's what you are." He turned. "Glantz, take the whore out of here."

The small bedroom was by now full of Gestapo. Two of them stepped up to Golitsyn and seized his arms, slamming him back against the wall. The other two went for Nina Andreyeva. She jumped up from the bed and tried to run to the window. They caught her. She struggled, raking their faces with her nails.

"She is under arrest. We have no warrant for you, General, or Marshal or whatever you are. I warn you, *once more . . .*"

Golitsyn lunged forward, shaking off the two men who had been holding him as though they were rag dolls. He went for Trakl, his enormous frame shaking with rage, his arms swinging wildly.

"You will not do this. . . ."

The Gestapo man reeled backward, his head ringing from the blow Golitsyn had dealt him. As he fell, he yanked out his automatic. As the Walther rose, Nina Andreyeva wrenched free and fell full length on Trakl.

Glantz turned and shouted at the SS men in the corridor.

"Don't just stand there . . . teach that great sack of Russian shit a lesson."

Two of the Gestapo agents pulled Nina Andreyeva away from Trakl as half a dozen SS clubbed Golitsyn to the floor.

"A lesson, a good lesson," cried Trakl, wiping the blood from his face. There were long scratches up and down his cheeks and across his nose. He spit across the room in a fury.

"Get her into the hall. Out of here. Glantz, go ahead. On my authority. You know what to do. And as for *him* . . ."

The rifle butts rose and fell methodically. At first Golitsyn tried to shield his head but it was no use. He fell, first to his knees, then down on all fours, his glasses smashed, bits of glass ground into his face.

"Sasha, for God's sake . . . don't let them do this . . . *don't* . . ."

Glantz hit Nina Andreyeva backhanded across the mouth. Two of the Gestapo men dragged her out of the room.

Trakl, wiping his nose, held up the other hand.

"Enough. We don't want to kill him. Not yet. . . ."

The SS men stopped the beating at once and left the room, Trakl following, and went out into the hallway.

Golitsyn swayed uncertainly, blinded by the blood that poured from his lacerated scalp. He heard the pounding of boots on the stairs. He tried to rise but could not. His shoulders felt as though a hot iron weight had fallen on them. There was no feeling in his left arm and an agony in his right. He was sure that the shoulder was broken.

Again he tried to rise but fell back, unable to get to his feet. The greatcoat caught on a chair and pulled it over. His legs simply would not hold.

He raised his head, trying to see through the blood. The room was empty, the door to the hallway still partly open, the door beyond that, leading to the landing, gaping wide. He could hear her still shouting as they took her down the stairs.

Once more he tried desperately to rise.

"Dushkin . . ." he cried. Then he saw Dushkin lying against a door in the hallway, his head smashed in. A howl welled up in his throat. He gagged, struggled against the pain, and finally got himself upright.

Trakl signaled his men to stop halfway down the stairs.

"Why are you doing this?" Nina Andreyeva cried. "Do whatever you wish with me, but let him . . ."

She was silenced by a hard slap across the face.

"That is exactly what we have in mind," Trakl spat. "Turn the whore to the wall."

Glantz took Nina Andreyeva by the shoulder, twisted her around, and slammed her against the wall of the stairwell.

Trakl glanced up to the landing, as though to make sure they had not forgotten to leave the door to the general's rooms open. "He's still conscious?" he asked Glantz.

His subordinate nodded.

"You bastards," said Nina Andreyeva, her face pressed hard against the wall. Glantz had her by the hair.

Trakl took out his Walther. Nina Andreyeva did not even know it until the snout of the pistol pressed into the back of her neck just below the base of her skull.

Trakl glanced once more up toward the landing. Then he pulled the trigger.

As Alexander Semyonovitch tottered across the room the sound of the shot cut across him like a whiplash.

A single shot. From the stairwell.

He reached the front door of his apartment, crashing dizzily into the walls half a dozen times, finally lurching out onto the landing with a bellow of rage.

Halfway down the stairs he saw Nina Andreyeva's body. She hung head down on the treads, one foot caught between the stair rails, a bullet hole huge and livid against the white of her neck. Trakl looked up at Golitsyn.

"My regrets, General. The whore tried to escape. Of course we had no choice."

For a moment a dense, absolute silence blanketed the stairwell; only the distant explosions from the Helmstauffer works could be heard.

Then, slowly, Golitsyn began to moan. The sound he made bore no relation to anything the Germans had ever heard before and for a moment they stood there dumb, shocked by the utter strangeness of it.

Trakl wiped off his leather coat and cleared his throat.

"Drag the bitch out by her feet."

"And him?" Glantz asked in a hesitant whisper.

"I've got no orders for him. He can hang himself for all I care. That's his affair. Now get to it."

Glantz nodded. He understood. Perfectly.

While Schreiber-Hartstein prepared to move the brigade of Russians to Gatow airfield and the waiting columns of Ju-52s, Gottinger proceeded as rapidly as he could into Berlin.

Because of the raid over the Helmstauffer works there were many roadblocks. At Buckow the car was stopped by a mixed squad of Orpo and military police and it was only with the greatest of difficulty and an enormous amount of threatening that Gottinger was able to get through. Twice, because of the low-power blue running lights he was compelled to use, the car almost went off the road.

The sky in the direction of the Helmstauffer works was aflame. Sirens sounded in the distance, and though the bombers had gone from the immediate area, the flak units kept pounding away. The car radio crackled with requests for fire equipment and ambulances.

Berlin itself was dark, blacked-out, and nervously expectant.

With infuriating slowness, Gottinger's car moved through the dark streets around the Tiergarten and, finally, into the Viktoriastrasse.

As he turned into the block where number 10 was located, Gottinger's heart leapt into his mouth. In front of the building were half a dozen cars and an ambulance with its flasher going full tilt in spite of the alert.

The street was lined with helmeted soldiers, all carrying rifles or submachine guns. He could see Zhilinsky standing just inside the building and a number of men in civilian clothes gathered around the rear of the ambulance.

He pulled to the curb, jumped out, and ran as fast as he could up the front steps.

"Here, here, stop, you . . ." called a helmeted, truncheon-waving Orpo barring his way.

"Hauptmann Gottinger, OKH, Operations Office. I'm in charge here. This is a Special Security Zone, you imbecile. What are you people doing here? No one is allowed . . ."

Out of the corner of his eye he saw Zhilinsky gesturing incomprehensibly to him. The back door of the ambulance was open and within, by the blinking light of the flasher, he could just make out two shapes lying on a stretcher, covered by blankets.

A stocky man in plainclothes pushed through the crowd.

"If you're in charge here, as you say, you'd better come inside at once."

"Who the devil are you?"

The man reached into the pocket of his leather coat and produced a little Gestapo identity disc. Inspector Trakl. Gottinger knew the name. The man was from Müller's office.

As he allowed himself to be guided into the doorway, Gottinger got a good look at Zhilinsky's face. It was enough to tell him that something terrible had happened.

It was the worst possible time—whatever it was. How was he going to get the other staff officers, not to mention Golitsyn himself, out to Gatow when most of them were standing in the street surrounded by Gestapo men and Orpo?

"There have been two deaths," said Trakl blandly.

"Two? The names?"

Trakl ignored the direct question and waved toward the building. "If that man there, that great general of yours, had not tried to interfere, perhaps none of this would have happened. No one would have been hurt." There was, however, a faint and distinctly insincere smile playing at the corners of Trakl's mouth.

"If you don't tell me who . . ."

"We came here to make *one* arrest," Trakl went on placidly. "Fully authorized, I assure you."

"*Who,* damn you?"

"The woman, Golitsyna. She was a spy. I'm sure you must have been watching her yourself, Captain."

Gottinger ignored the innuendo. "By whose authority did you

do this? Was the warrant cleared through Reichminister Rosenberg's office first?"

Trakl looked at Gottinger as though he'd gone mad.

"We obviously have nothing more to say to each other," he replied coldly. "You will please come with us. At once."

"I told you, *I'm* in charge here, not you. These men . . ."

"If you don't want them taken in too, then I advise you to do exactly as I say. We'll only need you for a few hours."

"You simply don't understand what you're doing. We're in the middle of a most important operation. Reichminister Rosenberg's office will verify our authority. Right at this moment there are aircraft waiting. Those men you've taken into 'custody' are staff officers. . . ."

"As I said," Trakl repeated as though he were talking to an idiot child, "we want only *you*, and then only for a few hours. If you are in charge here, then you must answer for what has happened. Don't make me use force. Believe me, I have ample authority."

Gottinger looked frantically at his watch. The Russians were already in their trucks and on the way to Gatow airport. Within an hour they would be loading, and unless there was another raid, they would be ready to go by midnight.

What the devil was he to do?

For a moment he felt venomously resentful that it had fallen to him to cope with such an insane situation. By rights, Schreiber-Hartstein should have been the one to deal with Trakl and his thugs. It simply wasn't fair. But there he was, and for the moment it was his problem and no one else's.

"One moment. I must give the necessary instructions. Then I'll come with you."

Trakl shrugged. "Be quick about it."

Gottinger went into the building. Zhilinsky was still standing there, ashen-faced.

"You heard?" Zhilinsky cried. "How could such a thing have happened? For what reason? No one understands it."

"Who else was killed? Who is the second?"

"Poor Dushkin. Apparently he tried to stop them when they broke into Golitsyn's apartment."

"My God . . . and where's the general? Was he injured?"

Zhilinsky didn't answer at first. Then he sighed deeply.

"You'd better come inside."

A door was open on the main corridor. A square of light fell into the hallway. Gottinger could hear the sound of Obriyan's voice and a deep, incessant groaning coming from the room.

The general was slumped in a chair, barely upright, his face blackened and bloody, both eyes swollen closed. Obriyan was working feverishly over him with dripping compresses and cotton swabs. On the table by the wall stood a basin full of bloody water. The room stank of alcohol. Obriyan was using vodka as an antiseptic.

"Trakl's men did this? To *him*?"

"Rifle butts. Very professional. Only the unimportant parts are broken. They could have kept it up for another hour before any real harm was done."

"Is he conscious?"

Gottinger honestly could not tell. The last time he'd seen a man who looked like Golitsyn had been at Buchenwald in 1939.

Zhilinsky nodded. "Yes, he's conscious."

"Does he realize what's happened?"

Zhilinsky nodded again. "He keeps saying it was his fault."

"So does Trakl."

"That Gestapo pig? He's lying through his teeth. They shot her down for no reason at all. She was executed, plain and simple. Obriyan saw it all."

Gottinger paused, thinking things over for a moment. The general went on groaning, a low, inhuman sound.

"Can he be moved?"

"You're not serious, are you? Look at him. He's in shock. He hardly has a pulse."

"He has to be gotten out to Gatow. As soon as I can clear the Gestapo out of here. Call ahead and have a medical team standing by to deal with him. If you can't get him to go with you peaceably, give him a shot of something to keep him quiet. There's an emergency kit in the locked bottom drawer in the kitchen cupboard. Just smash the lock. You won't have any trouble."

"She was the man's *wife*," Zhilinsky cried in outrage. "What kind of person are you?"

Gottinger's face was contorted with shame and the pain of his decision. But he simply had no choice. "Listen, Stepan Abramovitch, I am not a cruel man, you know that. None of us are—willingly. But Golitsyn simply must be taken to Gatow, no matter what condition he's in and no matter whether he wants to go or not. I have to go with that swine Trakl to Gestapo headquarters. You must get in touch with Major Reiman at once, before you leave, or someone else at OKH. Colonel Balthus or even General Schwenker if you have to. Tell them what's happened. After that, get the general and the rest of you out to Gatow as fast as possible. Do you understand?"

"Gottinger?"

It was Trakl, calling impatiently from the vestibule.

"In a moment. One more moment."

Gottinger turned back breathlessly to Zhilinsky.

"Do what I say. You must, Stepan Abramovitch."

He left the building almost at a run. From the top of the front steps he could see a dozen helmeted SS men dismantling a sandbagged machine-gun emplacement that had been set up at the other end of the street.

"Are you ready now?" called Trakl.

"As ready as I'm likely to be," said Gottinger and went over to the Gestapo car.

The room to which Gottinger had been taken was on the third floor of the Gestapo building. The colonel sitting across the desk, a small, pock-marked man with long white hands, fidgeted with a glass paperweight. Gottinger sat on a stiff-backed metal chair facing him. Inspector Trakl and three other plainclothesmen stood along the wall, their arms folded, like an audience. A small electric heater glowed red in the corner by the window. Gottinger noticed that there was an iron mesh over the window glass.

The colonel, a man named Hupfer, was trying to remain calm.

"I want your superior, not you, don't you understand me?"

"Don't *you* understand *me,* Colonel Hupfer? Your men have interfered with an extremely important and delicate operation. Without any authority whatever. Without any idea of what . . ."

"*This* is all the authority we need, Gottinger," the colonel said, picking up a sheaf of papers. "And I advise you to stop speaking to me in that tone of voice. You people at OKH seem to think you're above the law."

"The law is as it is made by those who have the power to make it. We all know that," Gottinger was astonished to hear himself say.

"Philosophy another time, Gottinger. Right now I want this Schreiber-Hartstein person. He is responsible and he will be brought here, do you understand?"

"Impossible."

"Don't say impossible to me. It is not impossible. It is imperative. Either he already knows about the business with that whore, in which case he's a traitor, or he doesn't, in which case he's a fool who has no business being in a position of command."

"I told you, it's impossible."

Colonel Hupfer jumped up in a fury.

"It is *you* who are impossible. Look at these, then tell me who is crazy, who is right and who is wrong. I assume you're an intelligent man, Gottinger. Here, look at these. . . ."

Hupfer pushed the sheaf of papers across his littered desk. On the top was a stapled bunch of dog-eared, typewritten pages. Even upside down, Gottinger could see that they contained a series of questions and answers. The other piece of paper, of a different size and color, was a photostat of a signal tissue.

Gottinger took the documents and stared at them for a moment.

"Let me make it easy for you," said Colonel Hupfer. "The woman was a spy. She was sent here by Soviet intelligence. We know that. You hold the proof in your hands. There is a transcript of her initial interrogation. She claimed that her prison convoy had been attacked by a unit of the Fourteenth Waffen SS, Galizisches Division. You will see on the second sheet a report from an excellent and alert young officer who knew at least what *his* duty was in such cases. He checked at once and found out that the Galizisches Division had no units operating in the area where the woman claimed her convoy had been attacked. Could anything be more obvious, more stupid? Unfortunately the garrison at Kolvo was wiped out by an air raid the next day and the unit at Bryansk—to which that confirming signal you're holding was sent—was also surrounded and destroyed almost at the same time. The Golitsyn whore was being sent to Bryansk for interrogation when your headquarters' people intercepted her. We didn't find out about this until just recently, but believe me . . ."

Gottinger's eyes narrowed. "If what you say is so, how can these documents possibly be valid? Where could you have gotten them, under the circumstances you describe?"

Hupfer stared at him, his fingers closing on the paperweight. A thin smile turned the corners of his mouth. "Let me remind you which one of us it is who is asking the questions here. . . ." He raised his voice suddenly. "Trakl, go at once and see whether this Schreiber-Hartstein person has been located yet. I don't understand why it should be taking so long."

Just as Trakl had reached the door, four staff officers and a man wearing a cuff title identifying him as from the office of the Reichsminister East pushed into the room.

The man from Rosenberg's office, who held the rank of full colonel, was white with anger. Behind him was Major Reiman, in field uniform, and carrying a machine pistol.

"How dare you," the colonel from Rosenberg's office demanded of the startled Gestapo officer. "Do you have any idea of what you've almost done?"

Hupfer drew back. Reiman, the snout of his machine pistol just slightly elevated, was staring straight at Trakl and the other two plainclothesmen.

"Gottinger, are you all right?" Reiman demanded. Gottinger nodded.

Hupfer began to speak but the full colonel cut him off.

"Not another word from you, do you understand? Or you'll all answer to the Reichsminister himself."

"This is an outrage," Hupfer exclaimed. "You can't come in here like this and . . ."

". . . and do what *you* do in *other* people's offices? The devil we can't."

"I'm going to wake Müller at once and . . ."

"Do that. As soon as we're gone. But I warn you, touch that phone before we've left and you're dead where you sit. You may consider yourself a dead man in any event, Colonel Hupfer. And the rest of you as well. The operation you've interrupted not only has Reichsminister Rosenberg's personal approval but that of General Schwenker as well." The full colonel saluted. "Now, good night to you. And if I were in your position I'd start putting my affairs in order at once."

Hupfer stood motionless, thunderstruck, as the group, now including Gottinger, turned and walked rapidly out of the room.

Trakl was the first to break the silence. "Those shitheads . . ."

Hupfer stared at him, then at the papers on his desk, then back at Trakl. His mouth moved, forming the name Schreiber-Hartstein, but nothing came out.

The second plainclothesman started for the door.

Hupfer reached for the phone. It was essential that the head of the Gestapo, Müller, be informed at once. But as he lifted the receiver, he stopped cold. It was three in the morning. What if he was wrong? What if he'd acted improperly? If he'd misunderstood? It was all Trakl's fault anyhow. Trakl and his damned Russian contact. He'd have Trakl's head for this.

But in the morning, in the morning.

There was no need to make matters even worse than they were by calling now.

The general's eyes refused to focus but he could nevertheless make out Obriyan's familiar face, hazy and indistinct and very close to his own. Obriyan was holding something; a hypodermic.

Let them, the general thought. Nothing mattered now. There was nothing they could do to him that would make any difference at all. The pain from the beating they had given him was meaningless; all of the individual pains had coalesced into one overwhelming pressure and that had given way before the intolerable weight of his loss. Had it been planned that way? He recalled a story he had once read, by a French writer long dead. A prisoner of the Inquisition is to be executed. Suddenly he finds a way to escape. He makes his way out of the prison, hope rising with each step. He is almost there. Light appears at the end of the tunnel. And his executioner as well. The final torment has been administered.

If she had not come back to him it would not have meant so much. He could have read of her death without emotion. She had been long dead and he had killed her. Those wounds had healed. Now they were all open again.

Dimly, he understood that it could not have been accidental. But who had been responsible? His own people? The Germans?

He winced. Something bit into his arm. A needle. He felt the sting, a momentary pressure.

"Be calm, General. Try to breath deeply. . . ." Obriyan's voice. A numbness filled his body. He saw Zhilinsky come into the little room with an arm full of clothes: a coat, boots, furs.

Then he lost consciousness.

Trakl came through the iron gates in front of the Prinz Albrechtstrasse building at a run, temples pounding, his face purple with anger. If Hupfer didn't have the courage to wake Gruppenführer Müller up, then he'd have to do it himself. He couldn't believe that Hupfer had actually backed down before the emissaries from that half-Russian degenerate Rosenberg's office. And someone had better speak to the guards at the front gates; the men from Rosenberg's had arrived fully armed. Obviously they'd been carrying their weapons when they'd walked in. Just how such a thing had been allowed, he couldn't understand. What would it be next time, he wondered?

Seething with resentment, and moral outrage, Trakl slammed past the astonished sentries and onto the pavement. Where the devil was Glantz? Hadn't he ordered him to wait with the car? How was he to get over to Müller's without a car?

Then he saw it.

Parked just a little further down the street was a long black staff Mercedes. Two men in leather coats stood by the hood. One of them was Glantz.

Trakl shouted, half in annoyance, half in growing fear.

Glantz didn't move. Neither did the other man. Trakl flamed. He couldn't believe what was happening.

Glantz still didn't move.

Trakl became aware—with that sixth sense that all good policemen have—that someone was coming up behind him on the dark street.

Three more men. One in SS uniform, the other two in civilian clothes. Police, obviously. He thought he recognized one of them. What the devil are they doing there? And what was the matter with Glantz? Had he been struck dumb?

Then the rear door of the Mercedes opened and a figure leaned out. The streetlight glinted from the braid on the cap and the shoulders. And the monocle.

Trakl froze. It was Field Marshal Keitel.

The Field Marshal gestured imperiously for Trakl to come over. As the inspector rushed up to the car, he saw that there was another man in the backseat—a much smaller man, with an almost chinless face, a small mustache, and narrowed, oriental eyes peering out from behind thick lenses. A schoolmaster's face.

Himmler.

"Inspector Trakl?" Keitel asked languidly. "Yes, you *are* Inspector Trakl, aren't you? You're the one who's responsible for this piggery, yes?"

Trakl's heart mounted instantly to his throat. The three men behind him had closed the gap and were almost on his heels.

Himmler leaned forward and wagged one finger at him.

"Flossenberg," he said. Loud enough to be heard outside the car.

Four pairs of hands fell at once on Trakl's shoulders and arms. He didn't even have time to protest.

Colonel Budyankov had arrived at Lake Byeleymostnoy two days after the armored train bearing Major Gelb and Major Chekarin's unit had reported in. Chekarin's depleted force had been augmented by levies along the way, units of old Kourbash's cavalry that had come with them from Tul, half a dozen more partisan groups, and four additional companies of NKVD Special Purposes troops that had been siphoned from units between Orel and the lake.

Budyankov's arrival preceded that of the trainload of prisoners by less than two hours. It was clear to Engineer Captain Babayev that Budyankov had simply been traveling in the van, and that the prisoner train was under his direct command.

Together with Major Gelb and Major Trepov, Babayev had gone to meet Budyankov at the railroad siding to the south of the camp. The last two cars of the train were loaded with prison uniforms and equipment for the guards, including a substantial supply of rifle and machine-gun ammunition.

Budyankov came bounding down the iron steps from his coach in high spirits, a heavy fur hat on his head, its earflaps up. He wore fur gloves and a pistol belt with a holster so large that it reminded Babayev of the old photographs of General Kondratenko during the siege of Port Arthur.

A light snow was falling. Not enough to delay the unloading. The workmen who had constructed the camp were put to work emptying out the rear cars. Budyankov introduced himself to the engineers and clapped Gelb and Trepov both on the back.

"If this comes off, you're both going to get a medal. And don't think that exercise at Tul will go unnoticed either. Too bad we can't do as much for every one of the swine."

"We lost a few men, comrade Colonel," said Gelb. "It was inevitable. The order was mine and I accept full responsibility."

"Both of you . . . stop scowling. Didn't you hear me? A medal. At the very least. For Major Chekarin too, in spite of himself. There's been a new development too—a bonus, you might say. An extra reward for all our good work. I'll explain it all later, in detail. Well then, let's get on with it." Budyankov pointed toward the barracks compound, a long sprawl of low wooden buildings surrounded by a double enclosure of log fences and barbed wire. "The guard towers are mounted?"

"As you ordered."

"And a close watch is being kept? What about the radio monitor?"

"Nothing. An odd signal that wasn't there a few days ago. But we can't pinpoint it," Trepov said. "There's no triangulation equipment here."

Budyankov smiled. "Nothing to be concerned about, I'm sure. Let's not worry ourselves. The nearest functioning German unit is presently one hundred and twenty kilometers away, caught in a salient around Wysnograd and being chewed up nicely by General Kuzin's tanks. I wouldn't worry about them, not for the moment at any rate."

Gelb nodded, feeling that a perfunctory agreement was the best course, even though he had his own doubts. Babayev followed suit. It was not their place to argue. Besides, now that the construction work was finished and the camp administration was about to be handed over to the professionals, perhaps they would be released to go back to Moscow.

"Now," Budyankov said as they walked up the path to the officers' quarters, "I suppose we had better get started straightening things out." He handed Babayev a sheaf of papers. "You'll remain for a while longer. Your orders are on top, as you see. The disposition of prisoners and guards, the daily regimen and duties, are all there. You will be temporary chief of works here, answerable directly to Major Gelb, who will also remain."

Babayev's heart sank. Not only was he being held there, unable to get back to the city and to some kind of sensible life, but he was being placed under Gelb's orders. A Jew. He bristled but held his temper.

Opening the orders, he read quickly.

"There must be some mistake," he said, shaking his head. What he had just read did not make sense. "These dispositions, the schedules, all of this . . . surely, comrade Colonel . . ."

"It's all in order, I assure you. And you will please see to it that everything is operational, exactly according to those orders, by nightfall tomorrow. It shouldn't take you even that long."

"You're positive?" Babayev simply could not believe what he had read. The whole thing seemed to him upside down. Absolute insanity.

"Please don't ask me again," Colonel Budyankov said, a hard edge to his voice this time. "That is *exactly* how things are to be done."

Babayev was in a fleeing mood now. He saluted as fast as he could and stumped off down the path, kicking snow.

Before Gelb had a chance to say anything in his defense, Budyankov took him by the arm.

"Really, you've done very, very well. Both of you. We've only got a little further to go, so let's pay attention to what we're doing. I want to see comrade Chekarin, of course. At dinner will do nicely. And Babayev. We shall have to explain things to him a little more. I'm afraid we've taken him by surprise, and he won't be able to function properly if he doesn't understand. Of course, there's no reason why he shouldn't." He paused. "Now, my dear Gelb, let's go and see about the ammunition personally. I want to watch the unloading and make sure everything is in order. After all, the ammunition is the most important thing of all, isn't it?"

For a little more than an hour, Schreiber-Hartstein had been standing at the end of the airstrip, watching the big, trimotored Junkers drift in through a heavy cloud cover. The runway was cleared but only barely; huge humps of ice and snow bordered the entire landing field, allowing barely enough room for the transports to set down. Half a dozen snow plows sat waiting for the next fall. It gave him an odd sense of tranquility to stand there in the freezing weather, his cheeks rubbed raw by the wind, his glasses frosting over everytime he was careless about breathing too hard. The sky was a pale white, and the light that somehow filtered through the endless clouds was little more than the faintest counterfeit of day. His ears had long since ceased stinging and were now numb, even under the flaps of his fur cap. He had not stamped his feet about for a good ten minutes and as he watched the last of the Ju-52s make their ponderous approach he wondered idly whether he would be able to move his feet at all now.

To his left he could see the low sheds in which the fighter planes and reconnaissance aircraft were hangared. Much farther down the field, well past the squat structure that served as a control tower, were five enormous wooden buildings, so heaped with snow that they appeared a part of the low hills against which they had been built. In these were the gliders and the tow planes.

Schreiber-Hartstein tugged back his glove so as to give himself a brief glimpse of the face of his watch. What difference did it really make? What did time mean in such a place? The only thing that mattered was the count. All of the transports were in. Two battalions' worth of Russian volunteers were down, the very last of them, the engineer section, coming in just then.

The Junkers dipped, caught for the moment in a crosswind, its landing lights blinking, then straightened out and touched down. Schreiber-Hartstein took a deep breath and turned, kicking the snow away, astounded to find that he could still walk.

From the headquarters building, another long wooden shack with a corrugated tin roof, came a thin trickle of smoke and the sound of voices. The wind howled, scourging the runway and sending up high clouds of powdered March snow.

They were all there—Beifelder, Gottinger, and most of the Russian officers. Even Stalkov and Kurenko. The only one missing was the most important—Golitsyn.

Schreiber-Hartstein had insisted that Golitsyn accompany him in the lead aircraft of the convoy. For the entire trip the General had sat slumped like a dead man in the bucket seat into which he had been strapped, his chin on his chest, his eyes closed, his mouth hanging open. Schreiber-Hartstein had attributed the general's condition to the drugs Zhilinsky had administered; they would take a few hours to wear off. It was regrettable but there had been no other way of getting Golitsyn on board. He had struggled and protested all the way from Viktoriastrasse to Gatow, and it was only because he had been weakened by the beating he had received from the Gestapo that Obriyan and Gottinger had been able to control him at all.

At first Schreiber-Hartstein had blamed himself for all that had happened. Perhaps if he had been more sensitive to the situation, the tragedy might have been avoided. He had reproached himself for it a thousand times over while the fleet of Junkers roared out over Poland and toward the front lines near Orel. He realized that he had been so preoccupied with the threat to the operation posed by the Gestapo's interest in Kurenko that he hadn't given the woman a second thought. Nor had he appreciated fully the effect that her appearance had had on Golitsyn. Even now he did not fully comprehend what had happened or why—only that the woman's death had fallen on the general like a hammer blow and that it seemed doubtful that he would ever recover from it.

He pushed open the door to the headquarters building and stamped inside. The room was heated by a huge iron stove from which ran a bewildering network of pipes. Maps cluttered the walls. The air was heavy with tobacco smoke and the acrid stench of ersatz coffee being cooked in a large iron pot toward the rear of the room where a door gave way onto the radio room.

He shook the snow from the collar of his sheepskin coat. The stiff leather creaked and complained. His gloves would barely come off; they retained the shape of his hands even when he threw them onto the table on which Stalkov and two others had been playing cards.

"The last one's down," he announced. No one stirred. Only Stalkov looked up but he too remained silent.

Beifelder, wearing a heavy woolen sweater, had just come out of the radio room, a pipe stuck in his mouth, a sheaf of papers in his hands.

"The meteorological station is sending. Can you imagine? In weather like this? It's actually sending."

"That's what it was designed to do," said Gottinger. "A triumph of German science. It tells us which way the wind blows. We should always seek to know that," he said with a sad smile.

"Certainly," said Zhilinsky. "No one would disagree."

"What about Alexander Semyonovitch?"

Beifelder shook his head.

"We put him to bed in the back. Obriyan is with him. Also two of our people." He paused. It was clear from his expression that he had little hope of the general's recovery.

"Still no?" said Schreiber-Hartstein.

"Still. I'm afraid . . ." His voice trailed off.

Stalkov shook his head angrily. "Why should one man matter so? Do you think they're going to know whether he's actually out there or not? Don't be foolish."

"Still," said Schreiber-Hartstein, "it would be so much better . . ."

"She fooled us all, that one," said Zhilinsky. "Her death was, for him, the one irrefutable argument. They gave her back to him . . . and then she was taken away again. What a disaster."

Kurenko stood up. "What do you intend doing with me now?"

"Why, nothing. You've performed brilliantly. You have our thanks. Without the two of you, none of this would be possible."

Kurenko scowled. He did not want to feel pleased with himself. With these men, at least, he felt a strange sense of comradeship that he found infuriating but undeniable. He kept remembering the long lines of prisoners—Russian prisoners—trudging along the roadside. He remembered the police captain, Sipyagin, and the others, Budyankov and Trepov. Were these men any worse?

He became aware that Schreiber-Hartstein was staring at him. Unexpectedly, the German took two steps forward and put his hand on Kurenko's shoulder. It was as though he had read his mind. He looked at him sadly and said, simply, "I know . . . it isn't easy."

Just then, Nikiforov came out of the radio room. In the corridor, a number of men in flying suits were shaking the snow from their boots. Nikiforov was red, excited.

"The weather's good . . ." he announced.

Beifelder nodded. "Kraus says it should hold."

"For how long?"

"At least another thirty-six hours."

"And at Byeleymostnoy?"

"The mists, as always. But good winds. And the temperature is steady."

"You don't actually expect a thaw this early in March, do you? It would be unheard of. . . ."

"In this country you don't take anything for granted, believe me."

They walked back across the snow-powdered runway toward the glider sheds. The last of the Junkers was unloading. The Russian volunteers dog-trotted down the field to the trucks that were waiting to take them to their billets in the nearby village of Kosmach. Kurenko looked up. The sky was now an icy blue-gray, the sun a pale golden smear high to the east. Nikiforov stomped along just ahead of him, delighted with the wind, the cold. With everything. Stalkov whistled a merry tune. Along the edge of the runway, mechanics in bulky coveralls were struggling with ice-covered Henschels, trying to get them serviced for the day's routine observation flights.

A few hundred meters from the glider hangars, they were met by the pilot, Bauer, and the four men who were to fly the tow planes. Kurenko had gotten to know the German lieutenant fairly well and was accustomed to his moods and his expressions. Now, he could tell, there was something obviously bothering the man. But Bauer said nothing, and continued on down the path.

"You wanted to see them, Herr Hauptmann?" he said at last as they came to the hangar doors. "Well then . . . if you please . . ." He signaled to his mechanics, who began pulling on the chains that controlled the doors. The doors swung open slowly, giving onto a vast, dense blackness.

They stood for a moment, at the threshold, trying to adjust their eyes to the gloom within the hangar.

Something was wrong. Kurenko stepped back. Nikiforov let out a whistle and even Schreiber-Hartstein appeared startled.

Within the hangar, just now swimming into view, was an enormous, hulking shape. A towering blackness with wings that spanned the entire width of the hangar.

"My God . . ." cried Nikiforov. "What *is* that thing?"

"That *thing,*" said Bauer solemnly, "is a Messerschmitt 321, my friend, called the *Gigant,* for obvious reasons. We have four of them. . . . All the same size, naturally."

"Why, it must be almost seventy meters across," cried the astounded Nikiforov.

Bauer nodded.

"And it weighs, gentlemen, thirteen thousand kilograms. Empty. Up to seventy-six thousand fully loaded."

"Insane," said Zhilinsky.

"Bauer, this must be a joke of some kind," said Schreiber-Hartstein, his voice barely above a whisper. "And if it is, it's in very poor taste."

"I assure you, Herr Hauptmann, this is no joke. *These* are your gliders. They will be towed by twin-yoked Heinkel Zwillings. Another monstrosity, but it can't be helped."

"It *can* be helped and it will be. At once."

Bauer shook his head, but only just slightly. He had no desire to get into an argument with Schreiber-Hartstein. After all, it had not been his fault, and he was damned if he was going to take the blame.

Just then the lights in the hangar went on and the magnitude of the disaster became at once plain.

The gliders were enormous. The bodies were huge, swollen and grotesque, capable of holding tanks, trucks, an 88mm gun. God only knew what else. The fuselage alone loomed some twelve meters high and the wings went out of sight in the shadows at either side of the hangar.

"Preposterous," said Beifelder. "Lieutenant Bauer, is it seriously suggested that such a behemoth be landed on ice? How can such a thing be done? Surely . . ."

By this time Bauer had turned away. His voice echoed from the hangar walls like a trumpet of doom.

"The smaller gliders were lost trying to bring supplies into Stalingrad. These, too, were intended for that purpose but they arrived . . . too late. It's simple, Hauptmann. We either use them or cancel the operation."

Schreiber-Hartstein stood there, his face gray, a small vein in his forehead beginning to pain him terribly. As though a nail had been pushed into his left eye. He pulled off his glasses and looked once again at the towering monster.

There was a long silence.

Then Nikiforov laughed.

"Once upon a time, long ago, when I was in good Czar Nicholas's service, gentlemen, I managed to get Sikorsky's first four-engined monster off the ground. That was a long time ago, and they said then that we would never do it. Such a monster could not possibly fly. Four motors? Hah! Can you imagine? *Ilya Mourometz* it was called . . . *but it flew,* Herr Hauptmann. *I* flew it." He turned on his heel, just too rapidly to see Bauer start to grin.

"Now, with your permission, let us go back where it's warm, have some of that foul coffee of yours and see what we can figure out."

Nikiforov had the slide rule, Kurenko the map, and Schreiber-Hartstein the day's weather reports. Bauer stood just behind them with the Me-321 flight manual, checking their figures against the *Gigant*'s known capabilities. From the radio room came a steady beeping, the signal from Stalkov's "windmill," the little weather station whirling its propeller blades in the trees above the frozen lake.

Nikiforov had taken off his sweater and was now alternating coffee with whiskey. His hands moved rapidly, guiding the protractor and the rule over the map. A pad at his elbow was already filled with calculations.

"So . . . read me again the elevation of the hill mask. The ones just to the north of the lake," he said. "Once again. I don't trust these old eyes on something so small."

"Three hundred and twelve meters above sea level," intoned Kurenko.

"So, so . . . just as before. And here, at the center of the lake, we have two hundred sixty-three meters." He began drawing long, flat triangles. First one, then another. "Bauer, can those monsters of yours manage a one-on-twelve glide ratio?"

"With a skillfull pilot, yes, just barely."

"So . . . we have a one on twelve then. Good. You see, here? A nice shallow glide. So, we will hit with not too much impact. A ten percent factor perhaps. No more."

"But fully loaded there will be almost seventy thousand kilograms."

"The ice can take it. Remember, our best icebreakers are almost powerless against a mere two meters of ice. It *will* hold, believe me. It will hold."

Stalkov's face clouded. He was thinking of another time, another place. He whispered, "Yes, yes. At Kronstadt. I was there. The shells landed. Some of them didn't even break the surface of the ice."

Nikiforov scowled darkly. "Kronstadt? You were *there,* Boris Trifomovitch? We should have known then, shouldn't we? What kind of a revolution we'd made. It devoured its own children from the start, didn't it?"

Kurenko was too young to remember Kronstadt. He had been no more than two or three when it had happened. The sailors of the Kronstadt naval base in the Bay of Finland outside Petrograd had rebelled against the new government, claiming that it had not moved fast enough, that it was not truly revolutionary. Moscow had sent Trotsky to crush the rebellion and he had done so, with much bloodshed and brutality, attacking straight across the ice of the bay.

"On which side were you, Boris Trifomovitch?" Nikiforov asked quietly.

"The living side," Stalkov replied.

"Ça se voit," said Nikiforov.

"It's always the best side," said Stalkov with a grin.

Kurenko stared at him. Kronstadt had always seemed to him a watershed. The first time that the revolution had compromised itself for the sake of expediency. For survival. Just as it had twenty years later when Stalin had made his pact with the Nazis. And as it had done so many times between those two points. Trotsky, it was whispered, had never been the same after Kronstadt. He had been forced to exterminate those with whom he agreed in order to preserve a government that was already veering dangerously from the path he thought it should take.

So Stalkov had been there. Kurenko closed his eyes, trying to imagine the last battle, the attack across the ice floes. Whirling snow. Silent explosions and geysers of black water and ice.

Schreiber-Hartstein's voice cut in on his brooding.

"The weather signals show the temperature is holding. Well below freezing." He turned to Kurenko. "According to your measurements, we have at least one and a half meters of ice on the lake at the landing point. Are you sure? I must ask you to consider. You must be positive."

"I'm sure, Captain. There's no question about it." He recalled vividly the feel of the weighted line in his hands, the way the knots had slipped by his gloved fingers. Had he counted correctly? Yes, he was positive. And hadn't the measurements checked against the auger length? One and a half meters, at the very least.

He tapped his pencil on the table.

"Absolutely, Captain. Solid enough. More than solid enough."

"Then it's up to you, Lieutenant Bauer. And you, Major Nikiforov."

"It will hold," said Nikiforov.

Bauer lit a cigarette. Everyone waited for him to speak. Finally he said, "All right, if we must, we must. The little DFS machines would have been far better, but if the data is as it is, if the temperatures hold, then . . . yes. If you say so, we go."

"How long before the Zwillings are ready?" asked Schreiber-Hartstein.

"Eight hours. No longer."

"That's just as well. The men need some sleep, some food. And time to check out their equipment." He looked at the clock on the wall. "From here to Byeleymostnoy . . . how long?"

"Two hours at most, even with a stiff head wind," Bauer said.

"Dawn is at what time?"

"First light at 0650."

Schreiber-Hartstein studied the weather projections. The report predicted a cold, bitter day, but without storms of any kind. Little turbulence was expected. The damn thing was so sensitive. . . . He remembered talking once to a Luftwaffe captain who had been in on the glider attack on Eben Emael and how he had told him that the slightest crosswind could mean the difference between being on target and winding up in a canal. And the gliders they had used were one-twentieth the size of the giant Messerschmitts. Nor had they ice, dense forests with high firs, treacherous winds, and the white mist to contend with. . . .

The white mist. That too . . .

But there was now no possibility of turning back. Even if Bauer and Nikiforov had said no, he would have gone ahead. He knew that well enough.

"All right, gentlemen. We proceed. Captain Beifelder will contact Major Dietrich of the Sixteenth Waffen SS, who are to link up with us in the forests west of the lake after we take the camp. Unless there's a problem there, we leave at 0300 hours tomorrow morning."

Kurenko stood well back in the corridor while Schreiber-Hartstein fitted his key to the lock. Beifelder stood to one side, little beads of perspiration on his forehead.

"Has the drug worn off yet?" Schreiber-Hartstein asked.

"An hour ago, according to Doctor Seibert," Beifelder replied glumly.

"What was he given?"

"A sedative, that's all. Strong enough to fell an elephant, but it was necessary. Otherwise they would never have gotten him to Gatow."

"Then it was all against his will?" Schreiber-Hartstein asked.

"There is no 'will' left," Beifelder replied. "The beating caused no real damage to the body . . . but the will? Gone, not a shred left."

Kurenko whistled. Damn them all. What did they expect *he* could do in such a situation?

Schreiber-Hartstein turned the knob. "He *must* lead the men. They'll follow no one else. The entire operation will collapse if he doesn't lead. He must . . . he *will*."

"I wish I could be so sure," said Beifelder.

"He'll snap out of it, Martin. He's got to."

The room was dark and very cold. A single oil lamp burned on a table next to the general's cot. For a moment Kurenko did not even see Golitsyn sitting there. There was only a gray, blanket-wrapped shadow. Not a man.

"Alexander Semyonovitch? Do you feel better now? Shall I have the doctor come in to look at you again? Do you want something hot to drink?"

"I don't need anything," Golitsyn said dully. Kurenko winced at the hollow sound of the man's voice. "No more drugs, for God's sake."

"You needed a sedative," Schreiber-Hartstein began.

"Much more than that was needed. Trust was needed. Honor was needed. Above all, honesty was needed. Why don't you leave me alone? What good am I to you now?"

"Look, I've brought Kurenko to you. He's been waiting here with the others."

"Let them wait forever. I'm finished, Reinhardt Gavrilovitch. Understand that. You should not have brought me here. I didn't want to come."

"There is no question of choice in this," Schreiber-Hartstein said gently. "Too much depends on you now, Alexander Semyonovitch. You must go on."

"Must I?" Golitsyn began to laugh, slowly at first, the laugh dissolving into a rasping, sobbing noise horrible to hear.

"Vasya . . . explain to them that I cannot be forced."

Kurenko reached out, trying to touch the man, to reassure him. It seemed to him the only thing he could do.

Golitsyn rose suddenly and came two heavy steps forward, enfolding Kurenko in a violent embrace. Kurenko was not a small man but for a moment he vanished entirely in the general's arms. He thought he felt the general's fingers fumbling briefly at his belt. . . . No . . . impossible . . .

A chill swept through him. He pulled away.

It was hard to see in the dim light of the room. He looked quickly at the general's hands. They were open and empty.

The tension eased for a second.

Then Golitsyn began to weep. It was a terrible thing to see, that great ugly face contorted and stained by tears, the huge body racked by sobs. Kurenko stepped back. Now, at last, Budyankov had what he wanted. It was truly finished. He was ashamed to intrude on such a sorry private spectacle.

"General . . ." began Schreiber-Hartstein.

"No, Reinhardt Gavrilovitch. Not another word. You are a decent man, I know that, but you've lied to me in spite of yourself. And you've lied to yourself as well, which is worse. You have all been living in a fantasy. In the terrible real world, Reinhardt Gavrilovitch, there is no such thing anymore as honor or honesty. The madmen have taken over the asylum and the keepers are in the cages."

Schreiber-Hartstein sat down, ashen-faced, on the cot next to Golitsyn, and for a few long moments held his own head in his hands. Kurenko stood there, wishing he could disappear in the smoke of the lamp.

Finally Schreiber-Hartstein took his hands away. For one second, Kurenko thought he too had been weeping.

"All right," the German said wearily. "What can I say to you? Alexander Semyonovitch, you're right. It's no use, is it?"

"You can have me shot if you wish," Golitsyn said. "I won't blame you. Yes, you should do that. No one would dare say a word against you if you did."

Schreiber-Hartstein stood up.

"I'll come back in the morning, Alexander Semyonovitch. We'll have our breakfast together. For now, I'm going to send Doctor Seibert in to see you. He will give you another injection so you'll sleep."

"I'll sleep without an injection," Golitsyn said, his voice dead and hollow. He had stopped weeping now; the tears were drying up. He pulled the blanket around himself. "Yes, sleep would be good now."

The general leaned back against the rough wallboards of the room and closed his eyes.

"Good," he intoned again. "One may as well sleep."

15

An exile,
I linger and suffer!
Oh! When may I discard this life?
Who shall lend me the wings of a dove
That I may fly away and rest
At last?

Kondrati Ryleyev
Written on a maple leaf
before his execution,
July, 1826

Alexander Semyonovitch went slowly over to the frosted window and cleared away a little circle with his breath. Only a little of the runway was visible, a few meters of black earth bordered by spectral blue landing lights which had just been turned on. A *Stork* drifted weightlessly down, driven from the sky by snow flurries.

The silence in the room was as heavy as the air. The snow swallowed all sound; it was as though he had gone deaf. Once, he knew, he would have found it incredibly peaceful. Now, the silence only intensified his pain.

The room was hot. The small iron stove in the corner glowed cherry red. His body streamed with sweat. His temples throbbed.

He pressed his forehead to the smooth, cold windowpane, hoping to clear his mind. It didn't help. His body ached but the ache was nothing compared to what he felt within, where no medicine could reach.

He let his gaze wander as far as it could down the runway and off into the dark. He had always visualized his life as a long road curving up over a broad horizon, like the edge of the world. Along this road he could see himself and plot the periods of his life. The runway was like that. The two images coincided, the real and the imaginary, like the split field of a camera range finder. He saw his road running on its long curve through a swarming mass of figures and events. There—an almost unrecognizable child standing small and wretched at a narrow point, cringing under the discipline of the seminarians who had taught him. Poor child. A dull tolling of bells filtered momentarily through the falling snow, then was gone. A figure, large as a haystack, stood farther up the road; himself, as he had been during the revolution. Understanding nothing. Farther on, he saw himself as he had been on that day in the fields outside Strasneshev, struggling with Nina Andreyeva's wooden harrow. There were horses along that stretch of road, and the smell of gunpowder. But not doubt. He had known by then exactly where he was going.

He saw his other selves just as clearly, as he had been in China, as he had been on his return to Moscow. Like chess pieces ranged along a long, narrow board. He looked from one face to another, all of them his own, searching for a glimmer of understanding.

What dead, grim, fanatic faces, he thought. Could they be mine, *all* of them?

But there were not as many faces as he had imagined. Long stretches of the road were dark and impossible to make out. Somehow, it seemed that his life had been far shorter than he had thought. He knew, though, where the wrong turning had occurred; it had been on the day he had presumed a capacity to make moral judgments and had begun to act on them. Decisions had been easy after that. He had swung like a pendulum from one extreme to another. Everything had been simple, clear. But not better.

He blinked. There was Nina Andreyeva, standing on his curved road, where, otherwise, there were only multitudinous counterparts of himself. She stood, small and quiet, between the blue lights of the landing field, smiling indulgently and kindly, as though she had understood all along what a child he was and had forgiven him everything because of it.

She raised a hand and beckoned not to him at the window but to the figure who stood at the end of the path, just before it curved out of sight over the gray horizon. At first the figure hesitated, then began to move toward her, slowly to begin with, then with a more and more resilient step.

Alexander Semyonovitch took his face away from the dark windowpane. The gas lamp hissed behind him on the table. Little drops of water had condensed above his eyebrows; he rubbed them away with the back of his hand.

"Ninotchka . . . ?"

It was his own voice, soft and hoarse, barely recognizable. The only way possible had been through her. He had known it, truly, but had lied to himself over and over again. None of the rest really mattered. Only those lies and the injury he had done her. And himself.

He looked back through the circle on the windowpane, now beginning to frost over again. Opaque and glistening, like a mirror.

She was still there, between the blue landing lights with a soft curtain of snow behind her.

"Ninotchka . . . come, you'll injure yourself standing there. How cold it is . . . please . . . come. You will come, won't you?"

He reached into his pocket for the single cartridge he had taken from Kurenko's pouch when he had embraced him before. The metal casing was warm from the heat of his body. It felt smooth and the smoothness was reassuring.

"Ninotchka?" he said again, and took the cartridge from his pocket, held it up to the light. Only one.

He would have to do it right the first time.

The room seemed terribly crowded though there were less than two dozen people there—most of the battalion staff, Bauer and his pilots, the air field commandant, Major Wilcke, and the group of officers from Berlin. The lamps smoked and in the next room the radio kept up its dismal whining, the dull *beep-beep* of the meteorological station signal like the chirrup of some primeval cricket lost down a well.

Zhilinsky leaned back in his chair and began to smile spasmodically in that desperate way that condemned men will sometimes smile. This cannot be happening. Such a thing is impossible. It is absurd. Therefore it is also intensely amusing. See, I am amused, I am laughing. Therefore there is nothing to be concerned about . . . do you see?

"So he absolutely refuses? You're sure of this, Hauptmann?"

"I am sure, and in any event even if he were to change his mind and agree to go, I would not allow it."

Stalkov leaned across the table, his face dark, angry.

"But if he *were* to change his mind . . ."

"It's out of the question."

"Then it's all finished, isn't it?" said Zhilinsky, his voice even higher, more distraught than before.

Bauer shook his head and whistled, lit another cigarette, and immediately snuffed it out. "This is idiotic," he said under his breath. "There is an entire battalion waiting out there—planes, tugs, equipment that could be used elsewhere. . . . If you please, Hauptmann, we must know. . . ."

"Not to mention the Sixteenth Waffen SS who wait for you in an exposed position and cannot possibly secure themselves unless you do carry it off. It's unthinkable that they should be abandoned."

"What's left of them," Nikiforov said. "All right. For my part, I say we do it without him. Of course it's not up to me."

"Gentlemen . . ." Schreiber-Hartstein interrupted. "Stalkov is right. You are all right. It *is* unthinkable that we abandon the operation at this point. Too much depends on it. Not only the fate of the entire Russian army of liberation, not only the lives of the Sixteenth Waffen SS, not only the lives of Captain Beifelder and the others who've put their heads on the block in order to obtain consent to this venture. It goes far beyond that, and you all know what I mean. If there's to be a change in the *Ost* policy, if there's to be an end to this insane slaughter," his voice was now shaking and he faltered, lapsing for a moment into silence. Bauer stared at him in astonishment. Though Beifelder and the others from OKH knew the depths of Schreiber-Hartstein's passion, it had never occurred to Bauer or the others that there was anything more to the Russian volunteer force than a military expediency. In a way, what Schreiber-Hartstein was now saying was treason. Elsewhere, it would have been punished summarily as such.

Before Schreiber-Hartstein could recover his voice, there was a rapid, agitated knocking on the door of the operations hut. Nikiforov sprang up and pulled the door open.

One of the men who had been assigned to guard Golitsyn's hut stood there, a wild look on his face.

"You must come at once, Herr Hauptmann."

"What the devil?" Nikiforov burst out.

Schreiber-Hartstein's head turned so sharply that the clicking of his bones could be distinctly heard.

"The general, sir," said the guard. "You'd better come quickly."

It was only a dozen meters or so from the operations shack to the hut where Golitsyn had been quartered. Schreiber-Hartstein led the way, Kurenko and Stalkov right behind him. The door to the hut was open as was the door to Golitsyn's room within.

The guard would not go in but stood, terrified, by the open door.

Golitsyn lay on his back on the cot, his right arm dangling over the side. On the floor by his spread fingers lay the pistol that Schreiber-Hartstein had provided for him in Berlin.

There was a neat hole in Golitsyn's right temple. The left side of his head, where the bullet had exited, had ceased to exist.

Schreiber-Hartstein, his face white, his hand trembling violently, picked up the note that lay on the floor beside the still-smoking pistol.

"Samsonov was right. It is impossible to live without honor, even if the fault lies elsewhere. I blame none of you, but it is impossible to go on this way. Try to understand."

Schreiber-Hartstein read the note aloud in a suffocated voice. Then he put the paper down, went to the door, and ordered the guard inside. He slammed the door shut and locked it.

"How could such a thing have happened? There were no bullets for the pistol. I myself saw to that. He could not possibly have . . . ah, but he did, he did. That's the truth of it. My God, he *did*." He turned to the dead man and in a very low, calm voice said, "Forgive me, Alexander Semyonovitch. You must forgive us all."

Kurenko furtively touched his belt. His fingers moved quickly to the little cartridge pouch just behind the holster; it was there, he thought, that he had felt the general's fingers for that one fleeting moment when the general had embraced him.

And then he knew.

Stalkov sat down heavily at the little table at which Golitsyn had written the note. The pen still lay there, uncapped. Stalkov picked it up and held it to the light as though to examine it more closely.

"One bullet, no bigger than this nib . . ."

"Mother of God," said Beifelder. "After all of our work, for it to come to this."

"No, no," said Schreiber-Hartstein, a deathly calm in his voice. He turned to the guard. "Who else knows of this besides yourself?"

"No one, sir. I went directly to you when I saw what had happened."

"No one else heard the shot?"

"The wind is very heavy, sir. I barely heard the shot myself and I was just outside the door."

Schreiber-Hartstein stood there for a long moment. Everyone watched him. No one spoke.

Then Schreiber-Hartstein pointed to the body.

"So . . . so . . . cover the face please. At least that much respect should be shown." He went to the door and turned as though blocking the exit. "Boris Trifomovitch, will you stand please."

Stalkov, a puzzled expression on his face, did as he was asked.

"Yes," said Schreiber-Hartstein, studying him up and down. "I think it can be managed. If you will agree, Boris Trifomovitch, all of this can be patched over, at least for the time being. With your help, we will be able to carry it off after all, I think."

"What are you saying, Captain?"

"Sit down, gentlemen, wherever you can, and I'll explain to you exactly what I have in mind."

At exactly 0300 hours the first of the twin-yoked Heinkel tugs lifted grudgingly off the runway. The landing field was deep in darkness. A light rain was falling and it was impossible to see the tow line behind the Zwilling slowly going taut. When the giant glider far behind it on the runway lofted slowly and silently into the air it seemed more an act of magic than of science. The huge dark shape strained for the first few seconds against an invisible force, then suddenly rose with perfect, accepting grace, as though all at once its monstrous weight had been forgiven and it had been set forever free of gravity.

At regular intervals the four other Heinkels roared down the runway, their five motors straining, the double fuselages trembling as though about to pull apart. They vanished swiftly into the stygian, rain-swept sky, each followed at a great distance by a spectral bat shadow, deep-bellied and impossibly huge.

As the last of them rose out of sight and the pale blue runway lamps blinked off, Gottinger pulled his coat collar tighter up under his chin, thanked God he had been left behind, and wiped the rain from his cheeks. Then he went back to the radio shack to monitor the meteorological reports and to make sure that contact was maintained with the two Waffen SS battalions waiting in the woods southwest of Lake Byeleymostnoy.

Vassily Kurenko had never had such an experience before. There was no sound, no vibration, no sense of power straining to keep the huge bulk of the glider aloft. It seemed impossible that he was on board an aircraft of any kind. The sensation was far more like being adrift on some placid night sea. There was only a hint of motion, an occasional dip or swing as an unexpected air current pushed up at the enormous wings.

In the rear of the *Gigant* almost two hundred men of the First RONA Engineer Battalion, all in ghostly white jump suits, sat with their backs to the canvas walls of the glider. Some slept, others smoked, though it was against Lieutenant Bauer's strict injunction. A few sang softly to themselves; it was the sound of fear, soft but distinct. Had the men been just then rushing across a bullet-swept field with an "*Urra*" on their lips, death would have seemed irrelevant, almost impertinent. But there, in the silent night sky, its presence was ponderous and near to paralyzing.

There was too much time to think and to question. And too few answers to be found.

Kurenko looked up into the pilot's compartment high above the hold. He could just barely make out Schreiber-Hartstein's lanky figure crammed into the copilot's seat next to a pale-faced protégé of Bauer's, a lieutenant named Thiel. Nikiforov, in his major's uniform, a heavy sheepskin and white coveralls, stood behind the pilot, watching his every move. He had wanted to fly the glider himself but Bauer had said no. Now his resentment had given way to fascination.

In the cramped gunner's compartment directly behind the cockpit, and almost hidden from Kurenko's view, were two other figures.

The first was Stalkov, his beard concealed by the windings of a long Luftwaffe silk scarf. He wore the general's uniform with its three stars, the general's greatcoat, and a pair of steel-rimmed spectacles from which the lenses had been removed. Next to him, propped up against the bulkhead and dressed in an identical outfit was the body of General Golitsyn.

Kurenko had held the general's feet as they had hurriedly carried him to the hangar. He would never forget nor forgive the infuriatingly tranquil expression on the dead man's face.

What right had he . . . ?

Only the five men who had been in the general's room three hours before when the suicide had been discovered knew that it would be Stalkov, almost as tall as Golitsyn, almost as massive, who would lead the attack across the ice. The men would see a huge figure lumbering forward through the white mists and they would follow unhesitatingly. Later, after the attack had succeeded, there would be time enough to gather around the general's body and salute the first martyr of Russia's new army of liberation. Then there would be a funeral in the forest, with full honors, full ceremony. Tragedy would be transmuted into legend. Dead, Alexander Semyonovitch Golitsyn, would become an even more potent force than he had been living.

A radio sputtered. The operator strained to hear over his headset. Now and then Schreiber-Hartstein glanced questioningly at him. The man would nod, hand the captain a sheet of paper covered with figures; the latest meteorological reports from the weather station.

So much depended on the direction of the wind, the density of the mist, and the temperature. If they had had the far lighter DFS machines there would have been no cause for alarm. But with the *Gigants* everything was critical. Twenty-five tons compared with four. Six times the weight, five times the impact factor. An almost impossibly shallow glide that would barely clear the top of the hills to the north of the lake.

If they were lucky.

The map on the radio operator's table showed the release point—almost four kilometers back over the hill mass—to accommodate their altitude of over 3,000 meters.

For some reason it had not occurred to Kurenko, or as far as he could tell to anyone else, that there was a good possibility that the caravan might be intercepted by Soviet fighters. The air corridor from Kursk to Byeleymostnoy was by no means clear. Half the Luftwaffe groups in the area were grounded, frozen in, their oil thick and unusable, the fields still covered with snow for lack of adequate plows.

In the silence, Kurenko waited for the whine of a Lavochkin's radials, the snarl of an I-16. In that terrible silence, he tried to understand just how in God's name he had come to be in such a position and how it was that he felt not revulsion but such a terrifying, unwanted excitement.

In his mind's eye he set one next to the other, the dour German Balt and the stocky colonel with the ruined hand. He conjured up their voices, imagined them contending with one another, explaining themselves. It was absurd. He resented them both equally. Hated them both for what they had done to him and for the moral bankruptcy of their actions. Schreiber-Hartstein was propelled not by any real sense of justice, but by the belief that the only way for Germany to win the war was to convince the Russian people to take up arms against their own government.

And Budyankov and all the rest of them—the Sipyagins, the Gelbs, the warders, and the guards? For their own purposes, they would murder their own people, burn villages, and God only knew what else. To ensure the success of a deception, they would not blink at machine-gunning prisoners and innocent men. Out of fear, they condemned and imprisoned thousands of men whose only crime it was to have been captured and to have escaped, or to have fought too long and too well on the wrong piece of terrain.

And they too did all these things in order to win. To survive.

Thank God he would not have time to think on that question for too long.

He was sure, as he sat there with the rain clouds flowing silently and darkly past the glider's cockpit windows, that he would not live out another day.

He had dozed off leaning against the canvas wall of the glider; the Zwilling's distant drone had lulled him into an uneasy sleep. When he heard the radio operator's voice and slowly came awake again he had no idea of how long he had been dozing. It could have been minutes only, or an hour or more.

The radio operator was counting backwards very slowly. At first Kurenko did not understand why, or what was happening. Then, as his eyes opened, as things came back into focus, he saw that Nikiforov was in a crouch high above him, by the little map table next to the radioman's position. He had a protractor in his hand and was squinting hard at the lines he had drawn, only barely visible by the hooded light of a tiny bulb suspended over the radio set.

Then he knew. They were approaching the release point.

For a moment he could not believe that it had actually happened—that somehow he was really there and that in the next ten minutes he would come spinning down out of the sky and crash onto the frozen surface of Lake Byeleymostnoy. A crash. Possibly through the ice. . . .

"Twelve . . . eleven . . . ten . . ."

He looked up at Schreiber-Hartstein. The man's face was a blank, a long rectangle cut out of slate. The two pale eyes did not even blink. The mouth did not move.

Kurenko could hear sounds behind him in the craft's vast hull. The men were adjusting their harnesses, checking their weapons.

"Seven . . . six . . ." intoned the radioman.

He could still hear the distant roar of the Zwillings, not only their own tug, but those behind them as well. He thought he could see the huge bat shapes of at least two of them high and to the right, just at the edge of the field of vision afforded by the overhead canopy.

He listened hard for that sound. As long as it was there, nothing was irreversible. The glider was still attached. They had only to bank and head north again.

The clouds thickened outside the windscreen. The rain had let up and there was only a hazy streaking on the glass now. They were still far too high to be in the mist.

"Three . . . two . . ." said the radioman. Nikiforov tensed. Bauer leaned forward, straining to see.

"One . . ."

There was a sharp, metallic click as the tow cable dropped loose of its mooring. Something slim and dark whipped away far to their front and vanished almost instantly; the tow cable itself.

Suddenly there was no sound at all, only their own breathing and the rustle of the men in the hull behind them.

Lieutenant Thiel's face was knotted in concentration. He gripped the control stick until his knuckles went white. Yet there was no change except for the silence. The huge glider rode the air majestically as before, as though it had not even noticed that it had been cut loose.

"Hold . . . steady to your bearing . . ." Bauer said softly.

Schreiber-Hartstein turned to the radioman. "Twenty-seven thousand megacycles," he said. "Pick up the weather station."

In a moment, the radioman had found the signal. Nikiforov took down the beeping noise, translated the code into figures almost instantly.

"The wind, it's good. Just as it should be."

"Hold to . . ." said Bauer again.

Then, for the first time, Kurenko had a definite sensation of altitude loss. They were coming down, very slowly, in a deep shallow glide. Outside, he could still see nothing, only a vague darkening below and somewhat ahead; the land mass, the hills that masked the mist-bound lake.

Suddenly, Nikiforov's voice cut through the silence like a razor.

"That *can't* be right," he cried, pushing at the radio operator. "Turn up the volume. Get the signal again, clearly this time."

He waited. Schreiber-Hartstein did not turn. Thiel bit his lip and a thin dribble of blood started down his chin.

"Again," insisted Nikiforov.

"What the hell's the matter?" demanded Bauer.

"The temperature. I'm getting a surface reading of five degrees centigrade."

"There must be something wrong with the station. What did you have before?"

"Ten degrees below." Nikiforov was sweating now. "It must be wrong, it's got to be wrong."

"If it isn't," said Thiel between clenched teeth, "we're going right through."

"It's impossible, I tell you. Not this early in the month. It was *fifteen below* yesterday."

"So . . . we're a hundred and fifty kilometers farther south and in a valley. Who knows what's true and what isn't," said Bauer grimly.

The glider continued to drop. Now Kurenko could see the land below quite clearly, coming up at them, dark and shapeless. Ahead, not far off, a vast patch of light gray began to form. It was the lake. They were aimed dead at its center. Perfectly on course.

Bauer laughed. "What are we worrying about? Are we idiots?

How long would it take to melt ice two meters thick? Are you all crazy?"

"Crazy or not . . . this huge thing," shouted Nikiforov.

"You'd better hang on," said Thiel. "We'll be in the mist in less than a minute."

"Exactly on course," said Schreiber-Hartstein. "My compliments, Lieutenant Thiel."

"Thank you, sir."

"Yes, yes, we all thank you. What a perfect job. . . ."

It was starting to grow gray, the horizon lightening, everything slowly becoming visible. The peninsula was a dark sickle against the lighter area of the lake.

"Keep checking your damned plot," Thiel cried.

The sweat poured down Nikiforov's beefy face. "What's the altitude, for Christ's sake? Give me that at least."

"Fifteen hundred meters."

"Angle of descent?"

"Eight degrees."

There was a long silence. Then Nikiforov breathed out a whistling sound of relief.

"Almost dead on, Thiel. You'll hit within fifty meters of target if you can hold it."

"Oh, I can hold the course all right. But what's going to hold this monster up when we land in that champagne bucket down there? That's what I'd like to know."

Schreiber-Hartstein didn't seem to hear or, if he did, his thoughts were faraway and untroubled. He looked at his watch and shouted back into the hull in Russian for the men to get ready.

Then, suddenly, the white mist was all around them; the glider's bulbous nose settled into it like a submarine's prow going down into a cloudy sea. Kurenko realized that the light he saw was actually the faint dawn glow reflected off the ice and into the mist.

All at once he felt the temperature change through the glider's canvas hull. Nikiforov hadn't been wrong. There was an inversion of some kind, a pocket of warmer air trapped under the mist.

"Brace yourselves," Bauer shouted. "Thirty seconds at most."

The lake rushed up under them. The mist whipped by in long, diaphanous streamers, parting here and there to show the surface of the lake just barely visible in the dim, steel-colored dawn light.

Kurenko gasped; he saw below them, with terrifying clarity, wide pools of water glistening on the surface of the ice.

He had no further time to think; the hull of the *Gigant* smashed down onto the ice with a grinding roar. For a second, the wings remained true and horizontal. Then the hull of the glider heeled over to the left. Only Thiel, strapped in, and Bauer, who had wrapped his arms around the seat, remained upright. Nikiforov shouted in pain as his head slammed against one of the tubular steel body struts. Blood spurted over his face. Schreiber-Hartstein crashed against the radio table.

"Get the hatch open," Bauer shouted. "For the love of God . . ."

Kurenko scrambled to his feet, groping past the stunned Bauer, trying to find the hatch control lever.

The glider lurched again, throwing him off his feet a second time. There was a slow, violent cracking sound from somewhere below him. The ice was giving way. He could see a black opening, like a long canyon, spreading out fanwise from the nose of the glider. Bauer, who by now had recovered his footing, wrenched at a loop-shaped steel handle. The big clamshell doors began to grind open.

Behind, in the hull, the men had regained their balance and began pushing forward along the ramp.

"Stay back there—you'll put too much weight in the nose. The clamshells will jam."

Schreiber-Hartstein, blood streaming from a deep cut on his head, shouted at the soldiers to get back. They hesitated, then halted, their faces were as white as their coveralls.

The doors opened a little wider, gripping at the ice like hands. The mists and the pale gray dawn light flooded in. Kurenko clambered down the ladder to the ramp, snatching up a machine pistol. He could see clearly how far over the *Gigant* had heeled. Its left wing tip still rested on solid, uncracked ice. There was a deep fissure ahead and a gaping black hole just to the left of the hull. Somehow, they had not gone through on impact. The giant wing span had saved them.

Out of the corner of his eye, Kurenko saw a huge shadow spread silently over the ice. The second glider was coming in, almost on top of them.

Another crash, like a hundred oil drums coming down a hill. Was it possible that they had not heard the noise at the camp? The mists, Schreiber-Hartstein insisted, would absorb the sound. In any event, there would be no way of telling, from the south shore of the lake, just where the sound had come from. A distant artillery barrage. Nothing to be worried about.

And then . . . all would be silent.

Kurenko ran forward. There was a light snow cover on the ice that gave good footing. Behind him the giant hull was emptying out. The men spread in a fanlike formation and made straight for the wooded peninsula that screened the landing spot from the camp compound.

The third glider came down. Then the fourth. All neat, perfectly spaced. The last of them hit hard and almost went through. The hull was in, through the ice and almost up to the cockpit. The doors hadn't had a chance to open, to grab. But the men were coming out through the top of the fuselage, through the smashed cockpit windows which were still a few meters above the ice.

A huge figure in a flapping greatcoat strode forward through the mists, well ahead of the first line of advancing troops. His arm was raised in a magisterial, silent gesture of command: Follow me. The pale and icy light glinted from the steel frames of his eyeglasses and the barrel of his submachine gun.

The men smiled grimly to each other and nodded.

"Grandpa's off for a walk. We'll have to hurry to keep up."

"Did you ever see such a stride as that?"

Zhilinsky's company was the first to reach the north shore of the peninsula. It took only a moment for the men to scramble up the snowy slope and vanish into the woods. Behind them, on the ice, streams of men in white coveralls moved rapidly in a long line, fanning out as they reached the shore, and disappearing into the woods. Exactly as they had planned and practiced it at Dabendorf.

A heavy machine gun company under a junior lieutenant named Levashev took to the point, to establish a covering fan of fire. Next to it, a mortar battery under a Kirghiz with an unpronounceable name stood ready, although Schreiber-Hartstein's orders were that fire anywhere other than on the guards' quarters be held at all possible cost. Under no circumstances were the prisoners' compounds to be shelled, even if the guards and garrison force retreated there.

The first attack group had gone forward with Major Obriyan and was already swinging wide in a loop through the woods, so as to come out just to the east of the officers' quarters south of the main compound. The second wave, under Levashev's command, was at the center. A third group, roughly a company and a half in size, swung to the south to cut off any retreat and complete the encirclement. It was on those men that everyone waited; until they were in position, no one else could move.

Crystals of ice formed in Kurenko's hair. He hunkered deep down in the damp snow near Nikiforov and checked the mechanism of his Schmeisser. Nikiforov wiped his mouth and spat blood into the snow.

"So, hold your breath now, little Vasya . . ." said Nikiforov, squinting into the swarming mist.

Kurenko held his breath. What an insane position to be in. Even if the attack failed and he were taken prisoner, he would probably be shot before he could get anyone to listen to him. He remembered the way it had been during the civil war. This would be far worse.

He could barely make out the men of his company around him; their coveralls and the heavy mists hid them almost completely. Through the last line of snow-laden trees he could make out the slope that dropped down to the camp and the buildings themselves just beyond . . . the huge prisoners' compound with its rows of low sheds, the guard towers and palisades, the paths fanning out to the woods and quarries to the southwest, the guards' quarters, from which a few lights were just beginning to show.

His hands were sweating badly. The temperature was unbelievable . . . well above freezing. A freak of nature. He pulled his lined gloves off and thrust them into his belt, hefted the Schmeisser, and waited.

He squinted into the southern sky. As he watched—as though *because* he was watching—a green star-flare flowered lazily high above the woods just south of the guards' quarters.

"On your feet, little Vasya," cried Nikiforov, jumping up and scattering snow all around. "For God, for country, and for that great horse's ass, Golitsyn."

Firing erupted all along the hillside. The heavy machine guns on the peninsula opened up, their tracers describing a lazy glittering curve that first fell short of the guards' quarters and then moved slowly up and began scything back and forth across the walls.

As he ran forward, Kurenko could hear the solid chunking of the Kirghiz's mortars. A series of black-orange puffballs erupted over the barracks. He could see men tumbling out of the already burning building, falling directly into the raking fire of Levashev's machine guns, now crossed by automatic weapons fire from Schreiber-Hartstein's men, who had just come charging out of the woods.

Even over the drumming of the machine guns and the constant slam of mortars, he could hear the shouting.

"Urra . . . Urra . . ."

Far ahead, the huge figure in the flapping greatcoat strode along like a colossus, firing a tommy gun from the hip.

So far, Kurenko had not fired a shot, but to his astonishment, he heard himself shouting too.

"Proshkin, get the radio shack. Knock the antenna down."

Wherever he looked, he could see RONA troops rushing down from the snowy woods, firing as they came, charging in the old-fashioned way, straight into the teeth of the fire now spewing from the guard towers.

But not a man fell. They rushed on, now close enough to lob grenades. Kurenko could see the guards up in the towers and make out the scrambling black forms that fanned out from the smoky ruin of the officers' barracks.

Then Kurenko too began to fire at the high wooden towers, sawing away at the supports. As he fired, his anger overwhelmed him. They were entitled to no quarter, those men up there. They had given him none. They had been ready enough to drive starving men to the camps in the north where, but for Budyankov, he too would probably long since have died.

What did he owe to such people? Nothing.

He kept firing until the tower began to buckle. A body pitched out of the ruin, tumbled slowly over and over, and was swallowed up in the deep snow.

The demolition squad had reached the log and wire palisades and was placing charges under cover of a cross fire from Stalkov's group and Obriyan's machine guns. By now, the guards' barracks were in flames. The mortars on the point had ceased firing. Only a few men had gotten out and these were being methodically picked off by Obriyan's sharpshooters as they struggled through the knee-deep snow.

Men from the demolition squad plowed back through the snow, trying to get clear of the walls. A geyser of smoke jetted up, lifting the logs as though they were so many toothpicks. For an instant, great loops of wire described glinting arabesques against the sky.

With a shout, the men of Obriyan's company rushed through the breech and into the prisoners' compound, still firing at the now-silent guard towers. It seemed to make no difference to them that they were firing at their own countrymen.

All around them the snow was spotted with the crumpled, bloody bodies of the guards and the camp officers. Stalkov had given the order; the camp staff was to be wiped out, down to the last man. There would be no way to take prisoners on the long trek through the forests to the rendezvous with the remains of the Sixteenth Waffen SS.

A sergeant of Obriyan's group ran by, the white sleeve of his coveralls bloody. He was the first RONA casualty Kurenko had seen.

Then they came to the palisades. A gaping hole, burning at the edges, opened onto the prison compound and the long rows of low, tar-paper-roofed sheds.

Kurenko stopped for a second as the men of his unit rushed through the breach. He rubbed the sweat from his forehead. He could hardly believe what he saw. From the aerial photos it had been impossible to appreciate the true size of the place.

There were over a dozen sheds, each at least fifty meters long. The place must have held almost a division's worth of men.

Men who could have been in the lines, fighting the fascists.

Men who were imprisoned because they had fought too well, too hard.

Men who were no different than Kurenko himself.

Kurenko swore and ran forward.

Fifty men of Obriyan's and Zhilinsky's attack squads were drawn up in a circle around the prison barracks. The rest were inside the sheds, bringing the prisoners out.

Schreiber-Hartstein was talking quietly to Stalkov and Zhilinsky. The German captain's head was still running blood from the gash he'd received on landing but, somehow, his eyeglasses had remained intact. His short, steel-gray hair looked like dirty ice. He had lost not only his helmet but his *Feldmutze* as well.

Schreiber-Hartstein looked across to where a stretcher lay on a little rise, the body covered with a gray army blanket. Then he turned to Zhilinsky.

"Who would have believed it?" he said in a choked voice. "You're sure that this is correct?"

"I can't be positive, of course, Reinhardt Gavrilovitch, but it seems so. Only two killed, seven wounded. That's all." Zhilinsky swallowed hard.

"Out of two battalions? A sign from God, yes? Reichminister Rosenberg will really have to take note now, don't you think?" He glanced quickly at Kurenko. There was one more casualty to be added to the list; they both knew that. "And what about the guards? Were any taken alive?"

"Your orders, sir . . ."

"What orders? I gave no orders concerning the guards."

"Excuse me, Herr Hauptmann. Major Stalkov gave the instructions before we left. I simply assumed . . ."

Schreiber-Hartstein's face darkened. "I suppose he was right. There was really no alternative."

"We couldn't have taken them with us, Reinhardt Gavrilovitch. Or left them here either."

They watched the prisoners being brought out of the barracks, a long line of men in ragged blue uniforms, legs wound with strips of cloth, jackets stuffed with newspaper to keep the wind out. Few of them had head covering of any kind.

"They look strong. Good, good. They're still soldiers, you can see that. They can't have been here too long. Obviously, they're men with spirit, with soul." Schreiber-Hartstein seemed to be talking almost to himself. His eyes shone, his expression was one of transfiguration.

"Get them together," he said. "All of them. Never mind the formation. I want them to know who we are. And assemble our men too. They should know . . ." And here he glanced quickly and reluctantly at the stretcher. *"They must know what has happened."*

"You're going to tell them now?" Zhilinsky asked in a whisper.

"It should be done, don't you think? In the flush of a first victory?"

Zhilinsky nodded but he could not look Schreiber-Hartstein straight in the eye.

No one had given so much as a single order. The prisoners had drawn themselves up into ranks in the hard-packed snow field between the two rows of barracks. Behind them the Russian troopers had gathered, two battalions strong, ranged in their white coveralls against a background of burning palisades. Long streams of smoke trailed up into a sky still full of mist only just then being pushed by the early morning winds from the face of the lake.

Kurenko looked up and down the long, shapeless lines of prisoners. There was something about their faces that disturbed him, though he could not put his finger on just what it was. He had expected . . . What? Bewilderment? Pathetic surprise? Like the prisoners let out into the light for the first time in the performance of *Fidelio* he had once seen at the Bolshoi? What he saw instead were flinty, set expressions. Stern and concentrated. Well, why not? Hadn't the prisoners in the convoy looked the same way? Anger. That's what it was. Why shouldn't these men look the same? Perhaps some of them were even the very same men.

Schreiber-Hartstein stood next to the stretcher, looking down at General Golitsyn's body. When he raised his head to confront the silent ranks of soldiers who had gathered around him, there were honest tears in his eyes and his voice trembled so that he could barely be heard.

"Brothers . . . if any of you believe in God, we must consider this as a sign. Out of the entire two full battalions, only seven have been wounded and only three killed. One of the three was Corporal Pashkin, one was Sergeant Enukidze, and the third lies here at my feet . . . Alexander Semyonovitch Golitsyn. He has given his life for his cause, for our cause, which is as he would have wanted it. Which was as he *did* want it, leading his men into battle. We must carry on now with even more dedication than before. We have our duty, we have our honor. We will carry his body with us, and when we are able, we will bury our general with full honors. . . ."

Schreiber-Hartstein went on, slowly, deliberately, barely able to control himself. He told the assembled men of Golitsyn's crisis of conscience, of how he had finally agreed to place himself at the head of the liberation army, of its aims and of what must now be done.

He stopped to draw a breath. A voice came from the ranks.

"How can we trust the fascists?"

"This man is no fascist," cried Zhilinsky, putting a hand on Schreiber-Hartstein's shoulder. "He is a German, true, but before that he was a Russian, just like us. He served under General Pashkevitch in the Imperial Life Guards."

"We don't want *those* days back again either," someone said.

Zhilinsky shouted the man down. "I trust this man. I have said to this man that should he ever betray us, we will meet in the forest somewhere with guns between us. He understands that."

"I expect no less," Schreiber-Hartstein said. "But that day will never come. We will march together toward a new freedom."

There then ensued a long, deep silence. Only the crackling of the burning walls could be heard, and the faint susurration of the wind.

Kurenko's heart sank. How could anyone believe such things?

"All right then, lads. Who'll come with us? Anyone who doesn't want to join us, anyone who thinks he's better off with the Little Father's jailors, why, he's free to stay right here or do whatever he pleases. If you come with us, you'll be treated like men, you'll have your weapons back and maybe, just maybe, you'll get a chance to show that pipe-smoking bastard back in Moscow just what real Russian soldiers are made of." Zhilinsky paused, his hands on his hips. "I'm waiting. All those with us, let's see your hands. Anyone who wants to stay . . . over there." He pointed to the end of the field.

Slowly the hands began to rise, first a few, then more and more. Not a man moved out of line. Finally, there were a thousand hands in the air, blue with cold, fingers wriggling to keep warm.

"It's settled then. You can go by squads, back out to the gliders. Captain Kurenko will show you the way. There are rifles enough for all of you out there, and ammunition. We'll give you what extra clothing we can. You can take anything you can from the guards. We'll form up and move out within the hour. But first, brothers, we must pay our respects. . . ."

For a long moment, no one moved, no one spoke. A massive, grim figure pushed through the rear ranks and trudged with bent head to the stretcher; it was Stalkov, once again in his own uniform. He reached down and pulled back the blanket. The morning light washed over Golitsyn's dead face.

Then a man stepped from the ranks and walked slowly up to the stretcher, his rifle trailing. He paused, then went down on his knees and kissed the general's forehead. After a moment he rose, saluted, and with a desolate look on his face, moved past the little rise where Schreiber-Hartstein, Zhilinsky, and Stalkov stood.

Another man followed, then another. And another.

For fifteen minutes, the procession continued, one man at a time, until all of the RONA men had filed past. The prisoners hesitated, then, still bewildered by all that had occurred so rapidly, followed the example set by the soldiers.

As the last man shuffled past the body, someone began to sing in a strong, fervent voice. Others joined in. Then they were all singing, prisoners and RONA men as well. Even the few Germans who had come with them sang, though they knew neither the words nor the melody.

Kurenko glanced at Schreiber-Hartstein. The man was standing stock still. Tears were mixed with the blood still sliding down his gaunt cheeks.

As though he really believed. . . .

By eight that morning, the prisoners had been formed into company-sized groups and assigned, one each, to a company of RONA. They had been armed and clothed in the bullet-ridden sheepskins of the dead guards and officers. Before the winter morning sun had even begun to dissolve the eerie half-light of dawn, they were moving off through the silent woods to the northwest, and to their rendezvous with what was left of the Sixteenth Waffen SS Panzergrenadiers.

Behind them only a smoking ruin remained. The palisades had been pulled down, the shacks all torched. The lakeside docking facilities had been blown up. Demolition teams had set off heavy charges in the ruined gliders and reduced them to an unrecognizable tangle of steel tubing and metal scraps which the snow would soon enough cover. Heavy mist had rolled in, and with the typical perverseness of nature, the temperature had begun to drop again. The thermometer now stood at eighteen degrees below zero, centigrade.

Not a single aircraft passed over the forest all day. From the distance, now and then, came a faint coughing rumble which might have been artillery fire but might just as easily have been a storm brewing over the mountains. In this part of the country, Obriyan insisted, it was not unusual for snow to alternate with a freezing rain, for fog to cover the forests for days, and for thunder and lightning to lace the skies over the mountains with all the ferocity of summer storms. "Be thankful it's only cold," he said. "It could be much worse."

Schreiber-Hartstein arched his eyebrows, said nothing, and trudged on behind the stretcher-bearers carrying Golitsyn's body.

Kurenko was at least warm; he had taken the padded winter coat from a dead officer and pulled it on over his white coveralls. There was no point in trying to maintain camouflage discipline now. A company of men might, with proper clothing, fade away into the snow-covered woods, but it was impossible to conceal almost three battalions, no matter what they wore.

The prisoners from Byeleymostnoy had no whites, neither coveralls nor capes, and whatever winter camouflage clothing had been in the camp supply shed had gone up in smoke during the attack; a round from Pashkin's mortars had hit it dead center.

One thing still disturbed Kurenko as he stamped along through the forest just behind Stalkov. It was not his confused feelings of guilt nor his fear of what might happen in the next few days, for he had survived now three times when by rights he should have died and he had begun again to believe in his own immortality in much the same way he had when he was a child. No, it was none of these things but, rather, something small, something almost imperceptible. Something he might not even have noticed.

The dead officer from whom he had taken his coat had been an Asiatic, possibly a Kalmuk or a Turkoman. Nothing there to be concerned about—he'd seen many such in the ranks before Kolabyansk. But every other corpse he'd seen had been the same. The entire guard force, and all of the officers had been Asiatics.

And among the prisoners . . . not a single one.

At night they sheltered as best they could, spread out through the woods. The men dug burrows in the snow and erected shelters out of branches and canvas. Some wrapped themselves in their cloaks, huddled together for warmth under trees, and slept in the open.

Schreiber-Hartstein, Stalkov, Lieutenant Bauer, and a few of the other Germans sat around a small, screened campfire, poring over a map. Schreiber-Hartstein produced a flask and passed it around.

"*Schnaps*, gentlemen. Good, raw *Schnaps*. So . . . we have a little celebration."

"Perhaps," suggested Zhilinsky, "we should wait until we reach the Sixteenth and really have something to celebrate about?"

"And perhaps that time will never come, so why let good whiskey go to waste?"

Kurenko drank eagerly, savoring the brief moment of warmth the alcohol gave him. He choked, unaccustomed to the whiskey, which was much rawer than vodka. Stalkov laughed and slapped him on the back.

Kurenko shook. For some reason, the slap seemed like a deliberate, angry blow, a little too hard, a little too quick.

He glared at Stalkov, but the big man seemed not to notice.

"Another day's march," Schreiber-Hartstein announced. "By tomorrow evening we should link up. Then we'll see if some real cognac can be found, perhaps even champagne."

"It doesn't survive in this weather," said Lieutenant Thiel gloomily. "I was at Kiev last year when the Führer sent us a Christmas present. . . . What we needed was woolen socks and coats. What we got were fifty truckloads of French champagne, all frozen solid. Every bottle had burst."

"Get used to vodka," said Stalkov. "It keeps better in the cold."

Thiel gave him an odd look but Schreiber-Hartstein laughed and that was that. While Schreiber-Hartstein changed the dressing on his head wound, Zhilinsky put the maps away. There was nothing to do but eat what little food they had and try to sleep.

The temperature by then had dropped to twenty-one below zero.

All the next day they marched, the prisoners, the dog-tired RONA men, their officers, and the Germans. A deep, spectral silence hung over the forest; the only sound in the woods was the crunch of dry, hard-packed snow beneath the soles of two thousand boots.

Now and then they passed the ruins of an artillery piece, a few frozen corpses half buried in the snow, and once a downed plane, so badly burned that it was impossible to tell whose it had been. The strangest sight of all was the occasional litter—boots, canteens, a mess tin, sometimes a rifle or a tent, without a sign that anyone or anything human had ever been there.

They kept to the woods, carefully avoiding the few villages to their flanks. In the south stood General Yaroslavsky's Fourth Tank Army, in the north three divisions of Soviet infantry under General Ivanchenko. The corridor between them was the only way out from Lake Byeleymostnoy to the west. At the northwestern end of the forest, dug in against the eventual arrival of Ivanchenko's divisions, was the remains of the Sixteenth Waffen SS, less than a battalion's worth, waiting the promised linkup to bring them to strength enough to fight their way through the rapidly closing pincers.

It was late afternoon when the advance section of Stalkov's company first encountered the outer perimeter defenses of the SS positions. One moment there was nothing but white, close-packed snow, trees, and bushes, but in the next, slowly, without anyone even noticing it, the snow began to move and the snouts of antitank guns began to poke black holes in the white. Machine gunners in snow hollows raised their white covers just enough to see and be seen. Before he realized what was happening, the lieutenant in charge of the advance party found himself surrounded.

The SS held their fire. Contact was established and within minutes word was on its way to the main body of troops. There was no need for runners back to the main SS positions. Phone wires had been laid to the end of the echeloned defense rings. The word flowed back instantly.

Within half an hour, Schreiber-Hartstein, Bauer, Stalkov, Kurenko, and a dozen others were moving cautiously into a small clearing, escorted by two dozen Waffen SS carrying submachine guns. Schreiber-Hartstein had let his white cape drop open in spite of the cold so that his uniform could be clearly seen. The SS had never seen uniforms like the ones worn by the Russians and in spite of the fact that they had received clear orders concerning the linkup and knew it to be their only hope of ever breaking out, they were openly distrustful.

"Hold it . . . you wait here," said one of the SS men, a gray-faced, haggard lieutenant with a deep and livid scar down the side of his head. His eyes could barely be seen behind the slits of the ski goggles he wore. He whistled once, then a second time. Sharply.

From the trees on the other side of the clearing came three men, an officer and two soldiers carrying Schmeissers. The officer was tall, gaunt, and walked with a limp. A bandage covered one eye; he wore no camouflage, no helmet, only a crushed *Feldmutze*. Binoculars hung from his neck and clanked against his belt buckle as he walked.

Kurenko knew well enough what it said on that belt buckle; he'd seen them so many times before. What a bitter joke it was now, that inscription.

"Gott mit uns," was what it said.

Schreiber-Hartstein, seeing the officer's rank, the two oak leaves and bar of a Stürmbahnführer, a major, saluted quickly and briskly. The SS man's hand moved so brusquely it was hard to tell whether he was returning the salute or simply gesturing at his men to lower their weapons.

"Hauptmann Reinhardt Schreiber-Hartstein, OKH, Berlin . . . at the moment, Stürmbahnführer, in command of the Second and Third RONA, and a thousand new"—he paused and allowed himself a faint, self-satisfied smile—"recruits."

The SS officer introduced himself.

"Heinz Dietrich," he said. "What the devil's taken you so long? We expected you this morning."

Stalkov, who had come up behind Schreiber-Hartstein, said, "The men we freed at Byeleymostnoy—if the Stürmbahnführer pleases, are not in as good condition as they might be. It was necessary to slow down a bit to allow them to keep up."

Dietrich looked grim and annoyed. "How many did you say you have?"

"Roughly a thousand," said Schreiber-Hartstein. "We've broken them up into companies and parceled them out to our own men."

"Are they fully armed?"

"They have rifles and grenades. And about three hundred sub-machines guns among them."

"Russian, I suppose?"

"Yes."

"And ammunition?"

"One or two drums apiece, plus what we've brought along for your men."

"And when those give out we'll throw rocks, I suppose?"

"My men will fight," Stalkov replied quietly. "They will not allow themselves to be taken prisoner again, you can rest assured of that."

"Well, it's all better than nothing," said Dietrich. "You've brought your own food, I hope. We're eating bark here. When we can find it."

"No food, I'm afraid."

"A damned shame." Dietrich's expression softened for a moment. "Forgive my manners, Captain. It hasn't been easy here. We're glad to see you, really."

Then Dietrich noticed the stretcher, the body covered with a gray blanket.

"You've brought your dead along? We've got quite enough of our own."

Schreiber-Hartstein shook his head.

"General Golitsyn was killed in the attack. One of three . . ."

Dietrich whistled and went over to the stretcher. Before Schreiber-Hartstein could stop him, he pulled the blanket back to look at Golitsyn's face. No one had made any attempt to disguise the wound. Dietrich understood at once what had happened and pulled the blanket quickly back.

Schreiber-Hartstein cleared his throat in the awkward silence that followed.

"We thought that . . . perhaps . . . there should be a full funeral, with all military honors. . . ."

"With all honors, of course," Dietrich agreed grimly. "Yes, by God, you're right. It will be good for the men to see it. Even here."

"So I thought."

"Tomorrow. In the morning, then. As soon as we can manage it," said Dietrich. "After breakfast."

Over the next half hour, the RONA troops, the German fliers, and the prisoners moved into the SS position.

"You're damned lucky you got through," said Dietrich.

"We didn't see a single Russ. Didn't even *hear* them," put in Bauer.

"Strange," said Dietrich. "When we came through that way the first time, they were all over us." Dietrich raised a tin cup of hot water in which some bark had been steeped for flavor. "Stalingrad tea," he said. Schreiber-Hartstein had no stomach for it.

The two men sat in a small tent that had been rigged up between two trees, studying the map. Stalkov and Zhilinsky and half a dozen others crouched by the tent walls, listening, smoking the last of their cigarettes. No one offered a smoke to Dietrich or to any of the other SS officers.

The RONA men and the prisoners had been spread on a company-to-company basis among the remains of the SS battalions. The perimeter guard had been reinforced in the same way. Dietrich had insisted on it. He was not about to have two separate lines of command. Stalkov agreed at once. No one even asked Schreiber-Hartstein what he thought.

"We go . . . here . . . in the morning," said Dietrich, pointing to the map and a narrow corridor between the known Soviet positions to the north and the south. "If Ivanchenko has slowed up for even half a day, we'll get through without a fight."

Schreiber-Hartstein knew what the SS man was thinking; if we hadn't waited for *you,* we'd have had an even better chance. But it wasn't true. The Sixteenth simply wasn't strong enough to fight. They'd had no choice but to wait.

When the meeting was over, Schreiber-Hartstein produced a flask of whiskey again and passed it around. By the time it reached Dietrich there was hardly any left. Obriyan fought to keep from grinning. Fighting alongside the Germans didn't mean he had to like them, and this Dietrich was a bad example of the worst type.

Stalkov and Kurenko walked out of the tent together. The sky had cleared and through the gaps in the snow-covered branches overhead a vast array of stars—brilliant, cold, and distant—could be seen. The temperature had eased a bit. It was still fiercely cold, but the cold was bearable now at least—no worse than it had been that fall during the early snows far north at Kolabyansk.

"You stay with me, *malchik,*" said Stalkov, clapping an arm around Kurenko's shoulders. "You know? I like you, Vasya. You've got guts."

"I do? I thought that all I've done so far is try to stay alive."

"That takes something too," replied Stalkov, unrolling a tarpaulin and a blanket. All around them, they could see the dark, huddled forms of the SS men trying to sleep in the shelter of their ruined vehicles, under tarps, in crude shacks or lean-tos, or in simple burrows dug in the snow. They drew together for warmth, some of them; others lay in the open, alone, as though all they wished to do was to die quietly and peacefully in their sleep.

Stalkov wrapped himself in his blanket and leaned against the bole of a tree, his knees drawn up to his chest.

"I've got two cigarettes left. . . ."

Kurenko shook his head; he was exhausted, too tired even to smoke. The whiskey had left a small, warm center in his stomach.

"Suit yourself," Stalkov said. "But stay close, *stay close*."

"I'm not going anywhere, don't worry."

"Stalkov will look after you. . . ."

What an odd thing for him to to say, Kurenko thought, his eyes growing heavy. He rolled himself up in a corner of the tarp and prayed that it would not snow again. Just before he dropped off to sleep, he saw Schreiber-Hartstein and Dietrich walk across the encampment, conversing quietly. Almost as though they were friends.

Kurenko was awakened by a burst of machine-gun fire.

His eyes flicked open onto an ash-gray dawn blurred by large, wet flakes of snow falling all around him. For a second he could not get his bearings. Where was he? What was he doing in this place? His face was covered with snow rapidly turning to ice. He reached out. There had been someone there when he'd fallen asleep. Stalkov. Where was he now?

Another burst of gunfire, nearer this time. A sudden clamoring of voices and a deep, clanking sound.

Kurenko struggled to his knees.

"Stay down, *malchik*. Don't move. . . ."

It was Stalkov waving brusquely with the barrel of his submachine gun.

Then Kurenko saw why.

In the streaky light of the snowy dawn it was possible for the first time to make out the contours of the SS position. The remnants of the Sixteenth had sheltered in defilade behind a curving three-quarter ring of low mounds crested by fir. Through the trees, the dawn was just beginning to show. At the open end of the ring lay the forest route along which the RONA force had come. Across this wide path a solid wall of Soviet T-34s was now drawn up. Their guns were depressed for direct fire.

On the rim of the low hill ring could be seen the silhouettes of hundreds of silent horsemen. Beneath the trees and in full view. On the slopes of the ridges, dropping down into the bowl where the SS had lain in exhausted sleep, were hundreds of white-caped infantry, barely visible against the fresh snow cover.

Kurenko's knees gave way beneath him and, half in obedience to Stalkov's command, half out of shock, he pitched forward and lay face down in the snow.

All around the encampment, the SS and RONA huddled, motionless, barely awake, waiting for the deluge of fire. They were completely surrounded. Somehow, the perimeter defenses had failed, the pickets had been silenced. Not so much as a shot had been fired.

Then, as Stalkov remained standing, as though waiting for something, completely exposed to fire from all sides, Kurenko slowly looked about.

Among the white-covered infantry and the near slopes he saw other, darker uniforms and, at the same instant, glancing for the first time around the encampment, understood fully both the silence of the pickets and the unearthly stillness of the SS.

Spread over the hillside and the bivouac area were tight little groups of the men who had been taken from Byeleymostnoy. On the hillsides they waited, like the others, in shallow, scooped-out machine-gun emplacements. Within the SS positions, they had occupied a network of high points, on top of ruined vehicles, on tarpaulined piles of ammunition crates, positions from which their machine guns could sweep the entire area.

Anyone who so much as raised his head would be shot down in an instant.

The sentries' throats had been cut during the night. The prisoners had overwhelmed them and their RONA contingents in the dark, without a sound.

Stalkov turned slightly and, satisfied with Kurenko's position, nodded and smiled.

"Now, *malchik, now* we'll see . . ."

A voice from the hillside, first in German, then in Russian; Kurenko knew that voice. A violent tremor seized him. He would, perhaps, not die after all. Yet, in a way, this was almost worse.

"You have been disarmed," came the voice over a loudspeaker. "Resistance is futile. If you move, you will be shot at once."

A dozen meters away across the clearing, Kurenko could see Schreiber-Hartstein and Stürmbahnführer Dietrich, immobile, waiting.

A long silence.

Then the voice again.

"Do you surrender? You have no choice." It was unmistakably the voice of Colonel Budyankov.

Only Stalkov moved, slowly swinging the muzzle of his submachine gun around until it was pointed directly at Dietrich and Schreiber-Hartstein.

"Do as he says, Herr Hauptmann. There *is* no choice, not for you."

But it was Dietrich who stepped forward, not Schreiber-Hartstein.

"There is nothing heroic in suicide," he called out, as though to the wind, loud and in an angry voice. "You, up on the hill. We'll do as you say. Come down and you will have my surrender."

Dietrich began to move in the direction from which the voice had come. On the hillside a small, chunky figure came out of the dark overhang of a cluster of fir trees and began the shallow descent.

The two moved toward each other.

At the same instant as Kurenko saw Dietrich's hand jump up from his side holding his machine pistol, Stalkov's finger clamped down hard on the trigger of his submachine gun. The burst whipped across the clearing, caught Dietrich full across the back, almost cutting him in two. He sprawled forward in the snow.

Colonel Budyankov continued down the slope as though nothing at all had happened. Finally he stopped, cupping his hands to his mouth.

"Officers, forward. Russians there, Germans . . . there. All hand weapons will be piled up between you. . . ."

As the stunned RONA and SS moved to obey, the horsemen on the hillside moved slowly out from between the trees. They were irregulars, partisans, not cavalry, but there were even more of them than Kurenko had first imagined. The tanks along the edge of the forest road began to clank forward slowly, converging on the masses of Germans and RONA being herded together at the center of a steadily closing circle.

Budyankov, accompanied by another man whom Kurenko recognized at once as Major Gelb, came down the hill and walked over to where Stalkov and Kurenko were waiting.

"A perfect operation, Stalkov. Congratulations. Tell me, what of Golitsyn?"

"Blew his brains out. The body's over there. We brought him along for you to see."

"And the woman?"

"The Gestapo did as they were . . . asked to do."

Budyankov nodded gravely. "And the ringleader?"

"Over there," Stalkov said. "Your renegade Balt." He pointed toward a group of prisoners near the steadily growing pile of arms. Schreiber-Hartstein stood in the front rank, blinking against the brightening dawn, a sad, bewildered look on his face.

Budyankov gestured. Schreiber-Hartstein was brought over. Four Soviet soldiers stood behind him with their submachine guns cradled loosely in their arms.

Budyankov held up his withered hand.

"Leave him here, with us."

Schreiber-Hartstein looked from one man to the other. His expression was neither of anger nor of fear but of infinite sadness.

"Kurenko? Of course, we *knew*, didn't we?" Schreiber-Hartstein said without resentment. "But Stalkov? *You?* All along, *you*?"

"We do what we must, Captain."

"So," said Budyankov cheerfully. "This is the man? You, Captain, you were going to turn your government's East policy about, single-handed? And defeat us with our own men?"

"There will be others. I wasn't alone. It won't stop here."

"But perhaps it will," said Budyankov. "I admire your courage, Captain. And, in a way, I admire your motives too. Unfortunately, your superiors do not always agree with you. So far, we have three million graves to prove you wrong."

"There was a chance," Schreiber-Hartstein said quietly. "We did have a chance, you know that."

"I told you once, Captain, that one day we would meet in a forest, across the barrel of a gun," said Stalkov.

"But only . . . you said it yourself . . . if *I* betrayed *you*, Boris Trifomovitch. I did *not* betray you. It was you . . ."

"Who did what was necessary."

"All along," said Schreiber-Hartstein, so softly that it could barely be heard. "The entire thing . . ."

"Was planned? Yes, yes, of course," said Budyankov. "The camp, you see, was built especially for you and those fools over there. Everything, right down to the last board. For you and only you. The perfect target. Our own Potemkin village, if you will. And it worked."

"But the guards who were killed?"

"They," said Budyankov, "were the real prisoners. By dying they finally did their duty to their country. No less than front-line soldiers. They will be honored for their sacrifice, you can rest assured of that."

"What did you do?" cried Kurenko. "Give them blanks? Is that why we lost only three men while they were killed down to the last living soul?"

Major Gelb looked pained and did not reply. Colonel Budyankov, whose eyebrows had moved up almost imperceptibly as Kurenko had used the word *we*, exhaled a long, exhausting plume of frosty breath.

"Enough. We have three battalions of prisoners to take back. The transports are waiting."

"What will you do with them?" Schreiber-Hartstein asked.

"You and the other Germans will be sent to prison camps. You will be well treated, Captain, never fear. I have always had a soft spot in my heart for noble fools."

"And the rest, the RONA?"

"They will be tried and hung. What else would you do with traitors?"

There was no color at all in Schreiber-Hartstein's face. His muscles had gone rigid. His eyes burned.

"And that," said Budyankov, "will be the end of all of this. When our troops learn what has happened, when your Reichsminister Rosenberg learns of the debacle, not to mention Himmler, Keitel, and the others who've opposed your clique all along . . ."

"No," Schreiber-Hartstein said suddenly. He glanced over his shoulder. Behind him, now, lay a long, snow-covered space, open to the edge of the forest from which the partisan cavalry had descended. "You can do what you like. I won't go with you."

"What are you talking about? Surely, you realize . . ."

"I realize that you have betrayed not only me but yourselves."

With that, Schreiber-Hartstein turned and began to walk away across the clearing.

"Captain . . . you must come back," cried the astonished Stalkov.

A voice came back, shredded by the wind.

"Do whatever is 'necessary.' I will not go with you."

Stalkov threw down the Schmeisser and yanked his pistol from its holster.

"You *must* stop."

Schreiber-Hartstein continued walking, leaving clear black footprints in the snow. No one moved.

"I *will* shoot," Stalkov cried hoarsely. He raised the pistol and sighted down the barrel.

Without thinking, Kurenko threw himself at the outstretched arm. The shot went wild.

A gun butt slammed across the side of his head and he went sprawling into the snow. It was Gelb who had clubbed him down. Budyankov, his face flaming, shouted at him that he was under arrest.

Schreiber-Hartstein had not turned at the first shot. Stalkov stared for a second at Kurenko, now streaming blood from a gash in his scalp. Then he raised his arm again.

"Stop, Reinhardt Gavrilovitch, for God's sake, stop."

Schreiber-Hartstein kept walking.

Stalkov fired once, hitting Schreiber-Hartstein in the leg. The captain dropped to the snow, remained there for a moment as though hovering, undecided, then struggled to his feet and with an angular, lurching gait, continued on toward the forest. Behind him, a thin trail of blood marked his passage.

Stalkov's features were so compressed that he was almost unrecognizable. Budyankov stared. Major Gelb's hand lay like a weight on Kurenko's shoulder.

Stalkov took aim and fired again. A dark red splotch appeared on Schreiber-Hartstein's back. He stood transfixed, swaying, then—slowly, impossibly, he began walking again.

With a shout, Stalkov fired again and again. Each bullet, as it struck, seemed to push Schreiber-Hartstein forward and down at the same time.

As the fifth shot slammed into his back, he finally fell, a ragged, red-black mass in the snow, arms outstretched. No one moved. Two thousand men stood in a vast ring, watching in silence. Schreiber-Hartstein shuddered once. His hand moved as though he had at last found something worth grasping there in the snow. Then, face down, without turning over, he died.

Stalkov lowered the pistol. The chamber was empty.

Only Kurenko heard him. His voice was low and choked.

"That was . . . a good man," he said.

Then he threw the pistol from him as far and as hard as he could. It landed near the huge stack of rifles and vanished into the snow, leaving only a small black mark.

"He comes with me, this one," Stalkov said, helping Kurenko to his feet. "He's a fool, but no worse than the rest of us."

Budyankov nodded and turned away; he knew better than to speak.

Kurenko did not understand, and he knew then that he would never understand.

Stalkov put his huge arm around Kurenko's shoulder and the two of them trudged slowly across the clearing and up the little incline to the rise and the waiting lines of horsemen and the forest beyond. The sun, now fully risen, shone above the black latticework of branches and turned their icy tips to silver.

> Those who were born in our country's stagnant years
> Do not remember their way.
> We—children of Russia's years of dread—
> forget nothing.
>
> Alexander Blok